# DUCKETT & DYER

The One-Hundred Percent
Solution

ISBN: 978-1-7338943-4-0

PIN: 218— Ah-ha! Nice try!

10 9 8 7 6 5 4 3 2 1

You've read the fake reviews, now read what actual

human beings have said about

# DUCKETT & DYER
## Dicks For Hire

Read the other books in the

# DUCKETT & DYER

Series!

Or don't. I'm not the boss of you.

---

DUCKETT & DYER: DICKS FOR HIRE

THE ONE-HUNDRED PERCENT SOLUTION

---

Wait. That's it? There're only two?

We wasted an entire page on this!

Ink costs money, you know!

*To everyone who needs a laugh right now.*

# DUCKETT & DYER

## The One-Hundred Percent Solution

A NOVEL

BY

G.M. NAIR

∂s
∂F

www.ds-df.com

# CHAPTER ONE

## Just Another Story

One day Craig Breene would see it all. Quite literally, in fact. Almost every single possible thing. He would see so much, it would haunt him to the end of his days which, to his benefit, wouldn't be long thereafter. This would not be his choice. If he had a say in the matter, he would have done things differently. Instead, his life would veer so horrifically off-course that he would have a hand in the collapse of existence and the end of all things.

All of that, of course, was yet to come. For now, he was just yet another office drone who had to get through lunch.

Not that lunch was a particularly large hassle, but the grease of the office cafeteria's sloppy joes kept dripping onto Craig's pad of graph paper. His notes and drawings were, bit by bit, consumed by stains ranging in color somewhere between orange and transparent orange.

"Aw, crap!" Craig whined, attempting to rub off the grease with his thumb. Failing that, he balled up the top sheet and added it to the small pile of similarly crumpled notes at the corner of his lunch tray. Another afternoon's work ruined.

Craig grumbled to himself as he finished up the last bits of his sandwich. Emptying his tray into the trash, he took the elevator back up to the fifth floor.

The doors dinged open into an office bustling with activity. The harsh, staccato clacks and carriage returns of typewriters elbowed for room alongside their buzzing modern brethren—line printers and telex machines. If someone had thrown a xylophone into a nest of angry wasps because they had been told it would be profitable, they would have built this office.

Consolidated Futures Inc.—established 1983—began as a small firm specializing in trading commodities futures for maximum return. Now, nine years later, they were a small-ish firm doing the same thing. Craig, always leaning more into the creative aspects of his personality, found the entire business model incredibly boring. He could barely wrap his head around the basic premise. Luckily for him, he wasn't hired to understand the point of the company. Instead, he'd been brought on to spearhead technology initiatives to advance financial analysis and improve profitability since he was pretty good with computers.

Craig sidled into his very cramped eight-foot by six-foot beige cubicle, and booted up his computer—one of the few new devices on the floor. It was why he'd really joined the company—access to their advanced machines. He'd do his best to do whatever it was they wanted him to do during the day, but Craig would do the things he really wanted to do at night. Though he'd have to keep it quiet. In any case, he'd keep his head down and concentrate on his work until the office was empty. Craig's computer finally finished booting up, the cursor on the screen barely materializing before his attention was demanded elsewhere.

"So, what's this?"

Craig spun around in his chair and was greeted by a six-foot mountain of a man. Marcus Espinoza had a strong, chiseled jawline, framed by a mop of brown curls Craig noticed almost daily—although he'd never tell Marcus. He also dressed sharper than Craig ever could, in a deep navy power suit. It's what all the other guys wore in sales and marketing, and they put Craig's faded polo shirts and khakis to shame. What all the other sales and marketing guys didn't have, though, was a crumpled piece of graph paper with oil and grease stains all over it. Craig's eyes widened.

Marcus unrumpled the paper with his thick, fumbly fingers, squinting at it before turning it to face Craig. "What is this, some kinda minotaur?"

"No, it's not a—" Craig yanked the paper out of Marcus's hands, before collecting the few scraps left in his strong grip. "It's not a minotaur. It's . . . just a different kind of monster altogether."

"Alright, well"—Marcus pulled up a chair from an empty cubicle and sat on it backwards—"what're you doing making monsters? Aren't you supposed to be working on our—whatever it is? Computational finance."

"Yeah." Craig pushed his thick glasses up his nose and turned back to his computer. "I'm . . . uh . . . working on it. This is something I do in my downtime."

"Dungeons and Dragons, right?"

Craig had met Marcus in college and invited Marcus to play with his D&D group—hoping the experience would spark something. It didn't, but they stayed close friends—which was the absolute least Craig could hope for. He had been the best man at Marcus's wedding—a bittersweet experience to say the least—and Marcus was the one who had gotten him the job at Consolidated Futures, touting Craig as one of the smartest guys he knew. And now Craig had to admit he was wasting the company's time and resources on a frivolous hobby. He wondered how Marcus would take it.

"No, not exactly like Dungeons and Dragons." Craig cleared his throat. "Well, similar. I'm trying to make a game. Like a video game. A text adventure."

"Text adventure?" Marcus cocked his head.

"Have you ever heard of Zork?"

"What the hell is a zork?"

"Oh, um . . . okay. Let's maybe back up a second?" There was a part of Craig that regretted trying to explain all of his stupid nonsense to Marcus, but there was another part that hoped just maybe they'd bond a little more over this. It was this second part that continued running its mouth. "It's—how do I put this—like an interactive story. Done mostly through text and pictures. Not like a regular Nintendo game. You get to tell the computer how you want to go through the story."

"Like a choose-your-own-adventure thing?" Marcus grimaced as Craig nodded. "Why can't you just make something cool looking, like Mortal Kombat?"

"I would, but the technology isn't there yet." Craig picked up the July '92 issue of Electronic Gaming Monthly he'd hidden between stacks of paper on his desk. "The stuff out there now—even dedicated arcade games like Mortal Kombat—is pretty barebones. The story I want to tell is incredibly deep and complex. It'd take hundreds of video game cartridges for just the initial levels."

Marcus sighed. "Alright. I'll bite. What's the big deal with the story?"

"It's gonna sound really dumb . . ." Craig looked down.

"Craigo." Marcus gave him a tap in the arm. "Try me."

Craig loved Marcus' openness. He didn't have to be as worried as he was about telling him everything.

"It's based on a story my mom told me as a kid," Craig started.

"Of course it is." Marcus was well aware of the close bond Craig shared with his mother.

"She used to tell me a bedtime story about something called the Order of Steel Knights who protected the Holy Realm against a giant evil monster who's bent on destroying everything. She was super creative. A real story teller."

"So, what's this monster look like?" Marcus leaned forward. "Giant green thing with a hundred arms and a hundred eyes?"

"Well, I haven't gotten that far yet, but I'll keep it in mind. Anyway, my mom told this story a lot, but often times she'd change different details or add new elements. Like these two legendary heroes the Steel Knights needed to summon to help them. Sometimes the heroes were best friends." Craig looked away. "When my parents got divorced, the heroes became worst enemies. Context aside, the Knights always had to bring them together to defeat the monster.

"So recently I got to thinking, what if all of these different versions of the story were all equally different universes in the same multi-verse system? Like in comic books?"

"Awright, that's a neat idea." Marcus nodded. "So what would the game be about?"

"In the game, you're one of these Steel Knights who discovers an elixir which allows you to jump between hundreds of different universes. Some are normal with minor changes. Some can be really strange. But they could be absolutely anything you could think of."

"What, like a universe where hamburgers eat people?"

"Yeah, okay . . . I guess that could be one of them."

"Hahah, awesome." Marcus smirked. "Sorry. Keep going."

"And while you're jumping through these universes, you find out this dark and terrible monster is also traveling from universe to universe and destroying each of them. You have to stop the monster. But the only way you can stop him is by uniting the two chosen heroes in each universe, using the items and knowledge you gain on your quests in different realities."

"Whoa." A wave of understanding washed over Marcus's face for a moment, as if he was really picking up on Craig's excitement. "That's actually pretty cool."

Craig smiled as a warm glow filled his chest. "Thanks, Marcus."

"But, you're right. It sounds really hard to put together. A thousand CD-ROMs wouldn't even do it."

"That's why I decided on doing it as a text adventure," Craig said. "Keeps things simple."

"Yeah, well, that won't sell. You think my little kid would wanna read everything that happens instead of something like Sonic the Hedgehog or Mario or whatever? You gotta have flash!" Marcus threw his hands up in the air, directing an invisible movie. "Animations! Battle sequences! Maybe make it 3D! That'll be what really moves units."

Craig frowned. Maybe Marcus hadn't understood what he was going for, after all. "I never really thought about it from a business standpoint before. I just wanted to make this thing for people like me to enjoy."

"Well, how else am I going to justify my investment in this amazing opportunity?" A grin spread over Marcus' face.

"What are you talking about?"

"Craig, this company makes a stupid amount of money doing nothing. *I* make a stupid amount of money doing nothing. It doesn't really make sense. We're just investing other people's money and getting a cut. We're not producing anything. Believe me, making money is nice. But if you make your game half as cool as it sounds, we could make a bunch of money *and* produce something a bunch of kids will love. It'd be nice to have that kind of impact."

Craig had never thought about it in quite those terms, but Marcus's point resonated with him. Leaving his mark on the world would be a dream come true, much more than trudging through investment technology mumbo jumbo. Not to mention, he would be able to work closely with Marcus on something they'd both be invested in. The thought sent a pleasant tingle down his spine.

"So, if I got the company to front you the money for better machines to keep you developing," Marcus continued, "could we go halvsies on your game?"

"Wouldn't we get in trouble for that?"

"We would, if I didn't do it all quiet-like. There's an empty room in the basement we can use. And when we deliver a kick-ass product, the board won't be able to thank us fast enough. Ask for forgiveness, not permission."

Craig nodded.

"So, are you in?"

Craig's eyes sparkled. "Yes, absolutely."

"Very cool." Marcus flashed a thumbs up at him as he rose to leave. "Now listen, put together a list of everything you need, we can go over it together and see how we can get this done, alright?"

"Yeah," Craig said. "Yeah. I'll do that."

The thumps of Marcus' thick brown dress shoes were swallowed up by the thick office carpeting as he strode away. Craig—truly, deeply happy for the first time in a long while—smiled as he swiveled back toward his computer and the blinking green cursor.

* * *

Craig's apartment was a sparse little box of a place in a small neighborhood known as Squalor's Wallow. The area was run down, but the state had promised several new infrastructure programs aimed at rejuvenating the area in the next five years. Nevertheless, Craig tried not to spend much time in the area to avoid depressing himself and mainly used his apartment to sleep and call his mom.

"Hey, mom."

It was the latter he was doing right now, because Craig, having had powered through ten more hours of work, found out he didn't really need that much sleep to function.

"Oh, Craigy! How're you doing?" His mother's sweet tones wafted through the headset. She had never really approved of his lifestyle, but they were still on very friendly terms.

"I'm okay, just really tired."

"Tired? What's wrong?"

"Just a really long day at work. People have been bugging me on a hundred different things. Sometimes I just can't take the stress. It's like I'm giving my life to this company."

"Craig." His mother adopted her stern tone. Craig could almost see her finger wagging. This was what she disapproved of. "I told you a hundred times, you need to quit that place. Come to the agency. You'd be appreciated here."

"I don't want to work for the government, mom. I want to stay here."

"Why? You seem to hate it." She paused. "Wait, is this about that Marcus?"

"Noooooooooo." Craig stretched out the word so much it turned into a yes.

"Oh, good god," his mother moaned, "for the hundredth time. I don't trust that kid. He's always been in it for himself, and he'll drop you as soon as things start to go south. Frankly, I don't even think he likes you very much."

"Not true, mom." Craig smirked. He always had come to Marcus's defense when he talked to his mother. It didn't matter that he'd found Craig a job or had stuck by him since college. She just didn't like him. But today, he had just the ammo to disprove her suspicions. "I pitched him my video game idea today and he's willing to back me. It might be a ton more work, but it's something that'll be fun."

"Video game? Like one of the Nintendos?"

"Kinda. It's an idea I've had for a while. It's actually based on the stories you told me when I was a kid!"

"What? The Steel Knight stuff? Oh, Craig. That was just a fairy tale. I never got all the details right. All you wanted to hear was stories about a knight and a monster. It'd be a miracle if I managed to tell you the same story twice."

"That's part of it!" Craig beamed. "Oh, I can't wait for you to see it. With Marcus's help, I'll get it done even quicker. It's going to be really cool."

"I dunno, sweetie. It's a cute idea and it's very sweet, but Marcus might just see the dollar signs. He might be using you for a profit. Believe me. I've met guys like him before."

Craig's mouth flattened. "You mean Dad?"

"In not so many words . . . yes. But that's beside the point. You don't need him to be successful. If you come work for the agency, you'll be paid really well and get to buy all the equipment on your own. No need to be dependent on Marcus."

"You don't understand, mom." She and Craig were not on the same page. Being linked with Marcus was the icing on the cake. "I just need to do these things myself. I'm not a kid anymore."

"I'm just trying to look out for you, Craigy. I've been there."

"I know, thank you."

"Alright, honey." His mother's tone zipped to hushed and impatient. "I gotta go. A fax just came through."

"Where're you going this time?" Craig knew his mom's job always kept her moving. She'd never divulge the nature of her business, but she often had to leave at the drop of a hat. All she'd tell him was it was government work.

"You know I can't say. But it starts with a 'Czech' and ends with a 'Slovakia.' At any rate, you just be careful, okay? Call me in a few days. I love you. Bye!"

"Love you, too, mom. I promise, I know what I'm doing. Stay safe."

Craig sat in silence for a long while before he realized he had absolutely no idea what he was doing.

# CHAPTER TWO

## You Don't Have To Be Dead To Work Here, But It Helps

The ID card's smooth plastic slid easily between Detective Rex Calhoun's thumb and forefinger. He flipped it around in his hand, allowing the black and red company logo to announce itself, although it hardly needed the introduction. Anyone who lived in this city longer than a week recognized the brand.

"The Future Group. What a surprise." Calhoun smirked.

But it wasn't a smirk of happiness. Oh, no. Rex Calhoun had never been happy. He was born a curmudgeon. No, his smirk came from the self-satisfaction of having been proven right. A smirk that only came from knowing you'd soon be able to tell your goddamn boss "I told you so."

But before he could say those words, there was work to be done.

Leaning back on his haunches, Calhoun studied the body. The cloudy eyes of a fifty-something man, separated only by a precise, gaping bullet hole between them, gazed at the evening sky. The corpse's face was a grim death mask at odds with the wide grin the man had on his ID.

It struck Calhoun as odd. What kind of twisted psychopath actually smiled in their work ID photo? Certainly a different kind of psychopath than the one who murdered this guy in the middle of an apartment complex.

The corpse was the third in a set of dead bodies Calhoun had championed as linked, despite being repeatedly reprimanded by Chief Braddock. Braddock refused to attribute the killings to a single person. To be fair, the victims and methods had all been wildly different.

The first death was the most high profile. A state senator had been found slumped over her desk after a long night. Since she had been a bit up there in years, it was ruled an unfortunate cardiac arrest. No one looked into it further.

Two weeks later, the next one turned up: an agent at a highly reputable commercial and industrial real estate firm. His death was not quite as inconspicuous. His head had exploded. Ballistics had identified traces of a high-powered sniper rifle.

At the time, Calhoun had been side-lined. He'd just closed a particularly troubling case regarding gangland activity in the neighborhood of Squalor's Wallow. The gang activity wasn't what was troubling him, however. It was the fact he couldn't remember much about it. A whole week of his life had been wiped from his memory. He hadn't told anybody about it, but he did see a doctor. The most probable cause was a series of mini strokes, but Calhoun refused to believe that. Even though he had managed to single-handedly bring a key gang member to justice, Calhoun was still as much a grump as ever. The copious amount of paperwork didn't help matters. Paperwork that was still unfinished. But these new killings caught Calhoun's eye and, eager to prove to himself that he was sharp as ever, he went on a digging expedition.

He paid the senator's body a visit in the morgue and gave it a more thorough examination, enlisting the help of Carrie McDermott, an ambitious CSI on loan from the 35th Precinct, where the senator's office had been located. She was young, but capable, and Calhoun saw something in her. But he couldn't say exactly what—or why. Yet another thing he couldn't remember. It set his teeth grinding.

Calhoun knew his faith had been well placed when McDermott managed to find a pinhole wound in the back of the Senator's neck, something even the medical examiner missed.

Or covered up.

Given the lack of any damage or evidence of struggle in the senator's office, Calhoun and McDermott conjectured she had been secretly injected with some sort of slow-acting poison during the day. But, since it had been so long since her death, a tox screen wouldn't return any reasonable results.

When Calhoun brought this theory up to Braddock, the man called him crazy, demanding he remove himself from the investigation and finish his pending paperwork immediately. So, of course, Calhoun called in a few favors and amassed whatever records he could find on the senator and the real estate agent. There was very little overlap. As far as he could tell, the two of them had never been in the same room together, let alone the same building.

The one piece of connective tissue catching Calhoun's eye was the commonality in their line of work. The senator had tirelessly championed corporate rights and had submitted multiple bills to the State Senate advocating for increased subsidies for The Future Group. She ranked the company among the greatest institutions of the new millennium. Likewise, the real estate agent —while he still had his head—brokered several large real estate deals for The Future Group over the past decade, granting them the rights to run industrial piping through and around most of the plots they owned.

It had taken Calhoun around three weeks to find this tenuous link, but it was something. He had been planning to drill into the specifics of these land and piping deals when he heard about the death of Arthur

Birch. The man who was found lying face up in the center of the Berman Towers Apartment complex, on his way to work . . . at The Future Group.

Calhoun had called McDermott up immediately and demanded she meet him on the scene.

Around the central plaza of the complex—past the aesthetically pleasant shrubbery—uniformed cops milled about, cordoning off the immediate area and herding residents back toward the streets or into the lobbies. The low buzz of their voices actually made for calming background noise. Though Calhoun hoped none of them would squeal to Braddock that he was stalking around.

Calhoun stood, but seeing the body from a higher vantage point did nothing to help. He glanced across at McDermott, whose thin fingers danced across a tablet, scrolling through information she thought would be relevant. Unlike Calhoun, McDermott was usually the talkative sort, but she remained eerily silent while deep in the weeds. He wondered what she was thinking.

"So what're you thinking?" McDermott asked, disengaging from her tablet and coming up for air.

"I dunno. I was waiting for you to tell me something." Calhoun cleared his throat.

"You're the detective, Rex. I'm just the girl with the tablet."

"But this clinches it, right? There's something fishy going on at The Future Group."

"They're a business, Rex. Someone might be targeting them."

"Someone who kills a state senator? One of their biggest land brokers and . . . uh . . . whatever this guy did?"

McDermott stabbed at her tablet. "Arthur Birch. Manager. Human Resources."

"Ah, Christ." Calhoun ran his hand over his bald head, tipping his hat. "The poor schmuck."

"It's kind of a rough link, Rex. I still don't think Braddock is gonna buy that it's some sort of serial killer."

"Well, Braddock doesn't have to *know* about it. Besides, it's gotta be a serial killer on the loose. Who'd want to murder an HR guy, anyway?"

"About ninety-nine percent of the American workforce," Carrie shot back. "They're there to protect the company, not the employees."

"Noted." Calhoun frowned. "Irregardless, I think there's something worth looking into." He pivoted on his heel and strode away. "I'll see you back at the station. If anyone asks, I wasn't here. And if Braddock asks, I *really* wasn't here."

"Where are you going?"

"Where do you think?" Calhoun called back as his powered his way across the apartment plaza, shoes occasionally scraping against the concrete. "I'm gonna ask The Future Group a few questions."

\* \* \*

The Future Group was the city's oldest and most beloved company, despite nobody knowing exactly what they did. Whatever service they performed or product they produced, The Future Group made a big splash with it in the mid-nineties and had been riding that wave as a powerhouse of the local economy ever since.

Despite its reputation for inscrutability, The Future Group was a very charming mainstay in the local culture of the city. In addition to donating a large chunk of its considerable profits to general public works, the company employed much of the citizenry and boasted the highest retention rate of any company in the nation.

No one ever left The Future Group—apart from dying, a condition that had recently become more relevant—and it was very clear why. Employees often sang the praises of the company's great culture and benefits, even if they hadn't been asked about them. The refrain was always the same: they loved what they did (whatever it was) and none of them would even *think* of working anywhere else.

And then there was Michael Duckett.

He was a despondent worker-bee who sat in a beige cubicle on the fifty-third floor of The Future Group's monstrous glass and steel tower, which loomed over everything from its position in the center of the city. Each floor's windows were floor-to-ceiling, allowing Future Group employees to take in the whole city at once as they walked to-and-fro. Nothing was beyond their reach or visibility. Michael's particular cube, however, was equidistant from every window on his floor, making the soft caress of natural sunlight an unattainable goal and fresh air the fever dream of a lunatic.

Today, in the stuffiest of stuffy cubes, Michael hunted and pecked on his keyboard, slowly manipulating numbers for a purpose he didn't fully understand. He often wished he had a job where he could actually help people. To do some good and make an impact. But he realized a long time ago, those jobs didn't pay. The Future Group did. And with his roommate Stephanie Dyer still trying and failing to drum up business for a fly-by-night detective agency, Michael needed all the pay he could get. So he stuck around at a job that was the bane of his existence.

However, Michael had found a new, more invigorating reason to come to work. As one of the thousands of people employed at The Future Group, he was given access to the company's wealth of historical public and private data it had acquired through . . . various means and channels, and he was taking advantage of it.

A few weeks ago, Michael and Stephanie had hurtled through the vast, strange expanses of the multi-verse that, up till then, Michael didn't know existed. Despite the panic that consumed him—as it would any rational being—Michael and Steph had managed to find a way home. He never thought he would be glad to return to the drudgery of The Future Group, but he was. At least for a week. Then it became irritating all over again.

The entire experience, though, was hard to forget. Michael wanted to have washed his hands of the entire situation and move forward unabated, but it was naïve of him to believe he could. While he wasn't jumping at every little noise that sounded like an eyeball-handed cow monster or giant robotic Franz Ferdinand, Michael *had* changed.

Mid-way through their journey across the bizarre and terrifying alternate universes, Michael had been forced to address his shortcomings as a person and a friend. He'd realized he focused too much on what could go wrong and his own neuroses to the detriment of his and Stephanie's friendship. It manifested in his constant annoyance with Stephanie—which, still, was often warranted—but prevented him from really seeing her as a person. It took a complete emotional breakdown for him to realize she'd been burying the pain of her parents' deaths beneath her façade of flippant irresponsibility. She didn't feel like a capable adult and was scared of failing if she tried. But the moment of vulnerability disappeared as quick as it came, and Steph was back to her normal jokey self. But Michael remembered, and resolved to be a better, more attentive friend.

To that end, Michael had been scouring The Future Group's databases for articles on the death of Stephanie's parents. Sure, he had considered asking her about it but, given her hesitation to discuss anything substantial, he figured a covert search would be less painful for both of them. Maybe once he understood the circumstances, Michael could craft the perfect set of words Stephanie would want to hear. His job may have been unfulfilling, but he could at least use its resources to become a good friend. Unfortunately for him, searches for the Dyer family in The Future Group Archives turned up no leads.

What Michael *had* stumbled upon were documents detailing other activities of The Future Group. While looking up old newspaper articles for traces of Stephanie's parents, he'd found small excerpts of coverage regarding something called **LXR** Chemicals and their co-funding of The Future Group's major donations to a nearby prison. Weird, certainly, but not out of character for The Future Group. They were probably screwing somebody out of money, somehow. It wasn't any of Michael's concern, though, he'd be fine just as long as his checks were clearing. It was the knee-jerk response of a jaded millennial, and he was terrifyingly used to it.

"Hmm." He shook off his laments and pushed up his glasses. Perhaps he could start searching for—

A sudden movement behind him triggered Michael's highly toned office reflexes. He yanked the offending program off-screen and switched windows back to his work, simultaneously whipping his head around to see who approached.

It was no one. Just a few other office drones he didn't recognize passing by his cubicle in overly jovial conversation. Michael breathed a sigh of relief. If anyone found out he was misusing Future Group resources, he'd be in trouble. It normally wouldn't phase him, but his recent experience with eviction was one he'd like not to repeat. His current place was a barebones Private Investigation office in the seedy borough of Squalor's Wallow, which—with some uncomfortable compromises with Stephanie—doubled as an apartment.

Michael chuckled as he switched back to his search. Two evictions in two months. Yes, it was the same old struggle in the makeshift Duckett and Dyer household, but after the craziness of a few weeks ago, it seemed everything had settled down and was finally going smoothly.

"Hey, Mike-ster."

Until now.

"Gah!" Michael jumped out of his chair and nearly his skin. He spun around to face Ravi Patel, who managed to maintain a grin through a long sip of coffee. "Ravi, what the hell?"

"Sup, buddy?" Ravi slid into Michael's cube, extending the word "buddy" as if he was entering a Paulie Shore impression contest. He peered over Michael's shoulder. "Whatcha working on?"

Michael nonchalantly fell back over his keyboard and monitor and attempted to hit the power button with his elbow. After flailing for a bit, he turned back to Ravi as if everything was hunky dory. He cleared his throat. "Um . . . nothing?"

"Didn't look like nothing." Ravi took another sip of coffee, and then, like a switch turned off in his head, his interest in Michael's doings was gone. "Anyway, just dropped by to tell you the good news!"

"Good . . . news?" Michael raised an eyebrow.

"I was gonna wait until the All-Hands Call today to let you know, but since you never come to those things anyway . . . I made Manager today, baby!"

"What?" Michael could scarcely believe his ears. Ravi Patel was one of the most irritating, useless sacks of shit he'd ever had the misfortune of knowing. The man took forty-five minute bathroom breaks. Michael didn't know what he did in there, but it sure wasn't pooping! And he made *manager*? "That's . . . good news!" Michael did his best to sound slightly positive.

"Yeah, man. The Future Group is awesome. It really takes care of us, y'know?" Ravi smiled an empty smile.

"It sure does," Michael deadpanned. He always got his number-crunching done, but he never put in the overtime the others in his division did. Michael couldn't quite understand how everyone else at The Future Group always seemed okay with putting in extra hours or working the weekends with smiles on their faces. Smiles like Ravi's. Maybe Michael was just defective. Lazy. But he was okay with that.

But there were times Michael had seen Ravi return to his desk and stare blankly at his computer screen for hours at a time. All the other times, he was socializing or in the bathroom. If that counted as overtime, Michael should have won employee of the year. It's not like they were doing anything important, especially in light of the grand, existential scheme of things Michael had been introduced to in his trip across the multi-verse.

"By the by, Mike-ster." Ravi was on his way out of the cubicle before he leaned back in. "The call's starting in thirty. You gonna come to the conference hall, or take it at your desk?"

"Hm?" Michael, still awkwardly positioned over his computer, tilted his head. "I think I'll take it here."

"You sure, man? We'd love to have everyone all together. Craig says he's got a bunch of important announcements about this week's new, final release. It's gonna be a show!"

"Yeah, I'm sure it is," Michael said. "I'll still take it down here."

"Alright, that's coolio." Ravi flashed a thumbs up, even though he was visibly disappointed. "But if you change your mind and wanna pop on up there, we'd love to have you. Just consider it, okay."

"Okay," Michael said through gritted teeth.

Ravi began to walk off with his coffee again but turned back, as if he had forgotten something. Michael knew what was coming. It made him grimace just thinking about it.

The employees of The Future Group had developed a particular quirk. They would always follow up any request—or any communication, really—with a simple phrase.

"Thanks, in advance."

Michael tried to will his face into a neutral position, if not a smile, but he failed. Ravi looked like he had nothing more to say, but once again, he refused to leave. He leaned on Michael's cubicle wall and slowly swirled his coffee while clearing his throat.

"Thanks." Michael sucked air in through his teeth. "In advance."

Ravi winked and shot him a wide smile before strolling away.

# CHAPTER THREE

## Ad Nauseam (Again)

Stephanie Dyer relished the satisfying clunk of the staple gun as it discharged into the telephone pole, before stepping back to admire her handiwork. The neon pink paper screamed against the stark brown of the pole, demanding her attention—and any passerby's.

She crossed her arms and nodded to herself. Steph had put together this new ad at the last minute, and while it wasn't as great as the launch campaign for her fledgling detective agency, it was certainly one of the top twenty ads she'd produced in her lifetime.

Of course, this flyer—along with its hundreds of sisters posted across the city and the internet—weren't strictly for the agency itself. They served a different purpose, one likely to make Mike a bit upset. But it was for his own good. She had a duty to fulfill.

Normally, Steph would have chuckled at the classic duty/doody dichotomy, but the disturbing events of the last month took precedence.

How could they not?

Weeks ago, through a disaster of time and space that may have very well been her fault, Steph had been propelled through a wide variety of super-neat alternate universes before landing two months in the past. There, she was confronted by a version of herself from an alternate universe. One which existed three years in the future.

Yeah. It was as confusing as it sounded.

The logic wasn't important and was, quite frankly, beyond her. What was important was that her alternate-future-self had told her Mike's life was in danger, as were the lives of all Mikes across the multi-verse.

And if that hadn't been the crap icing on top of an extremely shitty cake, the other her had also been very persistent that the two of them continue operating their detective agency. Why? She didn't say, other than a stereotypical warning of "grave consequences." Initially, Steph had no reason to distrust her other self, and she jumped at the chance to fight crime. But during the eight weeks spent living underneath her bed while waiting for timelines to sync, she had the opportunity to think.

She hated that. Steph preferred to be a "woman of action." She hadn't expected to mentally untangle a bunch bizarre sci-fi rigmarole when diving headfirst into forming a detective agency. Unlike the stuff she'd seen in cartoons, this weird logic puzzle gave her a headache. Probably because her life was on the line.

And Mike's life, too. Without the intervention of the newly branded "Duckett & Dyer: Dicks For Hire," Mike would fall victim to whatever mysterious disaster had befallen all the other Mikes in the multi-verse. And that's why Steph had to ensure the agency's success.

Or did she?

The more she thought, the more she realized—no matter what her alternate/future/whatever-self said—dragging Mike heedlessly into the rough and tumble world of private investigation was counterintuitive. If Mike wasn't killed by some criminal or accidentally shot, his anxiety would likely cause a heart attack at the mere sight of any super cool action set pieces that were bound to come up. And, come to think of it, why would Steph trust a parallel version of herself, anyway? Steph knew herself and knew she wasn't as reliable as she should be.

And Mike would agree.

She'd been a shitty friend. Even after what they'd gone through. Or, rather, what she'd forced them into against his will: traveling through a rainbow of different universes fighting Cow-Men Supreme and a terrifying "Normal Al" Yankovic. It should've been a bonding experience, but she couldn't bring herself to tell him about her deepest worries. Sure, she'd mentioned the painful memories of her parents' deaths, which happened a few years before she and Mike met as kids. But she never once brought up the disappearance of her brother. It was the most heart-rending part she didn't want to relive. They had been best friends. And he had vanished without a word. Without a trace. She knew he couldn't have abandoned her, but that was the only logical explanation. Her brother had never been found.

This multi-verse nonsense made her realize a lot of the shortcomings Mike had identified in her—as accurate as they were—stemmed from what had happened to her. She had just been a kid, but Steph remembered taking in the full weight of her family's loss like a gunshot to the chest, even at 6 years old.

She bit her lip. Her buried and forgotten feelings were bubbling to the surface, and Steph couldn't stand that. She didn't want Mike to know anything about it. He would see her differently, and she would feel weak. Not like a woman of action.

It wasn't like Mike would understand anyway. He didn't even know Steph once *had* a brother. And he didn't have to. She didn't need to burden him with all that. He probably wanted no part of it. Hell, Mike didn't even want any part of this detective agency. And maybe he was right not to, Steph decided. Despite the warnings of the future, she'd protect Mike and keep him away from this dangerous mess if it killed her. Better her than him. She certainly wasn't about to lose another best friend. She'd changed, promising herself to be reliable and consistent.

So Steph was going to do the only thing she really knew how to do—piss away money so the detective agency would become unviable. Of course, she could've just quit the detective biz outright, but that would've involved admitting she was wrong. She'd never done that before, so Mike would demand an explanation, and then it'd become a whole thing. It would be easier the roundabout way, allowing Steph to keep her pride. And it'd make for a cool little caper.

It'd be fine. As long as Mike still worked for The Future Group, they'd have enough cash to land back on their feet, and he would be safe.

Steph shoved her staple gun into the deep pockets of the oversized, comfy green coat she'd found amongst her brother's old clothes almost twenty-five years ago. It was the only thing left from the time before she met Mike, and it comforted her greatly. She may not have her family, but she still felt like her brother was there. He'd help Steph keep Mike alive. She knew it.

Steph dusted off her hands—well, the sleeves covering her hands—and pulled the lapels tight to shield herself from the chilly November breeze. Saving Mike would be a tough job, but doody called, and Steph had accepted the charge.

She chuckled to herself.

* * *

A few blocks later, after her stack of flyers visibly thinned, Steph turned a corner and found her favorite raving derelict—a man with tousled brown hair and bleary eyes she only knew as 'Homeless Joe.' Homeless Joe sat cross-legged on the cold sidewalk with an empty coffee cup at his feet. His upturned "The End Is Nigh" sign was propped up against a nearby mailbox. Joe had a few problems—most specifically, toting his sign around town and shouting conspiracy theories at people—but he was otherwise a decent dude and could always use some help, so she felt a sort of kinship with him. Steph reached into her pockets and removed whatever meager change she could find, tossing it into his coffee cup. "How's it going, Joe?"

"We're treading ever closer to the edge of destruction, Stephanie. The end is approaching. Not just the end of us, but the end of all things. Korthuu is coming. We must find the answer. The chain that links everything together."

"Aw, that's great." Steph flashed him a smile without actually listening to him. "Anyway, I'm going into this coffee shop to spread my literature around." She waved the stack of papers in her hand. "You want a latte or something while I'm in there?"

"Maybe just a coffee. Black with sugar."

"Black with sugar? Man, you're weird, Homeless Joe." Stephanie winced. "but I'll see what I can do."

"Thank you."

Steph nodded and turned into the coffee shop. The tiny set of bells above the door jingled, but their sound was lost in the hustle and bustle of the clientele. It was the morning rush just before work. Steph wasn't usually up this early, so she had forgotten it was a thing.

As Steph pushed her way through the crowd, the barista called out an order. "Nicolynn! Small Skinny White Latte. Nicolynn!"

Steph sighed and got in line. She wasn't much of a coffee person, but she knew she especially didn't like Skinny White Lattes. She was only here to drop off some of her flyers for maximum exposure, and, based on the crowd, she wasn't wrong. There were a ton of young attractive people here, any of whom could fill the position she had in mind. And perhaps other positions. But she'd burn that bridge when she came to it.

"Ace! Large cappuccino! Ace!"

It took a while, but eventually Stephanie reached the front. Leaning on the counter, making doe eyes at the guy behind the register, she plied her trade. "Hey, you. How's it going?"

"Hi, how can I help you?" The man's eyes smiled back at her, gleaming pools in a sea of dark skin.

"I'm Stephanie Dyer, you might have heard of me. Anyway, let's cut to the chase: how's about I buy you a coffee sometime?" Despite her other commitments, she had to try.

"Um . . . uh . . . I work at a coffee shop."

"So?"

"I . . . don't need coffee."

"Yeah, but, like, it's not *about* the coffee." Steph tried to reassert herself. "It's just like—y'know what? Forget it." She brandished her papers in the air. "I've got some flyers I'd like to spread around, you guys got a place for that?"

"Uh . . . yeah, back there." He pointed at a table near the front window.

"Cool. Thanks."

"So are you going to buy something, or . . ."

"Yeah. Whatever. Give me a large black coffee, with sugar."

"Are you still hitting on me?

"What?" Stephanie blinked. She thought that ship had sailed.

"It sounds like a euphemism. Because, like, I'm black and you want some sugar?"

"No? What? *Now* you think I'm hitting on you?"

"So you actually want a black coffee with sugar? That's ridiculous."

"I didn't ask for your opinions, buddy." Stephanie slammed a couple of bucks and some change on the counter. "Just give me my shitty coffee and I'll be on my way."

Stephanie trudged back to the front window to address what she'd really came for. On a small table filled with pamphlets and handouts for weight loss, guitar lessons, and weird religious propaganda about a flying space octopus, she found a small space, dropping her stack of flyers.

Turning around, she took in the bustling crowd of the coffee shop—who apparently cared less about holy octopi, much less her advertisement.

So, she took matters into her own hands. "Anyone here want a job?" she yelled.

A dozen ears perked up.

"Get in on the ground floor of an amazing start-up! No experience required."

A dozen more.

"And we pay handsomely!"

In a stampede to the front of the shop, soon everyone was perusing her flyers. If she had a lot of takers, Steph could easily spend all her budget on salary, close the detective agency, and summarily save a bunch of trouble without admitting defeat. Mike would be safe—and none the wiser.

"Stephanie. Large Black Coffee . . . with sugar? Stephanie!"

Steph sidled back up to the counter and grabbed her drink, watching more and more people look at her ad. She smiled to herself. Perhaps her luck was turning around. An attractive woman with dark raven hair and blue eyes, swished by in a pantsuit.

Steph decided to try her newfound luck. "Hey sexy lady, can I buy you a coffee?"

The woman scrunched her face up behind her glasses, holding aloft her coffee cup. "I . . . uh already have one."

Steph swatted it out of the air, sending her cup flying and spilling coffee everywhere. "Hey sexy lady, can I buy you another coffee?"

As the woman stormed off, wiping herself down, Steph was left wondering why that didn't work. Maybe she'd have to workshop her pick-up lines.

# CHAPTER FOUR

### Firing Solution

Michael turned back to his computer when he was sure Ravi had left a 500 foot radius around his cube. He didn't want to be surprised by another pathetic attempt at having him attend the quarterly All-Hands Meeting in person. Those calls were bullshit anyway. Michael had more important things to do. He'd rather spend his day searching for information that actually mattered to him and Stephanie than hear the company's CEO Craig Breene squawk about how The Future Group was actually a family with an important corporate mission to help the future of the world. And how their profits were continually through the roof. It was the same old schlock delivered through the teeth of Breene's static, almost creepy smile.

The only time Michael had ever seen Breene frown was in their face-to-face meetings during Michael's early days of employment. Breene—after insisting Michael call him "Craig"—told Michael he sat down with all his employees, or "family members," this way, but Michael hadn't bought it. Breene said he wanted to make sure Michael was becoming "a company man," and Michael sought to avoid that on every possible level. Michael couldn't give two shits about The Future Group or its "corporate mission." In fact, he wasn't even sure what its mission was—except a bunch of hogwash. Michael only showed up because he didn't enjoy the idea of him and Stephanie starving to death. The pay wasn't phenomenal—and Michael had the sneaking suspicion that everyone else was being paid more than him—but it kept him covered. If anyone other than The Future Group offered him a higher salary, he would have taken it in a heartbeat.

Breene, however, had no idea Michael wasn't showing up every day for his health. So while Michael persisted in being content to do his job and nothing more, Breene goaded him further toward spending extra hours and joining in on more team events. Michael smiled and nodded through another nauseating talk about how he wasn't living up to company expectations and could do better.

All of it furthered Michael's feeling that he was increasingly out of control of his life, merely another cog in an incredibly useless and infuriatingly inscrutable machine. He could only hide behind a mask of fake enthusiasm. Surely, he had everyone fooled.

His phone rang, and Michael nearly jumped out of his chair. The trilling three-toned ring repeated a few more times before the auto-answer system picked up.

The Future Group had, in its early days, implemented an automated answering system for all employee phone lines. If an internal call was made between employees or management, the receiving phone would automatically pick up and broadcast the call on speaker. According to Craig Breene, the practice emphasized the corporate family's ability to always listen. Much like a real family.

Michael didn't know what kind of family Breene came from, but it certainly wasn't "real".

"Hello everyone." Breene's voice beamed enthusiasm over the

tinny speaker. "I'm so glad you could all join us today for The Future Group's Quarterly All-Hands Call. I have a ton of good news for us, especially regarding the upcoming release.

"It is also a pleasure to see all your smiling faces here in The Future Group auditorium, which just reaffirms just how much of a good investment we've made in our family."

Michael rolled his eyes as the sound of applause followed.

"Now, speaking of family," Breene's voice continued, "our HR Manager Arthur Birch is unavailable today, otherwise he would be making this announcement. But I'm happy to say, given the impending success of our release, we're anticipating a large influx of new members in our family very soon. So we're going to need more senior staff. Thus, everyone in this room right now has been granted a full promotion and a very considerable raise. Just another way for us to say thanks, in advance!"

Michael's eyes widened. This *was* good news. After so many years, he'd finally make manager, just like that idiot Ravi. Maybe things weren't so bad around here after all.

"Unfortunately, this reshuffling of duties will mean there will be some organizational adjustments, and we will sadly have to let some underperforming members of our family go. The following employees have been laid off"—the pause hung in the air interminably—"Michael Duckett."

When no other names followed, Michael rocketed up out of his chair.

"What?" His voice echoed across the empty floor. As everyone had vacated to the conference hall for the meeting, no one heard Michael's subsequent volley of curses. What the hell was this? They were firing him? For what? Sure, he'd been a bit distracted recently, but he finished all his work on time. This was outrageous! The anger was quickly followed by fear. What the hell was he going to do? How was he going to get paid? What about health insurance?

"We wish Michael the absolute best and thank him for his years of service. We're certain he will find greener pastures elsewhere." Breene's voice maintained a surprising cheeriness Michael didn't share. "Now, let's move on to our earnings . . . "

Anger returned, replacing the fear—much to Michael's benefit—and he roared, picking up and slamming the phone receiver back down, hanging up on the call. A few seconds later, it rang again, and the phone's auto-answer system continued the call.

". . . which have been considerable. The release of Kor—"

Michael didn't hear the latter half, as he had already stormed his way through the cubicle maze on the way to the central elevator bank. That asshole wanted him to attend in-person so badly, he was going to oblige.

Using the express elevator, Michael made it to the 97th floor. The hallway curved around the vast conference hall containing thousands of The Future Group's employees for the *important* company-wide announcements. There were no windows, and most of the walls were paneled with thick polished wood, rather that the transparent glass of the working floors. It felt claustrophobic and isolating. The interior designer had probably nailed the feeling The Future Group was going for. Michael had been up here once before and was so turned off by it all, he refused to return, on principle. And—because it was less annoying to take the calls from his desk.

Michael burst through the wide double-doors, leaving them swinging in his wake, and every employee in the bright white stadium-style seating of the hall turned to face him. He'd never made such a scene before. His heart pounded.

"What in the actual hell?" he yelled down toward the conference room floor, where Craig Breene, in a simple black button down and jeans, stood, presenting a high-definition stylized PowerPoint detailing recent acquisitions of The Future Group. A spotlight, positioned directly above him, illuminated the stage and made the air around Breene seem to glow.

"Oh, Michael! Hello!" Breene's voice boomed through his lapel mic and around the rotunda through strategically placed speakers mounted on sterile white walls. "Is this about the organizational adjustments?"

"You're goddamn right it's about that," Michael shouted. His voice felt tiny and fragile when compared to Breene's artificially amplified exuberance.

"Yes, well, I'm sorry, Michael. Let's not beat around the bush anymore. You know this is for the best."

"What are you talking about?" Michael could barely hear himself. He was surprised Breene could.

"Can someone get him a mic?" Breene motioned to the back. In seconds, an assistant approached Michael with a microphone, and he reluctantly accepted it

Breene pulled a stool on stage and sat down, leaning on one knee. "Michael, I just want to talk. What did you like about your job here?"

Michael dug his nails into his palms to keep himself from blurting out the word 'nothing', opting instead for a more diplomatic outright lie. "I enjoy the work. And the people."

Breene paused, as if waiting for a laugh track. When none came, he continued, "Well, Michael, that's never come through. And I'm sure you're not surprised about that. We've gone over this a number of times. And, frankly, we're disappointed in you. We tried to give you the benefit of the doubt over the past few years. We really believed you could become a part of The Future Group Family." The last phrase felt like it should have come with a trademark symbol in the corner.

"Michael—what I'm saying is—The Future Group might not be the best fit for you." Breene's tented fingers slid into each other's' gaps, allowing neither hand to escape from a vice-like grip. "All of us are working toward a common goal that will soon be realized, for which we've provided several monetary bonuses, with bigger rewards to come.

You've never showed us the kind of dedication worthy of those rewards."

"But I got all my work done. On time and efficiently!" Michael surprised even himself, being so protective of his work product. "I may not have stayed late nights, but I got things done. That's gotta count toward dedication. I should be the one getting a promotion, too! You're firing me and not friggin' Ravi?"

"Hey!" A small voice sounded from the far end of the rotunda, muffled by the sea of faces. "Mikester, that's not cool!"

"It's not about the work, Michael. I thought we made that clear. It's that we don't believe you fit the company culture we've worked so hard to establish. Case in point: bashing good old Ravi, there. He's the kind of enthusiastic manager that The Future Group needs."

"You've got to be kidding me." Michael furrowed his brow.

"Unfortunately, no. We would appreciate it if you could be out of the building by five o'clock." Breene's smile persisted.

Michael glanced at his watch and spoke into the mic. "It's 4:45."

"Well, then I suppose you should better get going," Breene said. "If you need any assistance, I'm sure security would be happy to help." He caught himself and added, "Also, if you could clean your desk of any personal effects, so we can prep for a new hire, that'd be great. Thanks, in advance."

"Thanks, in advance?" This was the final cherry on top that broke the camel's back. Not being fired. Not being humiliated in front of all his former co-workers and on a quarterly call that would be filmed and archived. No, it was hearing that insufferable phrase, once again, causing years of downright frustration to pour out of Michael's mouth. "No! To hell with "thanks, in advance!' How about 'kiss my ass, in advance?' How about that? I've busted my goddamn butt for years at this shitty company, putting numbers in spreadsheets for no reason, and you're going to fire me? To hell with you! Do you want to know what I really think about you and this whole Future Group bullshit?"

"No," Breene cut him off bluntly, "We don't think that would be productive. So if you could head out, we'd really appreciate it."

Michael tried to stifle the frustrated howl bubbling at the back of his throat before attempting to leap down the stairs in anger. However, the hall was so wide, he barely made it two-thirds of the way down before two members of the support team grabbed him by his arms and stopped him in his tracks.

Breene cleared his throat. "So are you quite done?"

\* \* \*

It didn't take long for Michael to gather his things. He never brought in any personal items, preferring to leave his desk barren, lest he get too attached to it. A laughable notion to be sure. All he placed in the box he'd stolen from the office supply closet was a bunch of office supplies he'd stolen from the very same closet. No one gathered to say goodbye, although Michael wasn't sure what he expected. It wasn't just that they were still in the meeting. In the four years Michael spent here, he actively avoided trying to make any unnecessary friends. A thought crossed his mind—maybe Breene had a point. But Michael quickly smothered it with impotent rage. He slunk into the elevator with his box, attempting to comfort himself. At least he would never see this cursed place again.

The elevator spat Michael out into the building lobby, covered from floor to ceiling with green marble tiling only broken by repeated tessellations of the company's triangular red logo. Out past the elevator banks, Michael scanned his ID for the last time, opening the glass dividing gates that separated the riff-raff of the common people from the business being performed in the tower. Over the corrugated edges of his box, Michael stole a sideways glance at the reception desk. Empty. Maybe even Erica, the front desk girl, had been promoted out of her current position.

No, Erica wasn't at the desk, but another familiar and terrifying face was. Detective Rex Calhoun stood in the reception area, tapping his foot and glancing at his watch with his standard grimace.

The gruff, bald detective had confronted Michael weeks ago after he and Stephanie had hurtled through the multi-verse. Calhoun didn't seem to remember too much about how their paths crossed, but he had—in no uncertain terms—threatened the two of them with jail time if he caught them trying to play at their brand of "crime solving" ever again.

Whatever Calhoun was here for, Michael didn't want to be a part of it. Worse, Calhoun was yet another reminder of the stress Michael wanted to avoid. A direct confrontation was out of the question. If he was to evade Calhoun's detection, he would need to be as cool and subtle as possible. Unfortunately, Michael defaulted into panic mode and employed the first plan that came to mind. He raised his box of stolen goods a little higher to obscure the lower part of his face.

Luckily, Calhoun was too engrossed in waiting for the missing receptionist to notice Michael slinking by. Michael smiled to himself, proud he had managed to evade a real detective. Then—the box smacked straight into the lobby's glass front door before bouncing back into Michael's head with a loud thwack. Rogue pens and binder clips leapt from the open box and scattered across the floor.

Startled, Michael opted to raise the box even higher to cover his entire face as he dashed out the door. Peering through the box's handle holes, Michael saw Calhoun shake his head and make his way to the elevator bank, jumping over the glass dividing gates.

Michael exhaled fear out of his system, leaving only anxiety behind. He used it as fuel to speed-walk across The Future Group courtyard and hide beneath the statue in the center. Michael passed this thing every day on his way to work but paid it no attention, until now. The towering black obelisk, extending out of multiple, concentric, brass bowls, gave him a brief moment to drop his box and breathe, head between his knees.

Once he collected his bearings, Michael peered out from behind the statue's plinth to see if Calhoun was still in the lobby. He couldn't really see through the glare of the glass doors, but his mind told him to make a run for it anyway. Scooping up his box, Michael dashed across the courtyard, narrowly avoiding the giant brass statue in the middle. Escaping down a set of side stairs flanked by tall shrubbery, he managed to make it to the relative safety of the parking deck where he could breathe easy. Slumping beside his vehicular deathtrap—a 1982 Mercury Zephyr affectionately known as the "Garbagemobile"—Michael let out a sigh, equal parts irritation and relief.

But what was Calhoun doing here anyway?

# CHAPTER FIVE

## Severe Corporate Audit

This was a bunch of horseshit. Calhoun ran his palm down his face as he looked around for someone he could talk to or, even better, yell at. Despite The Future Group being a multi-billion dollar business, it couldn't seem to afford to staff a reception desk. Was everyone here just a gang of idiots?

Calhoun's suspicions were confirmed when an employee carrying a cardboard bankers box slammed headfirst into the glass lobby doors. If this was the kind of talent The Future Group was hiring, Calhoun would have his work cut out for him. Shaking his head, he opted to bypass the absent secretary and vaulted himself over the glass entry barriers toward the elevator banks.

"Hrm." Calhoun grunted as he loomed at the touch screen buttons. It had options from one to ninety-seven—and a basement, grayed out and inaccessible. Calhoun jabbed his finger at the highest number, but it refused him entry and flashed a lock symbol. A cartoon version of The Future Group's logo walked onscreen and chastised him with a waving finger and a stern but playful look. Calhoun ignored the pop-up password box and instead stormed down the rows of elevators. The last bank would take him to the top. So, he waited, back against the cold marble wall, until he heard one ding. He rushed past a janitor with an oddly wide smile pushing a garbage bin and slid into the open elevator. As Calhoun rode up, his ears popped every fifteen floors or so.

He exited at the top—floor ninety-seven. It was an enormous space with thick, curved wood paneling in lieu of external windows. No emergency exits, either. That had to be some sort of fire hazard. As the elevator doors clicked closed behind him, Calhoun turned to see a massive throng of people flooding out of the large presentation hall in the center of the floor. The crowd split up, with each mass heading toward a different elevator bank. Calhoun pushed through the sea of bodies filled with shiny, chatting idiots. They all seemed to be real happy about something or another. Every time he took two steps forward, the tide of people forced him five steps backward. It was as if they didn't notice him at all. And if they did, they didn't care. He had half a mind to pull out his gun and start firing into the air to get their attention.

Unfortunately, it didn't come to that. Although there were a lot of people, they were well organized, and within a few minutes, the floor was clear of anybody save for a few stragglers. Calhoun found his bearings and proceeded into the presentation hall The Future Group nerds had filed out of. Calhoun hoped the top floor housed a boardroom of some kind, so he could find someone with authority he could speak to. Instead, a vast rotunda greeted him, with concentric seats surrounding a wide stage. The house lights were on, illuminating the already white room in an almost blinding glow.

"Huh." Calhoun scanned the hall. It was bigger than he had thought. It could fit a few thousand people, easy.

"Hello!"

"Jesus!" Calhoun nearly toppled over. A balding man in a black button-down shirt and jeans smiled widely beside him. Where the man had come from, Calhoun didn't know. It was like he'd popped out of nowhere.

"How can I be of service?" It was an odd response to finding an angry man in a trench coat and hat on a private floor, but at least Calhoun wasn't being shot at, so it was one of the better welcomes he'd received.

Calhoun pulled out his badge. "Detective Rex Calhoun. City PD. I was looking for whoever's in charge here."

"That would be me." The man extended his hand. "Craig Breene. Founder and CEO of The Future Group."

"You're Breene?" Calhoun arced an eyebrow. He'd heard a lot about this financial savant, but he expected him to be older. Even though he was bald, this guy looked like he was barely pushing forty.

"Yes, I know. I look younger than you'd think." Breene read his mind. "I appreciate the compliment. Now, how can I help you, detective?"

"Well, we have reason to believe The Future Group is connected to a series of deaths that have occurred over the last few weeks. They may be murders."

"Murders?" The smile dropped off the man's face. His grimace was pained and uncertain, as if he had never gotten used to frowning. Calhoun could teach him a thing or two about that.

"What can you tell me about your firm's ties to State Senator Elaine Clegg?"

"Oh, Senator Clegg." Breene held his hand up to his mouth. "I heard about her death and was saddened, to say the least. She was one of our biggest supporters in the state legislature. But I thought her death was of natural causes?"

"We have reasons to suspect foul play."

"Well, I met the Senator once at a function and gave her a tour of our facilities here a few years ago. But other than that, we've had no contact with her."

Breene sounded sincere, and there was no way for Calhoun to dispute it. He pressed on. "What about Edgar Brauer? EM Industrial Real Estate?"

"I personally don't deal with our land and building holdings. You'll have to talk to the Property Department on Floor 49. But you say we've had dealings with this Mr. Brauer, and now he's dead?"

"Yes."

"Are you sure?"

"His head exploded."

"Hm. I suppose that would do it."

"And what about Arthur Birch?"

The words shook Breene's façade, although it wouldn't surprise Calhoun if this was just an act. "Arthur, oh, no! He's our Human Resources Manager. I knew he was out today, but I didn't know why."

"Sorry to be the bearer of bad news, but we found his body. He was shot on his way to work this morning."

"This . . . this is awful." Breene looked down before meeting Calhoun's gaze once again. "And it is of the City Police Department's opinion that all these deaths were perpetrated by the same person?"

"Well . . ." Calhoun wanted to avoid claiming any specifics, since he didn't have any official department backing. "That's what we're trying to find out."

Breene's face turned dark, edging into a scowl. "You think The Future Group is involved."

"If you aren't involved, then at least you're being targeted."

"If that is the case, I'll have to phone up Chief Braddock and demand extra protection. I will not have my employees exposed to harm in any way. Nor will I have them subject to baseless accusations."

"Whoa." Calhoun threw up his arms and backpedaled. "No need

to phone Braddock. I'll have you know he and I are on . . . uh *very* good terms. I'll make sure your request gets sent up the pipe myself."

"Excellent." Breene's face returned to its tight artificial smile— probably its natural state. "See that it does."

Calhoun was going to see that it didn't. "But you're certain there isn't anybody in this whole organization that would want to harm The Future Group or its supporters?"

"Oh, no. Everyone at The Future Group is very respectful of our mission. We're all working together for our common good. And no one would execute such a betrayal."

"Uh huh. No one. Not any disgruntled ex-employees?"

"Well, our employees generally stay with us for life." Breene's face transformed again, this time to a quizzical grimace. "Except one. We had to let him go quite recently. You just missed him, in fact."

Calhoun raised an eyebrow. A lead. It was small, but it was something. And it would distract Breene from even thinking about alerting Braddock.

"Hrm. He may be a person of interest in the case." Calhoun flipped open his notebook. "Any information you have would be helpful. Would you be able to share his name with me?"

When Breene did so, Calhoun nearly bit his lip in two.

# CHAPTER SIX

## Virtual Insanity

"Attack Supreme Cow Monster," Craig enunciated as he typed in the direction. The green wireframe on his screen—which vaguely resembled some sort of minotaur—flashed, and a message appeared.

```
You have done 20 damage to Supreme Cow Mon-
ster.
```

```
Supreme Cow Monster attacks you with Staff.
```

"Counterattack," Craig typed, voicing the written word.

```
Counterattack successful.
```

```
You have slain the Supreme Cow Monster and
have defeated the last of the Cow Cult guarding
the temple. Proceed inside?
```

Craig typed a "Y."

The screen flashed again, and the image of crumbling steps and a minotaur-like monster, lying on the ground and bleeding, was replaced by a lavish rotunda. An upturned hemisphere, the rotunda was lined with multiple levels of stone chairs circling an enormous flame, burning brightly on a carved dais. At least, that's what it was supposed to be. Right now, Craig had only designed the green wireframe model, a mess of lines and angles looking more like a static neon blueprint with no substance. Even the fire was just jagged green lines jutting into the black air. An angular porcupine, rather than licking, roiling flames of death.

Craig's terrifying interdimensional monster would sit beyond the "flame," when he'd finished the level. The player—the Steel Knight—having rallied the heroes on various endangered worlds, would came face to face with the beast threatening to consume them here in this final chamber. But Craig had barely gotten to the point where he could design the monster.

He'd been having trouble with it for the past three years. Between learning to code, creating graphics, fleshing out mechanics, and charting the various stories and worlds that had to be created for his game, Craig had made precious little progress. He was now completely certain he and Marcus had bitten off more than they could chew. They had siphoned a great deal of Consolidated Future Inc's money, and without anything to show for it, there would soon be hell to pay. Marcus had made that very clear.

To make things worse, he had been promoted at his real job. Craig was now in charge of the technology initiatives for several different departments with hundreds of employees. At best, his days were filled with juggling employee tech requests or telling them why their requests were at best unreasonable—and at worst, impossible bullshit. It left little time for putting together an elaborate multi-faceted roleplaying game.

Thus, Craig had cloistered himself in his make-shift basement office late on a Friday night. He kept himself in the dark partly because it allowed him to focus on the computer screen and partly because he wanted to ignore the piled boxes of computer components strewn across the floor.

"Craig!" Marcus stormed in and flipped on the light switch, flooding the room with harsh florescent light. It reflected off the limestone walls, making the room glow a bright, heavenly white.

Craig was so shocked he might have hissed.

Marcus approached his desk, with a package in hand. Another computer component to add to the pile, Craig supposed. "Please tell me you've made some progress on this."

"Uh . . ." With a few keystrokes, Craig jumped out of his program and back in again, back to the start. "Well, it's not much, but I'm working on the final boss."

"Okay, and what else?" Marcus asked.

"Well, nothing. There's nothing else. I'm working backwards from here so I can create the multiple other worlds that lead up to this."

"What?"

"I was thinking of making the next world a futuristic slum world with cyberpunk aesthetic."

"No, I mean, what? You've done nothing else?"

"I've been busy doing my actual job, Marcus!" Craig didn't want to snap at him, but he was at his last frayed nerve. "And I've been spending all my free time learning how to design a 3D video game because you thought it would sell better!"

"Don't you pin this on me." Marcus grabbed Craig by the shoulder and spun him around in his chair so they were face to face. "I'm risking my neck here basically embezzling money and piping equipment down here to fund *your* video game. And I'm also working my ass off up there to keep my numbers up. Because if I don't, the board is gonna come sniffing around down here and we're both going to be out on our asses! And I got a little girl to feed!"

"You should've thought of that before—" Craig clammed up immediately when he realized what he was going to say.

"Before what, Craig?" Marcus leaned down toward him. "Before what? Before my wife died?"

"Hey, Marcus, c'mon, I'm sorry." Craig shouldn't have even thought that. He knew Marcus was having a tough year—even tougher than his—and it pained him to see Marcus hurt so much, especially when Craig was adding to it.

Marcus took a breath and ran his hand through his thick hair, "Listen, man. I'm really sorry. I'm just . . . it's too much right now, okay?"

"I know. I get it. But I've been working as hard as I can." Craig tried to understand Marcus' frustrations, but all he could hear was his mother's judgements. She had told him this would happen. Craig's faith in his friend was crumbling—and vice versa—and it hurt more than he wanted it to.

"I just don't wanna get us in any more trouble than we're already in. We need to make our money back—and quickly—before someone finds us out." Marcus thrust the package toward Craig. "Here. Maybe this'll help."

Craig turned the box around in his arms, inspecting the slick packaging. The words Virtual Boy were emblazoned on it in long red lettering.

"It's a Nintendo," Marcus explained. "One of the new ones with the goggles. They told me it was gonna be the hottest toy of 1995."

"Yeah," Craig said. He'd seen the previews in the March issue of EGM. "I know what it is."

"I got it for my kid, but she hates it. Makes her eyes water. I thought maybe you could strip it for parts or use it for research or something."

Craig didn't know what he would do with it, so he offered a quiet smile. "Thanks, Marcus. It's pretty great."

"Alright." he nodded and started toward the door. "I gotta pick Ace up from soccer practice, so I'll see you later. Just don't burn yourself out. You want the lights on or off?"

"Off, please."

"You got it." Marcus flipped the switch on his way out, bathing Craig in darkness.

* * *

The Virtual Boy proved quite useful. As a gaming system, it was terrible, but as a visualization tool, it worked wonders. At least it did after he changed its eye-destroying red display into a more pleasing green one with a few clever bits of re-soldering that only took half a day. The rest of the day, Craig set up a method by which he could use the headset—the controller was a piece of crap—to help him navigate the worlds he was creating in real time. Even if they were just wireframes for now, it'd help him generate levels more quickly. And since he had hundreds to do, every little bit would help. At the very least, it was a peace offering from Marcus, and it soothed Craig's worries.

Craig sat down in the swiveling chair before his computer and connected the headset to the desktop tower by way of a few stripped wires he need to replace at some point. Grabbing the keyboard he'd adapted into a control pad, he lowered the headset onto his greasy hair and secured it tightly with a newly-attached strap. His vision now obscured by a vast, unending black, he tapped a few buttons. The black vanished, replaced by a rainbow of different shades of green. He was well within the central rotunda of his final boss level. The static green flames of the fire on the dais stuck out like spines in front of him, illuminating the rows of identical, but empty, wireframe chairs.

Craig kept an eye on the timestamp in the bottom left corner of his field of view—a safety precaution to ensure he didn't lose track of time. September 17th, 1995, 12:07pm. He had a bit of time before he wanted to get lunch, so he cracked his knuckles—the real world sound muted and tinny through his headset—and got to work.

His fingers flew across the keyboard, importing several different polygonal models and forming components of his pan-dimensional monster. Insectoid legs, hundreds of them—accompanied by eyes, jaws, and arms—all positioned uncomfortably on a bulbous, rotting body.

Certainly something beyond the realm of human understanding. But, as Craig pulled back and admired his newly built terror, he wondered. Was it too much? Or not enough? Eh, either way, with this new system, he could quickly remodel it if need be. For now, all it needed was a name.

A faraway buzzing and crackling drew his attention. It wasn't anything in the level, since he hadn't yet added any audio—that was another future headache. It must have been coming from outside. A burning sensation flashed across the back of his hand, causing him to yank it away.

The display went dark with the increased flurry of sizzling and popping. Craig could smell the first few drafts of ozone wafting through the air. The computer was overheating, or worse, outright burning! Craig panicked, fumbling at the headset, but he could not remove it in time. A surge of electricity coursed through the wiring and into Craig's skull, sending fireworks across his otherwise black vision. He smelled his own hair burning as he lapsed into unconsciousness. Everything went well and truly black.

* * *

Craig awoke hours later, only knowing the time due to the timestamp in the lower left corner of his vision. September 17th, 1995, 17:42pm. Although he could not see—ostensibly because he still had the Nintendo headset on—his bare cheek felt the cool cement floor of the basement and the lukewarm drool pooling outside his mouth. What the hell happened? Did he need to call himself an ambulance? What if he hadn't woken up and Marcus only found him tomorrow morning? Craig would have asked more questions if he hadn't been distracted by the visuals flickering to life before his eyes.

He was still in the ancient stone temple of his final boss monster, but now, instead of rough wireframes, the structure was fully realized. The green flames danced and crackled on the dais. He could practically feel the rough cracks in the stone walls. It was all . . . real, for the lack of a better word. It felt impossible. It was exactly as Craig had seen it in his head. He half expected to turn around and see his nameless horror charging at him. Wouldn't that be a sight! Hell, if Marcus could see this now, he'd be floored.

Speaking of which, Craig was still lying on the floor in the real world. He pushed himself up and clawed at the rough ground around him until his fingertips hit hard plastic. The keyboard. Taking it back to his desk and re-righting the chair without the use of his eyes was difficult, but Craig didn't want to lose view of his level. Sitting back down, he found he could move about, flying all around the temple, although he felt a bit uncoordinated.

Ah, yes. He felt around the outer edges of the keyboard. It was upside down. He would have to just turn it and—the keyboard flew out of his hands and clattered on the floor, sending his in-game view tumbling out of control. By the time he had reasserted himself, the temple was lost. Gone completely. It would have been devastating had Craig not found himself in a surprising new locale.

It was a vast desert wasteland he had never seen before. A few cliffs and canyons towered in the background, and wisps of sand blew in the gentle breeze. But the most striking feature of the new world: it was in color. The temple had been lit in all green, like the Virtual Boy's display, so Craig might not have noticed it. But this desert completely surpassed the headset's abilities, rendering the landscape in soft, undulating variations of brown, with the occasional pink and green cactus blossom popping against the blue sky and blooming white clouds.

As Craig stood in his own personal Oz, a wind picked up around him. Of course, he couldn't feel it, but Craig could see the shifting of the ground, the flying grains, the rustling of dead bushes and the tumbling of weeds.

Squinting in real life, Craig could make out a commotion off in the distance in his video game. Several figures were moving and kicking up quite the dust cloud. It looked like a fight. He could not make out who was fighting whom, as it seemed to be an epic struggle.

Craig reached for his keyboard, eager to fly over and see what the fuss was all about, but the winds grew stronger; the ground textures began to shake. Confused, Craig turned around as a wall of sand, rock and chunks of earth rushed toward him.

Once again, everything fell into darkness.

But this time, Craig was fully conscious.

"What the—" He swiveled his head around in the real world, as if looking for some answers in the virtual one. But he found nothing. "What the hell was that? Am I dead? Was that some kind of hallucination?"

To his surprise, the darkness answered back.

"No, Craig Breene. That was destiny."

The darkness had a deep, soothing voice with a bit of a rough edge, like James Earl Jones after smoking two packs a day for a year. It was exactly what Craig expected darkness to sound like. Nevertheless, it surprised him.

"Who are you? What's going on? How do you know my name?"

"All good questions, Craig Breene. They will be answered in time. But now, I need your help."

"My help?" Craig tilted his head as if the darkness could see it. "For what?"

"The worlds you have just seen are but a sliver of what is known as the multi-verse."

"The multi-verse? Are you serious?" Implications exploded across Craig's brain, adding to the list of questions he had already proposed. The multi-verse wasn't just some weird meta-concept posited by physicists and illustrated by comic book artists? What was out there? What kind of worlds existed? But Craig kept quiet, swallowing his excitement.

"Yes, Craig. Come with me and I'll prove to you exactly how serious I am."

The empty black of the display vanished in an instant, replaced by the floor of a forest illuminated only by thin rays of sunshine piercing through the canopy. But this was no ordinary forest, as everything was out of scale. Craig felt like an ant amongst towering trees, with trunks as thick as an apartment building. He spun around in time to see a giant black fluffball dart out of his field of view. Even the animals here were huge.

"Where . . . where are we?"

"Yet another world of the multi-verse," the voice answered, echoing through Craig's brain. "Care to see another?"

The voice didn't wait for Craig's response. Suddenly, he was in the midst of an exotic alien market, where strange, otherworldly creatures bartered over fruits he did not recognize. A small child with grey skin and seven eyes snuck a stone fruit from a vendor's basket before running away, giggling.

"This is unreal! How're you showing me this?"

"I have had much experience with the multi-verse, Craig Breene," the voice said. The display left him in darkness once again. "I sense your equipment has been granted the ability to pierce the veil between worlds. If we work together, I can show you how to traverse them all. And move throughout their timelines."

"That's amazing!" Craig bit his lip. "This could change the world. I could see everything. Every possibility. I could predict the future."

"There is much more to show you, so much more," the darkness continued. "But there is something out there that limits our abilities to view certain universes and their timelines. Even the future of your own universe is blocked off to me."

Craig furrowed his brow. "What do you mean?"

"Something is preventing me from fully accessing your universe. It may be the same anomaly causing other realities to wink out of existence with surprising frequency. To put it in more certain terms, the multi-verse is in danger. The stability of existence is being threatened. And only you and I can save it, Craig Breene."

Craig's jaw dropped. In the space of a few minutes, everything he knew about life had fallen away. The meager work he'd done for Consolidated Futures, even the video game he set his heart on designing, paled in importance with what was before him now. It was like his mother's fairy tales, only now, he was the hero. The Steel Knight. Craig Breene could finally make the difference he'd always wanted to. Not just for the world, but for existence itself.

He'd definitely have to tell Marcus about this.

# CHAPTER SEVEN

## Secretaries and Lies

The Garbagemobile wobbled and jerked down the highway, the steering wheel actively resisting Michael's attempts to direct it to the proper exit. He had often thought of installing sails on the damn thing, as they would be a more reliable way to control it. The car eventually acquiesced, allowing Michael to yank it off the highway and into the colorful borough known only as "Squalor's Wallow."

Squalor's Wallow wore its name well. It was a small section of the city inhabited by burnt down husks masquerading as buildings, with windows made primarily of plywood. The roads weren't in great condition, either. Potholes littered the street and, rumor had it, those that had been fixed were filled with a mixture containing human bone meal. Needless to say, a rusting 1982 Mercury Zephyr felt right at home here. With a screech akin to a hundred records scratching at once—if all the records had been "Sounds of the Slaughterhouse"—the Garbagemobile halted when Michael directed its front wheels into a set of particularly deep potholes by the curb of an old brick building. The three-story structure seemed to be standing only due to some arcane ritual cast on it in centuries past. Or perhaps the convenience store occupying the ground floor was just strong enough to bear the weight of the upper levels. Still, as Michael slammed the single functioning door of the Garbagemobile, a brick fell off the crumbling edifice and shattered on the sidewalk beside him with a loud clack.

"Fantastic." Michael craned his neck up to see a tiny new gap below the third floor window that concealed the operations of Duckett & Dyer: P.I.s for Hire LLC. He approached the front door of the building and pushed through, ignoring the remnants of yellow caution tape stuck to the frame. The door held fast. Michael scrunched his face up in frustration and shoved again. It gave a bit. One more shove and—

"Hey!" A voice yelled from inside the building. A voice Michael didn't recognize. "Stop that!"

The front door creaked open, and the scene on the other side baffled Michael—which seemed to be happening more these days. A line of men and women had taken up residence in the narrow hallway, snaking all the way up the stairs. The most striking thing was exactly how attractive these people were and how well-fitting all their clothing was. Michael couldn't help but feel a mix of sheepishness and jealousy spreading throughout his body.

Unsure how best to react, Michael issued some curt apologies as he pushed forward and followed the line all the way up two flights of rickety, termite-ridden stairs to find—surprise, surprise—it ended upstairs at the door to his and Stephanie's new office/apartment hybrid.

"Excuse me, uh . . . ma'am." As he reached the top of the staircase, Michael tapped on the shoulder of the nearest girl, a blonde woman in a pencil skirt. "Do you, um . . . could you tell me what this line is for?"

"Oh." She turned with a breathy whisper. "It's for the . . . secretary position."

"Right," Michael glanced back over his shoulder before addressing the line as a whole. "That's why all of you are here? To apply for a secretary position?"

"Well, yeah." A brown haired man, whose eyes were as blue as the waters of the Amalfi Coast and whose shoulders were as broad as the coast itself, leaned out of the line.

"*All* of you," Michael repeated, before asking the obvious. "Why?"

"The starting salary was listed as $80,000," offered another muffled voice from somewhere in the line. A dull pain started forming between Michael's eyes.

"We'd be stupid not to try," the blonde woman said. A general hum of agreement pervaded the rest of the line. "Even if we didn't agree with some of the . . . specifics."

"Of course." Michael bit his lip and rubbed his temples. "Excuse me for just one second."

Michael walked to the beginning of the line, cutting off a tall black-haired man in a half-unbuttoned shirt and suspenders.

"Hey!" he said. "Wait your turn."

"Sorry. I . . . uh . . . I live here," Michael pointed at the door's frosted glass emblazoned with the gilded Duckett & Dyer: P.I.s For Hire logo—a logo Michael had not approved of in the first place. He grimaced at the bright red graffiti that replaced the word "P.I.s" with "Dicks" in all caps. It was embarrassing. Michael hated it. Stephanie promised to clean that up, but he knew how much Stephanie's promises were worth. Speaking of which . . .

"Steph—" Michael started to bellow, but found himself cut off as the door to the office slammed open, nearly shattering the glass and sending Michael into a flying stumble, bowling him into the line of people.

"This is discrimination!" From behind the door, a raspy voice Michael did not recognize yelled. It belonged to a heavyset older woman who subsequently stormed out of the office with such force, Michael worried about the integrity of the floors. "You're lucky I don't just sue!"

"I'm sorry, Maureen, but you just don't fit the profile!" Another voice, this one annoyingly familiar, carried from inside the office. With the help of the other members of the line, Michael hoisted himself to his feet.

Maureen suppressed a growl before pushing Michael aside with surprising ferocity and clomping down the stairs. This time, Michael maintained his balance, dusted himself off, and moved to occupy the doorway. "Stephanie!"

In the small waiting room outside the larger office, behind a hastily assembled desk that hadn't been there when Michael left in the morning, sat Stephanie, her hand clasped firmly around a banana. She grinned like an idiot. Through a mouthful of banana, she said, "Oh, hi, Mike. You're home early."

"What the hell is going on here?"

"That's a great question." Stephanie gulped down the remaining fruit mush and tossed the peel into a nearby waste bin. It landed atop many leftover pieces from the desk. Too many. "Let me answer it with another question—"

"No, no." Michael cut her off at the pass. "None of that. Why are you interviewing secretaries? And why was that older lady yelling at you?"

"Well, she just didn't fit the profile, Mike."

"Profile? What prof—" Michael stopped and turned around to take in another view of the line of beautiful men and women that had queued up in front of their office. Everything clicked. "Goddamnit." Michael stepped through the office door and slammed it closed. "Were you planning on tricking these people into sleeping with you?"

"Um . . ." Stephanie avoided Michael's piercing gaze, hiding her face behind a large manila folder overflowing with resumes. "I wouldn't say 'tricking,' really. The ideas just kinda came together. You see, I put up some ads with requirements—"

"Typical." Michael threw his hands in the air. "I should've expected you to pull something like this."

"You're not understanding me, Mike," Stephanie said. "I just wanted to hire a nice assistant to help with the day-to-day around the office! If there was a spark then certainly we would explore that avenue. But who's to say—"

"How'd you spell secretaries in your ad, Steph?" Michael knew the answer, but he wanted to drill down on it. "Was it with an X? Was it 'sex-cretaries'?"

Stephanie bit her lip. "That was a typo."

"Shut it down, Steph. You're not sleeping with anyone in this office. You do remember we *share* a Murphy bed, right? The bed's structural integrity is tenuous as it is."

"Fine. I'll use this new reception desk instead." Stephanie patted the particleboard monstrosity in front of her. One of the side panels fell off, clattering to the floor. She looked down at the mess she had made. "Okay. Maybe I'd use the main Detective Desk."

"You're using nothing!"

"I was trying to kill two birds with one stone, Mike. I get the chance at a hot date, and we get some help around the office. It's win-win, because this detective job is keeping me really busy."

"Is it?" Michael cocked an eyebrow. He wasn't wholly against Stephanie's detective agency. Their experiences across the multi-verse had showed, even though Steph's ideas didn't always make sense, she was still trying, and he needed to be more open to that. Michael realized this "detective agency" was her way of taking responsibility and attempting to chip in, and he really didn't want to deprive her of that. But he needed to draw a line somewhere. "How many cases have you gotten since you started?"

"Well, there was that one with the old lady's cat. And, uh . . . the multi-verse thing!"

"Neither of which we got paid for."

"You gotta spend money to make money, Mike. And I think we're just gonna need a bit more of your seed capital to get this off the ground. But if we're out of money, maybe we should just—"

"Yeah." Michael cleared his throat, still feeling the burning shame from his meeting earlier. "About that. I . . . uh just got fired. So I don't think we'll be able to pay your secretary $80,000."

"Oh." Stephanie's face fell. She pushed some of her short blonde hair out of her eyes. "Oh, man, what? I'm sorry, Mike. What happened?"

"I don't know. They were handing out raises and promotions because of some 'new release.' But I got nothing except the sack." Michael's mouth flattened into a line. "I don't really want to talk about it."

"Okay, okay," Stephanie waved her hands, "let's shut this whole thing down and figure this out. I'm here for you, Mike. Remember that."

Michael noticed, recently, instead of her usual devil-may-care attitude, Stephanie had been expressing more sympathy to Michael's struggles, rather than pushing him to fix it with a crazy scheme. It was a weird new dynamic he wasn't used to. If Michael didn't know better, he would have thought he was dying.

Stephanie walked over to the office door and stuck her head out. "Position's cancelled, babies. Get outta here!" The groan of a hundred disappointments made it through the crack in the door. "Maybe come back in three or four months." She slammed it shut. The rest of Steph's hastily built desk came apart, its components clattering to the floor. "I'll fix that later."

With a caring arm draped across Michael's shoulder, Stephanie escorted him from the small front reception area to the main office, a large well-appointed room that dwarfed the apartment they used to live in. The dark navy walls were accented by tasteful wood paneling harkening back to the 1970s. A Murphy bed lurked, unseen, in one of the side walls between wooden doors leading to a large closet and the bathroom. At the far end, beneath the wide windows, a large hardwood desk—which Stephanie referred to as "the Detective Desk"—sat stolidly in comparison to the mess of pieces left in the reception area. She plopped the folder full of secretary resumes down on the Detective Desk and turned back to Michael.

"I hated the job," Michael started without prompting, "but I liked the job security. I made enough to cover us. Now I don't even know if anyone else around here will take me after being fired from The Future Group. That name carries some weight."

"These things happen, Mike," Stephanie said, "but we'll figure it out. Maybe you can—"

"What? Help out with your detective agency? Nope. Not happening." Michael waved away the offer. He wasn't yet that desperate, even though his name was on the door. And the lease. And the insurance. And a lot of other things Steph probably hadn't told him about yet. "The only way I'd join this dog and pony show is if someone put a literal gun to my head."

"Alright, of course not. I was just saying I've got a bit of cash squared away I was going to use for the secretary. Maybe you can use some of that."

Michael nodded. She was trying to help, but it was a *bit* short-sighted. "Thanks, Steph. That might work for a bit, but we need to get a solid source of income fast, or else we're going to get evicted from this place."

"Didn't we just have that same problem, like, a month ago?"

"Yeah. It's becoming a thing." Michael hung his head. "I just don't want to think about this anymore."

"I feel ya." Stephanie patted him on the shoulder. "But y'know what'd make everything better right now?"

"What?"

"A slushie." Stephanie started toward the door. "The store downstairs has some killer ones. What flavor do you want? On me."

Michael smirked at the notion. "Grape, if they have it."

"I gotcha covered, buddy." With a click of her tongue, Stephanie was away, the tails of her oversized green jacket nearly getting caught in the closing door. The gust of wind caused by the slam, however slight, toppled the folder of secretary resumes teetering on the edge of their desk. A sheaf of papers flew up for a second before slaloming down through the air and skittering across the floor.

"Ugh." Michael ran his fingers through his hair and set to work, picking up each resume. After about five minutes of this nonsense, the manila folder was back to its proper thickness and made a satisfying thwack when Michael slapped it back on the desk. Quite pleased with himself, Michael smirked and turned around to find a woman slinking in through the crack in the office door.

"Oh, uh, sorry, ma'am. We're not actually hiring any—" Michael started. The rest of his words caught in his throat as he noticed her striking blue eyes, rivaling the man from earlier. "I mean, uh, hello."

The woman smiled a reserved, but alluring, smile and said nothing. Her black hair was tied back in a ponytail as taut as her skirt suit and she carried a black portfolio clutched to her chest. Another 'sex-cretary' applicant, for sure.

"I'm not here for the secretary position, Mr. Duckett." As her attire implied, she was professional and to the point. And she . . . knew his name? This was a better foot than Michael had started on with most women. "I'm here to enlist the services of your . . . organization." She delivered the last icy word only after she surveyed the office through her steel-rimmed glasses.

Okay. So she wasn't hitting on him as he had hoped. Of course she wasn't. That was a ridiculous assumption. Michael cleared his throat. "I'm sorry? You want to hire me and Steph? For, like, a *case*?"

"Yes," She confirmed. "And you might want to sit down for this."

# CHAPTER EIGHT

## Spies Not Entirely Unlike Us

"Are you serious? You want to hire us?" Michael looked around as he sat down on the opposite side of the Detective Desk, searching the walls for cameras. "This isn't part of another internet prank show?"

The woman tilted her head, squinting. "You're really not selling yourselves very well."

"I've been told I'm not good at the client-facing aspects of business. It's really Stephanie's baby. You might want to wait for her. I just pay the bills." Michael looked away. "I mean, I used to."

"Then why is your name first on the door?"

"She said it didn't rhyme otherwise." Michael shrugged.

The woman, still clutching her portfolio, sat down in the wooden rolling chair reserved for clients—had the agency come across any. "In any case, yes, we'd like to hire the two of you for a job."

"Uh . . . great." Michael nodded. "And who is 'we,' exactly?"

"We are a collective of people who have been monitoring threats to this world," the woman said with a voice like cold steel. "There are more impending dangers to humanity than you realize, and we're the only firewall between your continued existence and total annihilation. Our success depends on us remaining anonymous."

"Oh." Michael exhaled. "Kay. There's a lot to unpack there. So you're, like, a spy or something?" This kind of thing would have phased Michael in the past, but after hopping through dimensions and facing down a monstrous cow-man, being tracked down by a super-secret spy agency was almost mundane. In fact, it was a more believable scenario than an attractive woman actually hitting on him and was much easier to swallow.

"Not exactly, but if that helps you, sure." The Woman—it was quite clear she wasn't going to divulge her name—slipped him a wry smile. It didn't make Michael's heart flutter; rather, it added to his confusion.

"And why you want to hire a couple of—let's face it—shitty detectives?

"Oh wait." Michael smirked. "Let me guess. If you told me, you'd have to kill me?" It was a tired joke, but this whole thing was straining his suspension of disbelief, anyway.

"*I* wouldn't have to kill you." The Woman cleared her throat and pointed to the window behind Michael. "The sniper we've positioned across the street would."

Michael glanced back to see a single dot of red light wobble daintily about on his shoulder. His heart jumped into his throat, as his limited amount of fake bravado evaporated. "Oh, sweet Jesus!" He let out an entirely too high-pitched scream before dropping to the ground and cowering on the floor beneath the window out of the sniper's sightline.

"Relax, Michael." The Woman sounded almost bored. "He's not going to kill you. Just think of it as proof."

"Alright! Alright!" Michael yelled into his knees, muffling his words. "I'll help you! What do you want?"

"Will you let me finish this time?" Michael saw her eyes narrow as she leaned over the desk and loomed over him.

"Yes. Anything! I don't want to get shot in the head."

"I figured as much. Now relax." The Woman bent down and picked up his glasses. They'd clattered to the floor in the commotion.

Michael unfurled himself and took the glasses, but insisted on remaining on the floor. Just in case.

"Alright. Good. Now, our organization has had some trouble with certain contacts we've attempted to embed in the field. It appears they've been compromised."

"Compromised how?"

"Certainly you've heard about"—the Woman tilted her head down and lowered her own glasses—"the murders?"

"Murders?"

"Have you been reading the news? State Senator Clegg?"

Michael shook his head.

"A real estate agent's head exploded."

"I don't recall hearing about that."

"Ugh, so you probably haven't even heard about this." The Woman removed a rolled up newspaper from the portfolio and unfurled it on the desk. Michael caught a glimpse of the front page.

### PSYCHO KILLER?—QU'EST CE QUE HEY!

### FUTURE GROUP EXEC SHOT DEAD IN BROAD DAYLIGHT. POLICE BAFFLED AS USUAL

"The Future Group?" Michael gulped. "That's where I used to work!"

"Yes, I'm aware. That's why I'm here. My organization has been investigating The Future Group for some time now. Given their contacts with the organization, we enlisted Senator Clegg and Edgar Brauer—the real estate agent—to provide us with intel. We suppose they were summarily eliminated because they were found out."

"Eliminated?" Michael screwed up his face. "By who? The Future Group?"

The Woman nodded.

"Oh, come on." Michael scoffed. "They may be a bunch of workaholic weirdos, but they're not murderers."

"Michael." Her voice carried a tang of pity. "How much do you know about Craig Breene?"

"He's the biggest, most sanctimonious holier-than-thou asshole I've ever met."

"Well, that's true, but there's more to him than that."

"You think he's responsible for these three murders? Hah! I don't think you can condescend people to death. And why would he kill one of his own execs?"

"Arthur Birch was one of ours, too. In the deepest of cover. He was on the verge of revealing The Future Group's timetable to us before he was assassinated."

"Their timetable? For what?"

"That's what we need you to find out. There is one more agent of ours that has access to the intel, but we can't risk a data transfer that might compromise their location or identity. You and your associate need to make physical contact . . . before they're eliminated."

"You want me and Stephanie to race against an assassin?" Michael's chin retreated so far back it felt like it was about to merge with his neck. "We'd be killed!"

"Worst case scenario, yes." The Woman shrugged. "Brutally, thoroughly, and probably repeatedly. But that's a risk we're willing to take."

"Oh, as long as you guys are okay with it, that's just great! I'm glad you're hiring us as bait."

"You're not bait, Michael." The Woman rolled her eyes. "We're hiring you because you have an 'in' at The Future Group that could be useful. Find the agent. Record their information"—she paused, before adding the most relevant detail—"we're willing to compensate you handsomely."

Now she had his interest. "Okay. How handsomely are we talking? It better be a lot. We've got bills to pay. This office isn't cheap."

"Don't lie to me, Michael. It's clearly very cheap. But don't worry. You'll get what you need." The Woman coaxed a thick manila folder out of her portfolio and slid it across the table. "This file contains several physical documents on the identity of our agent and what we know about The Future Group. It's all the information I could get cleared, but for security, it will ignite approximately ten minutes after I leave."

"Whoa. Really? You guys can do that?"

"We can do lots of things, Michael." The Woman rose, straightened her skirt, and scooped up her portfolio before striding toward the door. "We hope you can too."

Michael said nothing as he watched the Woman glide away, despite the ever-present creak in the office's floorboards. Then, a thought struck him. Michael had something he needed, and this was just the opportunity he was looking for. His hand shot into the air. "Wait!"

The Woman turned, her body already halfway out the door. "What?"

"I need your agency to help me . . . with a request."

"You're in no position to make requests, Michael."

"A favor then, please." Michael grabbed a red pen from the desk drawer nearest him and yanked a resume off the top of the sex-cretary folder, jotting down his favor on the back side. He quickly jogged to the door and handed it to the Woman.

She stared down at it over the top of her glasses before folding it and tucking it away into her portfolio. "Okay. I'll see what we can do."

"Thank you." Michael smiled.

The door slammed shut and Michael felt his muscles finally un-clench, allowing him to slide down the nearby wall and onto the floor. The door creaked open and he tensed back up as the Woman's head peeked in. "By the way, if you don't complete the mission, we'll kill you."

"Fantastic." Michael nodded. "Thanks for the follow-up."

"Just making sure, you know. If I wasn't clear before."

"No, I got it. You can go. Don't forget your sniper."

The door shut again and Michael clambered to his feet. His first order of business was to dash to the window and yank down the venetian blinds. After a few moments, he peered through the slits and across the furthest rooftops. He saw nothing. No glint of a scope. No stealth suited sniper. Although, to be fair, if the sniper was any good, Michael wouldn't have seen them anyway.

Letting the blinds clack back into place, he exhaled for the first time in what felt like hours. Michael's glance then strayed to the desk and the top-secret spy folder on it. The floorboards barely had time to groan before he rushed out the door with the information in tow. He had a job to do, and the only person that could help was downstairs getting slushies.

# CHAPTER NINE

## Imperious Rex

"So, let me get this straight." Stephanie had always thought of herself as patient woman, willing to give people the benefit of the doubt. But, recently, she had begun to find even she had limits. She stared dead into the eyes of the teenage cashier—the bags beneath his eyes a fair bit darker than the rest of his face—and drummed her fingers on the counter, which they occasionally stuck to. "You're telling me you don't have *any* taquitos?"

The kid—he couldn't have been much older than sixteen—shrugged. "I haven't put them in the heating machine yet. Sorry."

"You haven't put them on the heating machine yet?" she repeated. The kid wasn't sorry at all! She leaned over the counter but stopped herself from slapping him. "It's 4pm! What kind of fly-by-night operation are you running here?"

"We don't get a lot of call for taquitos." The cashier's long, straight hair swished with the same listlessness of his entire demeanor. He reached across the counter, his fingers just barely brushing the bright yellow cover of a "Coding For Dummies" book before Steph's hand slapped it away.

"Listen . . ." She squinted at the tag on the kid's shirt to discern his name. "Ka. . . shir. Listen, Kashir. You're making this very difficult for me!"

"I don't know what to tell you, lady." He threw up his hands in resignation. The sleeves of his over-sized convenience store tunic slid down his arms. "I can start them up now if you want."

"Fine, then. Make it quick." Steph crossed her arms. Hopefully, she could get out of here fast. Mike was upstairs feeling down and out and she was wasting time at the convenience store under their office watching his grape slushie melt while waiting for taquitos. They were Mike's favorite, so Steph thought she'd surprise him with one. It was the least she could do after he got the sack. But maybe it was a godsend. Mike could find another job—a job he actually liked—and she could shutter the detective agency, keeping him safe.

"They gotta defrost, dude. Come back in twenty."

"Twenty minutes? That's insanity!" Steph shouted. As luck would have it, a customer service phone number on the counter caught her eye. After memorizing it for future use, she stabbed at the sticker with her finger. "Alright, kid. We'll see what your manager has to say about this."

"I am the manager." The kid smiled.

Steph would have slapped the lanky little bastard's face off of his skull if the tinkling bell above the door hadn't stayed her hand. To her surprise, a panting and disheveled Mike stood in front of her, his glasses askew and his deep black hair sticking out this way and that. He'd seen better days. It didn't help that he was waving a folder in the air like a madman.

"Mike!" Steph gasped as she steadied him by the shoulders, making sure he didn't cough up a lung. "Whoa, what's the matter? You okay?"

"There—there was . . . woman"—he struggled—"who came to . . . case . . . gotta help. Ass . . . in."

"Alright. I got none of that." Steph slid the melting slushie across the counter toward Mike. "Here's your slushie. Take a breath and calm down."

Mike slapped the folder down on the counter and grasped at the slushie, taking a long swig. Steph wondered if the potential brain freeze was worth it.

Once the icy, sugary mix finished sliding down his throat, Mike caught his breath, fixed his glasses, and exclaimed, "A case! We got a case!"

"Really?" Steph was surprised at how surprised she was, but pushed past it. "Hot dog!"

"The hot dogs haven't defrosted yet, either," Kashir interjected.

"Quiet, you." Steph glared at him before turning back to Mike. A new case would really be something. Another old lady's missing cat might just take Mike's mind off of losing his job. And it wouldn't be too dangerous. "So what's the sitch?"

"This attractive lady. Just walked into the office after you left."

"A sexy lady walked in to the detective office and gave you a case? Was she a knockout poured into a red dress? Did you know she was trouble the minute she walked in?" Steph cocked her head and smiled, raising her hand up to her neck. "Did she have legs up to here?"

Mike slapped her hand away. "I'm serious!"

"Okay, sorry." Steph rubbed the back of her hand. "I'm done."

"Good." Mike took another sip of his slushie. "Because we might be in some real trouble here."

"Was she from the secretaries' union?"

"No! She said she was—" Mike paused, looked around at the convenience store—empty, aside from Kashir who had taken to scratching off lotto tickets—and grabbed Steph by the lapels of her jacket. He dragged her into a nearby aisle, where he whispered the end of his sentence. "Some kinda spy."

"A spy?" A tingle of adrenaline ran down Steph's spine. This was cool. But if Mike was telling the truth, the case had the potential to be a problem. Steph had never been more conflicted. "Like a real 'spy' spy?"

"A real 'spy' spy. They had a sniper on me just to make sure I'd cooperate! I nearly crapped myself."

"A sniper? Are you okay?"

"Yeah. Yeah. I'm fine. The lady said it was just a warning."

"Good." Steph let out a breath. "What'd she look like?"

"She . . . well, she had these eyes," Mike said.

"Good job. Your description of this lady is that 'she had eyes.'"

"I was distracted, okay? She was beautiful!"

"You think all women are beautiful."

"So do you!"

"Yeah, well, I appreciate the female form." Steph flipped her hand. "You're just desperate."

"Could we get back to the matter at hand?"

"Yeah, yeah, okay." Steph nodded. She knew this could become a clear risk to Mike's life. It could very well be the thing her alternate future self warned her about. The thing that would cost Mike his life, just like all the other Mikes in the multi-verse. Not knowing terrified her, but she couldn't overdo it and insist they not take the case. Then Mike would know something was up, which would open up a whole 'nother can of anxious worms. And Steph wasn't ready to explain it to him. She'd just started wrapping her own head around it.

So, for the time being, Steph would have to play it straight. Ironically, it meant she would have to slip into joke-mode. Lucky for her, it was something she excelled at. "So . . . who was it? CIA? NSA? FBI? Oh man, are we going to be part of an X-File? I want to meet the Smoking Guy."

"It wasn't the X-Files!" Mike's palm hit his face. "The Smoking Guy? He's not even a real—forget it. She wouldn't even give me the name of the organization."

"Well, then what did she want?"

"Someone is killing guys they embedded in The Future Group."

"Oh. Uh, wow. So it's probably a good thing you got out of there, then." Steph bit her lip. As dangerous as this situation was, it may have already helped Mike dodge a literal bullet.

"She wants us to find her last remaining agent before they're killed, too. She needs the information they have."

"What kind of shady shit is The Future Group up to?"

"I dunno, but the lady gave me a secret file that's supposed to start us off on the right foot."

Steph pointed over his shoulder. "You mean that file?"

Mike turned and, upon seeing what Stephanie saw—Kashir flipping hungrily through the manila folder—dashed over and yanked it out of his hands.

"What do you think you're doing?" Mike shrieked, holding the folder in the air, out of the kid's reach. "This is sensitive information!"

"Uh, looks to me like a bunch of resumes and headshots of sexy people," Kashir said.

Steph jumped and yanked the folder out of Mike's outstretched hand. Splaying it open on the counter, she found a crisp resume and the small black and white headshot of Maureen Whelan, the older mom-type chick who just wasn't—*wasn't*—her type, glaring back at her. Steph flipped through a few more pages, featuring candidates she'd already evaluated. "Mike, this is my secretary folder."

"Wait, what?" Mike blinked. "That means—aw, crap!"

Before Steph could utter another word, Mike had her by the cuffs of her loose jacket sleeves, dragging her outside and up the stairs to the office.

"I took the wrong folder!" Mike yelled, "Hurry up!"

Mike almost took the door off its hinges as he slammed it open. Steph peered over his shoulder and, sure enough, there was another manila folder on the Detective Desk.

But it was on fire. Along with the rest of the desk.

"Hm." Steph clicked her tongue. "That's not good."

She noticed Mike's reaction to fire bore a striking similarity to his reactions to women. He had always been confused about how to proceed and ended up flailing his arms in an erratic fashion while running around, desperately looking for a solution that didn't exist. When one couldn't be found, he ended up with his shirt off, but no less confused.

Mike blanketed the desk fire with his loose shirt, hitting it repeatedly until the flames were smothered. As far as Steph knew, Mike had never hit nor smothered a woman with his shirt. That was really where the analogy broke down.

By the end of the whole ordeal, the top of the desk and the critical intelligence folder had transmogrified into a pile of ashes beneath a sweat-stained powder blue dress shirt. Michael's bony chest heaved beneath his white undershirt.

When she figured it was safe to interject, Steph asked, "Did those papers self-destruct? Like on TV? They can do that?"

"Goddamn it." Mike banged his fist on what remained of the desk. A cloud of ash poofed into the air and into his lungs. After a brief coughing fit, he continued. "That was our only lead! What the hell are we supposed to do now? Just wander around looking for a murderous assassin?"

"Chill out, Mike." Steph placed a hand on his shoulder. "We'll figure something out."

Mike spun around. "Steph, the lady threatened to *kill* us if we didn't get this done! You think a lead'll just fall in our laps?"

Steph had no words. It looked like Mike's life was going to be in danger, no matter what they did. Honestly, she didn't know where or how to begin, but she had to believe things would work out. That sense of misguided hope, in the utter chaos of the universe, was the only thing pushing her forward. She'd just have to trust in it, once again.

And, once again, it delivered.

"What the hell is wrong with you two?" A familiar angry roar reverberated through the office. "A *detective agency?*"

Steph and Mike turned to the entrance to find the hulking, trench-coated form of Detective Rex Calhoun looming in the doorway. He was angry about something. Then again, he always seemed angry about something. This time, it may have been because he couldn't kick down Mike and Steph's already open door.

"Oh, look who's here, Mike." A smirk crawled up Stephanie's cheek. "It's Black Columbo."

"You." Ol' Rexy stormed into the room like a tornado filled with dynamite. He pointed at Steph. "Shut up." Rex swung his finger over until it was so close to Mike's face he could have been picking his nose. "You. What the hell did I tell you the last time we met?"

"To . . . uh . . . to stay out of your business?" Mike stammered.

"Right. And what do you do? You turn around and open up a goddamn *detective agency!*" Rex stole the fedora off his head and dashed it to the ground. Steph didn't think that was necessary. Everyone in the room already knew he was upset. Nevertheless, Rex said, "And now you're messed up in a whole Future Group murder spree. I need this like I need a boil on my ass."

"Whoa, whoa, whoa." Mike threw up his hands. "We didn't kill anyone."

"I know that, you idiot." Rex dragged his fingers across his face. "You don't have enough brains between the two of you to tie a shoe."

"Don't exaggerate, Rexy." Steph gestured at their feet. "Clearly Mike and I have tied three out of our four shoes. Why are you here?"

"Because if I wasn't the one investigating this, Nervous Nellie over here"—Rex returned his finger to Mike's face—"would be hauled downtown for questioning."

"What?" Mike stumbled back a bit. "What did I do?"

"You got fired," Rex spat.

Mike cringed a bit at the reminder.

"I dunno how you managed to screw up such a cushy job, but you did. And if any of the other idiots on the force were looking into this, they'd say you'd have a plausible motive to kill a bunch of Future Group nerds." Rex leaned over and stared past them into the office, taking long, large sniffs at the air. "Was your desk on fire?"

"It's been taken care of." Steph cut him off by stepping into his field of vision. "So what's the deal with all these murders?"

"Nuh-uh." Rex grimaced. "If you're thinking of looking into this: don't."

"What makes you think someone hired us to look into this?" Mike shuffled his feet. He was trying hard to look nonchalant but failing. Steph didn't know why. Even if Mike did spill the beans about his sexy spy lady, Rexy was the last person who'd believe him.

"I dunno. But I can't be too careful with you two yahoos. Stay the hell away from me." Before Rex could say any more, the staticky crackle of his belt radio pierced the conversation

"All units. All units. Possible 10-54 at Industrial Port, near LXR Chemical."

"LXR Chemical." Mike cocked his head. "That's a Future Group subsidiary."

"What?" Rex froze in place. "Are you sure? Are you absolutely certain?"

"I mean, I think so. I saw some documents . . ." Mike trailed off.

"Okay, Rexy, now what's a 10-54?" Stephanie smiled.

"It's nothing," Rex shot back, all too quickly. "Not important."

The radio burst to life again and Rex frowned. "The guy's just lying in the gutter. Wait. Scratch that. Unconscious. Still breathing. Downgrade to a 10-53."

Rex's stoic face devolved into one barely masked his explosive irritation. Steph had never smiled wider.

"Don't. Follow. Me." Rex punctuated each word with a violent thrust of his ever-extended pointer finger. He pivoted on his heel and stormed out the door, which he slammed with unnecessary force.

Mike turned to Steph, uttering words she never thought she'd hear him say: "Alright, let's follow him."

# CHAPTER TEN

### Askew To A Kill

Calhoun couldn't have gotten out of Squalor's Wallow fast enough. The sun clocked out as he sped through traffic toward the industrial district, and by the time he reached the crime scene, it was already well past twilight. He drove past a loose conglomeration of towering pressure tanks and smokestacks illuminated only by the neon green LXR sign cutting through the night.

His front tire jumped the curb as the car screeched to a halt. Uniformed officers scurried about the place—an alley between two large loading docks—setting up lights so they could properly survey the area. Carrie McDermott was already walking up to him as he shut his car door. He was glad to see at least one of them had made it on time.

"McDermott, any idea what's going on here?" Calhoun rasped as he powered toward the alley, McDermott only a few steps behind.

"They wouldn't let me through for some reason," she whispered, rubbing her arm. "And they haven't even brought in an ambulance for the guy. It's really strange."

"*Who* wouldn't let you through?" Calhoun's question was answered as they reached the edge of the crime scene. Two of his colleagues waited there with crossed arms, keeping them on the wrong side of the caution tape.

"Lin." Calhoun grumbled as he bounced his glare from one to the other. "Brook. Care to stand aside?"

"No can do, Rex." Lieutenant Lin remained rooted to the concrete, his posture even stiffer than his starched collar. "We can't allow you in."

"Bullshit. We've got as much right to be here as you do. Let us through." Calhoun reached down to duck under the caution tape, but Detective Brook's hand shot out and grabbed his shoulder.

"Calhoun, I think—"

"Shut up, Brook." Calhoun slapped the hand away. "Nobody wants to hear what you think!"

"Listen, Calhoun," Lin started. He was a good deal younger than Calhoun, but he'd rocketed up through the ranks due to his workaholic tendencies. That, and Captain Braddock seemed to really like him. "I've gotten strict orders to keep you and Ms. McDermott from interrogating this victim and dragging him into whatever crazy ideas you've been concocting."

"Yeah!" Brook added. Unlike Lin, Brook was a useless sack of lazy shit who didn't know the difference between his ass, his elbow, and a hole in the ground. What he was doing here was beyond Calhoun's understanding, so he was just going to ignore him. "You stay right where you are."

"Yeah, I don't have time for this. C'mon, McDermott." Calhoun barreled through the middle of Lin and Brook, making sure to elbow Brook in the nose on his way. McDermott, though a little unsure, followed him past the broken caution tape.

The sea of blue uniformed officers parted and Calhoun found the victim, a thirty-something male, slumped on the side of the alley, his head lolling. He certainly wasn't dead, but he was hopped up on something.

Calhoun grabbed his shoulders, shaking him into coherence. "Sir, can you tell me your name?"

"Wha? Huh?"

"Your name!" he growled.

"Eric . . ." The man moaned. "Bunting."

"Eric Bunting." Calhoun swiveled around. "McDermott, see what you can do with that."

"Already on it," she said, fingers flying across her tablet.

As Eric Bunting collapsed back into unconsciousness, his drool adding to the already disgusting puddles on the alley floor, Calhoun turned to the uniformed officers surrounding him. "What happened here? How'd he get like this?"

"We found him with a dart in his neck," one cop said.

"Dart? What kind of dart?" Calhoun asked. "Where is it? Did you take it out of him?"

"That's enough, Calhoun," Lin's voice was overshadowed by the cocking of his gun. "Bunting will be fine. I'm ordering you to step back immediately."

Calhoun was about to reach into his coat, but thought better of it when the uniformed officers all pulled their guns on him. Brook was the only one who didn't have his gun drawn, instead sporting only his usual confused look.

"Are you crazy, Lin? What the hell are you doing?"

"My job, Calhoun. The same thing you should be doing."

"Eric Bunting! He's on the board of directors of LXR Chemicals." McDermott raised her eyes from her tablet, finally taking in the current situation. "Oh, uh . . . what's going on here?"

"Just a little disagreement." Calhoun put his hands in the air. "Lin,

I have it on good authority that LXR is a subsidiary of The Future Group. You're going to want to let us go. We might be on to something."

"Well, that's a doozy of a coincidence," Lin mocked. "Too bad, no dice."

"That didn't come up in any of my digging." McDermott sidled over to Calhoun, her hands slowly rising. "Who told you that?"

"Uh . . ." Calhoun looked away. "A . . . source."

"Well, that's specific," Lin said. "Trustworthy?"

"He better be," Calhoun grumbled.

"Oh, so it's a he!" Brook added.

"Never mind who it is!"

"But that doesn't fit the MO, Rex," McDermott whispered. "Maybe this one's not our serial killer."

"Or maybe there's no serial killer at all." A jovial, lilting voice snaked through the crowd of policemen. Calhoun stiffened, knowing exactly who it was—and how much trouble he was in.

A broad-chested mountain of a man in a pin-striped white shirt and suspenders emerged from behind the crowd of police. He gave Lin's shoulder a gentle tap, and Lin obeyed the silent command, lowering his gun.

"I'll take it from here, Lieutenant." Captain Leslie Braddock was only a few inches taller than Calhoun at six feet, but his thick mane of well-coiffed red hair added a bit more height over Calhoun's bald head, allowing him to loom. "A man could have died here tonight." Braddock's handlebar mustache bristled, the mouth beneath twisting in displeasure. "And you're concerned with baseless conspiracy theories rather than proper police work?"

"Well . . . I . . . uh . . . no." Calhoun hated being at a loss for words, especially in front of McDermott. What kind of example was he setting? And he could hardly abide Brook seeing him on the back foot.

He'd never hear the end of it. So Calhoun would have to try. "If you've seen what we've seen, you'd have to accept—"

"Calhoun, I *have* seen what you've seen. Craig Breene of The Future Group called me directly earlier tonight. He laid out everything you said to him when you went down there—without a warrant, I might add." Braddock frowned. "The man's the head of the city's biggest and most valuable institution! He deserves our utmost consideration and ought not to be harassed."

"That's bullshit. I didn't harass anyone!"

McDermott shrugged. "You do have a bit of a prickly demeanor."

"Carrie McDermott." Braddock wheeled around to the young CSI, his tone no less angry. "Don't think you're blameless in this either. I spoke to Detective Hobson, and she said you've been parading around as Detective Calhoun's right hand woman."

"I'd . . . well, I'd hardly use the word 'parading.'"

"In any case," Braddock continued, "you two continue to chase ghosts even after being repeatedly warned to stop. And now I find you barging into a crime scene, accosting an incapacitated victim, and starting an armed standoff with Lieutenant Lin and officers from our precinct?"

"Standoff?" Calhoun shouted. "*He* drew *his* gun! I didn't do shit."

"I don't want to hear it, Calhoun! You were a good cop, but you went way out of line on this one. McDermott, too. I've had enough of this nonsense. You're both officially relieved from duty. Permanently."

"What?" His and McDermott's echoing voices sounded surreal to Calhoun, but no less surreal than being let go from a job he'd put his blood, sweat, and tears into for several decades. Also, losing the pension was going to derail his whole retirement plan. "But, Captain—"

Calhoun was stopped by Braddock's outstretched hand. "If you don't leave immediately, I'll have Brook and Lin run you both downtown for tampering with a crime scene. Head back to the station and turn in your badges and guns."

"I don't have a gun." McDermott whimpered.

"Turn it whatever it is you do have, then. I'll be taking over all your investigations from here on out. And I will be quashing whatever silly serial killer narrative you're peddling."

"But what if there's another Future Group related death?" Calhoun said. "What then? The blood'll be on your hands, Braddock!"

"Calhoun, I'll be taking every precaution to make sure that doesn't happen." Braddock motioned to Brook and Lin. "And I will be respectful of the citizens of this fine city while I do it."

"Don't you friggin' touch me." Calhoun reared as Brook approached. He nodded to McDermott. "We're going."

Calhoun stormed out of the alley, stepping over Eric Bunting's comatose body, with McDermott in tow. As they reached his car, McDermott shot Calhoun a sorrowful look, and Calhoun had no choice but to give her one in turn. He cranked the ignition and, for the first time in his life, Rex Calhoun slunk away, tail between his legs.

* * *

Michael ground the Garbagemobile to a halt when he saw the squad of police cars and uniformed officers crowding a well-lit alleyway in the distance. They were far enough away, so the high pitched squeal of the car's rusty brakes did not draw the cops' attention. Pulling off the main street—an avenue wide enough for semi-trucks to sit five abreast—Michael maneuvered into a loading dock and shut off the car.

"Great. We can't even get close enough to see what's going on without Calhoun getting on our asses." Michael indicated the far off alleyway with an irritated wave of his hand. "We're gonna need a higher vantage point."

Michael got out of the car. There was a chill in the air, so he rolled down the sleeves of the replacement button-down shirt he'd donned just before leaving. After a quick survey, it was clear the highest point within reach was the looming hulk of the LXR Chemical building. "Up there." They'd have a clear view down to the alley. That is, if the giant neon green sign didn't blind them.

"Well, we'd be a safe distance away from Rexy," Stephanie said, "if he throws another tantrum."

"But we won't be able to see shit at that distance."

"That's where you're wrong, friendo." Steph levered herself up and out of the Garbagemobile's passenger-side window. The window was the only egress since that door—a rusted yellow number from a completely different car—had been haphazardly welded onto the otherwise red chassis. Steph traipsed to the rear and slammed on the trunk. It popped right open. After pushing some junk out of the way, she waggled two halves of a broken set of plastic binoculars that, as Michael recalled, had come from a children's fast food meal. "Ah, eh? Always prepared."

"Wonderful. Let's go."

Michael made sure to stick to the shadows, pulling Stephanie back into them whenever she began to wander off. The main plant was large, and it took them several minutes to find a back entrance out of view from the main road. Unfortunately, it was padlocked.

"Ah, goddamnit." Michael grabbed the lock and shook it, to no avail. "I don't suppose you have any idea how to get in here."

"Mike, please." Steph scoffed, almost offended. "What do I look like? Some kind of amateur?"

Michael's eyes flitted down toward the broken toy binoculars in her hands.

She shoved the binocular halves into her jacket pockets. "Notwithstanding. Let's see what we're dealing with here . . ." Stephanie bent down to get a closer look at the scuff brass lock, clucking her tongue. "Ah. A Stanco. This might be easier than I thought."

"What're you talking about?"

"Stanco locks have an exploitable structural flaw. They've corrected it in the newer models, but this one looks old enough."

"How do you know so much about locks?"

"I used to help my friend Spider Johnson break into condemned hospitals," she said, as if that sentence made any sense. "It's a victimless crime. But let's not dwell on it." Steph extended her hand. "Can I borrow your cell phone?"

"You don't have yours?"

"I forgot it at the office."

"What happened to 'always prepared?'" Michael raised a coy eyebrow as he passed his folded cellphone over. "Who're you gonna call?"

"Ghostbusters!" Stephanie smiled back at him, before launching into an air guitar solo.

Michael rolled his eyes as Stephanie made guitar sounds with her mouth for a good thirty seconds. "Alright, alright. Relax."

"Sorry, Mike. It's like a little lightbulb in my head goes off every time I hear someone say that. Besides"—Steph nudged him with her elbow—"it's like a cute little in-joke for us."

"Is that how you see us? The Ghostbusters?"

"Yeah. You're Egon, and I'm all the cool funny ones smashed together."

"Gee, thanks."

"You can be Ernie Hudson if you want."

He shrugged. She'd been pulling this same joke since they were kids. It warmed his heart a little. Even after all the crazy shit they'd been through, she still found fun in the little things. But, if he was being honest . . . "It's 2013. Ghostbusters has been played out for years."

Stephanie gasped as if she'd been stabbed. "How dare you!"

"Let's just move past it. Who are you calling?"

"Oh, right. No, I'm not calling anyone." In one fluid motion, Stephanie wound up, and lobbed Michael's cell phone at the lock. The cellphone blew apart, sending plastic and silicone pieces flying in every which direction.

Michael stood, mouth agape, hands extended in gnarled claws as if trying to grasp the meaning of the situation. "What? Why?"

"Wait for it . . ." Stephanie pointed at the door just in time to see the lock disengage and clatter to the ground. "Older Stancos can't handle sharp impacts at high velocity."

"But . . . my phone."

"Oh, stop living in the past, Mike. We've got a job to do." Steph opened the door and slunk inside, leaving Michael to pick up the pieces of his shattered phone.

Once he realized the device wasn't salvageable, Michael trailed Stephanie down the pipe-and-vent-lined underbelly of the chemical plant. The place was creepy as all hell, with little room to maneuver. Michael almost ran into low hanging pipes on several occasions. But, as his eyes adjusted, he managed to find Stephanie halfway up a flight of stairs to a set of metal catwalks that snaked between enormous cylindrical tanks.

"So what does LXR do?" Steph asked when he caught up.

"What?"

"Like what chemicals do they actually make?"

"Beats the hell out of me," Michael struggled to think of an actual product or ingredient they produced. "But if they're secretly owned by The Future Group, they probably also do nothing."

"Then what are all these tanks full of?"

"Do I look like a chemical engineer?"

"No, you look unemployed."

"Gee, thanks."

They reached the third floor of the hanging catwalks which were situated terrifyingly high above the plant floor. The cylindrical chemical tanks were even bigger than Michael had expected close up, their range of pressure gauges and computer controlled panels lending air of legitimacy. The two vats had U-S-1 and U-S-2 spray painted on them in stenciled letters three times Michael's height. Whatever LXR was making, it certainly wasn't nothing.

"The agent we're supposed to find might be able to tell what's going on here," Steph said as they approached the door to the roof. "If he's not dead."

"Calhoun's radio said he was just unconscious. If the police have gotten to him already, I think he might be safe."

"So how do *we* get to him?"

"Steph! Wait a second." Michael spotted something off. He beckoned her over to the computer terminal on the chemical tank closest to the roof door. It was on, displaying something like a flow chart but super-imposed on a map of the city and the surrounding areas. If Michael was reading it right, the network was piping all of the substance produced in this plant—something called U-S—to two different locations: a prison outside of town and . . . The Future Group tower. "Okay, this is really weird, Steph. What the hell are they making here?"

"Good question," she said. "Here's a better one: who logged into this computer . . . and are they still here?"

"That's two questions, but they're still very unsettling."

"C'mon, let's check it out," Steph glanced at the roof exit, then, extending an arm, added, "just stay behind me."

Steph pushed the door open, the crisp air of the November night rushing in. Michael did as he was told and peered over her shoulder. An expanse of blocky, asymmetrical HVAC units stood guard over the rooftop, bathed in the emerald light of the towering neon LXR logo. A few red maintenance lights placed at regular intervals made the whole affair feel like Christmas a bit earlier than Michael would've preferred. As they stepped out onto the roof, a flock of pigeons decided it was in their best interest to flee the immediate area, spooking Michael further.

"Relax, dude." Steph placed a hand on his shoulder. "I got your back."

"That's what I'm afraid of," Michael smirked as the two wound their way through the maze of humming ventilation boxes toward the side of the roof facing the alleyway.

"Hrm. It's certainly a good view." Michael peered over the edge, taking an eyeful of the height, and summarily backed away.

"Here," Stephanie chose that moment to toss Michael his half of the broken binoculars. Michael, of course, fumbled with it, causing it to bounce around from hand to hand. He finally caught it in his armpit while struggling to maintain his balance. Michael, arms flailing wildly, would have gone over the ledge had Stephanie not launched toward him and grabbed his shirt, yanking him back to safety.

"Oh, geeze," Michael whisper-shouted. "That was a close one. I could've died!"

"Sorry, sorry, sorry!" Steph thrust up her hands in apology. "My mistake."

Michael had been expecting a flippant brush-off, but she seemed incredibly sincere. "Not your fault. Thanks for grabbing me. I should've been more careful." Michael exhaled. "Let's just see what we can see and get down from here."

Stephanie raised her monocular to her eye and Michael did the same. Across the way, past the bevy of flashing red, blue, and white lights that turned the view into a veritable kaleidoscope, a group of policemen helped a wobbly man in a disheveled suit to his feet, leaning him against an alley wall. "Hm. That must be our guy. Recognize him?"

"No," Michael said, but it wasn't just the alleged agent he didn't recognize. Aside from the uniformed cops, there were two suited detectives—one lanky, balding white guy and another prim and proper man of Asian descent. Both of them flanked a mountain of a man, with a mane of slick hair and a waxed moustache. This cop, with the fiery hair of a god had, for some reason, decided on wearing suspenders. And nobody was calling him on it. He had to be in charge. "Wait who the hell is that? What happened to Calhoun?"

"No idea. But we better find out what they're gonna do with our agent. You think he was shot?"

"I can't tell." It looked like they were dusting him off. He seemed to be recovering nicely as the officers herded him toward an ambulance. "They're moving him. We need to get back to the Garbagemo—"

A blinding pain that sparked against the back of Michael's head made him see stars until he finally blacked out.

# CHAPTER ELEVEN

## Big Boned

Stephanie whipped her head around as Michael's pained yelp echoed across the rooftop. Just in time, she saw his body collapse to the floor at the feet of the attacker towering over him. Well, 'towered' was a strong word, as the guy was only about five foot four at best, but he was still intimidating, nonetheless—mostly due to his awesome mask.

Printed on the thick black knit pulled over his face was a fierce white skull. A pair of red lenses, reminding Steph of opera glasses—but a little more sinister—protruded from the eyeholes. The only more concrete indication that this was the assassin Michael and Stephanie had been looking for would be if he had yelled "I AM THE ASSASSIN YOU ARE LOOKING FOR." But that wasn't the sort of thing admitted in polite company.

Steph stumbled backwards as the assassin emerged from the shadows, allowing her to get a better look at him. Stephanie eyed him up and down, and could only squeak out a few words from her otherwise dry mouth. "Boy, you're . . . uh . . . chubbier than I expected."

Yes, the macabre skull mask and threatening demeanor had initially diverted attention from the assassin's skin-tight bodysuit, stretched taut on a body straining the limits of the fabric. "Good for you, though. I wouldn't be comfortable in skintight anything. But this whole look? It's kinda working."

"Leave." The assassin's voice was garbled, as if post-processed by something beneath his mask. He gestured to Mike, laying on the ground. "Take your friend and go. This isn't your problem."

"Oh, yeah?" Steph had recovered from her shock, now determined to be on the offensive. "Well, the second you knocked out my friend, you made it my problem. I'm not gonna let you kill him."

"I'm not going to kill him! He'll be fine." Even through the mechanical garbling, Steph could make out the assassin's irritation. It was a tone she'd become very familiar with. "Just leave!"

"Nuh-uh. Not until I get some answers. Or until I beat 'em out of you." She pushed up the baggy sleeve of her jacket and raised her left fist. "Say hello to Warren Harding"—then her right—"and the Teapot Dome Scandal."

There they stood for a good minute, a twenty-four-year-old slacker in a faded green jacket and baggy jeans and a short, chubby assassin with a terrifying skull mask for a face. In another world, they would have made an excellent sitcom pair. Hell, based on Steph and Mike's terrifying ride through the multi-verse, a world probably existed with that premise.

Steph usually dismissed people's criticisms of her rash decisions or acting before thinking, but—this time—a thought crossed her mind. They may not have been entirely wrong. Because, before Steph had time to move or even blink, the assassin's rifle appeared in his hands, leveled straight at her face.

Her hands shot into the air. "Right. Crap. Forgot you probably had a gun."

"I told you," the assassin garbled, "this doesn't concern you."

"Alright, buddy, alright." Steph spoke as if she was talking to a child. "I get it, but we're detectives. We're concerned about whatever we've been paid to be concerned about. And right now, that means you."

"Paid?" The gun barrel wavered. "Who hired you?"

Stephanie shrugged, her hands still in the air. "Uh, some lady, I guess."

"What?"

"Mike's the one who talked to her." Steph waggled her chin in the direction of her prostrate friend. "Said she was some sort of spy? Frankly, I can't be sure she exists."

"Why would they hire *you*?" The assassin lowered his gun in confusion.

"Well, it's in the name. We're Duckett & Dyer: Dic—"

"Shut up." He raised the gun again, angrily. "You two don't *know anything*."

"Listen, Chunky Cheese," Steph said, with a bit more belligerence than prudent when talking to an armed assassin, "we know enough. We know you're running rogue killing all of Michael's old bosses from The Future Group. And we're here to stop you."

"You're wrong. I didn't kill anyone!"

"Says the guy with the gun."

"The Future Group took everything from me. They're not what you think. And if I have to go stop them myself, I will." The assassin lowered his gun a final time. "I don't want to kill you. But if you don't stay out of my way, people will die."

Stephanie lowered her arms and clenched her fists once again, "Oh, I don't think—"

The assassin shot from the hip, and a loud bang filled the air as

Steph fell to the ground. She gathered her wits for a few seconds before realizing she hadn't been shot. Instead, the assassin's bullet had hit the metal casing of the HVAC unit behind her.

Letting out a sigh of relief, she looked around to find the immediate area empty, save for Mike's body. The assassin was nowhere to be seen.

"Hrm." She grunted as she moved over to Mike, to find he was indeed still breathing. "Gone without a trace. Like Batman."

Or maybe not. Over Mike's breathing, Stephanie picked up the telltale sound of two leather-encased thighs rubbing together. She smiled to herself before rocketing to her feet and rushing into the maze of rooftop boxes.

Three rows away, Steph noticed the faint glint of light off the assassin's mask lenses.

"Hey you!" Stephanie yelled.

The rubbing noise stopped.

"Get back here!"

*Swssh-swssh, swssh-swssh, swssh-swssh-swssh-swssh-swssh*

The rubbing noise increased in frequency and Stephanie gave chase, closing the gap a little.

Despite his lumpiness, the assassin was deceptively quick, bounding his way across the rooftop, rifle in tow. The man bobbed and weaved with the grace and elegance of a dancer through the HVAC unit and other rooftop boxes of inscrutable purpose. Stephanie, despite her comparatively slender frame, bobbed and weaved with the grace and elegance of a cinderblock, slamming her shoulders and torso into the obstacles time and again. Eventually, she slowed down and clutched her side. It seared with the pain of a stitch.

"Hey! Wait!" Steph exclaimed between breaths. "I just want to talk! I'm sorry for fat-shaming you!"

The assassin either didn't hear her or, more likely, did not want to answer. With one final burst of agility and speed, he vaulted himself over a wall and across the gulf of an alley onto the roof of an adjoining building below.

Steph, using her remaining stamina, jogged up to the wall just in time to make out a dark blob dashing over the rooftop across the way.

"Damn it," she pouted. "I knew I should have brought the grappling hook."

As it stood, Steph figured there was only one thing to do. With slow, deliberate motion, and despite the pain that ran across her midsection, Steph backed away from the edge of the roof and into a starter's position. Her feet kicked up dust and debris as she rushed headlong toward the crevasse between the two buildings, ready to take a leap of faith. It couldn't be nearly as wide as it looked.

Steph reached the brink of the building and pushed her feet off the ground, just before a force on the collar of her jacket brought her crashing back down onto the roof—and to reality.

"Are you insane?" Mike yelled, a bit of wheeze in his voice. "What the hell are you doing?"

Steph pushed herself up and beat the dirt off her sleeves. "I was going to jump the alley and chase after the assassin!" She pointed across the gap, but the masked, jump-suited mystery man had disappeared. "Well, now look what you've done. We lost him."

"I just saved your life, you idiot!" Mike removed his glasses and massaged his eyes.

"I could've made it," Steph countered.

"Remember the last time you tried to make a jump like this and you almost cracked your skull?"

"No . . ." Steph couldn't recall that incident, but made a note to look into it later, if she remembered. "How's your head, by the way?"

"Not great. I should probably go to the doctor." Mike rubbed his temple with the heel of his palm. "But you said the assassin was here?

Was he the one who knocked me out? Did you get a good look at him?"

"Yeah," Stephanie said. "He was fat."

"Fat?"

"Yeah, I don't wanna be a jerk or nothing, but you don't really expect a super assassin to have manboobs."

"He had . . . manboobs," Mike's voice fell to his usual exasperated deadpan. "That's what you got out of this?"

"Well, his assassin suit left nothing to the imagination."

"Great. Fine," Mike re-donned his glasses. "Did you manage to get anything *useful* out of him?"

"He was really pissed off at The Future Group."

"Wait, *at* The Future Group? He wasn't working for them?"

"He said they took everything from him."

Mike furrowed his brow, "Wait, Steph, what if we got it all wrong? What if—" Mike's thought was interrupted by a loud bang as the rooftop door slammed open. Police, brandishing guns, flooded the area.

"Oh geeze!" Steph shouted.

"We surrender!" Mike's hands shot up in the air within seconds. "We didn't do anything!"

"Then who are you?" The well-built, red-haired Adonis of a man stepped out onto the roof. Steph didn't usually have a thing for older men, but this guy could get it. "And what are you doing here?"

"Uh, we're building maintenance," Steph said, the first thing she thought would get them out of this mess. "and we're here doing . . . building maintenance."

"Right." The man was not fooled. "You don't look like maintenance people."

"We left our uniforms at home."

"You're those two PIs Detective Calhoun told me about, aren't you?"

Mike opened his mouth to offer a rebuttal, but nothing escaped

"Don't worry," the man said. "I'm not gonna arrest you. I did some private work here and there when I was about your age. Mostly security. I know what it's like." He extended his strong, meaty hand. "Captain Leslie Braddock."

Stephanie took it. "Stephanie Dyer. And this is my associate Michael Duckett. We're Duckett & Dyer: D—"

"PIs for Hire!" Mike jumped in, now certain there wasn't any danger.

"Pleasure to meet you." Captain Braddock beamed. "Now, we seem to be working on the same case. A victim of ours was tranquilized by a dart in that alleyway down there. Anything you've found could really be of help. That is, if you choose to share it. You're well within your rights to refuse."

"Uh, well, he seemed to really have it in for The Future Group," Steph said. She felt a bit of comforting camaraderie between them and Captain Braddock. Although, truth be told, she enjoyed the back and forth of Ol' Rexy a bit more. In any case, having a real ally on the police force might just help her keep Mike safe.

"The Future Group?" Braddock cocked an eyebrow. "Are you certain?"

"Yeah, definitely. Also, he was really fat."

"Hm. Good to know." Braddock turned to the nearest uniformed officer and began issuing orders. "Go and tell Lin we need as many men as we can spare. We need to deploy several squads to The Future Group Tower posthaste."

The officer departed, taking his colleagues with him. Braddock spun back around to address Mike and Steph again. "That was incredibly helpful. You've done us a great service."

"Oh, all in a day's work, I suppose." Steph waved him off.

"Now, if you'll excuse me, I'll need to coordinate some re-sources," Braddock said. "I'm sure you'll find your way out."

"Steph," Mike said, after Braddock confidently strode off the roof, "I think we made a big mistake."

"What're you talking about?"

"If that fat assassin of yours had a bone to pick with The Future Group, he might not actually be the assassin. He might be the agent we're looking for."

Steph grimaced in embarrassment. "And if he's going after The Future Group, I just lead the cops right to him. Crap."

"We need to get to him before they do." Mike began to jog off the roof.

"Yeah, I think you're right," Stephanie followed suit, thundering her way across the chemical plant's metal catwalks. "Mike, you might have to go back to work."

# CHAPTER TWELVE

## Blue Skies

Craig Breene had never felt better. Things had been going swimmingly for the past two years. It felt silly to attribute all his success to a random voice in the darkness, but he couldn't have done it any other way.

After his sudden introduction to the multi-verse, Craig's excitement began to subside, replaced with a cocktail of anxiety and self-consciousness bubbling in his gut. Telling anybody about this fantastical, ridiculous scenario—though proven real by the guidance the voice had given him—could have Craig committed to a mental institution. Craig opted not to tell Marcus—nor his mother—the truth, choosing instead to brand it as a virtual reality simulation taking in real-life scenarios as input and spitting out logical outputs.

His mother had her doubts, obviously, and insisted he bring his "invention" to her agency, where the government could put it to good use. Marcus, on the other hand, was all in. Perhaps more so than he was about the video game. Of course, he had the bright idea to put it to use on lucrative stock speculation. It was a rather petty use to this life changing technology, but Craig went with it since Marcus seemed convinced this was the right avenue. And besides, who needed a video game about the multi-verse when one could traverse it all by themselves?

Since Craig could see into any sort of alternate universe he wanted, he could view closely related universes in the near future to see if investments were wise and pass the results off as a tightly run simulation. The two of them managed to net over $100 million dollars in the first year alone, enough to buy out their old bosses at Consolidated Futures Inc. and take over the entire company. As the new bosses, Marcus and Craig reorganized the firm as The Future Group—hailed as one of the biggest success stories of 1996. Soon after, they acquired a square mile of real estate around their current office building to construct their own modern tower. They called it One Future Plaza. Construction completed on their giant tower complex in early '97.

While Marcus was in charge of the day-to-day financial and administrative drudgery that he was actually good at, Craig set to work refining his system. He had used system upgrades as an excuse to get Marcus to fund more and more advanced components. Over the past few months, Craig transformed the entire basement into a single state-of-the-art supercomputer. Now, from his position in a central throne—for lack of a better word—flanked by towering machinery, Craig could commune directly with the voice in the darkness.

On a more personal level, the most important thing to Craig was Marcus's happiness. And the boundless easy riches their company produced saw to that. Since Craig got to spend time with him, even in the boring business of setting up a large conglomerate company, he was happy, too. He'd wished they hadn't been separated by mountains of paperwork and office walls, but beggars couldn't be choosers. Realistically, since the two of them were content, it was the best of both worlds.

Now it was the best of all the rest of the worlds Craig had to be concerned with. While Marcus funneled him investment picks to advise on, Craig, under the guidance of his shadowy advisor, learned how to traverse the strange corners of the multi-verse. He had seen so much. From cyborg samurai in a glittering neo-Tokyo to the medieval world the voice introduced to him earlier. Apparently it had the giant human-eating hamburgers Marcus had joked about so long ago. Once Craig got up the nerve to tell him the truth, he'd love to take him on a tour.

But there were more dire things to focus on at the moment. As the voice in the darkness told him, the multi-verse was in danger. According to him—or it—several universes had been wiped from the face of existence, and Craig needed to find a way to stop it. Otherwise, he and Marcus and everyone in the universe could be dead in the near future. With the help of the voice, Craig had been running actual simulations to find a possible solution, but everything he could come up with left a large percentage of multi-verse destroyed, causing the structure of existence to weaken and collapse into itself. He needed to find a stable, all-encompassing fix.

"This latest run has only a sixty-three percent effectiveness," the voice echoed. "Hardly enough to see us through to survival."

"Rrgh," Craig growled. "What the hell are we doing wrong?"

"I believe there must be a base misunderstanding between the simulations you are creating and the information I am trying to feed you. As well as we work together, we might not be speaking the same language."

"That's super frustrating."

"The cracks that have formed in your universe's shell allow us to converse, but they aren't permeable enough for me to send my psychic essence through."

"So you're some sort of psychic race!" Craig smirked. The voice in the shadows knew quite a bit about Craig—through observations, they said—but offered very little about themselves. They said it was in order to promote objectivity, but every drip of information was a gold mine.

"Hah!" The darkness chortled. "Very good catch, Craig Breene. Soon, you will know more about me than I do about you."

"I just don't understand why you can't show me your corner of the multi-verse."

"Because I have lost my home universe to the instability, Craig. I now exist only in the space between worlds, hoping to prevent that which has happened to me."

"Oh," Craig said. This was news to him. And suddenly, he felt bad about his prying.

"Do not worry. Once I find a way to pierce the shell of your universe, we will become well acquainted. Shall we run another simulation?"

"Sure." Craig set up another run, inputting coordinates of several distinct universes and adjusting variables between them to create a lattice of interdimensional interactions, hopefully keeping the structure steady. These ranged from things as massive and conceptual as the speed of time to the mundane, like the placement of certain individuals in different universes. Craig recalled his mother's bedtime stories about a fictional set of heroes. Maybe she had been right! Come to think of it, he hadn't called her in a while. He made a note to do so soon, once he was less busy.

Though the voice helped him view different universes and their various timelines, he was still very much a rookie and lost without its guidance. Just as well. The multi-verse viewer was powerful and not to be left in the hands of a novice. Craig had once tried to access his own universe's future through the viewer's powerful time slider and was disappointed when met with only darkness. Something—the threat the voice was speaking of, perhaps—prevented him from seeing his future, even if only to help his relationship with Marcus. It was profoundly irritating. He was limited to accessing things that would help the grand universal scheme and keep his company in business. Certainly the voice had its own reasons for keeping him on the straight and narrow. Whatever it was, it kept him busy.

"Heyo, Craigo. How's it going?" Marcus' voice filtered past the headset.

Craig disengaged the headset with a click and lifted it off his head, finding Marcus standing in front of the giant armchair Craig had cobbled together out of computer towers and thick cabling. In Marcus's hands, a big box of donuts and coffee waited. Wedged under his armpit was a folder of papers.

"Marcus! Good morning."

Marcus set the food and papers on the nearby desk and began to pour two cups of coffee. He handed Craig one with milk while stirring his own: black with sugar.

"Craig, I don't mean to pry," Marcus said, wrinkling his stubby nose, "but it looks like you've been here all weekend. Smells like it, too. What've you been doing?"

"Running simulations," Craig averted his gaze, sipping his coffee.

"But I haven't given you any info yet," Marcus slapped the stack of papers he'd brought in.

"These are for . . . my own personal use."

Marcus blinked. "Is it porn?"

"No!" Craig choked on his coffee. "No, it's not porn!"

"You can tell me if it's porn."

"It's not. It's . . . physics." Craig couldn't suppress his blush. It sounded like a lie even though it wasn't.

"Physics?"

"Yeah . . . it's become a bit of a hobby of mine. Y'know, ever since we stopped working on the game."

"Right."

"Well, I decided to get into simulating what would happen in a real multi-verse." This was as close to the real explanation as Craig could get without Marcus thinking him totally insane. "Turns out the structure of the system isn't one-hundred percent stable. Elements keep disappearing. It's a whole thing. Interesting problem to solve."

"Uh . . . huh . . ." Marcus squinted. "You've solved this problem?"

"Well, no." Craig rubbed his arm. "It's complex. I've only managed to hit a sixty-three percent success rate and that's hardly stable. The whole thing needs to hold together."

"I'll bet." Marcus furrowed his brow. "Listen, Craig, I know you're still hung up on your mom and her bedtime stories and you can run whatever crazy sims you want. But don't let it interfere with your real work, okay, man? We've got a multi-million dollar business to run here. And I'm hoping we can make it to a billion before the end of the decade. Don't make me regret my investment in you, okay bud?"

"Yeah, no, I got it, Marcus. Sorry."

"No sweat." Marcus returned his attention to the stack of papers, which he plopped into Craig's lap. "Now the analysts upstairs have pulled a lot of promising new companies for potential investment, so if you could run the real models on these and give us a success estimate by the end of the week, we'd be golden."

"Sure thing, Marcus. I'll get it to you then."

Marcus winked and clicked his tongue at Craig as he slid his way out of the room. Craig looked down at the stack of papers and sighed. What had happened to him? He'd wanted to create a product that left its mark on the world. Now, Craig was just raking in meaningless amounts of cash. And even though he was getting to spend time with Marcus, it was less friendly and intimate than he'd expected—or wanted. When Craig thought about it, it was actually kind of depressing, while Marcus—focused on the bottom line—would never notice the irony.

Craig re-donned the headset in order to get down to actual work.

"He doesn't respect you," said he voice of his shadowy friend.

"What?"

"Marcus Espinoza. He doesn't respect you. He doesn't know how important our work is. He's merely using you for monetary gain."

"You . . . you heard that?" A chill creeped up Craig's spine.

"It was hard not to. I know you care for him."

"I . . . I do." The words slipped out of his mouth as if he was being forced into saying them.

"But I've seen many other universes. In very few of them do you end up together. And even then, it matters very little."

His heart sunk. "What about this universe? My universe."

"I cannot see further into your future. Something is blocking me. I know you have tried, facing similar roadblocks. It is just as well, you should not be aware of your own future."

Craig nodded to himself. Overcome with a slight dizzy spell, his head felt foggy—cloudy—like he wasn't certain of what he was doing. Out of control. But it passed soon enough. "What can we do?"

"Perhaps this is due to our inability to solve the stability problem."

"How . . . how can we fix it?"

"We must continue our work," the darkness said. "I have found a way for us to improve our communication, as I mentioned before."

"Really?" Craig felt an involuntary smile crack across his face. "What?"

"Yes, once we can work together in true mental tandem, then we will be able to solve the multi-verse problem and get you the love you deserve. You and I can save the universe, Craig Breene. And Marcus, too. Check the papers he has provided you. There you will find exactly what we need."

"What is it?" Craig felt a strange yearning he'd never felt before. A hunger nothing else in his life could satiate. He wanted to know more. He felt a greed like no other. It scared him. It felt alien, but, at the same time, it felt so right. "What do we need?"

"A universal solution," said the darkness.

# CHAPTER THIRTEEN

## Back To Work

Michael wanted to say he had never committed a break-and-enter before, but that wasn't true. A few weeks ago, he and Stephanie performed a home invasion to confront an unsuspecting graduate student. Said confrontation spiraled out of control in the worst way possible, which was why Michael—plagued by stressful flashbacks of fighting cowmen and tessellated highway robbers—had very low hopes for this new attempt.

Stephanie had dragged Michael back to the detective agency in an attempt to find something she misplaced. As she dug through the storage closet near the bathroom, he was still struggling to wrap his head around what they had to do. "So, we need to break into my old office?"

"I don't like it either." Stephanie raised her voice over the clattering din of her search. "But it's not like you work there anymore."

"That's not the point, Steph." Michael leaned against the wall near the burnt remains of their desk, as far from the closet as possible. "It's The Future Group building. In the center of the city. People are going to notice us."

"Well, obviously we're gonna have to do it real quiet like!" Stephanie shouted back.

"That place is locked down tight with electronic locks and RFID scanners."

"You still have your ID?" Steph poked her head out from the closet.

Michael nodded. He had left in such an indignant hurry this afternoon that he'd forgotten to return it. It was still sitting in the cardboard box in the Garbagemobile's trunk.

"It's only been a few hours, they might not have deactivated it yet. Besides, you said they were concerned about some new release? Maybe that kept 'em busy."

Michael nodded. "You find what you needed in there?"

"Yeah." Stephanie grinned as she slid on a pair of shades. "Ready to roll."

"Sunglasses? That's why we came back?"

"Well, I couldn't find the grappling hook."

"You stashed that away in our old apartment, remember?" Michael harkened back to a few weeks ago when he found Stephanie—having gone missing for two weeks—breaking open their apartment wall as a sort of make-shift hidey-hole.

"I meant the other one."

"You bought *two*?" Michael wasn't sure why he was surprised.

"Yeah. Maybe it's in the trunk of the Garbagemobile." Steph nodded to herself. "I'll go check."

Before Michael could form a thought, she dashed out the door, her boots clomping down the steps. He let out an exasperated sigh and leaned onto the ash-covered desk to catch his bearings for a second.

Until he remembered he was sitting on ash—and he jumped up to swat it off his pants and hands. Michael stopped his ass-slapping dance when he heard the telltale rumbling of a cellphone on vibrate. Since his own phone had been unceremoniously destroyed about an hour earlier, Michael was understandably confused. He walked around to the back of the burnt desk and, following the sound, opened the top drawer to reveal the glow of a fancy smart phone. It continued to vibrate, displaying a "Caller Blocked" message. But Michael picked it up, having an inkling of whom to expect.

"Hello, Michael," the Woman said, her voice as silky, yet cold, as he remembered.

"Hello, uh"—Michael fumbled as he still did not know her name—"uh, you. How's, um, every little thing?"

"You tell me, Michael."

"Well, your file exploded earlier before we even got a chance to look at it. So that little wrinkle made things a lot more fun. But we managed to fight off an assassin on top of a chemical plant in the industrial district."

"So you made contact with our agent in the field."

"That was your guy? Well, then yes. Because the butt of his gun certainly made contact with the back of my head!" Michael rubbed the bump beneath his hair, wincing at the touch. "But it looks like I have a new phone now, so at least I've got that going for me."

"I understand you're under a lot of pressure right now, but I'm not appreciating this attitude."

"Well, I'm not appreciating your . . . face." Michael frowned. Even he knew he hadn't nailed that one.

"Focus, Michael. Were you able to extract the intel from our agent?"

"Not really, no!" Michael barked into the phone. "Except that the chemical plant we went to has started funneling their product to The Future Group tower and some prison."

"LXR?"

"Uh, yeah." Michael was caught off-guard by her guess.

"I see," she murmured. "Breene must be getting his ducks in a row."

"What ducks? What are you talking about?"

"Baby steps, Michael," the Woman chided. "Where's our agent now?"

"He seemed to have a real mad-on for The Future Group. I can't blame 'im, but now he's going to go in there guns blazing, if the cops don't catch him first."

"Hm." She grunted before falling silent for a solid minute.

"Hello?"

"Yes. Sorry. No. You're going to need to stop that from happening."

"We were thinking that, too. But I'm starting to feel like breaking into my former workplace and risking arrest isn't that great of an idea. Can you not send us, I dunno, some back up or something? Big guys. With guns."

"We can't risk making any overt moves at this time."

"Oh, of course you can't!" Michael scoffed. "What about my risk? Huh? Breaking into The Future Group isn't the kind of job I had in mind."

"Well, you have more than one risk, remember?"

The familiar red dot of a laser flashed upon Michael's shoulder. He looked back at it, more disdainful than anything else.

"Anyway," the Woman interrupted, "this has been a good talk. Best of luck. And, remember, if you don't fulfill this mission, we'll kill you."

"Yeah, no, you don't have to keep saying that." Michael nodded, his lips in a flat line, as the laser disappeared. "Good talk."

* * *

After shifting through the box in the trunk, Michael walked around to the driver's side of the Garbagemobile and rapped his knuckles against the window. Stephanie met his glare through her pitch black sunglasses and smiled sweetly as she rolled the window down in fits and starts.

"Oh, hi, Mike."

"Get out." Michael jerked his thumb over his shoulder.

"But, Mike—"

"No buts. Get out."

"Can't I drive at least once?" Steph pleaded.

"I *did* let you drive once. I don't want to scrape dead deer out of the radiator again."

"To be fair, that deer jumped out of nowhere."

"You drove us into the middle of the woods, off-road, at night!"

"I'm better at riding motorcycles. More maneuverable."

"Get out," Michael reiterated.

Stephanie sighed and relented, exiting the car and walking around to swing herself in through the window of the welded passenger-side door.

"Did you find your grappling hook?" Michael asked, fastening his seatbelt.

"No," Stephanie hung her head. "And I'll thank you not to bring it up. I'm really sad about it."

"Well, it looks like we're just going to have to do this the old fashioned way." Michael cranked the engine repeatedly, but it refused to turn over. But then, the tailpipe backfired, giving the Garbagemobile enough of a push to inch it forward, which in turn helped get the engine going. They were off.

* * *

The first thing Michael and Stephanie noticed upon reaching One Future Plaza, aside from the immense tower which dwarfed all other structures in a ten-mile radius—not a single light was left on. The entire building was a glass and steel black hole in the night.

The area surrounding the tower was a different story. A blockade of police squad cars, SWAT trucks, and emergency vehicles sat in a wide radius around the tower and its plaza. Armored cops standing guard packed copious amounts of heat.

"Uh . . ." Michael, who packed no heat, said leaning forward over the steering wheel.

"Looks like Braddock was good on his word," Stephanie said, placing her sunglasses atop her head.

"Maybe if we find him and explain our situation, he'll let us in."

"He seemed like an agreeable chap, but maybe we shouldn't push our luck."

Michael was taken aback by Stephanie's pragmatism.

"Hey, Mike," she asked after a second, "why's the building so completely dead?"

"Huh?"

Stephanie squished Michael's cheeks in her hand and wrenched his face toward the darkened building. "You were always going on about your work friends staying late. And you said they were planning on some 'new release.' So they should be in there, and I doubt they'd be working in the dark."

Michael jerked his head out of Stephanie's hand and rubbed his cheeks, "That's . . . a good point."

"If the building's really empty, that gives us a lot of time to poke around," Stephanie said. "Did you grab your work ID?"

Michael raised himself off the driver's seat and dug around in his back pocket, eventually extricating the hard, plastic card and thick red lanyard he'd fished out of the trunk earlier. "Yeah. But what if they check the records and see I've swiped in?"

"Meh. They've got bigger fish to fry." Stephanie nodded, forcing the sunglasses on her head to perch perfectly on her nose. "Let's go fool some cops."

* * *

They spent a good while slinking through the shadows around the perimeter of the police blockade, attempting to find the area guarded by the least gun-toting cops. After passing by several entry points staffed by SWAT members in tactical gear, Michael found the side entrance by the parking deck he had used to make his escape earlier that day. The way forward was surrounded by tall shrubbery and two plain-clothes officers on guard.

"Excuse me, officers." Steph put on her sweetest voice, violently clashing with her usual grungy green jacket and army boot aesthetic. "My adopted brother here needs to go to the bathroom. You mind if we go inside? We won't be long."

"Your adopted brother?" the white, balding cop in an ill-fitting, rumpled gray suit said, before turning to Michael. "What's his problem? Can't he use his words?"

He froze. He didn't know what Steph would say next, and, even if he disagreed with her choice, he wouldn't have enough time to come up with his own cover story. To make matters worse, Michael had seen these two cops before, just from further away. They had been in the alley with Captain Braddock.

"Well, geeze, that's a little offensive!" Steph didn't seem to notice and carried on with her charade. "Uh . . . he's mute."

"Is he with The Future Group?" the other cop, the young Asian guy with a far more prim and proper aura than his old counterpart, stared her down.

"He's the janitor," Steph said.

"You know this place has been locked down due to a terrorist threat?" the older cop barked. "No one except authorized personnel are to enter or leave. You can't get in without proper identification."

Michael reached into his pocket for his ID and began to hand it over, trembling. Steph yanked the card and lanyard out of Mike's hand and thrust it at the cop.

"How's that?"

"Hm." He flipped it around in his hands, as if examining a cursed object. "This . . . is you?" The cop turned the card outwards to face the two of them. On the red and black face was a picture of Michael from three years ago. His hair, usually a relatively chic mess, was slicked and matted down so much, the outline of his skull was visible. His older glasses dwarfed his face to the point where they should've just fallen off. Michael heard Stephanie stifle a laugh.

Wordless, he nodded fervently and crossed his legs. Conveniently, his anxiety often masqueraded as an intense need to pee.

"Well, nobody would lie about that." The older cop sighed.

His partner, the stickler, squinted, his piercing black glare darting from Michael to the card and back. Michael didn't know how much more of this he could take. After another scan of his eyes, the cop picked up his radio. "I'm gonna have to call it in."

"Listen, guys." Steph crossed her arms and cocked her head. "If this threat is preventing my brother—an American citizen—from exercising good bladder health, then the terrorists have really won."

"Lin." The older cop nudged his partner. "The kid just wants to piss. Let him in."

"It'll only take a second," Steph added. "We'll be right out."

"Fine, ID checks out anyway," said Officer Lin. "Go on. But be quick about it."

"Much appreciated, officers." Steph saluted. "My brother's urinary tract—and America—thanks you." She yanked him up the courtyard steps and past the high shrubbery.

Steph smirked when they got out of earshot. "You should act mute more often. It plays to your strengths."

"Wonderful," Michael muttered. They rounded a corner and emerged into the empty central plaza of The Future Group complex, which looked as dead as the building. During the day, when it was filled with Future Group employees milling about, it was fine, but now it was just a dark, empty expanse of cement slabs with thick, tall shrubs lining either side, preventing any sort of egress. In the center, the black obelisk reached toward the nonexistent stars like some sort of dark idol yearning for escape from the brass bowls imprisoning it. The whole thing gave Michael the creeps.

He rushed to the glass front doors of the building, motivated partly by fear, partly by curiosity, and partly because Stephanie's excuse to the cops had made him actually want to go to the bathroom. He scanned his ID on the card reader next to the entrance and yanked on the cold steel handles. But the doors didn't budge, despite the reader's friendly beep. Michael tried again. And again. And again. But the thick glass only vibrated; it did not give. Either they'd cut power to the entire building, or The Future Group indeed deactivated his card.

"Hey, Mike," Stephanie called out from far behind him. He turned around to find her standing beneath the onyx and bronze statue, fully enveloped by its creeping shadow. At some point in his manic state, she must have fallen behind him. "What's this thing supposed to be?"

"It's just some weird statue. It's been here forever." Michael raised an eyebrow and started walking back to Stephanie. "Why?"

"Well, it looks like they stole a satellite dish from a mummy's tomb." She turned back to him. "Except for this bit."

As Michael approached, he saw Stephanie running her hand over an inset area on the marble plinth of the courtyard sculpture. When his eyes finally adjusted to the darkness, he could make out what it was.

"Huh," Michael said. "Never noticed that before."

"You still got that embarrassing card on you?" Stephanie tapped a small, slightly discolored patch of marble that would have been imperceptible if you didn't know what you were looking for. It was another card reader.

"That doesn't look like what I usually swipe in with," Michael said.

"Might be a completely different system." Steph shrugged. "If we're lucky, they might've forgotten to erase you off this one."

Michael had his doubts, but it was worth a try. So he swiped.

With a hiss and a thunk, a side panel in the bronze statue's plinth slid down into the ground. A set of smooth stone stairs descended, lit only in an eerie green. It was way too super-villainy for Michael's taste.

"Bingo." Stephanie smiled.

# CHAPTER FOURTEEN

## Twists and Turns

"Uhhhh . . ."

As they wound through what were essentially concrete and stone catacombs beneath The Future Group complex, Mike's constant, confused groaning was beginning to get on Stephanie's nerves. She smacked him in the chest. "Would you shut up? I can't hear myself think."

Mike composed himself to the best of his ability.

"Better," Steph said. They continued tiptoeing through the maze of hallways lit only by an eerie set of green LED runners. Still, it was pretty cool. Steph wondered exactly what they'd find at the end of this. If there was indeed an end. What was The Future Group doing? And what kind of beef did that fat assassin have with them? With all this argle bargle going on, she'd have a real tough time keeping Mike safe. She also realized—now she could hear herself think—she was thinking too much.

"It's quiet in here," she whispered, breaking the silence and her train of thought. "Too quiet."

"You *always* say that every time we go somewhere quiet, and you just told me to shut up!" Mike snapped. "More to the point, what the hell is going on here? What is this place? How come I didn't know about these creepy tunnels?"

"I don't know, Mike," Steph hissed back at him. "Big companies are into a lot of shady shit. And maybe if you'd been a better employee, they would have let you in on the goods."

"Don't you start." Mike raised a finger.

"Relax. I'm just teasing you." Steph shot him a smile. "They never would've let you in on the goods."

"I mean, they might have."

"Would you really have wanted to be part of whatever this is? What if this is where they stash the bodies after they murder people? Or what if they're having sex with animals down here?"

Mike reared back. "Nobody's having sex with animals!"

"You don't know that." Steph thought it was as good a guess as any.

"Gross, Steph." Mike scrunched up his face and passed in front of her, taking the lead down the next hall, but he stopped in his tracks suddenly, causing Steph to crash into him. "Would you be careful?" he spat.

"Don't blame me for conservation of momentum," she said. "Why'd you stop?"

Mike waved his hand with a wordless flourish, indicating two large pipes—one yellow, one black—jutting out from the walls and began to run parallel down the ceiling. Both had labels stenciled at even intervals down their length: U-S-1 and U-S-2, respectively.

"Oh." Steph nodded. "Looks like this is where LXR is pumping their stuff."

"Yeah, but what *are* U-S-1 and 2?" Mike asked. "Maybe we should follow the pipes?"

"It's not like we have much choice." Stephanie started down the empty green hallway, keeping her eye on the pipes above.

Five minutes later, Mike and Steph had made considerable progress, taking only the branching paths the pipes suggested, though she was beginning to wonder if they were actually going anywhere. Soon, she began to hear a low hum, rising and falling in waves. She slowed her roll down to an inching crawl and raised a finger to her lips. "Shh. You hear that?"

"The creepy humming?" Michael asked. "Yeah, I hear it!"

"C'mon," she beckoned him. "Stick with me."

"You wanna go *closer*?"

As Steph tiptoed further, the hum increased in volume to a soft droning. It skeeved her out enough to lean back against the hallway wall. Whatever the noise was, it didn't sound inviting, so she inched her way forward until her hand hit a cold, lumpy patch of metal. A keypad.

"Hello, what have we here?" Steph stared down at it. It wasn't the usual nine-digit alphanumeric keypad. No, this one featured the letters A through I, along with the four cardinal arrow keys superimposed on the B, F, and H. "You know of any secret codes The Future Group has, Mike?"

"Steph, I barely knew my timesheet codes. Let's just follow the humming. There's no way you're going to guess—"

But Steph already had, the flat panel of wall before them sliding open with a hiss.

"How did you do that?" Mike asked.

"Konami Code. Up, up, down, down, left, right, left, right, B, A." It was what she always tried on keypads that allowed it. This was just the first time it worked.

"Y'know, Steph. Sometimes you amaze me."

Steph clucked her tongue at him as they moved into the room.

Above her, two U-S pipes dipped down from the ceiling and thrust themselves into the room, directing their gaze.

"What the hell is this?"

Before them was a large computer room, but not in the traditional sense of the phrase. The entire room was a computer. Each wall was covered from floor to ceiling with a computer console, standing guard around the full perimeter of the room—easily four hundred feet.

"Alright . . ." Steph surveyed the machinery. She dared not move. If she banged into the wrong thing—as she was often wont to do—she'd accidentally launch a nuclear missile, knock Google offline, or turn off the moon.

But her reticence was quickly overcome by the technological throne sitting in the center of the room on a circular platform. The sleek white chair did not look like it was built for comfort. It was all angles with very little in the way of padding. Bundles of meticulously organized wires trailed from the back of the chair out to the supercomputer walls. The U-S pipes had dropped and turned down into the floor, pumping their liquid into the chair's platform.

Directly above the chair hung a familiar piece: an inverted version of the black obelisk and brass bowl statue that Steph and Mike had entered on the surface.

"Okay, I know I said I was creeped out before," Mike said, "but now I'm really creeped out. What is this thing?"

"Only one way to find out!" Steph was already in the chair. She spied a set of clunky, red goggles hanging from the inverted obelisk and yanked them toward her. "Oh, neat! A Virtual Boy! I haven't seen one of these in ages."

"Steph, stop! I don't think this is a good idea." Mike reached out to her. "This thing could kill you."

"Uh, yeah," she said, placing the goggles over her eyes, enveloping her in a sea of black. "That's why *I'm* gonna use it instead of you." By touch she felt around the armrests of the chair, pushing buttons and rotating dials, errant missiles be damned. Despite her experimental combinations of inputs, nothing happened.

"What do you see, Steph?" Mike's voice sounded like a faraway echo."

"Nothing." Steph groaned. "Damn it, Nintendo. Now I remember how much these sucked."

She stabbed at a few more buttons before the throne booted to life with a low whine, followed by what sounded like a burst of energy.

"Now we're cooking with gas!" Stephanie said as her pitch-black view began to fill with wireframe models.

"You see something?" Mike asked.

"Looks like some sort of large temple," Steph tried to describe it accurately. "Big, wide area. Stadium seating and a giant fire pit in the middle. Torches and stuff everywhere. Kinda like Indiana Jones 2, but everything's green. Ugh, Temple of Doom was the worst."

Suddenly, a gust of wind wooshed, extinguishing the flames of the temple, and small red roundels of light coalesced in the darkness. The roundels appeared to pivot toward her, and a booming voice emanated from surround sound speakers installed on the seat above her head.

"I am Korrthu," the voice announced, "the Beast Who Walks Like a Man. God of the Etern—"

"Woof. It's some kind of fantasy RPG. Boring!" Stephanie bellowed to herself, as she rotated one of the dials she had found. The roundels disappeared as the screen wiped itself clean. "How do you get Mario Tennis on this thing?"

"That's what they're doing here?" Mike asked. "They're making video games?"

As Steph continued to mess with the dial, a series of graphics appeared on her screen, replacing the last with a surprising quickness. She saw a city—much like their own—its streets full of bustling people, an empty desert landscape that seemed to be evaporating into the sky, and a futuristic Tokyo populated by what looked to be half-human, half-robot samurai. This one got her blood pumping.

"Awesome. Now I got some sort of cyborg samurai game. I've always wanted one of these. Where's the start button?" Stephanie took a few more awkward stabs, but ended up nudging the dial one more time, blasting her out of the current simulation. "Aw man, no! Wait! Bring it back! I just—"

Stephanie blinked as the next view appeared on her screen. It was another desertscape, but this one was highly pixelated, as if the computer hadn't possessed enough processing power for high polygon graphics. Odd, as the other games had impeccable graphics. But now, the rocky ground and the few lone trees before her looked like pixelated approximations of themselves, much more in line with the capabilities of a Nintendo Virtual Boy. Something was off. It was familiar. Too familiar.

"Uh . . . Mike," It was so familiar because Steph had been there. Recently. She was observing another world of the multi-verse. A gem-like world, where she and Mike had been accosted by cowboys made of fractals, one of the many stops of their magical mystery tour from a few weeks ago. And if this machine could somehow see what they had seen, she had just opened up a whole new can of worms. "I think we might be in trouble."

"What do you mean?"

Stephanie yanked off the goggles, pulling herself out of the geometric wireframe desert and into the blinding light of the real world. She stared at Mike with raw and bleary eyes, despite her short time in the machine. "This thing isn't a Virtual Boy."

"Well, I could've told you that."

"I think it's a system that lets you view other worlds from the multi-verse."

Mike's jaw slowly dropped as if he was about to say something, but she knew he couldn't find the words. It was a full minute before his brain processed the information to the point of speech.

"Shit," he said. "How do you know?"

"Well, one of the 'games' I found looked exactly like that desert world we visited where everything looked like it was made of crystals. Remember? You threw up there?"

"Uh . . . yeah," Mike held his stomach. "I remember."

"Hold up," Steph tilted her head up. She could still hear the humming that they had heard earlier. "The hum."

"Yeah, computers hum."

"No." It didn't sound much like humming anymore, but rather a soft, undulating droning. "And it's not coming from here."

"You're right," Mike moved across the room toward the entrance. "It's coming from further down the hallway."

"Sounded like a ghost."

"It's not a ghost, Stephanie," Mike snapped.

"Fine, a bunch of ghosts!" Steph took a deep breath and stowed her attitude. "We've got to follow it, you know."

Mike bit his lip in resignation. "Yeah. I know."

With Steph taking the lead again, the two of them emerged into the hallway and moved toward the source of the sound. Neither said anything to each other. Usually Steph would offer a quip, Mike would come in with a riposte, she would hit back with a counter-riposte, and so on. But they seemed too humbled by the implications to even speak. To be fair, it made the whole investigation process faster, if less colorful.

They eventually stumbled upon their first set of branching passageways that could have led to exits, but they silently agreed to continue following the sounds. As they got closer, the droning resolved itself first into moaning, then into rhythmic, undulating chants. The sounds were too low and deep for either of them to comprehend the actual words.

Their journey ended as the hallway opened into a large antechamber with ceilings—at a best estimate—over twenty feet tall, which accommodated an arched set of double doors that could have belonged to a castle. While the arch was decorated in beautifully designed gold filigree, the doors itself were as black as midnight. No light could escape them. Even the bright green glow, filtering through the crack between the doors, was no match for its dark maw. The chanting, however, seeped out, as loud as ever, and in a language neither of them could place.

"Okay, well, none of this seems kosher at all," Steph hissed.

They paused and shrugged at each other in worried silence before turning their attention toward the door, as if hypnotized by the dancing green light and the alien rhythms of the chant.

It was at least a full minute before Steph, still gazing at the door, spoke again. "I'll go check it out."

"Nuh-uh!" Mike grabbed her shoulder. "No! I'm gonna check the weird shit out this time."

Steph wasn't about to let Mike wander headfirst into the unknown. For his sake, she decided that was her job. So she socked him in the shoulder.

"Oof!" Mike clutched the impact point and stopped himself from crying out. "What was that for?"

"Don't move. I'm the one checking it out."

"Okay, geeze," Mike backed off. "Fine, you go!"

Satisfied, Steph took tentative steps forward and pressed her hands to the door's black surface. Oddly cold to the touch, it felt like rough wood. Pushing it open ever so slightly as to not creak, Steph peered through the gap with one curious eye. She found a gargantuan rotunda with row after row of cushioned wooden seats occupied by an army of people in black hooded robes with deep crimson trim. This swarm of weird looking people chanted and swayed in the eerie green light flooding the space. A light emanated from the center of the room, where a man wearing the bleached skull of a bull stood atop an altar, leading the group in prayer over a pit of roaring emerald flames.

Steph narrowed her eyes. She had seen this place before, too. It looked suspiciously like the temple she had seen when donning the Virtual Boy the first time. Then, the lights went out, something strange announcing itself out of the darkness. She tried to recall what it had been and alert Mike, but only two words managed to escape her lips.

"What the . . ."

# CHAPTER FIFTEEN

## Feels Just Like It Should

LXR Chemicals was a small company making pre-mixed solutions for use in high school chemistry labs. But according to research provided by Marcus's analysts, their R&D department was on the cusp of releasing a new product. They called it the "Universal Solute," a synthesized chemical compound that dissolved into anything. They believed it would revolutionize the world. That is, if they could find a use for it.

Craig Breene, on the other hand, knew exactly what it was good for. As per the voice in the darkness, LXR's Universal Solute could create a "universal solution" that could seep into the cracks in the shell of the universe, allowing Craig and the voice to commune more fully. And when Craig and the voice put their combined powers together, they would be one step closer to cracking the case of the collapsing multiverse. Then, Craig could save the world, and Marcus with it.

It took a lot of calls for Craig to find someone at LXR who would speak with him. Perhaps if he had told them he was one of the founders of The Future Group—a multi-million dollar business—they would have been more receptive. But he didn't want to make a bigger splash than he needed to.

Once he did get someone on the line, they patently refused to give him a sample of the Universal Solute. They cited pending patents and the need to keep things under wraps until LXR went public. Even ludicrous amounts of money wouldn't grease their wheels. Craig thought they were fools, and the voice in the darkness agreed. None of them knew what was at stake.

So Craig tried a different route. Using his multi-verse viewer, he found the phone number of an LXR intern in a closely adjacent universe. One with seven-digit phone numbers. The thought crossed his mind to delve deeper into this universe, but the voice suggested there would be plenty of time to do so once they combined their powers. Craig felt compelled to agree. They could do more together than Craig could alone.

Craig called the young intern—a college student named Eric Bunting—and, offering him a hefty sum for a light act of corporate espionage, convinced him to bring over a small sample of the solute, under cover of darkness. Craig let Eric in and led him down into the basement, where he placed a heavy metal box on the desk.

"So, what do you want this for, exactly?" the heavyset boy asked, wiping his floppy blond hair out of his face. "It takes forever to make and it doesn't, like, *do* anything."

"Eric, you're a smart kid." Craig patted him on the shoulder. "You should know not to ask any questions. Just take the money and run."

"I mean, okay." Eric flipped through the wad of hundreds Craig had just handed him. "See you later, I guess."

"Good luck, Eric." Craig saluted. "One day, you'll be running that company."

"Hah!" Eric laughed on his way out the door. "I'm just there for the college credit. Once summer's over, I'm outta there. Peace!"

Craig turned his attention to the box on his desk. It was far too big for a simple sample of solute. And he was right; opening it revealed the few white, sandy grains of solute Eric provided needed to be suspended in an electromagnetic field. Likely, since it could dissolve itself into anything, it had to be kept from touching anything.

Now all Craig had to do was use it to create a universal solution. And that was a very simple procedure. There was only one step.

Just add water.

Craig had a small paper cup from a Future Group water cooler all ready. He opened the top of the containment box and, in one fell scoop, the water and solute got to know each other a little better. Craig swirled the cup around in the air, like a wine connoisseur aerating a glass of cabernet. Unlike said connoisseur, he gulped down the contents of the tiny cup in a second, crumpled the remains, and threw it in the wastebasket.

In the next few moments, he felt a slight tingling sensation run up his spine and burst across his head, giving him quick zaps of serotonin. The voice in the darkness said this would happen. It was all part of the process. Craig was just seconds away from unlocking the secrets of the multi-verse and saving every person, place, and thing that had ever existed.

He strode back over to his digital throne, a mass of hard white plastic paneling and ruddy wires, and sat down, donning the headset. Using one of the integrated dials on the throne's armrest, Craig turned the system on, and with the whir of fans and a friendly boot-up noise, the multi-verse viewing platform came to life. Once again, all Craig could see was darkness and the timestamp in the corner of his vision.

July 22nd, 1997, 22:13pm.

The time Craig's world ended.

"Is it done?" asked the voice out of the darkness.

"Yes," Craig said. Suddenly, he felt a strange sensation, as if something was wriggling through the thin crevices of his skull and into the folds of his brain. It was not at all like the serotonin zaps from earlier. No, this hurt, and for some reason, it felt much more sinister. Craig barely had time to contemplate if he'd made a grave mistake. His head surged with an indescribable energy, his eyes rolled over, and the darkness swallowed him whole.

*  *  *

Craig opened his eyes to a field of pure white. It was as if he was nowhere and everywhere at once. The only reason he didn't think he was dead? He could see the rest of his body.

"What . . . what happened?" His voice echoed through nothing.

"Welcome, Craig Breene," a voice said. It was similar to the voice he had spoken to through the darkness, but rather than hearing it through his computer's speakers, or even through his own ears, the voice vibrated through every fiber of his being. Instead of hearing the words, he felt their intent, which caused him to shiver.

"Is . . . is it you?"

"Yes, Craig. It's me. You've opened your mind to me and let us join as one. Don't you remember?"

"Yes, I . . . I remember."

Or did he?

"Good." The voice's deep baritone took on an unnerving, sinister quality Craig could not place. "Since that's settled, we must proceed to the business of letting me into your universe."

"Letting you in? What do you mean? That wasn't part of what we agreed on."

"Craig, I'd say I'm surprised that you're as naïve as you look, but I'm not. I had you eating out of the palm of my hand." The voice's words rushed through his blood and invaded every square inch of his veins. "I needed your universe and now you're going to be the one to help me acquire it. Well, your body is, at least."

"No! No, I won't." Craig shouted into the void, but his defiant shouts turned to tortured, angry screams as he realized the implications. "I trusted you! How could you do this to me? I wanted to help you save the multi-verse."

"Oh, but you are. I prune the multi-verse of weak, dying universes to ensure its stability. I'm a force of nature, Craig. A predator in the existential ecosystem. Universes are my prey. So I wouldn't feel too badly about it. In fact, I can stop you feeling badly at all! I've already got your physical form under my control. All I need to do is suffocate your mind." The voice was too matter of fact for Craig's taste. "And that's the easy part. I've done it hundreds of billions of times before to better beings than you. Don't worry. It's quite a simple process. You won't remember a thing afterwards."

Craig tried to run, but the white space gave him no place to go. He was running on an invisible treadmill.

"You see, I first start by diminishing your base intelligence. I'd already begun that bit. It's hard for you to notice, so I'll skip straight past that part and get down to the bargaining."

"W-W-What are you?" Craig stammered.

"Some people call me The Beast Who Walks Like A Man. I don't know why. I can take so many forms. Not just men. Others call me the God of the Eternal Feast. That seems more fitting, since I tend to devour their universes. I've always liked the sound of those two titles together, though. It seems very regal."

"You're . . . you're the monster." Craig's face fell, the obvious finally dawning on him. "The one from my game. From my mother's stories. You're the one consuming universes! How . . . how are you real? Did . . . did I create you?"

The voice sent a haughty lilt through Craig's veins as he searched for an answer he did not have. "Perhaps it is I who created you, in order for you to create me. Or both! Who knows, really? You see, existence is a tricky thing. Events sometimes happen in a roundabout order, or never at all. In fact, sometimes simultaneous things don't even happen at the same time. But I digress. Where was I? Oh, yes. The next step is the bargaining. This is the part where I offer to give you everything you want if you let me into your soul."

"What do you mean?" Out of the corner of Craig's eye, he could see thin cracks snaking inside the white façade. They were thin and far away, but they were there.

"Craig, what a ridiculous question. I can give you what you want. I know you want Marcus."

Marcus Espinoza, his longtime friend, appeared before him. Completely nude with not even a fig leaf to deal with his naughty bits. He proffered a coy wave. Craig tried not to stare, but he couldn't quite help himself.

"I can give him to you, and I can take him away," the voice said. Naked Marcus vanished. "And if you give me what I want, I can make it feel so good. You'll never miss your corporeal existence again."

"No . . . no. I . . . don't want that!" Craig yelled. "I don't want any of this! No more of your lies!"

"Well, then that leads us down the road to step three, where I take your memories so you don't know what the hell it is you do want. I prefer to let my thralls submit willingly, but sometimes you guys are pretty stubborn."

The cracks in the far walls split into deep fissures, and suddenly, Craig looked upon inky black. But he didn't know where he was or why it was happening.

"This way, you have no link to your former life, so there's nothing to keep you from connecting fully to me."

It happened so suddenly he didn't even notice. He couldn't remember anything. He didn't even know his own name! Was he even a he? He looked down at himself and didn't recognize the body he saw. The only thing he recognized was the thick black goop seeping in through the cracks in the world. The black encroached on his very being until he was standing on a tiny oasis of white in a sea of darkness.

"It's over, my friend." Something oddly familiar vibrated through his bones. Something strange he couldn't place. But it seemed . . . inviting, somehow? "I already have you. And soon, I'll have others in your old world. Once I amass enough followers, you will all let me through."

He wanted to respond, but he could not. He felt familiar but distant flashes of sadness and anger. Out of reach. Instead, he found himself kneeling down, aching to touch the rising pool of darkness around his ankles. It was warm. He wanted to be there.

"But I am not without mercy," the bone-rattling sensation continued, "I do so love to hear my thrall's last words. It gives me an insight into who they are, what they value, and—most importantly—their weaknesses. So I've left you enough free will for one last bit of light in your life. But not enough to break my darkness. Now what will it be? Who or what will you reach out for?"

"Mom," he said. He meant to call her. He should have called her. How could he call her? Whoever she was. He needed to call her. Now he would never get a chance.

"Mom," he said again. The word felt weird in his mouth. It could have had meaning once. Whatever it was. There was nothing there now. All he wanted was to succumb to the black, but he did not know why. It didn't matter.

"So that's who you would call for. Very enlightening, thank you."

The world shook. The void. The voice. They were the world.

It devoured him. He disappeared, bit by bit, under its surface. It was okay. He wanted it. It felt warm. It felt. . . right. Less of him existed, and each bit replaced by echoes of a name.

Korthuu.

And the void began to smile.

# CHAPTER SIXTEEN

## Company Culture

". . . actual fuck?" Peering over Stephanie through the crack in the giant double doors, Michael completed her thought. He took in the grand rotunda and the robed masses of chanting, droning people swaying almost in time with the green flames. The interior chamber was a nearly perfect sphere, almost five stories high, with rings of balconies overlooking the chamber floor, each flooded with hooded cultists. The better seats were, of course, on the floor, with wooden church-like pews in concentric circles around the dais, broken only by aisles between them. It looked like the stage of a TED Talk in hell. "What is going *on* here?"

"Looks like some sort of cult." Stephanie smiled up at him. She seemed to be enjoying this.

"Brothers and sisters of the Future!" bellowed the man in the center of the room over the quiet green pyre. The bull skull atop his head wobbled with his words. "Long has been our quest. But today, we stand upon the edge of salvation. Thanks to our tireless efforts, our Lord Korthuu is mere hours away from breaching unto this plane, and the cleansing of the Eternal Feast shall be upon us."

"There we go." Stephanie said. "They just want to release some sort of evil god to raze the Earth. Seems pretty cut and dry to me."

"Hail Korthuu!" The mass of hooded people droned in unison. "Hail Korthuu!"

"Korthuu?" Michael raised any eyebrow. "Wasn't there—"

Before he could cobble together his thoughts, a lone member of the group emerged into the center aisle and glided toward the bull-headed leader before the emerald flames.

"My lord," he said, his face hidden by the hood, "it must be said. Earlier tonight, I was drugged and accosted in the overworld. And while my loyalties lie only to Korthuu and the Universal Solution flowing through my veins, I cannot truly be certain I have not failed."

"My child." Even through the bull's skull, the leader's voice boomed and echoed across the stone rotunda walls. As creepy and insane as they were, these cultists sure had an ear for acoustics. "Worry not. Korthuu is aware. Even if you have caused action to be taken against us, your failures are forgiven. Come."

The leader beckoned the man onto the dais and removed his hood, turning him to face the gathered multitudes. Despite the distance, or maybe due to it, Michael recognized the man who he and Stephanie had spied in the dingy alleyway.

"Your service to Korthuu has been diligent, my dear Eric Bunting. You were there at our humble beginnings," the leader continued. "But, now, your essence will return to Korthuu so you may partake in the eventual glory of the Eternal Feast. Until then . . ."

The glint of a serrated dagger shot through the man's chest. His back arched and he let out a gurgling cry before crumpling to the floor. With one quick jerk of his leg, the leader punted the dead man into the green flames, which erupted into the air before settling back down.

"Thanks, in advance." The words stung Michael like acid in his face. By the time the flames subsided, the cult leader had lowered his bull skull into the flaming bowl, revealing a vacant smile emblazoned on the face of a bald forty-year-old man with glasses.

"Aw, crap," Michael whispered to himself.

"What?" Stephanie put her eyes back to the crack in the doors.

"It's Craig." He hung his head, as if he bore some responsibility. "It's my boss."

"Thanks, in advance!" chanted the cult.

"That guy?" Stephanie exclaimed a little too loudly for Michael's comfort. "The skull guy is your boss? The one who fired you?"

"Shh!" Michael grabbed Stephanie's wrist and yanked her away from the door, toward the rear wall. "Yes, damn it!"

"That's amazing!" Stephanie doubled over in a fit of guffaws, drowned out the repeated chants of "Thanks, In Advance." She looked up at Mike. "Oh, my God. I bet you wish they were actually having sex with animals now."

"Why would I wish that?" Michael's head bobbled in confusion.

"I mean, it would be better, right?"

"How would it be better?"

"It's a little more justifiable than trying to conjure up Korthuu, the Beast Who Walks Like A Man"—Stephanie provided sarcastic air-quotes for the god's title—"God of the Eternal Feast."

Michael's brow knit together, a few errant connections linking behind his eyes. The God. The Title. The bull skull. They were flashes of something familiar. But before he could say another word, a blinding, lime-green light washed over the entire hallway. The doors opened; the black and red hoods of the cabal all turned in their direction.

Craig Breene was staring daggers at them from his dais.

"Ahem." He cleared his throat. "I'm sorry. Are you quite done?"

"Uh . . . uh . . ." Michael stammered.

"Oh! Michael." Craig's voice dropped to a more casual tone, but he seemed somewhat disappointed. "It's you."

Michael froze, unsure of what to do. His mind was going a mile a minute in a hundred different directions. Everything was becoming a little too much to process. Fortunately, things were taken out of his hands, as two of Craig's hooded followers abdicated their positions in the wings and glided down to secure Michael and Stephanie's arms, dragging them down toward the dais.

The faces of the cultists, darkened beneath their loose black hoods, turned to watch as they were forced past, Michael's feet and ankles dug grooves into the carpeting. He turned to Stephanie, anxiety scrunching his face.

"Don't worry, Mike," Steph said, but she seemed less than convinced. "It could always be worse."

"How, Steph? How could it be worse?"

"The room could be filled with spiders?"

Michael growled and turned away from her and toward his impending doom. They reached the center of the chamber. Michael stared up at his old boss, who peered past a curtain of green fire, somehow still smiling. "I was told you'd be coming."

"Told by who?" Michael asked. "What the hell is all this? What's going on?"

"You're in no positions to be asking questions, Michael." Craig's voice was as even as when he conducted Michael's firing. "We gave you plenty of chances. But you denied us time and time again."

"What are you talking about?"

"Seriously, Mike-ster. We tried," came a familiar, irritating voice at his shoulder.

"Oh, you have *got* to be kidding me!" Michael scowled up as one of his captors lowered his hood to unveil Ravi Patel's infuriating grin.

"You just didn't want to hang with us," he said. "Craig made me your buddy when you first got hired. I was supposed to help convert you to the cause. But you never wanted to socialize. Never wanted to be part of the family. I tried so hard, Mike-ster."

"Oh, shut up." Michael sneered.

The cultist holding Stephanie dropped her hood to reveal a dark skinned woman with thick braided hair. "It's been years, Michael. We invited you to parties. After-work drinks. Company paintball sessions. You were just angry and aloof all the time. We wanted to be your pals!"

Michael could only stare at her and bite his lip.

"You don't even remember who I am, do you?" Her eyes narrowed. "I sat next to you for two years!"

"Well . . . I . . ." Michael sputtered.

"I'm Brianne! I invited you to all my parties!"

"Uh. . ."

"You see, Michael, The Future Group requires a team mentality." Craig spun around in place. The few thousand hoods in attendance lowered and revealed several familiar—but most unfamiliar—faces from the office. "We're a family here. We work to support each other in our goals. In our service of our Lord Korthuu. But you were never much of a team player. That's why we let you go."

"That's why you let me go?" Michael shouted, a nascent rage bubbling up inside him. "Because I didn't fall for your stupid cult?"

"This is the attitude I'm talking about, Michael. You just weren't the right fit for us or our values."

"Screw you! I was a perfect fit. I was a friggin' great employee."

"Mike," Stephanie whispered, leaning as far over as her handler would let her, "it sounds like you want to be part of the cult."

"I don't want to be part of the cult!" Michael snapped. "It's the principle of the thing! I'm tired of people telling me I'm not good enough. I'm good enough, damn it!"

The chamber was silent in the wake of Michael's whining.

Stephanie eventually broke the quiet. "Yeah, it sounds like you want to be part of the cult."

"We have precious little time to waste with this bickering." Craig's calm, corporate-approved demeanor dissipated, replaced by his booming anger. "These interlopers must be dealt with so that we may release Korthuu's true form!"

"Hail Korthuu!" The fists of thousands of cultists struck the air.

"Interlopers?" Michael tilted his head. Another flash of the familiar. Where had he heard the word before?

"Cast them into the universal flames, so their bones and essence can sustain Korthuu for their journey to our world!" Craig waved them forward, up onto the dais.

"Hail Korthuu," came the rallying cry once again.

"Hey, here's a better idea," Stephanie said as Michael's ex-coworkers began to jostle them up toward the giant bowl of green fire, "How about instead of killing us, you tell Korthuu to kiss my ass?"

The heat of the flames seared Michael's face and pulled sweat from his pores. Together, they sidled into the presence of hot, green death.

"Hey, Mike," Stephanie whispered, "how funny is it that this guy fired you, and now he's going to push you into an actual fire?"

"Out of all the jokes you've ever told, that was probably the most forced."

"Yeah, well, they can't all be gems."

"I'm sorry, Mike-ster," Ravi whispered over his shoulder. "For the record, I always thought you were a pretty cool dude. Even though you were kind of an asshole."

"Hey, Ravi." Michael's face contorted into a hateful, ugly grimace that came with an odd sense of liberation. "I hope you die."

"We're all dying, Mike-ster, but Korthuu can save us." Ravi's face began to shift and blur. Michael thought it was a trick of the heat, but as multiple eyes began to tear through Ravi's dark skin, and fangs began to elongate and pierce through his lips, Michael began to reassess.

"Ahh! Ahh! Ahh! Steph, I don't like this!"

Michael glanced over at Stephanie, who was witnessing her braided captor Brianne undergo a similar sort of transformation, but into an entirely different asymmetrical horror. The woman's eyes had rolled over black and her skin was beginning to slough off as her neck cracked and bent backwards, allowing her head to touch her back. Her lower jaw unhinged, lazily laying down her chest. Two separate tongues slithered out from the bottom of her throat. She hissed, "Korthuu has thanked us in advance by allowing us access to our most powerful forms."

"Okay," Steph said. "That is . . . not great."

The Creature Formerly Known As Ravi tightened his grip on Michael's shoulders, adding several other clawed appendages to the mix, and inched him closer to the fire.

"Michael." Craig said his name with the undiluted sweetness of someone who couldn't care less about what he was saying. His smile stretched at the edges, transforming a fake plastic grin into a horrifying, barely human rictus. "Please know this decision is purely professional. We wish you the best in your future endeavors as nourishment for our lord, Korthuu."

"Hey, Tim Cook," Stephanie piped up, sweat streaming down her face. "Before we go, how about I clue you in on one more thing?"

Craig, unamused, turned away. "I have no time for your nonsense."

"Well, I know something you don't know," Stephanie sang in the face of the hellish heat. "Look at all your followers. Your sons and daughters of Korthuu. You don't notice anything?"

Craig turned around and surveyed his loyal subjects. Michael followed his gaze and saw nothing but dark hooded faces in lockstep formation with one another. Craig returned to Stephanie. "What are you talking about?"

"Well, one of them is really kinda chubby."

A thunderous crack shattered its way through the perfect acoustics of the rotunda. Ravi's clawed grip on Michael loosed as his body crumpled to the floor, skidding down the dais steps. Michael turned back to see his ex-coworker's deformed head come to rest on the ground, its multiple black eyes frozen in shock. One had been replaced with a gaping bullet wound.

Stephanie took advantage of the distraction to wrench herself free from Brianne's clutches, pivoting harshly and shoving the cultist over the edge of the bowl and into the fiery depths of the sacrificial flame. The green fire roared into the air once again as the woman's screams were silenced.

"Huh. That was, uh, that's pretty dark." Stephanie peered over the lip of the bowl, allowing the sunglasses that had been sitting atop her head to slide off and tumble into the fire. "Aw, man! Those cost twenty dollars!"

"Who dares defile the Temple of Korthuu?" Craig whipped his head around until he found the barrel of a gun pressed up against his forehead.

Michael and Stephanie stared on in hushed silence as the skull-faced balaclava of their mysterious assassin emerged from a cultist's cloak, falling further to reveal his plus-size body.

"I dare," came the garbled voice, though there was not enough modulation in the world that could filter the anger those words expressed.

"Okay," Stephanie whispered to Michael. 'This is pretty badass."

"You'll never get out of here alive, you know." Craig's eyes narrowed. On cue, the thousands of cultists in the rotunda pushed back their robes and drew their own individual pistols, training them on the assassin.

"You gave everyone guns, too?" Michael squealed.

Craig ignored him, keeping eye-contact with the flat red lenses staring out of the skull's eye-holes. "Your move."

"You don't even remember who I am, do you?" The assassin, right hand still gripping the pistol, used his free hand to reach up and whip off the skull-mask. Beneath lay a face that was a combination of age, anger, and curls. And it was undoubtedly feminine, with a bit of extra mileage carving sorrowful creases under the eyes.

Michael narrowed his eyes in an attempt to figure out why she looked so familiar, but, as usual, Stephanie beat him to the punch.

"Maureen!" She waved both her hands. "Oh my God, hi!"

Maureen Whelan—the angry septuagenarian who had bowled Michael over while storming out of the detective agency earlier—shot Stephanie a punishing glare before turning back to Craig.

"Listen," Steph continued, "I know the secretary thing didn't work out, and I'm sorry about calling out your man-boobs earlier. I didn't realize they were actual boobs!"

Michael elbowed her in the ribs. "Shut. Up."

"Sorry! My bad. I can see you're busy," Stephanie yelled to Maureen with a dismissing hand. "We'll catch up later. You do your thing."

"I don't know who you are," Craig said, staring directly at Maureen, who refused to blink. "But these two seem to have some sort of relationship with you."

Maureen's face pulled back into a desperate, angry sneer. Michael could make out the soft glint of tears trickling down her cheeks.

"You took my son from me," she said.

"Oh. Uh, oh boy." Stephanie tugged at her collar. "This has gotten a whole lot darker than I'm actually comfortable with."

"You can kill me, woman," Craig said, "but rest assured you'll never stop Korthuu."

"I don't care about Korthuu!" Maureen sobbed through gritted teeth. "I want my son back, you son of a bitch."

"Korthuu enlightens all our lives. And when they are released upon this plane, then, they will bring rewards to all their children."

"I'll stop you no matter what it takes."

"You may try. The Future Group's influence is more far-reaching than you know. You may have killed the rest of the board, but we have acolytes everywhere."

A different sort of bang pervaded the rotunda as the large black doors Michael and Stephanie entered through slammed open. The already full chamber was flooded with armored SWAT officers. Each one held a corresponding cultist at gunpoint, and a separate group approached the dais.

"Oh, thank god. The cops are here." Michael let out the tension trapped in his chest.

As soon as the commotion died down, the now-crowded aisle between the door and the dais parted. Captain Leslie Braddock stormed down the aisle in a bulletproof vest, brandishing a gun. "And what exactly is going on here?"

"Leslie! Thank God you're here," Stephanie wheezed. "There is some seriously crazy shit that's gone down in the last ten minutes."

"They fired me and now they're all monsters and the monsters have guns!" Michael felt the words tumble out of his mouth in quick succession.

Braddock stared at Michael and nodded, before turning his attention to Maureen, who still held Craig at gunpoint. He, in turn, raised his glock. "Ma'am, I'm going to ask you to have to put the gun down. Immediately."

"Uh, sir." Michael raised a finger. "You might be missing the bigger picture here. Did you not catch what I said about the monsters?"

"Son." He faced Michael with an icy glare. "We'll deal with you and your 'monsters' soon enough, but first . . ."

Without even turning back to aim, Captain Leslie Braddock fired, hitting Maureen and sending her body flying off the dais and out of sight.

The SWAT officers lowered their guns and fell into lockstep with the cultists. Braddock turned back to Michael and Stephanie with a familiar, chilling smile. "Hail Korthuu."

Michael frowned. "Aw, crap."

# CHAPTER SEVENTEEN

## Escape From The Nightmare Factory

"Maureen!" Steph yelled as she saw her fall backwards off the dais. "You literal monsters!"

"I told you." Craig spun around to meet her gaze as she and Mike were—for the second time today—grabbed and restrained against their will, this time by actual police officers. "We have acolytes everywhere."

"Yeah, but that's just something you *say*," Stephanie countered. "Nobody actually expects you to actually have them."

"So you've been killing these people the whole time?" Mike butted in. "because the city police force is under your control?"

"Oh, no. Not all of them. The Universal Solution is a rare and precious resource." Craig chuckled. "We just focused on the important ones. Isn't that right, Leslie?"

"Hail Korthuu, sir," Captain Braddock said, his face a stoic mask.

"And besides, Senator Clegg and Edgar Brauer were liabilities. They had not accepted Korthuu into their lives. So although they had accepted our hefty bribes, when we found out they were becoming suspicious, they had to be terminated."

"Edgar Brauer's head exploded!" Mike shouted.

"Yes, well, some of our acolytes are more skilled than others, Michael. You of all people should know that."

Mike growled.

"What about Arthur Birch?" Steph asked.

"He was a traitor and we dealt with him accordingly. All in the service of Korthuu."

"You guys are insane," Steph scowled. "And I don't throw that word around lightly. Who the hell would want to willingly join you?"

"Everyone has their price!" Craig seemed almost gleeful.

"You bribed everyone?" Mike was taken aback.

"Bribe is such a dirty word." Craig paused in thought for a second. "But, yes, that pretty much describes it. Future Group stock is in constant climb, and everybody in this rotunda is a large shareholder. Capital is a powerful motivator, but once the truth of Korthuu is revealed to you by way the Universal Solution, material concerns melt away."

"How come I didn't get any of that stock?" Mike yelled. Steph rolled her eyes. He still felt so slighted by his exclusion from this crazy monster death cult that he was missing the wider picture.

"It was only for those who we knew would help usher in Korthuu's rule. It is thanks from them, in advance."

"Thanks"—the cultists chanted, this time, in unison with the cops, which was really disturbing—"in advance."

Stephanie glanced at Mike out of the corner of her eye. For some reason, he looked like he was going to blow a gasket, so she took the opportunity to grab the reins of the conversation. As long as they kept talking, they weren't turning into terrifying monster men, so she still had the upper hand. "You think a giant elder god is going to deliver you into salvation because this dude gave you some stock options as *thanks*?"

"Thanks," they chanted again, "in advance."

"Yeah. Alright. Enough of that!" Mike scowled and looked around. "This is really the worst god damn company I've ever worked for."

"Mike, this was your first job out of college," Steph nudged a correction. "It's the only company you've ever worked for."

"Craig," Captain Braddock said, "what would you like us to do?"

Craig pointed to Mike, then Stephanie. "They know too much and are not willing to be cleansed by Korthuu. Let them share the same fate as the assas—" Craig stopped midsentence as he gestured to where Maureen's body lay, or rather, had lain. In its place was a large bloody splotch, with a dotted trail leading toward a rope hanging from an air vent suspended high above the ground. Craig let out a frustrated wail. "Find her, you fools!"

The rotunda erupted into frenzied chaos. Using it to her advantage, Stephanie grabbed Mike's wrist and slipped into the crowd, leading them through the jostling mess and up the main aisle toward the doors. Before sneaking out, and against her better instincts but in service of her showboating style, Stephanie caught Craig's eye and flashed him a salute. His eyes glowed a bright red as he roared. But Steph was already chuckling to herself and dashing away after Mike, who, propelled by fear, was already far ahead of her.

"What the hell were you doing back there?" He yelled when she caught up.

"Uh . . . nothing?" Steph managed in between breaths, just before a torrent of human bodies in black and red cloaks rushed into the hallways behind them, carrying green flaming torches.

"Goddamnit!" Mike cried. "Did you taunt them?"

"In retrospect, yeah. That was a bad idea. Let's go!" The two of them picked up the pace, tearing down the maze of hallways. Steph led, but hoped against hope she hadn't made a wrong turn. It wasn't until they found the door of the secret computer room—still ajar—that she knew they would make it out. "The pipes! Follow the pipes!"

She and Mike raced forward, keeping their eyes on the black and yellow tubes.

"U-S!" Steph shouted as she read the pipes' stencils again. "You think that stands for the Universal Solution Craig was talking about?"

"I'm really not it the mood to discuss that right now!" Mike wheezed. They rounded the corner. "Let's just keep going!"

Within minutes, they were racing up the secret set of stairs they initially descended into this nightmare factory. At the top, they collapsed against the back of the elevator. It spat them out into the concrete expanse of One Future Plaza, splattered with the first drops of steady rain.

"C'mon! Let's go." Mike attempted to drag her away from the black obelisk statue.

Stephanie planted her feet in the ground. "No. You go."

The Korthuu cult was coming, and if she didn't distract them, neither she nor Mike would get away, and then things would really go sideways. But most of all, she did not want to risk Mike getting harmed again.

"What? What are you talking about?"

"Get the Garbagemobile and drive as far away from here as possible. Find Calhoun. He'll probably know what to do."

"Are you insane?" Mike yelled. The rain began to fall harder now, fogging up his glasses. "I'm not leaving you."

"Trust me. They're a hidden secret cult. They're not going to come out into the open before they release their monster friend. And we're not going to let that happen, are we?"

"No, of course not. But—" Mike's gaze was drawn to the statue, from which the elevator's dinging could be heard.

"Just go! I'll meet you!"

Mike's face crumpled in anger and confusion. He stared at Stephanie for a good few seconds before dashing away.

Steph now stood alone. She wanted to feel good with her self-sacrifice, but instead she felt . . . lonely, even with her brother's ratty green jacket clinging tightly to her as it began to soak through. Still, if she was the one thing able to keep Mike's death at bay, it'd be worth it. And hey, maybe she could talk her way out of it.

The secret door in the statue whooshed open to reveal Mike's ex-boss in full cult regalia, flanked by his ridiculous cloaked minions and dirty cops.

"We have you now," he said, extending a threatening finger.

"Yeah, alright. I'll give you that," Steph admitted. "But what're you going to do? Feed me to Korthuu? Y'see, I know your secret."

"And what secret is that?"

"I've seen your little Virtual Boy." Stephanie pointed to the statue. "It's hooked up to one of these, and its showing you the multi-verse. Korthuu is trapped outside of this universe. And they can't get through."

"Korthuu exists between worlds, cleansing weak universes in accordance with the laws of existence. Through our belief and the use of the Universal Solution, we shall break the barriers of this world and help our master sate their hunger."

"The power of belief? Sorry to break it to you, but you're not exactly Oprah."

Craig chuckled. "You know far less than you think."

"People tell me that a lot and it's starting to piss me off."

"Enough of this." He turned to his cadre. "Seize her."

The crowd of black and yellow hoods, supplemented by gun-toting SWAT cops, advanced on Stephanie and for a moment—just for a moment—she felt an actual pang of fear. That is, until she heard a familiar sound: a mangled blend of chugging and struggling that could only come from one place.

The Garbagemobile crashed through the line of trees at the far end of the courtyard, drawing everyone's attention. The hunk of red and yellow metal screeched to a stop near Steph.

"I'm *not* leaving you!" Mike yelled. "Now get in!"

Despite Mike's disobedience, a mad grin broke out on Steph's face as she ran to meet him, slipping in head first through the open passenger-side window.

"Go! Go! Go!" she yelled.

Mike obliged and hit the accelerator, which propelled them to a grinding, gurgling halt right in front of the harangued cultish masses.

Mike slammed the heel of his palm against the Garbagemobile's dashboard, "God dammit! You stupid piece of crap!"

In response, the steering wheel and driver's side dashboard erupted in the fluffy white plumes of airbags. The impact knocked Stephanie clean out.

# CHAPTER EIGHTEEN

## Right to A Speedy Trial

Michael's stomach wouldn't stop gurgling all the way to prison. Being chained up in the back of a paddywagon wasn't his idea of a relaxing nighttime drive, but it wasn't like he had any choice in the matter. Stephanie, on the other hand, seemed not to mind it. She was comparatively blissful, absently humming the Ghostbusters theme. Michael had long ago learned not to question her song choices, but he did have some words for her.

"This is the second time in the last few months that I've been in handcuffs because of this detective agency, but now we're actually *going* to prison."

"Well, Mike, if you hadn't come back for me like I asked, maybe you wouldn't be in this mess." Steph glared at him. Now that the tables had turned, he wasn't sure how he liked being scolded for his mistakes. Her glare vanished, replaced by a carefree smirk, before she added,

"We'll figure it out. Just shank the biggest guy in there as soon as we get in. You gotta establish yourself as a threat."

"I'm not shanking anyone!"

"Well, then good luck, new meat."

"That's not funny," Michael said. "I am terrified right now."

"Yeah? Well . . . so am I!" Stephanie forced the last few words out of her mouth.

Michael blinked. This was a new development.

"Sorry. I . . . uh didn't realize."

"We're being dragged off to who-knows-where by some freaky shape-shifting monsters and you didn't think I'd be a little scared?"

"Well, I, uh . . ." He hadn't been making good on his promise to cut Steph the benefit of the doubt.

"I don't want us to die or become zombies, Mike. I don't want you to die or become a zombie. Especially in prison."

"Well, yeah. I get it. Neither do I." Michael offered a solemn nod before turning toward the front of the truck. So the drivers could hear him, he yelled, "Well, they can't throw us in prison without a fair trial. This is America, y'know!"

Stephanie scoffed. "You think your cash-flush Future Group buddies need to deal with the courts? Please. Stop living in a fantasy world."

"I'm sorry, I didn't know I was working for a secret monster death cult with their tendrils wrapped around every rung of society," Michael said. "It's not the kind of thing you think might actually happen."

"Apology accepted." Stephanie tried to cross her arms, but couldn't, on account of them being chained together. She attempted this anyway for a few seconds before giving up. Then, a knowing look washed across her face. "Say, what about your sexy lady spy?"

"What about her?"

"If she really exists, can't we call her for help?"

"She exists! I'm not crazy. And no. She never gave me her number."

"Oh, right." Steph nodded. "Just like every other girl. I should have known."

The police van screeched to a halt, nearly throwing Michael and Stephanie against the front wall, had their arms and legs not been shackled to the floor. Instead, they just jostled around violently.

A minute later, the rear door opened into the dark night, illuminated only by lamps that sat atop a high set of fences. Two of their badge- and gun-toting captors entered the van, ensconced in shadow backlit only by the prison yard lights.

As Michael's stomach sank, Stephanie remained her usual self. "Which one of you two bozos was driving? That was the worst goddamn ride I've ever had, and this guy"—she jerked her head at Michael—"drives me around in a car that should've exploded years ago."

In recompense for her remark, the guards dragged them off the van quite brusquely, leading them through a maze of fenced off empty weight yards and toward the monolithic edifice of the City Penitentiary. It was oddly named, since it stood several miles outside the city limits, but the inaccurate title was the least of Michael's worries at the moment. The prison had been mentioned in the files of LXR. It was the second location that The Future Group had been pumping its strange Universal Solution—whatever that was. But why a jail? Michael had a few ideas, and all of them terrified him, but not as much as having to tell his mom he was in jail—if he survived.

The guards trudged Michael and Stephanie through the yards and several sets of gates requiring authorized buzz-ins before they split them up and sent them through opposite entrances.

"Wait, no!" she yelled. "You can't split us up! He's got a weak constitution! He'll freak out!"

"Stephanie!" Michael yelled back. "Be careful! I'll find you! I'll find you!"

"See? He's already freaking out! This is all cruel and unusual punishment, and it's not as sexy as I thought it would be!"

Michael caught a final glimpse of Stephanie's uncertain grimace before she was escorted out of his sight. He had little to no time to truly embrace his abject fright at the situation before his guard pushed him in front of what appeared to be an intake officer.

"Who's this?" The prison officer grunted.

"Cop killer," his guard lied with a straight face. "Caught him in the act over at The Future Group. Might've killed others, too. He's too dangerous to be kept in any holding cell. Gotta put him here before the trial."

Michael ignored the mention of a fake trial and did not celebrate that at least the appearance of the rule of law was alive and well in America. "I didn't kill anybody! Neither did my friend! I'd never kill a cop. Look at me. Do I look like a killer to you?" He attempted to tug at his sleeves to showcase his spindly arms. "I'm basically some sort of low-functioning nerd!"

The prison officer blinked at him. "Anything else you'd like to add?"

"Well, no." Michael didn't really know what else to say. "Except I, uh, I'm innocent. What are you going to do to me?"

"You'll be held here until your trial and you'll be provided food, clothes and adequate legal representation, as needed."

"Oh, good. I thought it was going to be much worse." Michael exhaled. A lawyer would be a godsend.

An ear-splitting shriek of agony pierced Michael's momentary relaxation. It echoed from somewhere in the prison before dissolving into frantic yelling and burbling begs for mercy. After another horrifying shriek, all went quiet.

Michael, his eyes wider than they'd ever been, glanced at the intake guard. "What was that?"

"Nothing," the guard replied, not breaking eye contact.

"What do you mean, *nothing*? What are you doing to people here?"

"Nothing. It was just a leaky pipe."

"That didn't sound like a leaky pipe!"

"Are you a plumber?"

"Well, no, but—" Michael was silenced by the intake officer's raised finger.

"Good. Then shut up." The officer turned to Michael's guard. "I'll take him in and get him kitted out. You go home and have a good night. Tomorrow's a big day."

Michael's guard smiled and nodded before throwing up a salute. "Hail Korthuu."

"Hail Korthuu," replied the officer.

"Are you *kidding me*?" Michael yelled, his voice echoing off the prison walls. He was pushed further and further away from the outside world. "Why would you even put on an act? Whose benefit was it for?"

# CHAPTER NINETEEN

## Last Resorts

Rex Calhoun grunted as he shoved the few personal effects from his office into a tiny cardboard box. Of course, he made a point to drain what was left of his desk whiskey before tossing the empty bottle on top of the framed photo of his ex-wife. When all was said and done, they really were the only two things of value he had here.

"That's it?" McDermott peered into the box.

"Yeah." Calhoun shoved it into her arms. "Do me a favor and throw it in the dumpster out back. Garbage truck comes by at noon today."

"What? No!" McDermott tossed the box onto a nearby desk. "I'm not your maid."

"Well, you sure as hell ain't a CSI anymore. So you might wanna start looking for a job. Maid's as good as any."

"Don't be a jerk. You're better than that."

"Yeah, but not by much." Calhoun spat, literally, on the floor of the office, which was still filled with the filing cabinets and folders amassed over a long career. "Listen, kid. I was a cop for 25 years now. It was all I knew, and it's been taken away from me. So *excuse* me if I'm a little salty about it."

"So you're just gonna walk away, huh?"

"That's right. How about you do yourself a favor and go see Hobson back in the 35th. Maybe she'll give you your old job back. As for me, I'm done with this shitty bureaucracy."

"But don't you think something fishy is going on? Braddock had no right to do this to you. To us. And now he pulled the entire precinct, along with all the SWAT resources, to staff The Future Group all last night? Everyone except us, who were the only ones to put them up as suspects."

"What, you think he's got some vendetta against me?"

"I don't know. But you're a good cop. Something's up."

"So what? You heard Braddock. I'm out on my ass. I ain't gonna be investigating anything."

"Why? Who's going to stop you?" McDermott gestured around the empty office.

Calhoun blinked.

"Kid," he said, "I like you. Never change."

McDermott smirked and flashed him a finger gun.

"Alright, kid. Where do you wanna start?"

"Well, if Braddock is doing anything suspicious, there might be a paper trail. Maybe we can connect him to the murders."

"Nah. He's always been a bit of a whip-cracker. He'd probably take a lot of care to cover his tracks." Calhoun rubbed his graying stubble, but stopped when a thought struck him. He slapped his palms together, as if the lightbulb in his head was powered by the clapper. "So let's look for the cover."

Calhoun dashed to the nearest desk and yanked the phone off the receiver, dialing someone who had access to the non-information he was seeking. "Anita?" Calhoun asked. "How're you? Yeah. Great. Listen, Braddock's been riding my ass for the past week to get some of our squad car GPS records for audit." Calhoun directed Carrie over to the desktop computer with a few curt jerks of his head. "Yeah. That idiot Brook got into an accident when he was chasing an ice cream truck last week, and we need to grab the data for insurance purposes."

"Ice cream truck?" McDermott mouthed.

Calhoun shrugged and resumed his conversation. "Don't worry about it. Just give me all the data you have for the precinct. We'll sift through it ourselves. Yeah, send it over to Carrie McDermott. I don't deal with this computer mumbo jumbo." His pause turned into his typical scowl as he was snidely berated. "I know it's the 21st century, Anita, get off my goddamn ass!"

Calhoun slammed down the receiver and motioned to the nearby computer. McDermott was on it in seconds, logging in and extracting an email attachment to the desktop. Calhoun had never been great with computers, mostly out of sheer stubbornness, so he just leaned over her shoulder as McDermott did her thing. "Alright, so if Braddock's been up to anything fishy, the GPS tracker in his car would record his location. That's why I tore mine out."

"Why?" she shot him an amused grin. "What have you been doing?"

"Nothing. I just don't like the idea of some random assholes pawing through my shit." Calhoun's eyes darted away, then back to the screen. "Like what we're doing."

"Point taken."

"Pull up Braddock's records."

McDermott was quick with her keystrokes, and in seconds, a map of the city popped up onscreen, smothered in a heap of light blue spaghetti corresponding to Braddock's whereabouts over the last week. A quick zoom indicated that there were large areas of blank disconnect between the blue squiggles.

"Looks like he shut it off at several different points in time," Carrie tabbed through the results.

"Yeah. That's what I thought," Calhoun frowned. "That bastard's been pushing 'accountability' on us and he's running around hiding his shit."

"Wait," Carrie flipped to an entirely different map. "This officer's map has blank spots, too." Then another. "And this one." Then another. "And this one."

"You're telling me we got more than one dirty cop in this precinct?"

"Well, I can't be sure, but—"

"Any way to find out where they were going at these times?"

"Well, I could export all the raw data and select all the coordinates at the times just before the cops shut down their GPS. That'd give me a decent radius around where they were probably meeting, and we could narrow it down from there."

"Yeah," Calhoun said, "that sounds like a lot of fun. How long is it gonna take you to do that?"

"I've already done it." Carrie smiled and waved her arm over the monitor like Vanna White revealing a vowel. The cluster of datapoints were mapped onto a new city grid.

Calhoun peered over. The dots congregated around One Future Plaza. "You've gotta be shitting me. They're in bed with those pencil-pushing geeks at The Future Group? No wonder Braddock yanked us off the case."

"Well," McDermott shrugged, "I guess if you're gonna be on the take, you might as well go with the guys who have the most money."

"Great. And if they're all in cahoots, and they're all there now, something big must be going down. So how're we gonna get in there?"

"Well, if we go in guns blazing, Braddock would have a plausible excuse to put us down," McDermott sighed. "And if this thing is as far reaching as it looks, we can't trust anyone else on the force. We need someone on the inside of The Future Group. But all of those guys are super loyal. Heck, I dated this one girl who worked there and wouldn't shut up about it. It kinda weirded me out the way she talked about that Craig Breene guy. So we need someone who hasn't drank their kool-aid. Do you know anyone like that?"

Calhoun's nails dug into his palms as he gritted his teeth. He did know someone like that. And the mere thought was so infuriating, white hot fire enveloped his vision, blocking out everything else.

"Uh, Rex?"

He could only hear the faint call of McDermott's voice.

"Are you okay? Your palms are bleeding."

# CHAPTER TWENTY

## Orange Is The New Black And White Stripes

Michael barely slept. After they took his clothes and replaced them with a scratchy orange jumpsuit, he'd been shoved in a small cell with a thin mattress and not so much as a "good night." Hell, at this point, he would've taken a "Hail Korthuu."

The one bright side: he seemed to be the only inmate in this wing of the prison. Michael recalled hearing City Penitentiary had a high occupation rate. Aside from a few violent criminals, it was mostly vagrants and disturbers of the peace. There had been several protests against it for that fact, but—if the news was anything to go by—they all seemed to have stopped a few years ago. Michael would have bet money on it being due to The Future Group. If all these inmates were missing, Craig Breene and his best friend Korthuu probably had a hand—or tentacle—in it. All that aside, his wing was deathly quiet all night, and Michael appreciated that minor kindness.

"Get up!" The voice startling Michael awake was as rough and scratchy as the thin blanket covering everything between his collar bone and calves.

"Whuz-what? Huh?" Michael shot up, bleary eyed, until the guard began rapping his nightstick along the cell bars. "Oh, god! Stop! I'm up."

"Alright, interloper," the guard growled. "We're taking you down to the Education Center."

"Education Center?" Michael blinked.

The guard didn't answer. Well, at least not verbally. He clanged open the cell doors and forced Michael up against the wall, cuffing him. "It's better than you deserve. We shouldn't reward interlopers with the truth of Korthuu. Now let's go."

"Whoa! Okay, okay, I'll come quietly." Michael had no other choice, following in shackles as the guard led him down the cell block. Its emptiness was somehow more eerie in daylight.

They trudged down several sets of metal stairs before entering a hallway with a service elevator. It transported them even further down into the bowels of the prison. This gave Michael ample opportunity to focus on absolutely everything that could go wrong. By the time they reached the so-called Education Center" his stomach gurgled to the tune of the William Tell Overture.

The guard led him into a waiting room that looked like something you would find on the Death Star. The sleek metal walls seemed almost brand new when compared to the older stone construction of the rest of the penitentiary. Although it should have smelled anti-septic, the actual scent of the place was bathroom-like, with a strong undercurrent of jockstrap. Michael winced as his handcuffs were chained to a link in the floor, forcing him to sit on a cold empty bench.

"Stay here," the guard commanded.

Michael glowered at him as he left, showing off his cuffs and lack of mobility as if they weren't obvious. After a few minutes, Michael's eyes drifted toward an open door on the opposite side of the room. It was slightly ajar, allowing him the briefest sliver of a glimpse of the chair within. It was quite similar to the VR chair he and Steph found at The Future Group. But this one looked less comfortable. For one, it was made of hard wood, and its backrest was constructed at an odd angle. Not good for lumbar support. Secondly, the metal shackles, array of syringes, and other torture materials mounted on it didn't come across as friendly.

When he finally noticed the two black and red pipes descending from the waiting room ceiling and curving into the torture room, Michael realized what was going to happen. After years of resisting becoming a Future Group Zombie through laziness and passive-aggression, they were finally going to make him one against his will.

And Steph's.

"Hello, new meat," Steph said, as the guard led her in and shackled her down next to him.

"Steph!" Michael shouted as the guard left. A wave of relief washed over him in a flash. He almost hugged her before he remembered he couldn't move. "Are you okay?"

"I'm fine. Just a little pissed off." She tugged at the chest of her matching jumpsuit. "These orange things suck. I thought we'd be wearing black and white stripes."

Michael would've scowled, but he actually found a little solace in her joke, so he smirked. "Of course. We're in jail, about to be brainwashed, and your biggest problem is that you can't dress like the hamburglar."

"It's not just the stripes. They took my br—" Steph stopped herself. "They took my lucky green jacket, man! I almost killed 'em for it."

"Yeah, well your old coat is only part of the problem. We gotta find a way to get out of here. I think they're gonna pump that Universal Solution into our brains and make us into Korthuu-worshipping assholes!" Michael did his best to gesture in the direction of the torture room door—and the hideous contraption beyond.

Steph gazed into the room and nodded. "Yeah. I was trying to figure out how to do that that all night, and I think we could always use our one phone call."

"A phone call?"

"Y'know. Like on TV? It's one of your rights."

"These monsters don't care about our rights! Besides, who're you going to call?"

"Ghostbu—"

Michael lifted a finger. "Don't you goddamn dare."

"Sorry! I told you it's like a freakin' lightbulb in my brain." She shrugged. "I just have to say it."

"You don't *have* to." He narrowed his eyes. "You just know it'll annoy me."

"That's why I have to! I annoy because I love." Steph grinned back. "But anyway, let's ask for the call. It's worth a shot. Guard!" Stephanie yelled.

The guard burst back into the waiting room, clearly not happy with either of them. "What do you want?"

"My friend and I were just processed yesterday, and we'd like our allotted phone call please."

"Phone call?" His eyebrows scrunched. "You don't get a phone call."

"Uh, yes we do," Steph said. "Ever watch Law and Order? Not the one with Ice-T. The other one. You owe us one phone call." Her eyes darted to Michael. "Technically two, but we'll settle for one."

The guard paused for a moment before tipping up his hat with a thumb. "How old are you?"

"Twenty-four," Steph said. "Why?"

"Good." A wolfish grin widened across the man's face. "Come with me. I'll give you your phone call."

"See, Mike? They're not unreasonable."

They were unshackled and led out of the waiting room down a set of hallways and back into separate room in the prison basement. An array of landline phones hung on the wall and the guard displayed them with a flourish of his hand.

"Go ahead. Make your call." He cackled and waltzed away, all too proud of himself.

"What was he so happy about?" Steph said once the guard disappeared around a corner.

Michael dragged his palm down his face. "Do you actually know any phone numbers off the top of your head?"

"Well, no," Stephanie said. "Do you think they have the white pages here?"

"Stop being stupid."

"No, you're right. Nobody has white pages anymore. Calhoun probably wouldn't even be listed."

"You wanted to call Calhoun? He could be dirty, too!"

"Rexy?" Steph leaned back in disbelief. "No way. He wouldn't fall for this bullshit. He's too much of a stubborn stick-in-the-mud. Kinda like you."

"I don't agree with the comparison, but I get your point," Michael said.

"Ah-ha! I got it." Steph snapped her fingers and slammed one end of the nearest handset with her fist, popping it into her free hand. "I *do* know one phone number."

Stephanie stabbed at the keypad, and soon, Michael heard an ancient sound he recognized as a dial tone, followed by muffled words.

"Oh, thank god you're there," Stephanie breathily exclaimed into the handset. "We're in big trouble, man. Real big. They put us in jail." A pause. Some muffled words. "The big jail. Outside of town. We need you to get us bail or break us out or something." Another pause. "It absolutely is your problem! We're paying customers, Kashir. And I was hoping for some better customer serv—hello?" Stephanie clicked the cradle down repeatedly. "Hello?" She turned to Michael. "Disconnected."

"Who the hell was that?" Michael waved his arms around frantically trying to make sense of what just transpired. "Who is Kashir?"

"You know. Kashir. The kid who works at the convenience store under our office. His was the only phone number I can remember."

"And you're on a first name basis with this . . . Kashir."

"Well, I guess. That's what it said on his name tag."

Michael exhaled long and loud. "Are you sure it didn't say *cashier*?"

"I . . . uh . . . hm," Stephanie started, ". . . can't recall."

"Great. This has gone from bad to worse at speeds I couldn't even imagine."

The guard, angry he wasn't able to stump a couple of Millennials with his phone number ploy, burst in with his gun raised. "Alright you two. Enough of this. Back down to the education center. Now. By the time your friend gets here—if he even does—you will reveal the truth of Korthuu to him."

A loud bang echoed across the prison walls. As the guard's limp body crumpled to the floor, Michael slapped his own chest, confused he wasn't the one shot.

"Hey, look at me when I'm talking to you," Steph chided the man's body, before looking back up at Michael. "The nerve of this guy."

"If this is the kind of service you provide, your detective agency isn't going to last very long," someone said.

Michael spun around to find the source of the voice. He was met by the attractive form of the mysterious woman emerging from behind a pillar.

"You!" Michael said. "What the hell are you doing here? And what took you so goddamn long?"

"Hey, I know you!" Stephanie pointed at the Woman. "You're the sexy lady whose coffee I ruined."

"What are you talking about?" Michael looked at Steph. "This is the lady that recruited me."

"We've met. Tangentially." The Woman's arms were crossed, but she bore a slight smile. "But we've got bigger fish to fry at the moment."

"I take it you've heard about The Future Group?"

"They're trying to summon a goddamn monster to destroy the world today!" Steph interjected.

"Yes, uh, we've known for a while. We've been constantly trying to stop them. But they're too well insulated."

"By money," Michael clarified. "And chemical brainwashing. That's what the Universal Solution is, isn't it?"

"Yes, partially," the Woman nodded. "That's why we still need your services. You're two of the very few un-brainwashed people who know the truth about them and can help us take them down. But we're running out of time. I promise you, you'll get all the answers you want, but you're going to have to follow me."

"Follow you?" Steph wrinkled her nose. "How'd you even get in here?"

"We have a network of tunnels," she said, slinking down a hallway, giving them no choice but to follow.

"We?" Steph asked the question Michael had been trying to get the Woman to answer since he first met her. "Who's we? Who do you work for?"

"Don't worry about it." She smiled and turned back around.

"Okay, fine," Steph said. "Then here's another question: can I buy you a coffee later?"

# CHAPTER TWENTY-ONE

## Stillness In Time

Marcus Espinoza was worried, for the first time in his life, about something other than family or finances. He was worried about his friend.

Craig had been acting strangely this past week. He'd been getting way out of his comfort zone in the basement and taking ownership of large parts of the company. Parts he used to hate: hiring, infrastructure, employee management.

Craig was spearheading a massive analyst hiring campaign, planning several upgrades to the tower they'd had under construction, and outlining plans for an inter-office phone system with an auto-answer function to "improve accountability."

Marcus didn't mind. He liked that Craig was broadening his horizons, but it just felt massively out of character, and Marcus thought he was in some way responsible. Maybe he shouldn't have gotten on

Craig's case about his little multi-verse simulation exercise. It was harmless. Craig enjoyed it. And Marcus had dampened his passion, trying to get him to focus on the money.

Marcus buried his head in his hands and sighed as he leaned on his temporary desk. He'd been moved to a small side room on the ground floor while the rest of the tower was under construction. All he had taken with him was a picture of his daughter and a desk phone, which started ringing.

Marcus' eyes darted to the phone's display. It was Craig. From downstairs. He bit his lip, deciding whether or not to pick up, when the phone made the decision for him and turned on its speaker. Marcus took it back. He hated this auto-answer system.

"Marcus!" Craig's voice beamed out of the speaker. "How's my best friend doing today?"

Marcus fumbled with the handset as he picked it up and put it to his head. "Fine. Fine, Craig. How's it going?"

"Oh, it's going a-may-zing-ly! I just got through some more analysis on those leads you gave me this week. I saw something interesting and I wanted to have a quick chat. You mind coming down?"

"Uh, sure, Craig." This was another change Marcus was weirded out by. Craig usually just sent his results up when he was done. Now he wanted to have a "quick chat?" Marcus preferred him as an introvert. "I'll be right down."

Marcus hung up the phone and got up, dusting off his suit. As he opened his office door, two young new hires walked by with smiles as stiff as their pressed shirts. They offered him a friendly wave, and he returned a weak one and went on his way.

As Marcus walked to the elevator bank, he could see a small construction crew outside in the plaza. They were setting up a statue Craig commissioned—a large black obelisk inside a set of concentric brass bowls. Marcus didn't care much for modern art, and this thing looked more like a satellite transceiver than anything, but it wasn't hurting anybody, so he'd approved it.

With a pair of quick, successive dings, Marcus was in the basement, walking through the long series of concrete corridors to Craig's office-slash-super computer. When he arrived, Craig was sitting in his giant white and gray throne, his feet kicked up on a bundle of wires serving as an armrest. He jumped up to greet Marcus with a smile, opening his arms in a wide embrace.

"Marcus! How've you been?"

"Uh, fine?" Marcus winced, pointing over his shoulder. "We . . . we just talked."

"So we did." Craig used a friendly arm to guide Marcus over to a desk pushed off to the side of the room, up against a wall of computer towers. "I wanted to speak with to you about something."

"I gathered, yeah. What is it?"

"When I was running some of my simulations on the analysis you gave me, I found that one of the small companies highlighted has tremendous investment potential. Like massive. We could quadruple our returns if we were to buy them outright."

"Buy them?" Marcus reared back. "Craig, we're an investment firm. We don't buy random companies. It'd look weird on our balance sheets."

"Then we do it in a roundabout way. I'm sure you know of some loopholes." Craig patted Marcus on the chest in a way he did not care for. "You're the finance guy. I'm sure you'll figure it out. But we just gotta buy this company. It'd be stupid of us not to."

"Why? What's the company?"

"It's called LXR Chemicals," Craig said. "They specialize in advanced chemical synthesis for industrial and research applications."

"What would we do with a company like that?"

"They've got a product they call a Universal Solute."

"What do I look like? A scientist? I don't know what that is."

"It's a chemical compound that can be mixed with anything. It's a stepping stone to developing a universal solution."

Marcus furrowed his brow, trying to understand. "What, like Hitler?"

"No, not like," Craig scoffed, "not like Hitler. It's a chemical."

"Hitler used chemicals," Marcus said.

"It's not Hitler, okay?" Craig was getting exasperated.

"Could be one of his clones," Marcus smirked. "I heard rumors that there's a secret organization that wants to make an army of Hitler clones."

"Marcus, this isn't a joke!" Craig let loose, throwing his arms in the air. "This is serious. We need to buy this company. It would be a massive liability if we didn't, and I don't want us stymied by your shortsightedness!"

"Whoa, whoa!" Marcus put up his palms and stepped back. It felt like Craig was about to throttle him. This was certainly new. "Mea culpa, buddy. Relax, alright?"

"Sorry," Craig said as he slid down into the chair behind him and took a breath. "I've just been under a lot of stress lately. I'm sure you understand. But things are gonna get better, real soon."

"Yeah, yeah, of course. I'm on your side, man," Marcus wasn't sure if he *was* on this new Craig's side, but decided to see if he could figure out what was going on. "How about you grab us a couple of coffees and we'll look into it. Together."

"That sounds pretty great." Craig smiled at him. It was a flat smile, but Marcus would take what he could get. "Y'know what? It's on me. Give me a few minutes and I'll go and grab 'em from the shop down the street."

Craig, a new man, jumped up and rushed his way to the door.

"You remember how I like it, right?" Marcus called after him in an effort to remain nonchalant.

"Milk and sugar?" Craig asked.

Okay. Something was seriously wrong. "Yep! Thanks!" Marcus nodded, forcing the words through his teeth,

"Great," Craig said. "And about the LXR thing—thanks . . . in advance." He flashed Marcus a gun finger before disappearing from view.

Black and sugar. Craig knew Marcus liked his coffee black and with sugar. It wasn't a weird choice. He was sure plenty of people liked black and sugar. Why did everyone always give him crap about it?

Marcus stopped his thoughts from running away from him. He had to focus. Something was up, and he needed to figure it out.

Marcus' gaze snapped to the giant computerized chair in the center of the room. Craig's simulation machine. Maybe something had gone wrong with it, frying Craig's brain. If he just took a look at it . . .

No. Marcus stopped himself. He couldn't. Craig had told him how complicated the whole system was, and only he knew how to operate it. Any other user's input could result in disastrous consequences.

Yes, but—Marcus moved back toward the chair—Craig had gone nuts, or something, and if this was the only way to find out what happened, so be it. He'd just have to be delicate about it.

Marcus plopped himself in the chair, and the first thing he noticed was that it was not at all comfortable. The hard, angled white seat made it feel like he was sitting on an awkward pile of computers. He shrugged and grabbed the headset—still the old Nintendo he'd gifted Craig a few years ago—and placed it on his head. He saw only black until he felt around for the keyboard and mashed some buttons. So much for delicate.

The thing turned on, but the screen remained black, except for a timestamp in the corner. It was today.

July 25th, 1997. 10:02 am.

Okay. Was this what it was all about? How did Craig run his simulations? Marcus fumbled around with the keyboard again. The screen lit up and displayed the very basement he was sitting in. It was an out of body experience. In the corner opposite the timestamp, a label said "UNIV-10E63.99721834512."

What the hell did that mean? Slowly, bits and pieces of Craig's conversations with him began to fit together. Craig had mentioned he was looking into some sort of science project involving the multi-verse. Something regarding simulations. Marcus didn't really understand the nitty gritty of it, but what he was seeing was too sophisticated, too visceral, too . . . real to be a simulation. Had Craig been lying to him this entire time? He wasn't running simulations at all. Craig was looking at actual alternate universes to get his investment information! But that couldn't be right. That was impossible. That was insane. Right?

Marcus started breathing heavily and dug his nails in to the chair's wired armrest. It took him a few moments to calm himself. He had to keep his wits about him. If this was an alternate universe, he was sitting in Craig's very same throne. Using the keyboard to pull back on this view showed the rest of the basement, but Marcus was a bit too overzealous. He overshot, clipped through the ceiling, and landed in the boardroom on the ground floor of The Future Group complex.

On one side of the massive wooden table sat a—presumably alternate—version of Craig and Marcus in nice pressed suits. On the other side were a few people he'd never seen before, but they all had their business cards in front of them. A gentle zoom in revealed the logo: LXR Chemicals.

Craig was looking into a closely related universe to see what would happen if they bought the company. If this was his method, it certainly explained his phenomenal predictive ability.

Marcus, essentially blind, traced his fingers around the keyboard to see if he could find a fast-forward button. After a few false starts, including one in which he turned the entire display monochrome, he found the right button and fast-forwarded in time to the deal-making phase. But an argument started. The representatives of LXR pushed away the offered contract and stormed out.

"Okay, looks like we lose this one," he said aloud.

A few more keystrokes allowed Marcus to slide into another adjacent universe: UNIV-10E63.99721834520.

The boardroom scene looked identical, but everyone was wearing festive party hats.

"Oh! This could be the one!" he said to himself.

But, no, again, the LXR representatives pushed away the contract and stormed out, this time more violently than before. Apparently, they had all put the party hats on for an unrelated reason.

Marcus tried again with another slightly adjacent universe.

In UNIV-10E63.99721834521 the boardroom was once again the same. But this time, after a few heated discussions, the head representative of LXR reached his hand across the table. Craig clasped it, gave it a vigorous shake, and they signed the contract.

And Marcus muffled an exclamation as he watched everyone in the room remove their outer skin, reveal the disgusting lizard people within, and proceed to have an orgy on the boardroom floor.

"Uh . . ." he said as he observed the disgusting lizard-on-lizard-on-lizard-on-lizard action. "I mean . . . close enough I guess?" Truth be told, Marcus was a bit unnerved by the minute amount of universe scrolling he had to do to get to one where everyone was a secret horny lizard person.

That aside, he'd have to figure out what happened after they bought LXR. Would they make as much money as Craig said? Marcus, getting a bit pro at this multi-verse hopping, locked this odd lizard universe in as his baseline and moved further forward in time. He was still in the boardroom, with Craig leading The Future Group in a company-wide earnings call. Craig was very vocal about hating these things, so Marcus typically headed them. But despite his best efforts, Marcus could not find his alternate-secret-lizard-self in the room. In any case,

The Future Group's profits had gone way up, especially after the LXR acquisition.

"Alright, I guess that's good? What else happens? What did Craig see?" Marcus spun the time dial further forward-a bit too far—and was greeted by a bright green screen.

"Whoa. Where'd everything go?"

He continued to look around but saw nothing but green. It wasn't displaying anymore. Not at this random time in the future. There was nothing there. Marcus looked down at the timestamp in the corner. July 30th, 2020. Twenty-three years in the future.

Dialing time back slowly, Marcus tried to pinpoint what happened. Maybe it was just a simple glitch. Eventually, the bright green nothingness began to fade away, replaced with fuzzy green television static that, after a blip, reverted to utter black. Increasing the speed of the rewind, Marcus saw the vast expanse of black slowly return to life as stars blinked into existence leading to a star smattered sky. He could feel the blood drain from his face as he realized what he was watching.

He was witnessing Armageddon undo itself. But on an incredibly quick timescale. According to the timestamp, it was only September 2016. That is, it would have been September 2016, if Earth and the sun still existed to determine the date.

But he did not have long to wait. Three years further into the past, he could see the form of Earth coalescing into a ball of molten rock and metal beneath his feet, the sun reasserting itself in the sky. Both the material makeup of the planet and the star were being funneled out of some dark, shapeless entity hovering between the two. Soon the view of space was obscured as the atmosphere returned, filtering the sunlight into a more familiar, calming blue.

But Earth's landscape was anything but calm and familiar. To put it simply, the planet was in tatters. Ruins of cities had been covered by dry, dead desert. There was no sign of any flora or fauna anywhere, much less any humans . . . or secret lizards. And it was only 2014.

Increasing his rewind speed yet again, Marcus blazed through a whole year, until he finally found himself in The Future Group Tower, fully completed. He was in a large auditorium somewhere in the building. The fact that it was there at all was a good indication that whatever had happened, hadn't happened yet.

Marcus couldn't feel it, but given the toppling of chairs and art falling off the walls, the entire tower was shaking.

Whatever had happened was happening now.

Marcus locked his place in time—freezing everything in its current position—and set about moving around in space. Clipping through the top of The Future Group Tower, Marcus soared above the city to figure out what was going on. And although he could see what was going on, he could not really fathom exactly what it was.

The city was in chaos, fires everywhere. Buildings crumbled, some frozen midway into collapse. A throng of panicked people were rushing away from the city center—away from One Future Plaza. Mixed among them were a few lizard men and women. Whatever was transpiring had broken down whatever barriers existed between the secret reptilian ruling class and the common folk of this universe. It had to be big.

And it was. Had it been in front of him, it would have been impossible to miss. But only after rotating his view around from the top of the tower did Marcus see it.

It was enormous. Almost the height of the tower itself. But its size was not important. The sheer horror it exuded was. The thing was a giant, corpulent mass with hundreds of multi-segmented insectoid legs and decaying green skin that seemed to slough off its body. Veins riddled portions of its upper body, twisting like vines around black eyes void of any feeling or emotion aside from anger. Between the eyes, at irregular intervals, lay large human-like sets of teeth, some with elongated canines, some with rictus smiles in mid-gnash.

Marcus' heart nearly stopped when the thing shifted its mass and pointed its myriad eyes directly at him, staring into the depths of his soul. A powerful sense of existential dread washed over Marcus and fear ignited in the pit of his stomach as a torrent of unwanted knowledge flooded his brain.

He could not throw off the headset fast enough. It clattered to the ground but remained intact. The same, however, could not be said of Marcus. He released himself from the seat and fell to his hands and knees, breathing heavily into the cold stone floor.

After several pained gulps of saliva and air, Marcus began to compose himself. He began to tell himself he hadn't seen a giant horrifying monster look directly into the very fiber of his being and found it wanting. He told himself it was a hallucination brought out by fear, and whatever he had seen wasn't real. Just a result of too much stress. That is to say, Marcus lied to himself.

But he couldn't for long. When the monster had looked at him, he had understood what was going on. It was coming here. To this universe, and their fate would be the same.

Craig had been used by the monster. Corrupted by it. It was in him now. That's why he was acting so weird. He wanted to corrupt others to help bring it here. And that meant Marcus and everyone else were in danger.

"Oh, Marcus!" Marcus's eyes widened as Craig's sing-song voice floated down the hallway outside. "I've got the coffee. Just the way you like it!"

# CHAPTER TWENTY-TWO

## The B-Team

Calhoun had never been the safest driver. Hell, he'd wrecked more than one car, but he still thought he was pretty good, statistically. At the moment, he was weaving in and out of cars on the highway like he was making the world's largest, most haphazard cross-stitch. McDermott was in the passenger seat hanging on for dear life. It was the first time someone had sat in his old partner's seat in a long time, and Calhoun didn't really mind it as much as he thought he would.

"Whoa, Rex! Watch out! Slow down, will you?"

He could've done with a little less backseat driving, though.

"Ain't happening. If Braddock is up to something, I want that shit quashed ASAP. I'm no fan of dirty cops." He pulled to the left to avoid the rapidly approaching bumper of a minivan. "The sooner we can get the information we need outta these two idiots, the better."

Calhoun took a sharp right onto the freeway exit for Squalor's Wal-low. Of course, the exit sign didn't say Squalor's Wallow, but nobody called the neighborhood by its original name anyway. In fact, Calhoun's brain had subconsciously replaced whatever was actually on the sign with Squalor's Wallow, so the point was moot.

He knew the neighborhood like the back of his hand and didn't have any problem finding the run-down building Duckett and Dyer squatted in. Calhoun pulled up to the curb with a sharp jolt and parked next to a fire hydrant. What were the cops gonna do? Arrest him?

He jogged past the convenience store on the ground floor and burst into the small adjacent door, McDermott trailing a few feet behind. Conquering the narrow lobby hallway and the three sets of rickety stairs put him at the front door emblazoned with the word "DICKS" in poorly spray-painted red. He was pleased to find the door closed this time. Using his boot as God intended, he kicked it open and stormed inside.

"Alright, you stupid bastards," Calhoun yelled to an empty office.

"I don't like to admit it, but I need your help and I need it now!"

"Uh. . . Rex?" McDermott peeked out from behind his shoulder, "where are they?"

Calhoun rubbed his forehead, causing his hat to go off kilter. "I don't know. This is a real shitty way to run a business."

"I'll say," came a muffled voice from behind the bathroom door. It creaked open to reveal an older, heavy-set woman in a skin-tight black jumpsuit. Judging by the bloody towels on the floor, she was cleaning a severe wound on her shoulder. Rex reached for his gun, but, even hurting, the woman was too fast, already training a rifle on them. "Hup hup. I wouldn't do that if I were you. I take it you're also looking for Duckett and Dyer?"

"Yeah, we are," McDermott confirmed, her hands in the air.

"Who the hell are you?" Calhoun rasped

"Let's just say I'm a concerned citizen."

"What kind of concerned citizen threatens a cop with a gun?"

"Ask your stupid questions later, Kojak." Her rifle was still unwavering. "Now, I bet you're probably here because you've realized The Future Group isn't staffed by a whole bunch of nice guys, which is the understatement of the century. So if you're going against The Future Group, I'm on your side."

Rex's eyes narrowed.

"Now if you agree to not do anything funny, I'll put my rifle down, and we can all have a reasonable chat about the infinite number of things you need to be aware of. Deal?"

Rex was caught between a rock and a hard place. He was at a disadvantage, but trusting a gun-toting septuagenarian with a bullet wound was craz—

"Deal," McDermott said from behind him. Rex turned to her with a bewildered scowl she returned with a shrug. "What other options do we have?"

"Well, at least I know one of you is reasonable." The assassin lowered her rifle and extended her hand. "Maureen Whelan."

McDermott shook it. "Carrie McDermott. CSI."

"Alright, enough of that." Calhoun waved his hand in an irritated circle. "Spill it. What do you know about The Future Group?"

"I work for a secret organization that's been moving against them for some time. But I was discovered by one of their men—Eric Bunting."

"LXR," Calhoun spat.

"Exactly. I learned they were supplying The Future Group with a dangerous chemical and decided to take things into my own hands. You can see how that went."

"They've got their fingers in the City Police, too," McDermott said. "What are they doing?"

"This goes beyond a precinct of dirty cops, Carrie," Maureen said, her voice grave. "The Future Group is a cult. And they want to destroy everything you and I hold dear."

"Destroy how?" Calhoun pulled back.

"You really wouldn't believe me if I told you. I don't really even understand it very well myself. There's a god they believe in—Korthuu—and they're trying to bring them to our world so they can cleanse it."

"You're right," McDermott scoffed. "I don't believe it."

"Sounds like a bag of horseshit to me."

"Fair enough. You're clever"—Maureen pointed to McDermott, then to Rex—"and you're a stubborn asshole. That's probably why neither of you were approached with an offer—unlike the rest of your precinct."

"What kind of offer?" McDermott asked.

"What else makes men believe in crazy shit? Money, and lots of it. And The Future Group delivers. But then they destroy your mind and let Korthuu take hold of your soul." Maureen paused. "It happened to my son."

McDermott put her hand on the shoulder of the angry old assassin. "I'm sorry."

"It's . . . it's fine. I've had years to come to terms with this. But it just eats at me that I wasn't even there to help him."

"We can't always be everywhere." Calhoun had a tough time being compassionate about anything, and this was the best he could muster. "Don't beat yourself up about it. It's not your fault."

"Thanks, but that's why I joined this organization. To take The Future Group down. To correct my past mistakes. If I can't save my son, I'll at least avenge him."

"So you know where they are," McDermott said. "Maybe they can help us."

"Yeah, I wish. But as soon as Eric Bunting and LXR made me, they went to ground. They could be anywhere. I don't blame 'em. It's safer that way. Especially since The Future Group is planning to release

Korthuu today. We're on our own and we might all be out of time."

"They're going to summon this god *today*?" McDermott cocked an eyebrow.

"Yeah. And they're gathering everyone loyal to them to witness and ease the transition. With their resources? Even my organization would be outnumbered and outgunned. We need a bigger team. And we need people we're certain aren't allied with The Future Group."

"Right." Calhoun wasn't sure about all this "god" business. In fact, he was pretty sure there wasn't any god, but if this lady wanted to take down Braddock and his cadre of corrupt cops . . . "I'm in. But I don't know who we can trust."

"Duckett and Dyer. They may be idiots, but they have no love for The Future Group. I can tell you that."

"You saw them?" McDermott said.

"We were both at the wrong place at the wrong time. I only managed to escape because they caused a distraction."

"Yeah," Calhoun grumbled. "They do that."

"I hoped they had made it out, too. That's why I came here."

"Well, uh . . ." Calhoun looked around. "They're not."

"Oh my god." McDermott put her hand to her mouth. "You think they could've been captured or killed?"

"I . . . I . . . don't know," Maureen hung her head.

There was a knock at the door. Maureen snapped out of her despair almost instantly, snatching up her rifle, finger on the trigger. Calhoun, similarly edgy, had his handgun out and ready at a moment's notice, as well.

The lanky, brown-skinned teen in the oversized shirt threw his hands up in the air. Suspicious, uncertain eyes darted back and forth around the room in silence until the kid spoke. "Hey, uh, are you guys looking for Duckett and Dyer by any chance?"

"Yeah," Maureen said, "do you know where they are?"

"Kinda," the kid replied.

"Whaddaya mean 'kinda?'" Calhoun asked.

"They . . . uh . . ." The kid flipped his hair. "Well, they just called me from jail."

# CHAPTER TWENTY-THREE

## Let's Talk About Sects

"So you knew The Future Group was a death cult?" Mike asked his strange and sexy spy friend who refused to identify herself. They were following her through a gross underground sewer pipe.

"Yeah! Did you know they could turn into freaky monster-faced goons?" Stephanie grimaced at the gunk squelching beneath her prison shoes. "By the way, this whole Shawshank tunnel thing is really friggin' gross. You couldn't have cleaned up a little?"

"Which question do you want me to answer first?" The spy lady was wry and condescending, which, in Steph's book, made her a great deal more attractive. Mama did indeed like. But unfortunately, the woman's face was currently framed in unflattering shadow, as their path forward was illuminated only by the fluorescent light stick she held aloft.

"How about we go with the monsters one?" Mike replied.

"Well, we didn't know they could turn into actual monsters." The Woman cleared her throat, the sound reverberating throughout the smelly pipe air. "So that's a new situation. We didn't realize Korthuu had the power to alter people in this universe. LXR's Universal Solute must be more powerful than we thought."

"Yeah, about that." Steph raised a finger, an admittedly useless gesture in the dark. "What the hell?

"As far as we can tell, Korthuu exists outside the boundaries of this universe." The splish-splash of the Woman's footsteps came to a halt and she whirled around, her face a mask of light and shadow. "How familiar are you with Multi-Verse Theory?"

"Uh, surprisingly familiar," Mike said.

"We . . . uh . . . studied it." Steph attempted a plausible alibi. "On the internet."

"That helps," the Woman continued. "Because the boundaries between universes have been weakened."

"You don't say . . ." Steph glanced away from the light and at Michael, who shot her a nervous expression.

"We don't know what caused it, but it's empowered Korthuu. Their influence can clearly seep into universes and corrupt them. From our research, the Universal Solute amplifies this. It's his key to breaking through the barriers."

"How?" Mike asked. "What does it do?"

"Back in the late 90s, LXR developed a rare product known as a Universal Solute." The Woman's sultry voice mingled with splashes of dirty tunnel-juice. "The same way water is a universal solvent, which can dissolve most chemicals, the Universal Solute can be dissolved by any kind of matter.

"But the solute is only part of it. You need something that can invade people's hearts and minds. Universal Solute plus Universal Solvent equals . . ."

"Goddamn it!" Mike grumbled. "You're telling me you just add water?"

"Basically. And then you've got a substance—a Universal Solution—that, when injected, makes beings open to any undue psychic suggestion from our friend Korthuu."

"This is . . . I mean, I don't even know what this is." Mike sighed.

"Then you're going to hate what comes next."

"Why? What comes next?" Steph asked.

"We're going to meet the team you're going to need to stop Korthuu from succeeding." The Woman's splashing stopped and she held her light up to the wall, revealing a large, rusted sewer hatch.

"What?" Mike barked. "There was nothing in our agreement that involved us amassing a team to take over some sort of horrifying inter-dimensional god!"

"Well," the Woman said as she spun the release valve for the hatch, "it's an evolving document."

The door swung open and the influx of bright white light was so intense Steph had to shield her eyes. Once they adjusted, Steph could see through the hatch into what looked like a well-appointed, classic-looking conference room. Polished wood walls surrounded a long boardroom table stretching at least thirty feet. It was positioned directly opposite a canvas projection screen displaying a map of the city limits. Around the table sat a few unfamiliar—and quite strange—faces. They looked worn and haggard and were covered in similar amounts of disgusting gunk, suggesting that they, too, had made the journey via pipe.

"Who're these guys?" Mike asked as he finally entered.

"Michael, do you seriously think The Future Group is the only cult in town?" The Woman said, as if it was obvious. "The other . . . let's say 'fringe' religions have been getting pretty antsy since their flocks were lured away with promises of large yearly salaries and huge bonuses."

"And the brainwashing," Steph added.

"And the brainwashing, yes. But not everyone was swayed. The Future Group rounded up and jailed any competing faith practitioners that could possibly pose a threat to them. When my organization found out about this, we set about recruiting them in our efforts through a back door we installed in this prison years earlier. The enemy of our enemy, you know."

Steph nodded as if she knew, but she was more intently focused on the who's who of people you wouldn't want to share a bathroom with seated around the conference table, each with a respective bright brass plaque depicting their affiliation. This was convenient, as Steph really didn't feel like shaking their hands. Her eyes scanned the table, reading each label.

There was a well-dressed man in a three-piece suit representing the Illuminati; a man in a burgundy hat and smoking jacket, who was glaring across the table at the Illuminati guy, represented the Freemasons; a skirt-suited woman claimed to represent the worshippers of some group called the Reptilian Elite; an actual honest-to-goodness armored knight from The Knights Templar; a man resembling a fat, forlorn Jesus in stained underclothes and an undone bathrobe who hailed from the Church of Infinite Sadness; a muscular black man from the Leopard Society, clad in a skin-tight leopard-print body suit and accompanied by a real, purring leopard at his feet that Stephanie desperately wanted to pet; and, finally, the coup de grace—a shabby, disheveled man in off-white robes who struggled to keep an octopus perched atop his head. He led something called The Order of the Cloud Octopus. Obviously.

"I'll spare the introductions, as time is of the essence," Mike's mysterious lady-friend said. "But you'll find most of the city represented here. However, we filtered out some of the more volatile sects. The Church of Euthanasia, the Nazis who want to clone an army of Superpowered Hitlers, Scientologists, Young Republicans . . . groups of that nature."

"But you *kept* the Cloud Octopus people?" Steph whispered behind her hand.

The Woman ignored her and motioned for Steph and Mike to sit. Steph and Mike purposefully moved to take the seat next to the suited Illuminati leader. It was the furthest place from the Octopus Man, who was beginning to give them the stink eye.

Steph looked up at the Illuminatus, who sat up straight in his chair with a good inch or two of height over her. "So, uh, how much do you know about what's going on here?"

The man gazed down at her through his thick spectacles, not in the mood for small talk. "Just as much as you do."

"Aren't you guys supposed to know and control everything?"

He forced an audible sigh. "Yeah, that's a common misconception. We were a Candlemakers Guild in the 1200s that wanted a cool name, and things just got blown out of proportion."

"So you don't control anything?"

"Well, we just control the worldwide production and distribution of LEDs at the moment," he said. "You gotta modernize."

"If that's all you do now, then why's the Freemason guy staring daggers at you?" Mike asked.

"I kinda . . . slept with his girlfriend," the Illuminatus looked away, eager not to continue this line of questioning.

Mike's mysterious woman cleared her throat and sat down behind her plaque, which was blank aside from a few scuff marks on the burnished steel plate. Stephanie noticed the seat next to her was unfilled and also sported a blank steel nameplate. All eyes turned to face her, and the murmur of the group quieted.

"Ladies and Gentlemen," the Woman said, "thank you for your patience. As you all know, the threat of The Future Group is upon us, and we've gathered you here today so we can stop it."

"Yes, but why now?" the woman from the Reptilian Elite cult said. She looked normal and unassuming enough, aside from the fact that she worshipped something called the Reptilian Elite. "If what you've told us is true, The Future Group is closer to summoning Korthuu than ever before."

"We've needed to gather a few remaining pieces of the puzzle. To that end, Michael Duckett and Stephanie Dyer here have been quite helpful. Through their investigation, they've found data that implies The Future Group has finally collected a critical mass of their Universal Solute and is preparing to break down the barriers of our universe and welcome Korthuu in as soon as this evening."

"Then we're too late!" The Reptile Lady banged her fist on the table. "We're all doomed. All because you had us wait for these . . . these yahoos!"

"Hey!" Mike interrupted. "We're not yahoos!"

"They are an integral part of this operation and their participation is necessary." Steph appreciated that the woman retained her cool, matter-of-fact demeanor.

"You keep telling us that, but you never justify it." She narrowed her eyes. "Well, it's a moot point anyway. The Reptilian Elite will reveal themselves any minute now. They will topple Korthuu and eat their followers' bones."

"Oh, that's rich. You actually think your secret lizard government will shed their human skin suits and help you fight a war? That's the stupidest goddamn thing I've ever heard," said the man with an octopus balanced on his head.

The representative from the Leopard Society scoffed. His leopard jumped up onto the table and lay in front of him, demanding pets, which it got. "If you have any better ideas, we would *love* to hear 'em!"

"As a matter of fact, I do," the Octopus Man said.

The Reptile Lady raised an eyebrow. "Name one." But, before the Octopus Man could rebut, she qualified herself, saying, "One that doesn't involve a sky octopus."

"Up yours! You all think you're so damn right all the time." His accusatory finger made the rounds across the gathered group, while his other hand scrabbled to balance his octopus. "But you're not. You're useless bums! The whole lot of ya!"

And that's when the fight broke out. The Reptile Lady lost her composure and leapt across the table. But the tightness of her skirt suit kept her from making any headway, giving the Octopus Man ample opportunity to use his living headpiece to give her an octuple slap. The Leopard Man tried to hold him back, but to no avail. Meanwhile, the Freemason and the Illuminatus took the opportunity to hash out their own, separate beef.

"She was the love of my life," the Freemason screeched, "you candle-making piece of shit!"

The leader of The Church of Infinite Sadness retreated to the corner to ball up in a fetal position, clasping his ears. "Why is everybody yelling? I don't like it when people yell!"

Steph and Mike could only exchange awkward side glances as the whole production unfolded in front of them. Steph liked crazy shenanigans, but this was pushing even her tolerance. Aside from them, the only other calm presences at the table were the Templar Knight, who continued to remain composed and motionless and, ironically, the wild cat, sitting on the table licking itself. The Woman, on the other hand, dragged her hands across her face and slumped in her chair. It looked like the first time she'd ever lost control of a situation.

A loud banging brought the group to attention, mid-fight. On the other side of the room, an older man in tattered clothing with a patchy five o'clock shadow trudged in. He used a large picket sign as a sort of cane, rapping the wooden handle against the wall. His stone-faced grimace proved he was in no mood to continue dicking around. As he approached the remaining chair, Steph noticed what was written in red, jagged letters on the front of the sign, and it was right. The end was indeed nigh

"Everybody shut the hell up!" He banged his fist on the table.

"Homeless Joe!" Steph shouted.

"You guys know each other?" Mike asked her, before turning to the Woman. "And *you two* work together?"

The Woman just gave him a playful shrug.

"Hi, Stephanie. It's nice to see you again." Homeless Joe gave her a warm, if tired, smile.

"Is this what you meant when you said the end was nigh?"

"Yes, but no one ever listened to me."

"I don't think shouting at people on the street was the best way to get your message across."

"Point taken." Homeless Joe turned back to the rest of the cult leaders who had slunk back to their seats, his face hardening. "Alright, you idiots. The Future Group and Korthuu are a very real, very credible threat. And if you're not going to stop this stupid infighting, they're going to continue to poach followers from you and, in the end, kill us all.

"Stop me if you've heard this one before," he continued. Complex, multi-layered diagrams projected onto the canvas screen behind him. "Existence is made up of an infinite number of universes each representing a unique possibility. So no matter how miniscule or outlandish, it stands to reason that any thought, idea, or concept created by a single conscious unit—human or otherwise—in any of these universes will birth a corresponding universe where that concept is reality. The more beings who believe in that idea, the stronger that universe or concept is.

"Korthuu is using that to their advantage. They live in the void outside the multi-verse. When they sense weakness in a universe's walls, they seep into the thoughts of a universe's inhabitants, corrupting groups of them until they generate enough energy through their belief to act as a beacon to home in on the target universe. And then Korthuu strips it clean. Their hunger sated, they move on to the next universe. That's why they're called The Beast Who Walks Like a Man, God of The Eternal Feast."

Time felt like it had stopped, allowing a dam to break in Steph's mind, and she knew Mike's had, too. Korthuu's two-part title, added to the first, contained a third title they were both unfortunately familiar with.

"Mangod!" they said in unison.

"What?" said the Woman.

"We've . . . heard of him before." Stephanie tiptoed around the fact she and Mike had met Korthuu's followers in a hellscape of an alternate universe populated by cow-men with eyeballs for fingertips and octopi for genitals. They had called them "interlopers." The very same thing they'd been called when they infiltrated The Future Group cult meeting. The time didn't seem right for what would be an extremely long story.

"But that's why Craig Breene is such an asshole!" Mike's face brightened. "Korthuu is using him to amass enough braindead followers to help invite themselves in."

"Like a Dracula," Steph added, desperate to contribute to the conversation.

"Exactly like a Dracula," Homeless Joe said, before letting his face fall. "But Craig Breene isn't an asshole. He is—was—a good man."

"Hold on just a second," Mike raised his hand, like this was a classroom. "How exactly do you know all of this, 'Homeless Joe'? If that *is* your real name?"

"It's obviously not," the Woman chided.

Homeless Joe let out a long sigh and leaned on the table, struggling under the weight of the explanation. "I helped found The Future Group."

"What?" Mike shouted as a wave of quiet whispers erupted across the table. Steph felt her jaw drop.

"My name is Marcus Espinoza, and I was Craig's friend . . . before Korthuu got to him." Homeless Joe—Marcus—launched into a tale so convoluted and outlandish, Steph could barely believe it. This raving homeless vagrant she had befriended was actually an ex-money manager whose friend had been corrupted by the very interdimensional being she and Mike were trying to stop. He'd spent the last sixteen years creating an organization to solve this very problem. And now it was down to the wire. "I should have stopped him then, but I couldn't. I was too scared. And it's been the biggest regret of my life. Which is why," he concluded, "we, as a group, need to figure out how to stop him now."

After brief murmurs of agreement, a hush fell over the room, as none of the other cult leaders could offer a suggestion. Before Stephanie could speak, Mike pre-empted her. "I . . . might have an idea."

Steph noticed Homeless Joe and the Woman share a look.

"We thought you might," he said.

Stephanie wasn't certain how she felt about not being the one to originate a crazy scheme, but she decided to roll with it.

"When we snuck into the secret catacombs under The Future Group tower," Mike said, "we found some sort of computer that Craig was using to view the Multi-Verse and commune with Korthuu. If we destroy that, we might just keep Korthuu from gaining a foothold and entering our universe. We just have to make it there in time."

"We'd tried that," Homeless Joe said, "Several times. Our agents who made it through couldn't crack the code to enter the chamber. Those that didn't make it back were captured and brainwashed. We had to relocate so many times to ensure our safety, it wasn't worth it."

"It's the Konami Code," Steph said.

"What?"

"The Konami Code. Up, up, down, down, etcetera? C'mon guys. None of you ever played Contra?"

"Oh, yeah, I'm pickin' up what you're putting down!" The Leopard Man nodded, his wild cat purring beneath his fingers. "I used to *slay* at Contra."

"Well, then, let's go," Mike pounded the table. "We don't have any time to lose."

"I like where you're head's at, Michael Duckett," the Woman said. Stephanie could see Mike almost blush.

"Mike, this could be real dangerous." Steph nudged him in hopes he'd step back from this ledge.

"No, Steph." He turned to her, a strange fire in his eyes. "You've been pushing me to take risks and dive right into things and now's my chance to do it and maybe save the whole damn world in the process. I wanted to do something important, and this is it. But I need you, because out of this whole collection of weirdos, only you and I are big enough weirdos to make sense of this."

Stephanie could say nothing to that. She felt a strange sense of pride and fear welling up in her chest, but she quashed it immediately. Mike was right. It was time for business.

The Leopard Man cleared his throat. "Alright, now that we're all on the same page, babies. How do we get back to the city in time to try out the skinny boy's plan?"

"The prison has several trucks and vans in its motor pool that could easily carry all of you," said Homeless Joe.

"But you'll have to get past The Future Group's indoctrinated prisoners," finished The Woman.

Everyone looked at Mike.

"Hey, I never said it was going to be easy."

"We'll help hold down the fort while you make your escape," Homeless Joe said.

"And, once you get into the city," the Woman said, "we'll try to send any resources we can scrounge up."

"That's all we can ask for." Stephanie took a deep breath and looked around the table. "So you guys ready for the fight of your lives?"

A hearty cheer went up from the assembled crowd, aside from the Freemason, who still had other issues on his mind, and the crying man who maintained his position in the corner. Mike met Steph's gaze and gave her a strong, solemn nod.

"Alright, let's get moving!" Steph threw her fist in the air just as a blonde woman emerged from a back room in nothing but her under-wear. This drew Steph's attention immediately, not to mention the rest of the room.

"Um, hi," she squeaked, tip-toeing toward the table. "Sorry!"

"Who're you?" Mike asked.

"Oh, uh, right, I'm from the Knights Templar," she said, pointing toward the armored knight in the seat around the table, who had not moved since Mike and Steph had entered. "I got here early and I really had to go to the bathroom. No one was around, so I just left my armor behind. Getting it on and off is a whole production. I guess I was in there longer than I thought. Anyway, what'd I miss?"

# CHAPTER TWENTY-FOUR

## Breaking In Is Hard To Do

Calhoun's foot was on the accelerator. McDermott's hand wrapped tightly around the passenger's side grab handle. As he made a rapid lane change, Calhoun caught a glimpse of Maureen the assassin and the wimpy convenience store kid—who was going on and on about something—in the rear view mirror.

"My dad wanted me to be an engineer, but I'm really into business and tech. And when I told him that, he forced me to work at one of his convenience stores to teach me a lesson about how business sucks. But the only thing I learned was how much *his* business sucks."

The kid had told them about Duckett and Dyer's unfortunate trip to the penitentiary. And if Maureen was right about this cult business, Calhoun'd need Duckett and Dyer's help. He was man enough to admit that. Or, at least, he was man enough to admit it after McDermott badgered him into it.

"Hey, uh"—the kid leaned over and tapped Calhoun on the shoulder—"could we maybe hit a rest stop or something? I need to pee."

"Shut up, stringbean," Calhoun growled.

"So what's your plan for when we actually get there?" McDermott winced as Calhoun cornered sharply onto the exit out of the city.

"Plan? What plan?" There was no time for a plan. "We're just going to wing it."

"When has that ever worked?"

Maureen leaned into the grate between the rear and front seats. "You want to break into a maximum security prison controlled by a powerful cult without a detailed plan of attack?"

"Alright, genius! You come up with something," Calhoun yelled over the roar of the engine as he overtook a slow moving pick-up truck that—in other circumstances—he would have pulled over for speeding.

"Oh, I don't know," Maureen shot back. "How about we walk in the front door and you flash your badge to get us in? No muss, no fuss."

"Well, that would work if Braddock hadn't kicked me and McDermott off the force yesterday!"

"Do the guys at the prison know that?" Kashir asked.

"Well, no." The words slipped out of Calhoun's mouth as he realized they had a point, which just served to make him angrier.

"So . . . we can just walk in?" McDermott asked.

"With my luck, it's not going to be that simple," Calhoun grumbled. He flipped on his lights and sirens, pushing his cruiser to its structural limits.

* * *

As usual, Calhoun was right. Although they had gotten there in record time, rolling their way past the prison's front gates, the guard at the entrance was proving to be a tough nut to crack.

"Unfortunately, Detective, the facility is on full lockdown," he said, blocking their entrance. "We're not letting anybody in or out for the remainder of the day."

"But I'm a goddamn cop." Calhoun flashed his badge, as if it still had real power.

"Yes, but these people"—the guard waved a limp hand at Maureen, McDermott, and the kid, his legs crossed tightly—"are not. In fact, I don't even know who they are."

"I knew we should've waited in the car," McDermott said.

"You know who I am, you little freak. You've seen my badge and my skinny little friend needs to pee, so if you would just move . . ." Calhoun tried to push past him, but the guard puffed out his chest and advanced on him instead, blocking Calhoun out.

"No one enters without the express orders of Captain Braddock."

"Shit, are you on his payroll, too? Listen, guys—"

"No." The guard's voice turned monotone. "We do not have to listen to interlopers. It is clear now that you are not here to help us serve the will of Korthuu."

"Oh, great." Maureen groaned.

"We will give you one chance to leave and be bathed in cleansing fire upon Korthuu's arrival. If not, you will be given glorious new purpose through the Universal Solution. Choose wise—AGH!"

Calhoun had drawn his gun and shot the guard in the knee.

"Rex!" McDermott screamed.

"Oh, relax." Calhoun waved her off and bent down to address the guard clutching his knee. "Alright, shitheel. I've got a glorious purpose for *you*. How's about you drag yourself back up and—"

The guard's face twisted and contorted so quickly that Calhoun barely had time to stumble and fall back. As the guard's eyes glazed over, pitch black, rows of clacking teeth erupted from multiple points in his face. An otherworldly shriek rattled Calhoun's bones. The man's arms and legs bent backwards and forwards at odd angles, setting off a cacophony of cracks and pops as new limbs sprouted and tore through his uniform with reckless abandon. Calhoun's jaw dropped as the thing stared at him with its lifeless eyes, more teeth undulating beneath its skin. Inches from his face, it roared, spittle flying everywhere.

With an ear-splitting crack, the beast's head exploded in a blast of bone, skin, and goo. It reared back before crashing to the floor, its limbs spread every which way. Calhoun looked back to see Maureen holding her own pistol. She slipped it back into a thigh holster.

"Okay, what the *shit* was that?" was all Calhoun could say.

"Oh, yeah. I didn't tell you they could turn into monsters."

"No, uh, that's . . . a detail you left out," McDermott said. She and Kashir had retreated to the far wall. Both were shaking.

"It was a need to know thing, and now I guess you need to know. But would you have believed me, anyway?"

"That's not even close to the point!" Calhoun shouted as he pushed himself up and toward to the seventy-year-old smirking assassin. "This is shit we should have known going in."

"Well, now you know," she shrugged, "and now we're going in."

"I oughta lock you up with the rest of these goombas."

"Yeah. Good luck." Maureen spun on her heel and waltzed past the guard desk and through the open barred doors.

Calhoun looked at McDermott, who had composed herself quicker than he had.

"I like her," she said.

"Shut up." Calhoun frowned and gestured to Kashir with his gun. "And you. C'mon. Let's find you a bathroom so you can stop pissing me off."

"I . . . uh . . ." Kashir stammered, glancing down momentarily. "Actually I think I'm fine now."

"Ugh. God. Just . . . keep away from me." Calhoun stepped over the former guard's body and followed in Maureen's footsteps.

Calhoun strode down the intake hallway with McDermott by his side and pushed through the heavy double doors leading to the main cell block. Maureen stood at the top of the landing towering over three floors of jail cells and overlooking an empty gen pop common area. The soothing taupe bars of each long array of doors popped against the darkness within. There were no prisoners here; the whole place was deathly silent. The only squeak came from a hanging overhead light creaking ominously in the distance.

"Where the hell is everyone?" Calhoun finally said after surveying the vast hall. "This place was supposed to be full of inmates!"

"If there's nobody here, what the hell was that guy guarding?" McDermott added.

"They must have been turning them." Maureen braced herself on the railing. "They're brainwashing all their prisoners and turning them into those monsters. To serve Korthuu."

"That's insane," Calhoun said. "With the number of prisoners here, they'd have the equivalent of a standing army."

"Plus the police force, plus the whole workforce of The Future Group, I'd say." The kid made his appearance through the double doors. "I swiped some prison slacks from an open closet, and this neat green coat." He twirled around to show-off his ratty garbage jacket.

"Great job, kid, nobody asked." Calhoun turned back to Maureen and McDermott. "So they've got an army of zombie goons that are going to help them unleash some other bigger zombie goon to destroy the city."

"Then the world," McDermott added.

"Then the universe," Maureen finished.

"Yeah, yeah, alright. Enough of that. If that's their plan, they've gotta be transporting these things to the city somehow." Calhoun clucked his tongue. "Probably disguised."

"Hm," the kid said, "what kinda food you guys stock here?"

"What? In prison?" Calhoun furrowed his brow. "I dunno. The

shitty kind."

"Yeah, but who's your *supplier*?"

"I'm a cop. I don't know these things."

"Well, whoever they are, they probably bring in food through your loading docks on big trucks. That's how we get stuff to the store. And we also stock the shitty kind of food."

Calhoun was impressed. "Kid, you might be right. And there're probably enough paddy wagons there, too. Let's go."

McDermott and the rest followed as Calhoun powered down the hallway toward the rear of the building. "Rex," she said, "if they are mobilizing, what're we going to do when we find them?"

"I don't know!" Calhoun snapped back as he quickened his pace. "I bust drug dealers and murderers. I don't have a contingency plan for monster invasions. I was just gonna shoot 'em!"

"How many bullets do you have, Calhoun?" Maureen checked her pockets.

"Not enough." Calhoun checked his magazine while on the run. It wasn't empty, but it certainly wasn't full. "We'll have to make do."

"You think Duckett and Dyer got monsterized, too?" Kashir asked.

"Well, if I see any stupid monsters, I'll let you know."

"You gonna shoot them, too?"

Calhoun clicked his magazine back into place. "Let's see."

# CHAPTER TWENTY-FIVE

## Too Young To Die

Marcus could do nothing except stand still as Craig—or whatever it was in Craig—entered the room with their coffees. He tried his best to smile, but it came out as forced. He hoped Craig wouldn't notice.

"Oh, man, sorry I took so long." Craig placed the coffees—secure in their cardboard caddy—on the table and turned around. "There was *such* a line! Mornings, am I right?" Craig's face fell when he found Marcus frozen on the opposite side of the room. His eyes darted to the giant throne of mismatched computer towers in the middle of the room and the Nintendo headset sitting on it, askew. Craig's face fell. "Oh, so you know."

Marcus took air in through his teeth with a sharp hiss.

"Oh, don't worry. I knew this time was coming." This definitely was not Craig speaking. It was something much more frightening. "Y'know, I've devoured a similar universe with a Craig and a Marcus. I know you saw it. They were a little different, but with the same nice flavor. This one though is fresh. It's intriguing."

"What . . . are you?"

"How many times am I going to be asked that question? Geeze." Craig's body wound its way toward Marcus in a spindly dance. "Fine. They call me The Beast That Walks Like A Man, God of the Eternal Feast. But you can call me Korthuu."

"You're . . . evil," Marcus stammered.

"I'm not evil!" Craig's hand pressed itself to his chest. "I'm merely a force of balance in the cosmos. It's just a fact of life. But if it makes you feel better to give me a subjective moral label, go ahead."

"Is . . . any of Craig still in there?"

"Oh, nothing of any use, I'd say." Korthuu flapped his hand. His arms seemed to be lengthening. Stretching, like taffy. "He loved you, by the way. I thought you should know that."

Marcus froze.

"He what?"

"He loved you," the thing inhabiting his friend replied all too matter-of-factly. "Quite a bit, actually. Never could get the courage to tell you himself. He was weak. Sad."

As a weird mix of fury, fear, and grief welled up in his chest, Marcus found he did not know what to say. Craig had loved him? He may not have been able to return that love, but Marcus kicked himself for being so wrapped up and self-absorbed in his own quest for success that he was blind to Craig's emotions. What kind of shitty friend had he been?

But it was too late. The friendship was gone.

Like Craig.

"But that's all beside the point." Korthuu waved away Marcus's human moment. "I'm here for your universe. I just need a few more things, and when I'm done, I'll pop on over real quick." Korthuu, now nearly fifteen feet tall due to his elongated limbs, stretched his grotesque mask of a face toward Marcus and caressed his cheek with a clawed finger. "Now, you're going to try to stop me. You always do. But everything you're gonna do is going to fail."

"W-why?" Marcus pressed himself up against the wall of computers, desperately avoiding making eye contact.

"Because nothing you pitiful lesser beings ever do matters. The universe is chaos, it's a fact of life. I'm the only orderly thing in it!" Korthuu snapped back into Craig's normal body and spun around like a child in a toy store. "I could kill you right now and it wouldn't make a difference. But it would rob me of turning you into part of my precious little workforce."

Marcus had turned his attention to the door—his only escape route—and, his back against the wall, began to sidle toward it. It felt infinitely far away, and he wasn't sure if Korthuu noticed. Marcus just had to keep the monster talking. He didn't want to die in this technological madhouse. Nor did he want to turn into a zombie slave.

Marcus blurted out the first thing that came to his mind. "Craig said the multi-verse is collapsing."

"That's above your pay grade, little man," Korthuu hissed. "I'm not sure you'd understand the implications. Craig did, that sweet boy. But look where that got him."

"If the multi-verse is collapsing, won't you die, too?"

"That's a problem for the future." Korthuu shrugged. "I'll figure it out. That's why I'm here, actually. I could never see into the future of this specific universe, and that tells me it's special. I love it. I need it. But I don't need you lot."

"What if I find a way to stop it?" Marcus said. "The collapse of the multi-verse?"

"Marcus, please. What you know could fit in a thimble." Korthuu snapped Craig's eyes back to Marcus. "You couldn't find the one foolproof combination to prevent existential collapse! Hell, you haven't even realized I know you're trying to escape!"

Shit.

Korthuu slithered Craig's body up to him and gave him a long, kiss. Marcus could do nothing but stare, wide-eyed and keep his mouth shut. It felt like Craig's lips were going to consume his face.

"Well." Korthuu finally withdrew and held Marcus out by his shoulders. "Now that I've gotten my goodbye kiss, you're free to go."

Marcus could only stand dumbfound as Korthuu, Craig's hands clasped behind his back, walked over to the throne of the multi-verse visualizer and plopped himself down. Korthuu placed the headset on Craig's head like a jaunty cap and kicked up his feet. He scowled when he saw Marcus remained frozen at the other end of the room.

"You're still here." The edge of Korthuu's frown dipped below Craig's chin. He waved a dismissive hand. "I said you could go."

"Just . . . just like that?" This had to be some sort of trick.

"Yes, damnit! No trick. No trap. Just go!"

"That doesn't make any sense. Why're you letting me go?"

"Marcus." In a snap, Craig's body was off the chair and right up against Marcus. He grabbed his cheeks and snarled, "Haven't you been listening to *anything I said*? Nothing you do matters! I've made my way in here now and you won't win. I've seen how other universes like yours fall. It's just a matter of time. And I've got plenty of that. Korthuu is eternal. Whatever you do"—he patted Marcus' face—"I'll come for you. Wherever your baby girl is. So do what we both know you want to do and run."

Marcus stiffened.

"RUN FOR YOUR LIFE," Korthuu snapped Craig's face into a hollow-eyed mask with insectoid mandibles for teeth.

Marcus bolted to the sound of maniacal laughter and didn't look back.

# CHAPTER TWENTY-SIX

## Meeting of the Minds

Michael and Stephanie waded their way through the last few yards of the Woman's secret underground tunnel, sloshing through more human effluence than Michael hoped he would ever see in his lifetime. It was comforting to know that, behind them, a few cult leaders were suffering the same disgusting slog, along with the Woman and the crazy vagrant Stephanie knew as Homeless Joe.

"How much longer?" whined the head of the Leopard Society, who had been complaining the loudest. His own leopard however, remained calm and even-tempered. "My tights are getting gross and this place smells like farts!"

"I don't know!" Steph yelled back, as if the darkness impacted everyone's hearing. "Shut up!"

"It should only be a few more meters," Homeless Joe said. "Sometimes, if you want things to be secret, you gotta put them in places nobody wants to go."

Homeless Joe was true to his word, and soon, Steph's flashlight, held above her head, finally landed upon the rusting hulk of an exit hatch.

"Jackpot," she said. "Hey, Octopus Man. Wrench that thing open for us, will ya?"

The Octopus Man, with one hand clutching his hat octopus tightly, lurched toward the hatch. With a creak and a groan, he freed the stuck hatch to reveal more darkness. It took Steph's flashlight to illuminate a single rusty metal ladder leading directly up into nothingness.

"Cool," Steph said. "Who's going first?"

Nobody made a sound, except for the leopard's soft purring.

"Alright." Michael cleared his throat. "I'll do it."

"What?" Stephanie seemed taken aback. "No. You shouldn't do it."

"And why not?"

"You have no idea what's up there!" Steph seemed oddly protective lately, and it was starting to get on his nerves.

"Well, neither do you. So we're even." Michael wasn't exactly sure what he meant by that, but it seemed to shut Steph up. He nudged her aside and grabbed the first rung.

"If you get mauled by a bunch of scary cult monsters, I'll never forgive you."

Michael ascended rung by rung, with a sense of purpose beating hard in his chest. Or maybe it was the fact his heart was not used to strenuous exercise. Either way, it kept him moving forward—until he hit the top and slammed his head against a hard iron barrier.

"Ow!" he cried.

"Mike!" Steph's voice was tinny and far away. "Are you okay? What'd you find?"

Michael felt around above his head, scrabbling in the dark. His fingers traced across deep grooves and notches carved into the iron plate he'd hit. The business end of a manhole cover.

"I think we're good!" Michael called. He braced his arms on the sides of the tunnel and his feet squarely on the rungs of the ladder. He held his breath and used his back to push against the cover with all the force he could manage. He was probably going to damage his spine in some way, but he lacked the upper body strength to push it up normally. After a few somewhat overdramatized grunts, Michael felt the cover lift up ever so slightly. Risking his balance, he removed one of his hands from the concrete tunnel wall and used it to help push the cover aside. Luckily it slipped, letting a small sliver of light cut through the darkness.

"Yes!" Michael cheered to himself as he returned to the comfort of the ladder. Another minute and he would have blown out a lung. After taking a second to catch his breath and rub his back, Michael returned to the task at hand, shoving his fingers into the slim crescent of natural light and heaving with the limited leverage of his wrist. The grating strain of iron on concrete greeted him as the manhole cover slid, slowly opening up nearly halfway.

Breathing heavily, Michael hoisted himself up by his forearms, and soon he was sitting pretty on the floor of a concrete hallway, close to a set of exit doors.

"Whoo!" he wheezed, before cupping his hand to his mouth and shouting down. "I did it! Let's get outta here!"

"Is it safe?" Steph's small voice called back.

"What? Yeah! Of course it's safe. There's no one- AHH!" Michael shrieked as a bullet whizzed past his head. He'd barely heard the crack of the gun, but he spun around to be greeted with a view down its barrel.

"Rex!" the voice of a young woman yelled. "What the hell? He's not a monster."

"Give me that." An older, chubbier woman in a skintight suit grabbed the pistol out of Rex Calhoun's hands. Michael recognized her, but he was in such a state of shock he couldn't process anything. "What the hell were you thinking?"

"I didn't know it was him. It could've been another monster. Hell, he might still be a monster." Rex leaned down on his haunches. "Kid, are you a monster?"

Michael finally found his words. "Jesus Christ, you goddamn asshole. What the hell! You could've killed me."

"Doesn't sound like a monster to me." A young, red-haired woman peered over Rex's shoulder. Michael could swear he'd met her before, but he couldn't place where. In any case, she seemed kind, which was a welcome change of pace from Rex Calhoun's poor bedside manner.

Michael heard the clanging of feet ascending the ladder below him and Steph's head popped out of the manhole like an excited gopher's.

"Mike, I heard screaming! Are you o—" Her head swiveled around to take in everyone else. "Oh, hey, Rexy. How's it hanging?"

"Yeah, she's definitely not a monster," Rex grumbled. "Unfortunately."

"Pfft. You love it." Steph's gaze landed on the redhead and her haughty grimace turned into a smile. "Oh, well if it isn't Carrie McDermott. You look as cute as ever! Mama do indeed like."

"Aw, gee. Thanks!" Michael could see a blush blossoming on her pale skin. "But. . . have we met before?"

"Uh. . . nope! But enough of the small talk. Carrie, would you help me up out of this hole? I seem to have a leopard breathing up my ass." Stephanie extended an arm to Carrie as Michael stood up and dusted off his prison jumpsuit. "And that's not a euphemism, this time."

"Thanks sweetie, owe you one," Steph said as Carrie helped her up. She fired a gun finger with a cluck of her tongue and turned back to Calhoun. "By the way, we've actually made a few friends in prison. They're a . . . colorful bunch. They'll be up in a bit."

"Seems like you made a few friends yourself." Michael nodded over to the motley crew behind the grizzled detective.

"Maureen!" Steph cried. "Good to see you. How's every little thing?" She went in for a hug and was promptly rebuffed.

"I'm glad you're okay, but you smell like piss and shit."

"Never change," Steph turned her gaze to the skinny Indian kid from the convenience store. Michael had to admit, she'd been right to call him. "How about you, Kashir? Fancy a hug?"

"I just stopped smelling like piss and shit, actually. So let's hold off on that."

Steph glanced down at what the kid was wearing, a familiar well-worn green coat. "Is that my jacket?"

"Uh . . . maybe?"

"Give it back!" she grabbed onto its tattered green sleeve and yanked.

"I think it looks better on me," he protested before Steph managed to rip it off him.

"Alright, stop," Michael said, intervening. "What are you guys doing here?"

"Well," Carrie said, "we were coming to break you out of prison."

"Nice work, guys. Real A-1." Steph donned her jacket, hugging it with the warmth one would reserve for an old friend.

"And we have a bone to pick with The Future Group," Calhoun continued. "We were hoping you could . . ." Michael could see him literally try to swallow his pride. It looked painful and unpleasant, and actually made Michael feel a lot better. "Help us stop them."

"Hahah!" Steph punched the air. "Rexy, I'd knew you'd come around."

"Don't let me regret it."

"Is it okay to come out?" A tiny voice whispered as the head of an octopus peeked out of the manhole.

"Okay." Rex blinked. "I already regret it."

"Rex, I know it's weird, and you've put up with a lot of dumb shit from us already." Michael opted for a steady non-confrontational tone. "But The Future Group has us outmanned and outgunned, so we need all the help we can get.

"Have you ever heard of the Cult of the Cloud Octopus?"

Rex gave Michael a look that was both infuriated and disappointed all at once.

"Well, it gets worse."

While each individual cult leader extricated themselves from the sewer below, Michael and Stephanie took turns trying to explain the ridiculous journey they had been on, while Rex kept shaking his head. Michael tried to convey the whole thing as simply and palatably as possible, but Steph exaggerated and embellished several details, winking and pointing at Carrie during most of her parts of the story. They covered the existence of Korthuu, the alternate reality terminal and its broadcasting statues, and the confusing bit about the Universal Solution. Luckily, they didn't have to recount the part about The Future Group and its monsters from scratch, otherwise they would have been there all night.

"If I hadn't had one of those four-armed freaks try to bite my head off a few minutes ago, I would've shot all of you and let God sort it out," Calhoun said when he could finally get a word in edgewise. "But apparently this god seems to be on their side, so we gotta take down these sons of bitches ourselves."

"We were hoping to make it to the prison loading docks so we could get transport back to the city in time to stop them from summoning Korthuu," said the Freemason leader.

"Good," said Carrie. "We were heading there ourselves."

"C'mon, we're not too far from it. Follow me." Rex whipped past the group, fueled by his rage and frustration, and stormed through the nearby doors.

From the corner of his eye, he could see Maureen in conversation with Homeless Joe and the Woman. It took him a minute to process that they had all been working together. Whatever their secret organization was, whatever their purpose, Maureen was their agent. Michael still didn't fully trust them, but the alternative was much worse.

"You guys, uh, all caught up there?" Stephanie asked. They turned and glared, but she didn't wait for a response. "Yeah, we'll all have a chat about this later. C'mon, let's go. I don't wanna have to spend another minute in jail."

Steph led the charge and Michael jogged beside her, with their increasingly large, strange, and unwieldly pseudo-militia following them.

After a few wrong turns and a few more doors, Michael and Stephanie finally found one that led onto a set of hanging scaffolding hanging above the prison loading docks. From the doorway, Michael spotted Rex crouching behind a crate.

"Rex, what the—"

"Shh!" Rex chided, his gun drawn. He waved them back. "Tell your idiot friends to stay low."

Michael and Stephanie turned around and, with a few rapid fire hand signals, alerted the cult of cults and the rest of the crew to remain inside. Michael and Steph moved outside, careful to inch across the scaffolding with the bare minimum of sound.

"We've got a situation," whispered Rex. Looking down, Michael caught a glimpse of what he meant.

Below them were hundreds of former prisoners equipped with body armor and weapons. They were lined up in formations so orderly that they all had to be under The Future Group's mind control. They moved in lockstep, filing into the backs of various trucks and paddy wagons for inevitable transport to the city. With them came several industrial barrels marked U-S.

"Alright, this may be a bigger issue than we thought," Michael said.

# CHAPTER TWENTY-SEVEN

## A Minor Dust-Up

"Well this is a fine how-do-you-do." Stephanie whistled as she took in the sight of hundreds of assembled troops, brainwashed inmates of the City Penitentiary. So far, neither she nor Mike—nor Rex—had been spotted, but in the back of her head, she wondered how long that luck would last. With the utmost care, the three of them re-entered the prison and broke the news to a group that looked like the dumbest version of the Avengers.

"There's no way we're going to be able to take out all these goons," Rex growled, still holding his pistol at the ready.

"Maybe we don't need to," Mike whispered. He reached out a gentle hand and pushed Rex's gun down. "We just need to hitch a ride on one of those trucks to get back to the city."

"Hm, that's not a bad idea," said the somewhat familiar Carrie McDermott, who was about Mike and Steph's age. Rexy seemed to have some sort of pre-existing relationship with her, but she made Steph feel funny in a good way. "Maybe we could split up and stow away on different trucks?"

"That's ridiculous," Maureen grumbled. "Us splitting up increases the odds of being caught by one-thousand percent."

"Yes, that's true," the Woman said, "but it's the only way we can keep hidden. They'll definitely see a big group coming. Let's divide into groups of two."

"Cool," Stephanie flashed a wolfish grin. "Carrie, obviously you and I will be together."

"Hey!" Mike cried. She winked back.

"Shut up the two of you," Rex commanded. "But you're right. McDermott and I will take one truck. Maureen, you and stringbean take another."

"My name is Kashir."

Stephanie elbowed Mike. "See! I told you!"

"I don't care what your name is," Calhoun continued. "Duckett, Dyer, you're together. And the rest of you crazies figure it out yourselves. I don't envy whoever's teaming up with the leopard."

There was considerable consternation among the cultish crowd, for good reason, but ultimately, Steph saw them start to break off into separate pairs. The Knight allied herself with the Leopard Man and his large cat, which wasn't going to be the stealthiest combination, but they'd make it work. And due to the tensions within the group, the Octopus Man and the Illuminatus opted to join up in a sort of rivalry against the Lizard Woman and the Freemason. They had lost the man from the Church of Infinite Sadness long ago, but he was probably off weeping in a corner somewhere.

Maureen took the brief planning period as an opportunity to scout the layout of the loading dock from the rafters. Upon returning, she laid out her decision. "Alright, the way I see it, there are six or seven different entry points to this motor pool loading area. We just need to spread out and bide our time until the last load of cultists is ready to leave. When their numbers have dwindled, we'll have a better chance to sneak onto our trucks."

Calhoun's head craned to deliver a withering look directly at Stephanie. "Especially if one of us messes up."

"Look, bro." Steph threw her hands in the air. "You haven't known me for very long. I'm not going to mess anything up."

"We'll see," Calhoun said through gritted teeth.

"Right, we'll stay up here and offer what support we can from the rafters," said Homeless Joe. "Maureen, I suppose we'll probably need that."

Maureen glanced over her shoulder. Joe was pointing at the large sniper rifle strapped to her back. Frowning, she detached it and passed it to Joe. She didn't seem like the type to hand over her weapons willingly, but recognized a direct order when she heard one.

"Okay, then," Homeless Joe said. "Good luck and godspeed. Hopefully we'll see each other again on the other side. But in a figurative way."

The newly formed pairs nodded to each other and set off toward their chosen points of entry, with Mike and Steph moving down a few floors. The way wasn't fully clear, and they found themselves ducking out of view of battalions of Future Group cultists more than once. Eventually, they made it to a hallway on the far right of the loading dock that was overstuffed with racks and bins containing oily car parts and rusting tools. They stationed themselves at either side of a set of double doors, concealing themselves behind a part of disordered shelves.

Through the small portholes in the door, they watched more corps of brainwashed, monsterized cultists goose-step their way onto waiting trucks. Repurposed from food delivery vehicles to troop transporters, their trailers had been sheared off, replaced with open-air seating. After boarding, they sat in orderly rows, calm and unblinking, as the trucks' engines roared, carting them away, only to be replaced by another truck, or police paddy wagon, lying in wait.

"Okay," Steph said, her hand on Mike's shoulder. "You ready for this?"

"Yeah, of course I am. What're you talking about?" Mike looked almost angry.

"I just don't want you to panic and get hurt or anything."

"Alright, Steph, that's it. What the hell's gotten into you? You've been really overprotective lately. I'm more than capable of taking care of myself."

"I . . . dunno," Steph lied, the visions of a dead Mike burning through her brain. That was the future her alternate universe self warned her about, and it was very close to becoming reality. And she would have failed to protect her friend. Another thing to add to a long list of failures for Stephanie Dyer. "I know you never wanted to be a part of this whole detective scheme from the get-go, and now I feel responsible for dragging you into danger."

"Well, stop. For the first time in a while, I actually feel energized. Like I'm doing something real. Something right. And maybe that's helped me be a little less scared. And it certainly helps that we're trying to take down The Future Group. They've pushed me down for far too long and this time I'm gonna push back!" He stood up in a dramatic flourish, knocking loose a large wrench precariously balanced in a box, like a baby bird in a nest. Unlike a baby bird, however, it hit the floor with a loud, ringing clang.

Mike shrieked as the formerly transfixed cultists outside pivoted toward the source of the noise, in sync. Through the windows in the door, they were snarling and gnashing their teeth. Their faces slowly gave way to second sets of teeth and other unnatural protuberances Mike surely did not approve of.

From somewhere high above on the mezzanine gantry Rex and Carrie had picked as their entry point, Steph heard a faint echo of a yell. "Goddamnit! What the hell did I tell you?"

"It wasn't me!" Steph yelled back. "It was Mike's fault this time!"

"It was an accident!" Mike yelled as he grabbed the giant wrench, assuming a defensive position. Steph took his cue and grabbed a crowbar from off the wall, holding it up like a sword as the first wave of cult monsters burst through the doors. In the short time between Mike's mistake and their entrance, the creatures grew more fists and legs per body than Mike and Steph could ever hope to achieve.

"Ahh! Ahh! Ahhhhh!" Every syllable out of Mike's mouth was a terrified scream, as he swung his giant wrench willy nilly and managed to bash in some of the deformed heads that were flying at him.

Steph was a little more methodical with her crowbar, but not by much. She took the time to sidestep the odd clawed arm that swiped at her or the tentacle that threatened to knock her off her feet. Both of them ducked and dived their way through the horde of advancing creatures, felling or injuring as many as they could and making their way into the open loading dock.

"A little help here?" Steph shouted.

"Screw it! Everyone else, cover them!" Steph heard Calhoun yell. Within seconds, gunshots rang out from every which direction. Maureen's former sniper rifle, now wielded by Homeless Joe, supplied a larger, louder bang that interjected between Calhoun's handgun shots, creating a sort of gunshot musical. Steph would've tap danced had she not been busy shoving her fist through the enlarging black insect eyes of a Future Group zombie.

Then, their own cult crew descended from the rafters. The Leopard Society's mascot roared at cultist jugulars, bounding from one neck to another. Stephanie couldn't be sure, but she thought she saw the octopus being used as an offensive weapon. The Knight Templar had the easiest time, hacking and slashing away at the monsters, sending limbs tumbling in a flurry of green protoplasmic goo. The remainder of the cult leaders, armed with only their wits, were less certain about how to proceed. They ended up battling the monsters through a combination of formal fisticuffs and flowery insults.

What followed was a rich tapestry of horrific violence that went on for far too long.

To Steph's surprise, The Future Group cultist numbers eventually dwindled to something more manageable. The monsters' weird mutations proved to be a disadvantage in large numbers in such a small space, with many of them tripping on tentacles or loose limbs and accidentally skewering each other with misplaced claws. It was a horrifying orgy of monstrosities, but it certainly made things easier.

Maureen and the Woman, both out of ammo, used Maureen's grappling hook to swing down from her perch and were beating the crap out of the remaining monsters with the butts of their guns. Rex Calhoun, on the other hand, was nowhere to be seen. That was, until a completely empty troop truck, horn blaring, sideswiped its way into the loading dock, crushing three monstrous cultists with an unpleasant squelching noise.

"Get in!" Calhoun yelled from the driver's seat. "No use killing more of 'em. Let's catch up to the rest."

The cult crew, octopus and leopard included, piled into the back of their very own troop transport, with Maureen claiming shotgun.

Steph and Mike were about to climb into the back as well until a realization struck her.

"Uh, guys. Where's Carrie?"

In a coincidence as convenient as the arrival of Calhoun's truck, the cacophonous cry of "help" came from the far side of the loading dock where Carrie and Kashir were being dragged, legs first, onto one of the remaining troop transports. It promptly sped off.

"Oh, yeah, Kashir was here, too," Steph muttered to herself.

The roar of the engine caught her off guard and she tumbled back, falling onto Mike and crashing to the floor as Calhoun and the remainder of their allies careened after Carrie and Kashir.

"Goddamnit," Mike rubbed his head as he pushed himself up. "What the hell? Did they just leave us here?"

"Rex must've thought we were already on. You know how impulsive he is."

"What the hell are we going to do now?"

"Uh, maybe we should ask them," Steph pointed over Mike's shoulder at the remaining monstrous cultists advancing on them, bones cracking into terrifyingly uncomfortable positions.

A monster with an elongated alligator-like snout covered in taut human skin lashed out and quickly had its head blown away. The Woman and Homeless Joe had grabbed rifles from the dead and were spraying and praying.

"Go!" The Woman yelled over the sound of carnage.

"We'll hold them off as long as we can!" said Homeless Joe.

Before Mike could make a sound, Stephanie grabbed his wrist and yanked them both into a bolt which propelled them away from the action and right off the loading dock into the yard below.

They both tucked and rolled onto the cold ground, kicking up a plume of dust and dirt that soiled their prison jumpsuits before coming to a stop.

"Keep moving!" Mike yelled. By the time Stephanie had gathered her wits, he was up and moving fast. Pfft. And she was worried about him. Steph smiled and took after him. However, a few monsters had broken off from the main pack and erupted off the edge of the loading dock, resuming their gangly, uncoordinated chase.

"Which way did the trucks go? There must be an exit somewhere!"

"Uh . . . uh . . . " Mike's head swiveled as the slobbering, growling monsters began to catch up with them. Finally, he spotted something. "There!" he pointed in the direction of the barbed-wire prison fence.

Steph followed his finger to find a small shed in the distance. The splintered remains of a gate arm were strewn around it, courtesy of Rex Calhoun. The dust his truck kicked up was still dissipating.

"Okay, let's go!" she said, taking a hard turn toward the prison exit.

"What happens when we get there?" Mike huffed, holding his side. "Even if we get outta here, the city is like fifty miles away! We can't run that far with these monstrosities chasing us!"

"We'll burn that bridge when we come to it!" Steph said through gritted teeth.

Despite their utter exhaustion, the monsters on their tail proved a potent motivator for Mike and Steph, and they reached the guard entry shack in record time. It stood empty and abandoned. The only sounds that moved through it were the wind and the encroaching monsters.

"Great. We're screwed." Mike gasped, hands on his knees.

Steph's face fell as she passed toward the guard shack. How could this be? Her alternate-future-self said she had come from three years into the future, so surely she would last as long in this universe. Or maybe this was one of the universes where she and Mike died before they reached their prime. If there were infinite universes, surely that would have to happen in some of them, right? Oh god, she was beginning to sound like Mike.

Before she got a chance to go further down that depressing track, her eyes caught sight of something spectacular on the other side of the shack. She smiled to herself and rushed toward it.

The universe had provided.

"Steph! Where the hell are you going? The monsters are here!"

Stephanie revved the motorcycle's engines and skidded around the shed, sending clumps of dust and dirt flying into Mike's face.

"Hop on," she grinned.

Mike wiped the dust off his glasses, "Do you know how to ride a motorcycle?"

"Is this a good time to argue about that?" she shot back.

"Fair enough." Mike hopped on the back and wrapped his arms around Steph's waist. "Let's goooooooooooooooooo." Mike's last strained syllable stretched into infinity as Steph gunned it.

# CHAPTER TWENTY-EIGHT

## On The Road Again

The rough, scratchy air whipped Michael's face. If he hadn't been wearing glasses, he was certain he'd have to squint, which made him even more anxious that Stephanie was driving without eyewear. And neither of them had a helmet. If he hadn't been hopping through universes just a few weeks ago, he would've been hard pressed to say he'd done anything more dangerous.

As Steph gunned the throttle, they reached speeds Michael had never imagined—given the lackluster performance of the Garbagemobile—rocketing onto the highway and bobbing and weaving through the few cars on the road. The dearth of traffic was helpful, as they could see the caravan of cult-laden troop transports in this distance. The last one in line appeared to be driving erratically and angrily.

"Calhoun," Michael confirmed to himself over the rushing wind.

"What?" Steph yelled back.

"It's Calhoun!" Michael matched her tone.

"I know!"

"I'll say one thing about him—" Michael started.

"What?" Steph yelled again.

"I said, I'll say one thing about him!"

"What's that?"

"He's really protective of that Carrie girl!"

"Of course he is. I think she's hot!"

"What?" Michael screamed over the roar of a passing car.

"I said I think she's hot!"

"Yes, that was obvious!"

"What?" Stephanie yelled.

"Never mind! Just keep going!"

Stephanie continued to accelerate, closing the distance between them and the trucks in record time. Michael had to hand it to her; she was doing quite well. Jockeying for position, she pulled up alongside Calhoun's truck. After passing the cavalcade of cartoon characters clinging to the back for dear life, Michael saw Calhoun hunched over the wheel, teeth gritted, ready to ram the other truck again. Hoping he'd reconsider, Michael threw up one of his hands and waved, the other still tight around Steph.

"Hey! *Hey!*" he cried out, eventually catching Calhoun's attention, prompting him to do the first un-ironic double-take Michael had ever seen in real life. Calhoun mouthed something that neither Michael nor Stephanie could hear, though it was certainly an angry swear word.

Stephanie, of course, gave him a wry salute then plunged ahead toward the cultist truck. With Calhoun falling behind, Michael got a clearer view of what lay before them—the rear bed of a truck overrun with cultists in military assault gear brandishing weapons. It was not a pretty sight. Toward the cab of the truck stood two figures, cowering in fear—Kashir and Carrie.

"Steph it's—"

"Yeah, I see them," she said, easing the throttle back and putting more distance between them and the truck.

"What're you doing?" Michael yelled. "We're losing them!"

"I'm doing something I've always really wanted to do."

"Oh, no." That's when Michael saw it. Ahead of them and the cultist truck was an empty car carrier trailer, perhaps fresh from a recent drop-off at a dealership, its ramp suitably lowered for what Stephanie was thinking of doing. Michael cringed in terror. "Don't tell me you're going to—"

She was. After the Cultist truck passed the slower moving car carrier, Stephanie hit the gas and rocketed forward. The front wheel of the bike pulled upwards, leaving the ground just enough to gain purchase on the lower part of the carrier ramp. The bike flew up the metal ramp with a clank, propelling them up and over the top, leaving them hanging in the air for an eternity.

Michael screamed the entire time.

The bike crashed down onto the trailer bed, taking two cultist monsters with it and sending Michael and Stephanie flying. Luckily, Kashir and Carrie were there to break their fall.

"Hey guys," Steph said from the floor. "How's it going?"

"Not great!" Kashir strained beneath the weight of Michael and Steph's bodies.

Michael pushed himself to his feet and stared down the six armored cultists flanking them on either side of the truck bed, ready to pounce.

"Steph, we've got a problem here," Michael said, receiving no response. "Steph?"

Michael turned back to find Steph lying on Carrie's lap, grinning like a madwoman.

". . . so then I found a motorcycle!"

"Steph!" Michael yelled.

"Yes! What? Sorry, sorry!" Stephanie bounded to her feet and took a stance beside Michael.

"Would you pay attention, please?" Michael snapped out of the side of his mouth.

"Relax, Mike," she whispered back, putting up her fists. "I fight better when I'm horny."

"How do you know that?" Michael put up his own dukes, as if they would do him any good in a fight against six literal monsters.

"Don't worry about it. You take right, I take left?"

"Uh, I guess?"

"Guys," Carrie called out from behind them, "What're we supposed to do?"

"Find a way to get into that truck and take control," Michael shouted, feeling authoritative and in charge for the first time.

"Got it, boss," Kashir said.

"Alright, let's—" Michael whipped around to find Stephanie already kicking ass and taking names. She had one cultist in a headlock and was repeatedly kicking them in the groin.

"Huh," he said to himself, "maybe she does fight better when she's horny."

Juking to the right, Michael avoided the swipe of a truncheon that would have bashed him in the head. This gave him an opening to drive his fist directly into the armpit of his assailant, sending the monster tumbling backwards. Meanwhile, another cultist transformed her arm into a giant bone scythe, which tore through her armor and clothing. She charged Michael with a feral yell. He stumbled back, falling over the first cultist he downed. This tripped the charging cultist and caused her to spear the downed cultist in the chest, draining him of his life force and leaving behind an empty husk.

The bone scythe cultist roared and attempted to advance on Michael but ended up ripping her weapon arm out of its socket in her fervor. She shrieked at the sky as green ooze poured out of her wound and onto the truck bed. Seeing his chance, Michael grabbed the disembodied scythe and used it to slice the monstrous woman's head off. It went tumbling off the side of the truck, crushed under oncoming traffic like an overripe melon.

Michael threw up in his mouth a little bit then turned his attention back to the last remaining cultist, who was beginning to foam at the mouth. Meanwhile, Stephanie had already dispatched two of her foes and was working on the third. She jabbed him in the throat to stun him, then spun his helmet around, effectively blinding him.

"Safety first," she said as she landed a kick to his torso that sent him flying over the back of the truck.

"Whoa!" Michael said. "Did you just kick that guy off the truck and say 'safety first?'"

"Yeah." She grinned. "Cool, right?"

"Very cool," Michael said. He felt galvanized and took a running start at his final foe, head-butting him into the back of the truck. Similarly, he reached up and yanked off the soldier's helmet, smacking him with it before punching him off the truck.

"Safety first," he parroted, before turning back to Stephanie, "How was that?"

"Meh," she shrugged. "You did it wrong."

"What?" Michael yelled as Stephanie turned her back on him, "What did I do wrong?"

"Just wasn't as good," she said.

"What do you mean it wasn't as good?"

"Listen, just keep practicing."

"Whatever." Michael looked over to the truck's cab where Kashir had just ripped a monster from the driver's seat, while Carrie angled in and took control of the wheel.

"Haha!" Kashir guffawed like a pirate as he hung off the truck's exhaust pipe. The sickening crunch of the monster's bones—or bone equivalents—passed beneath them.

"Good job, guys!" Steph called. "Let's stop this crazy train."

Carrie took Steph's direction a bit too literally, slamming on the brakes with a sustained squeal and sending the two of them flying head-first into the cab.

"Ow! Carrie, what the hell!" Stephanie rubbed her head.

"Sorry! I've never driven a truck before," Carrie said.

Calhoun's truck pulled up alongside them. He rolled down the window. "You guys alright?"

"Yeah, peachy." Michael massaged his arm and shoulder.

Maureen leaned over Calhoun's driving arm. "If you idiots ever try anything that stupid again, I'll kill you myself. But . . . good job."

"So what now?" Kashir asked.

"Well, we got two of their trucks, and killed a bunch of their monsters, so that's a pretty good start, right?" Carrie said from the cab.

"Yeah, kid, but there were around a hundred more of them headed to the city. If they reach there in the next hour or so, the show's gonna begin and then we're all well and truly screwed. So let's stop yapping!" Calhoun's truck started roaring away. "We don't have time to lose!"

Michael turned to Stephanie, hoping for some solace. "Do you think we'll be able to make it in time to stop this madness? What happens if we're too late?"

Steph put a comforting hand on his shoulder. "Don't worry, Mike. We won't be too late."

# CHAPTER TWENTY-NINE

## Hell On Earth

"Aw, shit," Stephanie said. "We're too late."

Their truck lurched to a halt outside the city limits. The already red afternoon sky had deepened into an unnatural and quite upsetting shade of crimson. Thin black clouds slashed streaks of void across the skyline. Michael had to squint to see it, but far above, a tiny green flame blazed in midair, tethered only by a thin glowing line that led down to One Future Plaza, presumably to the obsidian and copper statue in the center. The flame danced and flickered for a while before stopping completely, taking with it all of the city's ambient noise. He could no longer hear birds chirping, cars honking, or the mere rustle of tree leaves. It was a period of absolute silence. Michael looked to Stephanie and the others, but they were just as dumbfounded, daring not to speak a word to rupture the quiet.

Michael would have said the eerie calm was the worst part, but the devastating sonic boom and pressure wave that pulsed throughout the city in an instant was actually much, much worse.

Windows shattered. Trees uprooted, flying sideways into buildings causing massive structural damage. Fortunately, they were just far enough away from the city center to catch the very edges of the blast, but that didn't stop the sudden burst of wind from knocking them over and, indeed, knocking the wind out of them. The noises came rushing back. The screeching of escaping birds, the honks and car alarms, and most terrifying of all, the distant screams and explosions.

"That does not bode well," Stephanie whispered.

The green flame ballooned into a wall of fire that towered over The Future Group building by at least three stories. The flames parted, forming a sort of doorway into an orgy of roiling green nothingness, and a set of enormous black claws clasped each side. Then two more, and then a further two, the green tongues of flame licking at the mottled skin and muscle that held the claws together. Slowly, the dark form of Korthuu birthed itself into the universe: a humanoid frame with six muscular arms and a plethora of bug-like legs that oozed and crawled over the city streets. Their head, though, was the most horrifying part, playing host to a plethora of black soulless eyes darting every which way over what appeared to be a thousand jaws filled with rows of teeth—human and otherwise—with tiny arms stretching open their non-existent lips.

"Oh, goody," Michael said flatly. "Armageddon is here. Glad we didn't miss it."

"Okay, Plan B." Steph looked out over the group. "Does anyone have a giant robot? Kashir? I'm looking at you."

She was met with an appropriate, angry silence.

"Oh, well, it was worth a shot. But don't worry. It's not a total loss." Stephanie spread her arms, making a "calm down" motion.

"Not a total loss? Korthuu is here! We're all going to die!" Michael yelled, feeling his power and control slip away from the situation. He was too paralyzed to even try to claw it back. Maybe Steph had been right; he wasn't ready for any of this. He was just as scared and useless as ever. And, furthering Michael's breakdown was the fact that, despite Stephanie's attempt to calm everyone down, she was looking more freaked out than he'd ever seen her before. Steph was actually worried, and if that wasn't a sign of the end times, nothing else was.

"Well, kids, it's been a good run," Calhoun said, tipping his hat to the assembled group. "I'm gonna find the nearest liquor store and buy or steal enough booze to put down an elephant. Who's with me?"

"You're giving up?" Carrie yelped. "You can't give up now!"

"Actually, this is probably the best time to give up," Kashir said, which earned him a swift elbow to the ribs from Carrie.

"No! The Cloud Octopus will save us!" yelled the Octopus Man. "He is everything."

"Oh, would you shut up with that?" The Reptile Lady said. "There's no cloud octopus. The Reptilian Elite will be revealing their scaly hides soon enough. This is all part of their plan."

"And if they don't reveal themselves?" asked the Illuminatus.

"Well, then I'll just have to consider reconsidering my position."

"Perhaps you would feel safer in the loving embrace of the Cloud Octopus. He has arms enough for all."

Calhoun scoffed, "Listen to me, kids, if you're gonna go out, best cash it all in. You can't take it with you. So who's chipping in on the booze?"

Stephanie's uncharacteristic mask of hopelessness fell away in an instant. And Michael felt a strange sense of calm.

"You're right."

"Who? Me or the Octopus guy?" Calhoun asked.

"Both of you, really," Stephanie said. "I think I have an idea. Kashir, you like business and tech, right?"

"Yeah, I know a little bit." Kashir hung his head, embarrassed. "And one time I was in the school investment club and I had some spare cash to play around with e-stocks. Made a few hundred dollars . . . but then I spent it on porn."

"Who buys porn these days?" Steph scrunched up her face. "Never mind. I'm going to need you to come with me. I'll fill you in on the way."

"On the way to where?" Maureen asked.

"You know I always gotta be the center of attention." Steph smiled. "We go where the action is. The Future Group tower. Everybody saddle up, things are going to get hairy."

* * *

The call went out. No one was sure how far. It wouldn't be clear until days later that the entire world heard Korthuu's call in their head. Centuries later, interplanetary explorers would discover that alien races beyond our galaxy had heard it, too. How that came up in polite conversation would be anyone's guess, but one thing was certain, Korthuu was not speaking with their mouth—of which they had many. No, Korthuu spoke by vibrating the very fibers of existence in the universe, so not only did every living and non-living thing hear them, but they felt them shuddering their bones, flesh, cytoplasm, or mineral deposits in whatever form of communication was most pleasing. If Korthuu hadn't tailored their message, it would have been a haunting, discordant cacophony of syllables produced by gnashing teeth, flying spittle, and screams from the pits of hell. And that's no way to market yourself.

"Beings of this plane, your time is at an end. For those of you who have avoided the blessed cleansing of enlightenment, I am Korthuu, the Beast Who Walks Like a Man, God of The Eternal Feast. I have existed since the dawn of creation and have been fated to watch over the tapestry of worlds until its abrupt and untimely extinguishing. I exist outside of time and space and I possess a hunger greater than either of those things.

"I shall consume the energies of your existence until I am sated. But, lo, do not fear, for while I am without mercy, I am not without reason. For those of you who wish to bask in glory, submit your bodily flesh to me so that I may inhabit it as a vessel, adding your essence to my own. Though your bones may break, your organs may twist and pop, and your skin be flayed asunder, know that you will be a part of a better cause. One far above your mortal comprehension.

"My acolytes on this world have established themselves as a central pillar in this city. For those of you wise enough to join us, we will welcome you with open arms. For those foolish enough to resist, know there is nowhere you shall be able to hide from the all-seeing eyes of Korthuu. You will be found and you will be dismantled, atom-by-atom, to sate my hunger, while fully conscious. You will beg and scream and attempt to rip your own body to pieces to escape the agony, but no matter how deep you claw your nails into your skin or how successful you disembowel yourself, you will not succeed in relieving yourself from the pain that will last you until the end of this plane's concept of time. For here I will remain forevermore.

"But hear me once again and rejoice, for your individual existence may be at an end. But your purpose is only beginning. I await your decisions, which should be none at all."

\* \* \*

"Okay . . . that did not sound promising," Stephanie said as they steered their commandeered troop trucks around the ruined, disarrayed city streets. Cars were strewn across the roads, either abandoned, upturned, or on fire, which made their progress slow. Furthermore, the throngs of people running and screaming away from the horrifying extra-dimensional monstrosity threatening to flay them alive didn't help either.

"Oh, god. I feel . . . awful," Carrie braced herself on the side of the truck, shaking. Everyone else felt it, too. The overwhelming fear of hopelessness. The terrifying reality of coming to terms with the fact that absolutely nothing you do would matter. That nothing mattered. It was an intense and utterly unavoidable feeling. Kashir threw up into a nearby trashcan.

Michael, however, had not slumped into a pit of despair. While everyone else's knees shook and buckled, he remained standing. Because he knew that feeling all too well. He'd faced it day after day. The crippling realization of his utter insignificance and the unrelenting struggle of meaninglessness were things he ate for breakfast. And as he looked across the road at Stephanie who also remained standing—her worn out green jacket swaying in the apocalyptic breeze—he finally knew what she meant. They were the only two people who could fight this.

Steph met his gaze and nodded with a weak smirk, which he returned.

Summoning an energy he was, frankly, uncomfortable with, Michael clapped, drawing everyone back to attention. "Alright people, sit down and shut up!"

"Don't you tell me to shut up." Calhoun groaned.

"Whatever. Listen. Don't worry. We're gonna get through this."

"But you said it yourself! Korthuu's here," cried the Reptile Lady. "We've already lost. All that's left is to be mutilated alive!"

"No," Steph said. "We haven't already lost. We can't lose if we don't stop fighting. And goddamnit, I'm never going to stop fighting!" She thrust a fist into the air, before bringing it back down to rub her chin. "Unless, of course, I'm being mutilated alive. Then I'd probably have to stop fighting. Y'know. Logistically, it takes a lot out of you."

"You probably could've done without that last part, Steph," Michael said. "But she's right. We can still turn this around."

"Yeah, kid, then what's the plan?" Calhoun snorted.

"Uh . . . um . . ." Michael backpedaled. "Steph?"

"Right, it's all very simple. Mike, Kashir, and I sneak into The Future Group building and take control of whatever weird portal device they've built."

"How're you going even get close enough to the tower?" the Leopard Man said. "There're probably a thousand Korthuu-worshipping monsters guarding the entire compound." His leopard purred in agreement.

"That's where the rest of you come in," Steph continued. "You're our offensive line. Distract 'em. Make some noise and go on the attack."

"But there's only a handful of us!" Octopus Man whined.

"Well, then you're going to have to be smart about it," Michael added. "Don't let Braddock and his men just mow you down."

"Don't worry." Calhoun cocked his gun. "I'll take care of Braddock."

"Alright, everybody got it?" Michael asked.

There were tentative yesses, a few nodding heads and some outright shrugs.

"Good enough!" Steph yelled. "Break!"

The cult of cults filed into the back of Calhoun's truck, Carrie claiming shotgun. Before he took the driver's seat, Calhoun came to have one last face to face with Michael and Stephanie.

"You kids sure you know what you're doing?" he asked.

"Hell, no," Steph said.

"But when has that ever stopped us before?" Michael added with a shrug.

"I'm gonna be honest with you," Calhoun sighed. "This doesn't look like something we can win."

"Then we lose," Stephanie said. "With style."

"Good enough for me," Calhoun smirked—which was honestly kind of creepy—and hoisted himself into the driver's seat of his truck. With a squeal and a groan, they were off in a cloud of dust.

"Hey Mike." Steph turned to him. "Thanks for believing in me."

"Of course, Steph. It has to be us. We gotta do this together."

"Cute." As the dust cleared, Michael saw Maureen, a rifle slung across her back, remained. "Now let's get a move on."

"Maureen, what the hell? You're supposed to go with Calhoun."

"Not on your goddamn life. I came to get revenge for my son, and that's what I'm going to do. Even if I have to claw out every eye on that goddamn monster myself."

"Geeze, lady, chill out," said Kashir.

"Don't test me." Maureen pulled a pistol from nowhere. "Besides, I'm the only one of you bozos who knows the back way into the complex."

"Alright, alright, Maureen." Steph nudged the muzzle away from Kashir's chin. "You can come with us."

"Damn right."

"Okay, guys." Stephanie put her hand forward, inviting a team huddle. "On three, let's go Strike Force Omega!"

Nobody else put their hand in.

"C'mon!"

Michael, along with the rest of the newly christened "Strike Force Omega" just looked at her.

"Alright, fine, whatever." Stephanie sighed. "Let's just go."

# CHAPTER THIRTY

## Cult Classic

The truck's engine roared as Calhoun crested a hill. In the distance, the hulking, corpse-green eyesore that was Korthuu towered over the city, lashing out with their tentacles as they crawled through the skyline. The streets before them were in complete chaos. Cars were upturned and burning, and screaming throngs of people were flooding out of the city.

The truck slammed back down onto the asphalt hard, and Rex hit the brakes, screeching them to a stop in front of a burnt out husk of a pickup truck. The cult leaders in the back were none too happy about being smashed into the back of the truck's cab.

"Ow! Rexy, c'mon!" yelped the Leopard Man, clutching his head.

Calhoun ignored him, turning to McDermott, who had been hanging onto the truck's grab handle for dear life. "Well, we can't go that way."

"No shit," McDermott moved aside the strands of her hair that sweat had matted to her forehead. "What was your plan, anyway?"

"I was gonna wing it. Maybe drive this truck into Future Group Plaza and mow down any goddamn monsters I find. Then I'd probably find Braddock, break off his monster arm and shove it up his ass, then shoot everyone."

"Uh, that doesn't sound realistic."

"You're right," Calhoun said. "I don't have enough ammo."

"That aside, I think we need to approach this from a different angle. We're going up against a literal army of demon cultists. We need an army of our own. Because like it or not, you and I and the couple of crazies in the back are going to get bowled over real quick."

"I've always thought of myself as a one man army." Calhoun patted his gun but quickly realized McDermott was right. "Well, where are we going to get an army?"

"Nobody fights harder than scared people." McDermott jerked her thumb over her shoulder as the river of terrified, unwashed humanity continued to stream past the passenger side window. She then turned around, peering into the truck bed where the Octopus Man was readjusting his headwear and the Leopard Man was trying to remove the creases from his jumpsuit. "And nobody manipulates scared people better than religious leaders peddling a bunch of bullshit."

Calhoun sighed and placed his forehead on the steering wheel. "I really, really hate what my life has become."

McDermott opened the side door and popped out, swinging herself out to the truck bed. Calhoun followed suit on the other side with markedly less enthusiasm.

"Guys," McDermott said, "we need your help."

"Honey, we're coming with you to fight Korthuu," the Leopard man said. His leopard purred softly beneath his hand. "And we're probably going to die trying. What else do you want?"

"Yes, that's true. But look at these people." McDermott indicated the screaming mass of men, women, and children currently rocking the truck in their flight. "They're running scared, unsure of their place in the universe. Don't you think we should help them? Can't we show them that the path to salvation doesn't necessarily involve getting murdered by Korthuu?"

"By jove, she's right!" cried the Freemason. "If The Future Group can grow strong by amassing followers, so can we."

"We shall reveal to them the real truth of the Reptilian Elite!" The Lizard Lady stood up, galvanized. "And they will bow down before us."

"Up yours! These Suckers are mine," shouted the Octopus Man, whose followers were, indeed, called "Suckers."

"Hear me, my friends." The Freemason jumped up on the railing of the truck bed and launched into his sermon. "We see your fearful, poor, terrified masses, yearning to breathe free. And the Freemasons offer you the road to truth. A road that leads against the violence and death of Korthuu. Come join us, and we will take them down together."

This and other calls of proselytization rung out in a cacophony of competing voices from the back of the truck. But the strangest thing was not the oddness of the beliefs espoused. People were actually slowing down and turning around.

"The Reptilian Elite are merely waiting for the right time to shed their skins and strike out at the blasphemous Korthuu. But when they do, be sure that vengeance will be swift and brutal. Give into the truths of your Lizard Brain and secure your place in the Reptilian World Order."

"Yea, come and join us, and we shall defeat Korthuu and The Future Group bastards who raised them. The Cloud Octopus extends his tentacles from on high and will bless every one he touches. And even if we may perish, he will embrace all of us in his many, loving arms. The Cloud Octopus is love and life incarnate. He shall provide us the way forward."

"Hey, uh, why don't you come join the Illuminati. We control everything and will get you a great deal on some energy-efficient LED light bulbs. You could save up to 40% on your next electric bill!"

"No, screw that guy! He slept with my girlfriend!"

Over the next few minutes, the cult of cults amassed a huge throng of followers, eager and willing to help their chosen fake religion in the face of eternal damnation. It was a mass form of deathbed repentance Calhoun just simply could not believe. He lost all respect for every single person that stopped, but McDermott reminded him he did not need to respect them—just tolerate them, for the time being. Fair enough, and Calhoun could put his disdain to good use. He mounted the rear truck and turned to address the crowd.

"Alright, people. We are not going to stand idly by and let The Future Group and their monster take our lives from us! We got the power of, uh . . ." Calhoun looked at the ragtag group of freaks and losers surrounding him. The Leopard Man waved coyly. "The power of stuff on our side!"

A mighty cheer went up from the crowd, along with loud praises of various idiotic gods and lightbulbs.

"Now who's got weapons?" Calhoun asked the important question.

The crowd fell into a quiet murmur.

"Uh . . . I've got a stick!" one guy said.

"All I've got is thirty bucks," said another. "What can you do with thirty bucks?"

"Oh, goddamn it." Calhoun's palm hit his face. "Does nobody have a gun?"

"Guns kill people!" said a woman.

"Yes, I know." Calhoun grinned through his teeth. "That's what we're trying to do here. Except the people we're killing are *monsters* that are trying to kill *you.*"

"Can we not reason with the monsters?" said the same woman.

"You've gotta be shitting me, lady. Did you not hear what the giant hellbeast said? About flaying you alive?"

"I'd feel more comfortable if we tried to reason with them first. So I can feel like I tried to be a good person."

Calhoun turned around. "Which one of yours is she?"

The Octopus Man raised his hand and stepped forward. "The Cloud Octopus can only ensure your place in heaven if you banish the evil followers of Korthuu from this realm. Rest assured, you shall have the moral high ground in this fight."

"Oh, okay, then. I just needed to be sure."

"Fantastic," Calhoun said. "Are we all good here?"

"Yes," droned the crowd.

"Now where can we find some weapons before we all burn in hell?"

"I may be able to help you with that." The Knight Templar stepped forward, her voice an echoed muffle behind her helmet. "My order has a secret underground storage area for our armor and weapons. Since most of my brothers and sisters have been forcibly brainwashed by Korthuu, the equipment is probably all still there."

"Where the hell were you when I was asking for shit two minutes ago?" Calhoun glowered.

"Well, we don't have any guns. We're knights. So we basically have a cache of swords and shields. Plus some . . . other medieval weaponry."

"I've always wanted to be a knight." McDermott beamed.

"Then we shall make it so."

"Well, it's not ideal," Calhoun said, "but we better make do."

"Yea! Did I not say the Cloud Octopus would provide?" shouted the Octopus Man.

"All glory to the cloud octopus!" A large swath of the crowd chanted.

"Hey! They're our weapons!" the Knight protested.

"Yes, but the Cloud Octopus provided you to provide them to us." He smiled sweetly, before leaning closer to the knight. In her armored ear, he whispered, "See? I'm winning."

Even with the helmet, Calhoun could see her fuming.

"Alright, enough of this," he said. "Knight, take us to your stash. Let's see how many people we can arm. If you don't know how to use a sword, figure it out quick, because we're gonna pay The Future Group a little visit."

# CHAPTER THIRTY-ONE

## Tower of Terror

Stephanie, Mike, Maureen, and Kashir made the trek through the city toward the local convention center: a large, squat cylindrical building with stadium-style seating. The marquee sign they saw upon entering read "Psychic Convention Cancelled Due To Unforeseen Circumstances and Scheduling Conflicts." The entire building was deathly quiet, aside from the screams and destruction filtering in from the outside.

Steph's self-proclaimed Strike Force Omega—a name she still very much believed in—stormed their way up the Convention Center's fireproof concrete stairwells, emerging onto the roof.

"Okay." Steph took in a deep breath as the group huddled behind some aluminum vents and took stock of the situation.

The Future Group Tower loomed large, its slick modern surface reflected the darkening blood red clouds in the sky. It was only about a thousand feet away, but that distance seemed impassable, as the plaza around the tower was crawling with hooded cultists and armed, brainwashed prisoners who could turn into demonic monsters at the drop of a hat. Beyond the tower itself, Korthuu's horrifying eldritch form writhed and shifted in the spaces between buildings, gnashing their hundreds of teeth with a sustained low roar and loudly blinking their many eyes.

"Is this as bad as it looks," Mike whispered, "or is it worse?"

"Much worse," Kashir said, peering out from behind the ventilation pipes.

Steph turned to Maureen. "How'd you get in the last time?"

Maureen pointed across the way at an array of small vents marring the closest side of The Future Group tower from bottom to top. Steph noted that one of the vent covers was slightly askew.

"It's kind of warm in there," Maureen said, "but it's the easiest way. It's a big building with a lot of air to move, so we can easily climb through it. But it's still a bit of a tight squeeze. So clench up."

"Okay, all of that sounds real great," Mike squeaked. "But how do we get from *here* to *there*?"

Maureen scoffed and pulled out something Stephanie had been eyeing for quite a while. It was a state-of-the-art gas-powered grappling hook gun with a carbon-fiber arrow tip, an automatic gripping mechanism, and a computerized reel to maximize tension. The current eBay average winning bid for such a gun was around $14,350.

"Is that . . ." Steph could hardly contain her grin. "A Grapplematic GRS-1500?"

"Yup." Maureen patted the side. "With the additional steel cable, it's got a load capacity of a thousand pounds."

"Wow." That put the average bid up to a cool $17,000. Steph was almost drooling. "Can I hold it?"

"No."

"That's all well and good," Mike interrupted, "but we won't be able to use it with all those cultists running around down there."

"Yeah." Maureen grimaced. "That's the rub."

"Well, I hope Calhoun and the . . . uh, good cult leaders have a good distraction up their sleeves, otherwise we're screwed." Kashir pointed out the obvious before a huge explosion rocked the far side of the plaza, drawing everyone's attention.

"Like that?" Stephanie asked.

"That'll do." Maureen's eyes followed the herd of cultists suddenly streaming across the plaza, clearing a path for them. She fired the GRS-1500 with the greatest of ease. Even from this distance, Steph could see the arrow head pierce the vent system. Within a few seconds, the line went taut.

Maureen pulled out a few zip line handles and handed them to each of the participants. "I'll go first and remove the vent covering. I'll twang the line when I'm done. You guys follow."

"This is gonna be so awesome." Steph bounced up and down on her toes.

"Yeah. Real great," Mike said through his teeth.

"You afraid of heights?" Kashir asked.

"Not really. But falling? Definitely."

"This must be a great day for you."

"I've had better."

Kashir nodded and turned to Steph. "So once we're inside, I'm gonna need to get to a networked computer terminal. If it's got admin access, it'll be quicker."

"Mike, can you handle that?" Steph asked.

"Yeah, I, uh, I think I can. There should be several on my floor. If not, we can always use my old computer."

Maureen's line twanged three times.

"Great!" Stephanie hooked her zip line to the cable, and jumped into the open air, "See you guys on the other siiiiiiiiiiiiiidddddeeeee."

She saw Mike blink in astonishment as she flew away. As fun as this was, Stephanie couldn't help but worry that maybe her plan could go belly up and have the unfortunate side effect of them all being damned to a zombie-like living hell for all eternity. Luckily for her, the zip line ride wasn't long enough to sustain her train of thought for very long. She tucked in her legs and rolled safely into the vent where Maureen was ready to greet her.

"Not bad," Maureen grumbled. "You okay?"

"Yeah." Stephanie scooched into a more comfortable position, her back up against the flimsy metal walls. "I think so."

"Is Michael coming?"

"I dunno. He's probably prancing around right now, scared of the zip line."

"I don't know him, but that sounds typical," Maureen said. She donned her knit skull mask with the shiny red and gold lens mounts.

"It is," Steph admitted, then found herself surprised as more truths fell out of her mouth. "I'm actually kinda worried about him."

"Whaddaya mean?"

"I think he's gonna die." Steph felt the words on her tongue for the first time. They left an acrid taste.

"We're all dying, Stephanie."

"Yeah, but I mean much sooner than that. Don't ask me how I know—it's a long, crazy story—but I think when it happens, it might be my fault. This whole detective agency was my idea. I thought it'd help, but I'm just dragging him into danger."

"Kid." Maureen waddled over to Steph as best the vent would allow, and put a hand on her shoulder. "From what I can see, he may be a scaredy cat, but he seems to want in on this now. And it might be good for him to take that leap. You may have started it, but he's an adult and he's made his own decisions. And the best you can do is stick by him and hope things work out. The universe is a crazy place. Sometimes, in all the chaos, things *do* work."

"Thanks." Steph cracked a weary smile. That was what she needed to hear. "But how do you know Mike wants in on this for sure?"

"Well, for one thing," Maureen pointed, "he's zipping over to us pretty fast."

Steph turned around. Maureen was right. Mike, body fully extended, rocketed down the zip line, his eyes screwed shut.

"He better tuck his legs," Maureen said, before yelling, "TUCK YOUR GODDAMN LEGS!"

The yelling caught Mike's attention and his eyes opened just in time to see himself hit the side of the building at incredible speed. His arms and torso flew forward into the open vent, but his legs impacted against the glass and steel, bounding off and flipping him painfully through the metal corridor and onto Steph and Maureen.

The two of them got their bearings as Mike curled into a fetal position, cradling his aching legs.

"You idiot," Maureen growled. "Pay attention next time."

"Sorry," Michael said, tears in his eyes as he rubbed his knees. "Does anyone have my glasses?"

As Steph handed Mike his glasses—which had flown off his face from the impact—Kashir arrived, curling up into a neat little tuck that made his entrance a great deal less painful.

"What's wrong with him?" Kashir pointed to Michael.

"Don't worry about it. Let's go." Maureen beckoned them onwards with a wave of her hand.

The four of them crawled forward on their hands and knees. Maureen led with surprising efficiency, knowledgeable about every twist and turn in the system. It was warm and tight, as Maureen had indicated, and they were all beginning to sweat.

"How much further?" Mike complained.

"Not far. Hold your horses," Maureen called back.

Indeed, it was not much farther. Eventually, they hit the final vent casing, which Maureen turned and kicked out with a blast of her powerful thighs. The cover clattered to the floor. Maureen stuck her head out and craned her neck around. "Looks like all of your Future Group buddies are out playing," she confirmed. "Time to move."

The three of them had entirely less graceful exits than Maureen, but all of them wound up on the hallway floor in one way or another.

"I used to work on Floor 35. Everything I know is there." Mike looked around. The Future Group's hallways were decorated in a calming taupe, which somehow managed to soothe Steph's vibes.

"You don't know the other floors of your office?" Kashir asked.

"Listen, I just kept my head down and walked from my cube to the elevator, okay? It kept me from becoming a zombie, so I think I deserve a little credit."

Stephanie sauntered down the hall and around the corner, looking for any identifying markings. She stumbled upon a set of elevators, with the floor numbers painted in big friendly letters on the wall.

"Floor 20!" her voice echoed back. "That's what the elevator bank says."

"Okay, great. Let's take the elevators up 15 floors and we should be able to find some working computers in the cube farm," Mike started off toward Stephanie, but Maureen's hand on his collar kept him back.

"No elevators. Only stairs."

"What? But it's fifteen floors!"

"If there're any of them still here, they'll see us coming, and we won't see them."

"But I'm tired." Mike cried to himself as Maureen and Kashir walked toward Stephanie and the sadly elevator-adjacent stairwell.

Mike was right. It was a long, irritating trudge, and Steph was sweating more than she had been in the heating vent. Despite her size, Maureen bounded ahead of them, and Steph had to be impressed.

When they reached 35, Maureen, gun at the ready, tentatively breached the door and peeked through, surveying the coast for its clarity. With a nod, she ushered them in. In the corner of her eye, Mike stiffened upon seeing the infuriating sight of his former workplace. Although he now knew it to be a literal soul-sucking cult, Steph could feel the heat of Mike's boiling blood.

"Mike?" Steph tried to snap him out of his angry daydream. "Mike, you okay?"

"Just happy memories." Mike forced the words through his teeth, before proceeding down the first row of cubes, his head on a swivel. "Okay, let's go. There's probably a computer here somewhere we can hack into."

"Uh, I can't hack," Kashir said.

"What?" Mike stopped.

"I can't hack into a computer."

"But you said—" Steph started.

"I know code and financial systems. I'm not a hacker. Not every coder can hack into a computer. This isn't the goddamn Matrix!" Kashir shook off his rage. "Sorry. That just gets me so mad."

"Okay, okay, fine!" Mike said, shutting down the tangent. "Let's see if my computer is still here and I can log in."

Mike navigated through the cube maze by feel alone, Stephanie close behind and the others following him in rapt attention, as if he was leading them to cheese at the end. After a few corners, they approached his depressing cube.

Steph knew it was Mike's because his computer was gone. In its place was what looked like the remains of a fire that had been set on his desk, reducing everything to dark black ash that smelt of noxious, burnt plastic. On one of the walls of his cube which was still relatively taupe, the ashes were used to scrawl the word 'traitor' in dark, angry letters.

"Huh," Steph said over his shoulder, "that's the second desk of yours burned down today."

"You'd think it'd make me mad." Mike shrugged. "But it doesn't, really."

"But where can we find a computer with access to the network?" asked Kashir.

Mike thought for a second, then he had it. "Ravi," he snapped. "That idiot might just be of some use after all."

"Who the hell is that?" Maureen asked as he slipped out and jogged toward Ravi's cubicle.

"He was the guy who was supposed to convince me to become a crazy monster zombie. Also, he was an annoying douchebag." Mike dragged up a chair and moved Ravi's mouse to disengage his computer's screensaver. "You shot him. So, thanks."

Mike grimaced at the "enter password" screen. "I thought he would've left it unlocked."

"You think a death cult company wouldn't have stringent operating procedures, Mike?" Stephanie asked.

"Good point," Mike mumbled, rummaging about Ravi's desk. As he browsed through a few post-its and papers, the rapid pitter patter of gunshots and the roar of a terrifying hell beast kept the ambient soundtrack interesting. His search turned up nothing. "Dammit. He didn't leave anything."

"C'mon, Mikey," Steph pressed. "There's gotta be something."

"Wait a minute." Steph felt a lightbulb click on above Michael's head. Or maybe it was just the fluorescent lighting above flickering on and off due to electrical grid interference from the destruction going on outside. Steph watched over his shoulder as Mike typed in something he would never say aloud—the word "Mikester"—and hit enter. A dull login tone sounded.

"Success!" Mike threw his fists up in the air.

"Atta boy!" Steph beamed. Maybe Maureen had been right. Steph didn't need to worry about Mike. He could be a bit of an abrasive stick-in-the-mud sometimes and a bit of a panicky mess in others, but he was dependable. That's what she valued most about him. Steph hadn't realized it before, but she had never trusted someone as much since her brother disappeared. And she needed to make sure Mike could trust her. If they got out of this alive—no matter what her weird alternate-future-history dictated—Steph needed to back off and let Mike live his life, rather than try to control his every move and fix the outcome. Besides, when she put it that way, it sounded kind of manipulative.

A thunderous crash drew her attention as the ceiling on the far side of the floor collapsed in on itself. The lights that had before just flickered, immediately went dark, leaving only the natural light from the floors' far away windows—the dark red and purple of a nice evening's Armageddon—to keep the floor lit.

"What the . . ." Steph shielded her eyes from the dust and debris. Through the falling flaky mist and darkness, she could see the emerging form of humanoid body skittering across the floor on what looked like twenty spear-tipped insect-like feet.

"Hello, Michael." Craig Breene's voice slithered through the darkness.

"Oh, great," Michael said. "It's you."

"Craig." Maureen stood up straight, her goggles focused directly on Mike's ex-boss. There was a certain intensity Steph felt radiating from her, something she hadn't felt since they fought Craig in the underground rotunda.

"Yeah, hey Craig. Nice to see you again." Steph knelt by Kashir, who was still at Ravi's computer. She whispered, "Is the computer still working? Can you do the thing?"

Kashir hit the side of the monitor and it powered on. "Yeah, looks like it, but I don't know how much juice it has left."

"The computer systems in this building are the one thing they couldn't have fail," Maureen said. "It'll run till the whole world burns."

"Which could be real soon." Mike said. "Do your thing. We'll distract him." Mike cupped his hands over his mouth. "Nice legs, you dumb friggin' nerd!"

"Silence!" Craig's voice echoed throughout the floor, as if he had broadcast over the PA system. It was impossible to tell where he was exactly. "You shall all pay for your insolence in the face of Korthuu's glorious enlightenment. For it is Korthuu that gives me strength."

"How about you take your enlightenment and stick it where the sun don't enlighten?" Mike shouted, as if his words would have been dampened by the dark.

Steph watched as Mike's eyes darted around the ever-darkening floor, scanning for the signs of his former boss who had been turned into some sort of horrifying giant bug. Mike didn't waver. He stood hard and fast, ready to take on whatever was going to leap out of the darkness. She knew he could handle this on his own. Besides, Steph had some questions she wanted answered, and she needed to get them alone.

"Mike, this is your boss. Your fight." Steph sucked a breath through her teeth. "I need to go. There're some things I need to take care of. I can't tell you exactly what, but I need you to trust me."

"What?" Mike whisper-yelled. "You can't leave! We have to do this together."

"Don't worry. You can take him." Steph put a hand on Michael's shoulder. "I believe in you. You're better than you give yourself credit for. And I need you to believe in me."

Mike nodded. "Thanks, Steph."

Stephanie could have left it at that, but she couldn't help throw in another jab. "Besides, Maureen's here. If you get your ass kicked, I'm sure she can take him down instead."

"Great. Thanks." Mike smirked. "Fine, go. But if we survive this, we meet downstairs after it's over and go get drinks. You're going to owe me an explanation."

"That's a deal, buddy." After they shook on it, a gleam entered Stephanie's eye and she started to crawl back toward the stairwell. She wasn't going to stand idly by while Mike had all the fun. Besides, if she was definitely going to end up doubling-down on their detective agency— per the recommendation of her alternate universe self—she would be an idiot if she didn't pump the source of information looming over all of them. A source that could have answers about what was coming for Mike.

"Wait." Mike called out to her, his voice a hushed whisper. "Can you just tell me where you're going?"

"Oh me?" Stephanie smiled sweetly. "I'm going to pick a fight with an ancient monster god."

# CHAPTER THIRTY-TWO

## Plaza of Panic

The bombards had already fired off a flaming salvo of stone projectiles that crashed into the ground in front of One Future Plaza. They managed to take out a good chunk of cultist troops, many of which were still disembarking from their troop trucks. The subsequent explosion rocked everyone and everything in a five block radius. A wall of fiery twisted metal lay before the entrance steps to the plaza. Rex Calhoun gambled on the element of surprise, and it worked perfectly.

"Charge!" He roared from atop the white horse that the Knight Templar had wanted to claim for herself. Clanking his sword against his shield, he galvanized his light brigade to engage The Future Group on their home turf.

He couldn't see well out of his peripheries—nor could he move very well in the knight armor—but Calhoun heard the army of newly recruited citizens and their recently adopted cult leaders cheer as they leapt into the fray.

The Future Group certainly had numbers on them and they were certainly better armed, but they was not prepared for the guerilla warfare Calhoun's group deployed. Nor were they prepared for an assault by a standing army in fifteenth-century-style armor. Knights leapt out of buildings and from behind burnt out cars, striking hard and fast with swords, crossbows, maces, flails, and anything else the Knights Templar had hiding in their basement.

Calhoun didn't much care for all the crosses on their shields and armor, but he had to note it was having a pretty good effect on The Future Group goons, who seemed weakened by anything holy that challenged their god. The shields worked best at long range, but rapidly fell apart as they were struck by The Future Groups firepower and, well, monster power.

Speaking of which, their god, the multi-eyed, multi-armed monstrosity Korthuu, was causing their fair share of destruction downtown, trashing buildings and swallowing up fleeing citizens to add to their own gross mass. Calhoun grimaced and, with one hand, tugged on his horse's reins, switching his focus from the assault on The Future Group complex to Korthuu's hundreds of insect-like feet.

His horse burst forward, its hooves clopping quickly against the asphalt. Calhoun outstretched his sword and lopped off the heads and limbs of any deranged Future Group Cultist that got in his way. Some of the more equipped cultists had military rifles, whose bullets pinged against his armor at a distance, but luckily, never made it through.

As he got closer, Calhoun became increasingly aware of Korthuu's size. Sure, he knew the monster was big, but getting up close and personal with them gave him a whole new, unfortunate appreciation for their disgusting mass. He wondered for a second if he had been wrong to break away from his army to take on the monster itself. Calhoun had never been part of a war before, although he sometimes acted like he had. But this was a war for more than just the city—it was a war for his goddamn pride. And if he was going to go out, it was going to be in a goddamned, ridiculous blaze of—

Something enormous impacted his armor, not only knocking the wind out of him but knocking him clean off his horse. He clanked to the ground, bouncing twice before rolling to a halt on his back. Calhoun tasted metal—and it wasn't his armor. Blood was seeping out of his nose and trickling into his mouth, which also had its own share of blood to add to the party.

As the spots around his eyes cleared, he felt something long and spindly curl around his armor's visor, lifting it up and letting the full force of the ambient light singe his retinas. The flying spots slowly resolved into the grinning face of Captain Leslie Braddock.

"Braddock," Calhoun gasped. "You son of a bitch."

"Hello, Detective."

Calhoun found Braddock's smile unnerving. It distorted his cheeks, allowing his teeth to push out the very edges of his face. Calhoun then noticed there was nothing beneath Braddock's head, except for a thin purplish neck elongated to its very limits.

Calhoun gasped and did his best to sit up as Braddock's neck reeled back into his body some 30 feet away, hidden beneath one of those stupid black and red hooded robes draped over his otherwise reasonable attire. There he stood, arms akimbo, surveying the carnage with unadulterated glee. Beside him was Lieutenant Lin, in his taut gray suit, unmarred by the carnage around them. Crisp and clean cut as ever, his gun was aimed squarely at Calhoun's head.

Calhoun lowered his sword and looked around. "Where's Brook? I thought he was one of you guys."

"Brook?" Lin raised a stiff eyebrow. "No, he was an idiot."

"We killed him," Braddock said. "He was unworthy of Korthuu's light."

"Well, I can't really argue with that, so maybe take this as a thank you!" Calhoun lobbed his sword at them. It flew through the air straight and true, impaling Lieutenant Lin in the chest. His stoic façade was broken by a look of utter shock, and his face and body began to contort and twist as he fell forward, driving the sword deeper into his chest. Lin died writhing in pain, a deformed lump on the city streets.

Calhoun could barely hear himself yelling, but he was. And he found himself on his feet, running top speed at Braddock. He was inches from tackling the man when Braddock merely stepped aside and watched Calhoun fly past, stumbling to the ground under the weight of his armor once again. His helmet flew off, clattering to the ground and rolling away from him. Calhoun looked back up, but already Braddock—with superhuman reflexes—grabbed him by his arm and flung him back toward the main battle, toward the maddening crowd.

The sea of people opened up for him and, again, Calhoun crashed to the floor, this time on his shoulder, which he knew was going to hurt for weeks. He looked around for Lin's body and the sword it contained, in order to take the fight back to Braddock. When he finally found it, the sword was in Braddock's hands, leveled at his nose.

Calhoun raised his arms in the air reluctantly, with the one he'd landed on sending sharp pains across his side. The fact he was going to die with a busted arm angered him almost as much as Braddock being the one doing him in.

"Go ahead, Braddock," he said through gritted teeth. "Kill me."

"It's over, Detective Calhoun. But, no, I'm not going to kill you." Braddock tossed away the sword and smiled, his canines longer than Calhoun had remembered. In fact, his whole body was elongating, his clothes ripping and tearing to reveal mottled, rotting skin with an unnatural number of eyes and an even more unnatural number of spiky, serrated barbs. "I am going to consume you, adding your spirit to Korthuu's pan-universal glow. You should be honored. Korthuu is love. Korthuu is life. Korthuu is the essence of life and death."

"I oughta kick your essence."

"Charming, Rex, as always." Braddock's voice shifted into a disjointed garble that sounded quite like he was speaking through an old dial-up modem. "But the reign of our lord has just begun, and you will be one with them." His form grew increasingly more grotesque, until the only recognizable part of Braddock remaining was his handlebar moustache, now sitting atop a dozen mouths.

Calhoun grimaced. "You look friggin' ridiculous."

Braddock, now far beyond anything human, let out a disjointed screech that sounded like a velociraptor mating with a pig already in the process of mating with a vulture. The monster-Braddock reared its long neck back, its spines bristling, readying to strike its killing blow. In all his years on the police force, this wasn't exactly how he'd pictured going out. Not by a long shot.

It turned out he was right.

A deep, baritone grunting arrived, like a saw ripping through a tough piece of wood filled the air, just before the leopard burst into the open, knocking opposing cultists to the ground. Its thick, serrated teeth gouged into Braddock's neck, tearing out a chunk of protoplasmic flesh.

Braddock shrieked in pain and reeled back.

"Eat hot lead, assface!" Carrie McDermott, dressed like Joan of Arc, and the Leopard Man—his furry coat flowing out behind him—rushed out of the crowd, both astride Calhoun's runaway horse. The horse reared back with a loud whinny as McDermott brandished a weapon as big as her torso. She fired hot bolts of metal that punched holes through Braddock's monstrous body, silencing his wail and leaving him with entry and exit wounds Calhoun could see clear through.

"Where the hell did you get that?" Calhoun cried.

"I swiped it off a dead guy." McDermott leaned the large gun over her shoulder. "These guns got some nice firepower."

"Christ, kid." Calhoun pushed himself to his feet with his good arm. "You're kind of scary."

"I toldja to pull back a bit, girl," the Leopard Man said, holding the reins.

"You love it," McDermott smiled, before reloading her gun and firing another round into an approaching cultist monster. It sent them flying back 200 feet, impaling another cultist.

"Yeah, alright." Calhoun struggled to his feet. "Thanks for saving my skin."

"Day's not over yet, Rex. We've got a city to save." Another three shots, another eight dead cultists. Calhoun was honestly impressed.

Supporting his back with his armored gauntlet, Calhoun hobbled over and attempted to shoo the Leopard Man off his horse but was met with a stern rebuff.

"Nuh-uh, honey," the Leopard Man said. "Finders keepers. Now if you'll excuse me, I've got some bitches to slay."

McDermott leapt down from the horse. The Leopard Man dashed away into the orgy of spewing blood and gnashing teeth, his leopard bounding close behind.

Calhoun glanced at McDermott and sighed. "Y'know, I was really hoping to be the one to take out Braddock."

"Yeah, well"—she smiled—"get over it."

# CHAPTER THIRTY-THREE

## At The Mouths of Madness

"Hey!" The wind whipped at Stephanie's hair, tousling it beyond its usual messiness. Her brother's jacket flapped violently behind her as she clung fast to the railing of The Future Group Tower's top most maintenance deck. She cupped her hands around her mouth and tried again. "Hey! Hey, you!"

Hundreds of feet away, towering over everything in sight, the hulking mass that was Korthuu—The Beast Who Walks Like a Man, God of The Eternal Feast—began to pivot. Their eyes blinked in unnatural succession, and the various mouths lining their head—separated only by a thin film of rotting flesh—gnashed violently.

"Yeah, I'm talking to you, you fat piece of shit!" Stephanie yelled. "Where do you think you're going? I've got some words for your dumb ass!"

That last bit did it. Korthuu let out a screeching inhuman roar that pierced the blood red sky and sent chills through Stephanie's heart. Nevertheless, she held her ground as the writhing, lumbering beast turned and stomped their way toward her.

"Well, here we go, I guess," Steph muttered to herself before she came face-to—well, "face" wasn't accurate—face-to-grotesque with Korthuu. Their wet eyes, though all black, somehow focused on her small form.

"Hello there," Steph said.

Abject terror washed over her. Her skin grew cold and clammy, exacerbated by the tower's high winds. Conversely, her blood rumbled within her veins, as if it were boiling. Before her eyes swam a cavalcade of alien shapes, filling her with a roiling sense of discomfort that turned her stomach. Through all of it, Stephanie Dyer felt Korthuu's intent toward her.

"I am Korthuu! The Beast Who Walks Like a Man, God of The Eternal Feast! I am your savior. I will bring fire and blood and chaos to this realm and you will love me for it. And you dare stand against me, you small, insignificant, mammal? Who do you think you are?"

As Stephanie's body chemistry returned to normal, she shook her head and tried to collect herself, gulping down breaths of air as if she had been suffocating. Bracing herself again against the banister, she pulled herself back up to her feet, which she planted firmly on the ground.

"I'm Stephanie Dyer, you son of a bitch."

Korthuu blinked, but Stephanie continued staring right at them, her grip tightening on the railing. There was a long pause, as if she had caught them in thought. After a few moments, the unbearable sensation of Korthuu's mind-speech almost sent Stephanie to her knees.

"That name means nothing to me. You are nothing but another in a long line of defiant specks who will be consumed in my Eternal Feast."

When Stephanie regained her composure, she forced a smile.

Blood dripped from her nose and ran over her lips. "What if we make a deal?"

Stephanie again felt the sensation of Korthuu's speech wash over her, but this time in distinct, almost uncertain, spurts.

"You are in no position to bargain, small mammal. I've consumed hundreds of universes with inhabitants much stronger than your pitiful race. What do you have to offer me?"

Steph refused to let her knees buckle this time. She swallowed again, her saliva tinged with a coppery taste and her vision beginning to blur. "I'm the only one who knows your secret."

"What? How dare—"

"No, you've done enough talking. Or whatever the hell it is you're doing. It's time for you to listen to *me*, chuckles. I've got your number." Steph swallowed her blood, the acrid taste stinging on its way down. "You're not here to consume our universe. For your 'eternal feast.' If you were, you'd've done it by now. We'd all be atomized. Instead, you're just stomping around making a big old mess, while your Future Groupies—hey that's a good one, I should write that down—while your Future Groupies try to brainwash everyone in the world. You keep complaining about how hangry you are, but it doesn't look like you're trying to eat a goddamn thing. Now, why is that?"

There was no response from Korthuu. Stephanie could have sworn she saw a sweat droplet dripping down their face-equivalent, but that may have just been spots swimming before her eyes.

"Yeah. Don't answer. I already know. You're looking to lay low. Find a nice universe to hide in. Maybe control the populace to ease the transition. Slip in, pass a few hundred millennia and then be on your way.

"Because you're running from something else. Something that even you can't control. And that terrifies you."

Another interminable pause followed before Korthuu's words rumbled through every fiber of Stephanie's being. "You know of it. The destroyer of universes. Universes I use for sustenance. A being driven by fear and hate. It is unyielding in its hatred and will not sate its own hunger until every universe pays its penance. Every universe he visits dies and he leaves only husks in his wake. The Black King, the ender of all things."

"I've heard rumors." Steph swished her hand in the air. This was exactly what she was looking for. Now, thanks to Korthuu, she was getting close to finding out what this thing was. Know thine enemy, right? "Black King, huh? Sounds sexy."

Korthuu's chest—or central mass—puffed, and Stephanie could feel their anger boil her blood and sear her veins. "The Black King caught me unawares. But I am more powerful than him. I will destroy him and feast upon his bones!"

"Then why are you running?"

"What?" Korthuu's follow-up left less of an impression on Steph's body and mind. It was uncertain. Almost timid. "No. I'm not running."

"Yeah you are. You're afraid of not being strong enough to face it. Take it from me. I feel like that every day."

Another pause, but this one felt altogether more sinister. The high winds whipped around her and Stephanie had to stop herself from shivering.

"You, too, are scared." The mouth of Korthuu closest to her broke out into an eerily wide grin. "I can see into your heart and mind. You are scared. For yourself and your . . . friend. Michael Duckett."

"You leave Mike out of this!" Steph snarled.

"Bad things are following you, as much as things can follow in non-sequential time and space. The Black King seeks . . . you!"

"Yeah, well, bring him on."

"You have no chance. Your kind think I am a monster, but compared to it, I am mercy. You will fare poorly."

"Pfft. Poorly is how I do everything. But I suppose now you know he's after us, you've gotta leave this place."

"Oh, no." Korthuu's smile grew wider. "Not at all. If I consume your essences, they will be masked by my signature. He will avoid this universe and I will be safe."

This conversation was going south quick. Steph was hoping to out-maneuver Korthuu, but all she did was convince them to consume her and Michael. "No way, bozo. We'll never join your creepy little club."

"But you haven't heard *my* deal yet. I am Korthuu. I can give you every single thing your little heart desires. If your consciousness joins with mine willingly, I could give you your parents back. Your . . . brother back."

"Wh . . . what? How did you—"

"Ah, yes, my child. Korthuu knows more than you realize. I can peer into your mind and see your darkest parts of your soul. The loss of your family is a deep sucking wound that punctures through the shell you keep around you. Give yourself and Michael to me. He is nothing to you. He does not believe in or care for you. I will provide you your own pocket consciousness where you can find your true family. One who will be there for you." As Korthuu "spoke" into her feelings, Steph-anie watched as nubs began to sprout from holes in their tattered green skin. "You can exist there forever. It will be as perfect a reality as you wish for it to be."

"You . . . you can do that?"

"I can do whatever I wish." The nubs extended into gracefully dancing arms with elongated fingers that waggled toward her. "If you accept me as others have. We will be stronger. Stronger together."

"I can have my brother back?" Tears welled up in her eyes. She backed away, her exterior self pushing against the obvious horror. But what truly scared her was that a part of herself, deep inside, wanted nothing more than to go to Korthuu.

"Yes, child. Once I absorb you and Michael Duckett, all trace of you shall be eliminated from this universe, and I shall be safe to remain in this reality forever. And you shall receive everything in return."

The spindly arms and their many hands inched toward Stephanie's ears and mouth, and she stood uncertain of what would come next, but she was now certain about what she had to do. Whether it was Korthuu influencing her or her own broken inner self, she could not say.

Stephanie sniffled up her tears and took a big gulp. "Do it."

Korthuu's gangly fingers quivered with what could only be described as glee as they plunged themselves into her ears and mouth, wriggling into the crevices of her skull and the folds of her brain. Stephanie could feel her head surge with energy before her eyes rolled over.

Everything went black.

# CHAPTER THIRTY-FOUR

## Boss Fight

"Michael . . . Michael . . ." Craig Breene's garbled voice lilted, echoing across the office floor. "Where are you? I just want to talk."

Michael preferred that they didn't. He barely wanted to lay eyes on whatever horrifying monster Craig had turned himself into. But he did wonder how much was Craig and how much was Korthuu. In the meantime, he and Maureen darted from cubicle to cubicle under cover of darkness in order to keep Craig distracted from the real work Kashir was doing at Ravi's old desk.

"How long can we keep doing this?" he whispered to Maureen, who was cradling her gun in her lap.

"As long as we need, to get him either pinned down in a space that gives us the advantage or . . ."

"Or . . . ?"

"Until he kills us," she said, all too flatly.

"Can I at least get a gun?" Michael pointed to one of the myriad holsters Maureen had on her person.

"No!" She slapped his hand away. "We're not going to kill him."

"What? Why not?"

"There's something . . . inside of him that I want."

"What the hell does that mean?" As Michael said it, the explanation crystalized in his brain and his jaw dropped. "Craig Breene is your *son?*"

Maureen quietly elbowed him in the sternum.

"Oof!"

"Not so loud!" Maureen turned away and removed her mask. "He . . . used to be. Korthuu got to him and stripped everything I ever knew about him out. He's nothing but an evil, monstrous shell now. He doesn't even remember who I am."

Michael placed a hand on the shoulder of the assassin. "I'm sorry."

"Don't be." Maureen sniffed up a stray tear and shifted gears back to business. "Maybe you're right. We should kill him. Better dead than whatever that is. Here." Maureen thrust her set of red lensed night-vision goggles at him. "Put these on and pop your head up over the wall. Maybe we can find out where exactly he is."

"Okay." Michael let out a breath and slipped the goggles over his eyes, throwing everything around him into a beautiful tapestry of bright white and green hues, depending on the immediate lighting conditions. "Here goes nothing." Michael pushed himself up and grabbed the edge of the cubicle desk, pulling himself up into a half-crouch that still put him below the lip of the cubicle wall. He inched himself upward until his eye-line cleared the wall, revealing the entire floor in sharp, glowing relief.

To his far left, Ravi's computer glowed. It gave him a slight bit of comfort to know Kashir was still working. Slowly, he pivoted around, taking stock of the empty rows of cubicles stretching far and wide across the floor. The coast seemed clear until a giant pixelated blob covered his line of slight so suddenly it nearly blinded him.

"Agh!" He threw off the glasses. The terrifying sight of Craig's toothy smile greeted him, flanked by two insectoid mandibles, clicking and clacking in pleasure.

"Hello." Craig hissed as his head reared back on a caterpillar-like neck that illuminated itself and the surrounding area with rows of yellow and red bioluminescent pods. The pods ran from his head down to his torso, which was now a bulbous barrel-shaped structure sprouting multi-segmented legs with blade-like pointed ends.

"Craig!" Maureen shouted, drawing his attention as she brought up her gun and aimed for the head.

Craig's neck bobbed and weaved with incredible speed, avoiding each successive bullet. When Maureen's gun clicked empty, he roared and struck at Maureen with one of his scythe feet, goring her above her left shoulder—where she had been shot earlier. Maureen cried out in anguish as Craig raised his segmented leg—Maureen still impaled on the front—and whipped it back. A wet rip cascaded through the air as Maureen's flesh tore. Her body arced across ten rows of cubicles, trailing blood, before finally coming to rest somewhere by the eastern window. If Craig Breene had been her son, there was very little left of him.

Michael could barely comprehend what was going on because, on top of nearly being blinded by Craig's overload of the night-vision goggles, his ears were now constantly ringing from the close range discharge of a gun.

Things were simply not going his way. So, Michael did exactly what he always did when things were not going his way: he got up and ran. Trying to dig his newfound tinnitus out of his ears with his finger, Michael dashed through the cubicle maze, only occasionally squinting back to see that, yes, Craig's monstrous form was skittering after him, whipping his neck back and forth and destroying the cube farm one fabric covered metal frame at a time.

"Come back, Michael! There's still time to join us!" His voice carried a taunting lilt with a suspicious tinge of sincerity. "Your world's time is over. There is only Korthuu!"

"Korthuu can go to hell!" Michael screamed, half-out of fear and half out of trying to overshadow the ringing in his ears.

"Michael, Korthuu can make you as strong and powerful as you've always wanted to be! Just look what they did to me! We are one!"

"Yeah, look what he did to you. You look like H.P. Lovecraft took a shit and died." Michael ran past a cubicle and grabbed a loose keyboard, arming himself.

"You were never a team player, Michael. Being together makes us strong. Makes Korthuu strong. You're soon going to learn that, whether you like it or not. We'll be working together to make this universe into a sanctuary. We're stronger together."

"Strong enough for this?" Michael planted his feet and spun around, smashing the heavy mechanical keyboard into Craig's face as it rushed toward him.

Craig reared back once again to his full height, dwarfing Michael by at least seven feet. Craig's face was battered and bleeding, with one of his insect-jaws dangling off by a thread of flesh. But just as soon as Michael finished taking stock, Craig's face rearranged and healed itself, sealing up his cuts, reattaching the broken jaw, and popping out any loose keyboard keys embedded in his skin.

"I am more than strong enough, Michael," he hissed, but by the time his clouded-over eyes reformed into their normal deep-black pools, Michael had clambered over the cubicle wall and out of Craig's sight.

Crawling across the floor under cover of darkness, Michael slipped into another abandoned cubicle five rows away and bit his lip to stop him from crying out. He was hyperventilating, though. That he could not stop, no matter how hard he tried. Maureen was down, Stephanie was doing god knows what, and Craig could probably sniff him out, even now. His fingers dug into the carpet and would not let go. He didn't know what to do. He was going to die. Kashir would be next, and everything would be lost. Michael knew, in his heart, it was hopeless. He had ruined everything, once again.

Then he saw the phone.

\* \* \*

"Come out, Michael!" Craig yelled. "If you join us, we can make it painless!" His neck whooshed back and forth through the air, searching for his quarry. "I personally enjoy the pain, but to each their own. But if you resist our offer, you will never be more than the weak shell you are now. Didn't you always want to be part of something bigger than yourself? Help us remake the world, Michael. What could you do yourself that could possibly be better than that! You're not even strong enough to help your friend Stephanie."

Although Craig had expected a response from his goading, he was met with silence. An angry growl began to form inside his throats, before rising into his gullet. But before he could bellow, a trilling three-toned ring broke through the air. The source of the sound was five cubicle rows away, and Craig rushed over there, skittering across the floor and haphazardly over cubicle walls. By the time he reached the cubicle, his multiple kaleidoscopic eyes detected nothing except the faint green blinking of the phone system's auto-answer indicator.

"I'm more than strong enough to help Steph," Michael's tinny voice vibrated out of the phone's external speaker. "Hell, look at how well I'm distracting you."

Craig's head rotated all the way around his neck. On the far side of the office near the large painting that hung near the end of the cubicle farm, he saw a small figure waving.

Michael.

The roar Craig had held in finally burst forth as he turned, destroyed the phone taunting him, and leapt into the central aisle, bounding toward the last cubicle. When he slid to a stop, his blade-like claws gouging holes in the carpeting, he found yet another empty cubicle. The phone let out another three toned ring, and the auto-answer picked up.

"And besides," Michael's voice said, carrying throughout the floor, "there's a lot of things Steph can't handle, and I'm willing to help her confront those. But she's more than capable, too."

Another ring on the opposite side of the cube farm. Craig leapt toward it, but the auto-answer had already kicked in.

"In fact," Michael's voice said, "I'm sure she's kicking Korthuu's ass right now."

Another ring.

"Or is it your ass?"

Then another.

"Do you guys share an ass, too? That'd be weird."

Then another.

"How do you poop?"

Then another.

Then another.

Then another.

Soon the whole floor's cubicle phones were ringing. The auto-answer clicked in for an office-wide conference call.

"Between me and Steph"—Michael's voice roared across the floor in a trembling cascade of echoing—"you idiots have no chance!"

Michael's last word cascaded up and down each aisle, and when silence finally hit, an immense wave of audio feedback screeched through the air, leaving Craig's several auditory orifices ringing. He attempted to cover them up, but his legs were too long and spindly, with no flat surfaces to help.

Craig sucked in a lungful of air, circulated it throughout his system, and let out a tremendous bellow that shook the floor, destroying all the open telephones, and sending more ceiling debris crashing down.

When the dust settled, only one sound remained: that of a hanging dial-tone. It emanated from the handset Michael Duckett currently held to his face, five rows away. Craig snarled and crashed through the cubicles with little regard for the damage he was doing. Michael, true to form, was frozen in fear right where he stood. Craig could also see a thin, dark-skinned human cloistered behind him at the computer. This child was of little concern, as Craig would certainly consume him after he had dealt with Michael.

"You insolent little shit." He forced the words through teeth he had forced into angry serrated points. "You think you and your pitiful friends can out-think the natural balancing force of existence? Well you've already lost. Your stupid friend Stephanie Dyer is upstairs and has surrendered herself to Korthuu right now. You've failed."

\* \* \*

"Wh-what?" Michael filled with fear and uncertainty. This time not just for himself, but for Stephanie as well. Could Craig be telling the truth?

"Korthuu has made her an offer she simply couldn't refuse," Craig snarled. "Something you couldn't provide for her. And now she's ours."

"No, that can't be true. How could you possibly know?" Michael fought back tears of anger.

"I am Korthuu and he is me. He supersedes every little bit of the weak, worthless husk I was before his glory. I know everything that is going on at the top of this tower. Your friend is lost to you, and it is your turn to join us now." Craig's jaw unhinged from his skull and extended, revealing several rows of incredibly sharp teeth and pools of acidic saliva. Slowly, he advanced on Michael and Kashir, who had started screaming in tandem.

Suddenly a friendly ding sounded through the computer's speakers. Craig stopped in his tracks.

"Oh, sorry," Kashir said, turning back to the computer. "That's for me."

Kashir scrolled through his e-mail and read the latest message. Michael and Craig stood around dumbfounded.

"We did it! The transaction went through!" Kashir held up his hand for a high-five that never came.

"Transaction?" Michael asked. "What are you talking about?"

"Hold on, lemme just send one company-wide e-mail and . . ." Kashir typed up something real quick and hit send. "Okay. We're good. Steph and I bought all the shares in The Future Group that used to belong to any dead cultists."

Michael furrowed his brow and shook his head.

"Well, The Future Group—Craig—personally orchestrates buybacks of any free floating stock. But since he's a little busy right now, we nabbed it. Turns out Ravi Patel alone had huge amounts of stock, enough to give us a fifty-one percent stake."

"Huh. I guess he must've really believed in the company." Michael shrugged. "At least he was good for something. But that must've cost millions of dollars."

"Once Korthuu started wrecking up the place, share prices dropped pretty fast. Then I just sent an email firing everyone and demanding that they return their cumulative bonuses, since the company's gone under. Losing that kinda cash would shock anyone out of their brainwashing."

The half-centipede half-scorpion that was Craig Breene cleared its throats, bringing Michael and Kashir's attention back to the more important issue of the day. "Whatever action you've taken is just a meaningless gesture. And now you'll pay for it."

Craig raised his steely, pointed feet and struck out at Michael and

Kashir—but was stopped in his tracks by Maureen, who kept him at bay with her bare hands.

"Craig, sweetie." She struggled. "I don't know if you're still in there after all this time, but I'm sorry. I love you."

A small blinking object appeared in her hand and she shoved it into Craig's gaping maw.

"Run!" Maureen grabbed Michael's hand and dragged him toward the elevator bank toward safety. Kashir also did as he was told and vaulted over the desk and into the center aisle, dashing away as Craig exploded, incinerating the immediate area. Whatever smoky chunks of bone and flesh were left of him fell through the hole in the floor the grenade created, dropping through every subsequent level of The Future Group Tower.

When the dust settled, Michael, against his better judgement, crept over to the gaping hole and stared down it.

"Thanks, in advance! How about that?" he yelled, before turning back to Maureen and Kashir, who were shaking their heads.

"That was my son," Maureen said.

"Sorry." Michael hung his head. "It's just that Steph would've appreciated a badass line—" A sudden realization stopped Michael from running his mouth. "Steph! She's in trouble. She's upstairs with the rest of Korthuu. We gotta go get her!"

"Alright," Maureen grumbled. "Let's go."

"But she's thirty stories up!" Kashir said. "We can't climb that many stairs in time."

"We don't have to." Maureen pointed at them. "Kashir, get back down to the ground. See if Steph's plan worked, and if Calhoun needs any more support. Michael, you come with me."

"Where're we going?" he asked.

"Out the window." Maureen retrieved her grappling hook from its holster. "You'd better hold on."

# CHAPTER THIRTY-FIVE

## Cashing Out

"Hold the line!" Calhoun screamed as another wave of Future Group monsters advanced on their position. Despite their initial push, the cultists had regrouped and mutated into more powerful and terrifying forms that forced them back with the aid of whipping tentacles and gnashing, slobbering, disembodied jaws. The only thing holding them at bay were the few rifles Calhoun and the rest of his army had managed to swipe off of the dead cultists. The medieval armor just wasn't cutting it anymore. Even the Leopard Man and what had arguably been Calhoun's horse were retreating.

"This is madness," the Lizard Lady yelled as she, Calhoun, and McDermott took refuge behind a car upended on its side. "Where are the reinforcements from the Reptilian Elite? They should be here by now!"

"Maybe they're not here because they don't exist!" the Octopus

Man screamed from across the way, his hands cupped over his mouth.

"Shut up!" the lady yelled back. "I don't see any Cloud Octopus coming to help us, either!"

"Screw you!"

"Alright, alright!" McDermott interjected, as several of their allies gave them cover with some suppressing fire. "We just gotta hold out for a little while longer."

"How much longer can we wait, McDermott? We're getting killed out here." Calhoun grumbled, removing his armor plating which had been dented beyond recognition. Each piece of it clanked to the ground in defeat.

"We need to wait for Steph and Kashir's plan to kick in."

"Listen, kid, I wouldn't put all my faith in that girl or that skinny Indian kid." Calhoun reloaded a surplus rifle he had strapped to his back and fired blindly over the top of the car until it clicked empty. "We don't even know what the plan is."

"I do," McDermott whispered. "Steph whispered it to me on the way here."

"You?" the Lizard Lady asked. "Why you?"

"She said she thought I was cute."

Calhoun rolled his eyes.

"I *am* cute," McDermott said in an admittedly cute huff.

"Are you the same girl that blasted Braddock dead in the head with some sort of hand cannon?" Calhoun asked.

"I can be two things. Besides—"

McDermott had no time to finish, as the husk of a car they were hiding behind hurtled into the air. Behind it stood an enraged hulking mass of writing tentacles and exposed muscle that just happened to sport a handlebar moustache on a battered, bleeding face.

"Not quite dead, I'm afraid," the thing roared.

"Braddock!" Calhoun growled before turning back to his now exposed army. "Fall back!"

"No!" Braddock's tentacles formed into a muscly claw, grabbed Calhoun with its pincers, and raised him up by his collar until he dangled ten feet in the air. "Not this time."

"RRAGH!" The Knight Templar leapt out from her position in a side alley and charged at the thing formerly known as Braddock. Her longsword clashed against an onslaught of thin, dexterous arms that shot out of Braddock's back. The knight managed to keep them at bay, slicing off hands and forearms wherever she could gain purchase. Inching past his defenses with every slash, the knight was soon within striking distance of the monster's chest, but before she could raise her sword, another of Braddock's arms lashed out and wrapped its spindly hand around her neck and twisted it with a sickening crack. The suit of armor fell limp, and parts of it shed themselves, crashing to the ground, followed by the whole of the Knight's corpse.

Calhoun could barely utter a sound. He could do nothing except watch and struggle. The same could be said of the people all around him. The battlefield of One Future Plaza fell silent, save for the low gurgling growls of The Future Group monsters.

"Interlopers!" Braddock's garbled voice echoed through the streets. "Korthuu has no patience for the likes of you. Either you submit now and commune with us willingly or suffer a fate worse than death."

"Put him down," McDermott approached. Having scavenged another over-sized hand cannon, she pointed it at Braddock's head.

Calhoun looked down at her, pleading with his eyes to get her to back off, but she didn't.

"You're next, sweetheart." Braddock sneered with what was left of his mouth. "You're *all* next!"

Before Braddock could raise another tentacle, several buzzes hummed through the air. Some were continuous, others occurred in a discrete pattern, but they were all in sync. Like a swarm of friendly bees.

Then came the cacophony of music: different, discordant tones, some recognizable, others generic, providing a new soundtrack for the urban war zone. Ringtones. Hundreds and hundreds of ringtones, communing with vibrations for those who left their phones on silent. Calhoun, from his great height above the street, could see none of his people were getting paged. Rather, The Future Group monsters and cultists, still possessing their mobile devices either on them or secreted away in some sort of internal monster organ pouch of some sort, were receiving a call.

One by one, in an eerie pantomime of humanity, Calhoun saw tentacle bug monsters and broken human zombies alike perform the banal task of checking their messages. Some reacted with shock, others screamed, still others seemed to have their whole glazed-eye cult persona simply melted away as their bodies squelched their way back into a reasonably human form.

"What . . . what is happening?" Braddock was just as shocked as the rest of them. "This isn't right at all! This wasn't part of the plan!"

"Seems like you didn't account for Stephanie Dyer." McDermott smiled. "Calhoun! Catch!"

Calhoun met McDermott's gaze just as she lobbed the giant gun up at him. Despite his current breathing problem, he wrenched his arms away from Braddock's tentacles, caught it, cocked it and aimed it at Braddock's mustachioed monster head, "Eat lead, you rat bastard."

"Wha—" was all Braddock could get out before the gleaming tip of a medieval sword thrust its way through his chest. His multiple black eyes went even darker, and he went limp, crashing to the ground and bringing Calhoun with him as he fell.

"Hi-ya!" the skinny Indian kid—Kashir or whatever—yelled as he withdrew the sword from Braddock's monster corpse then proceeded to repeatedly stab it in the face.

Calhoun looked up from the ground and scowled. "Are you kidding me? I was just about to kill that asshole and this kid steals my shot! Where did you even come from? Why does everyone get to kill him except me?"

"Uh, excuse me." A bewildered man in a ripped shirt and khakis wobbled up to them, followed by a legion of former Future Group cultists covered in protoplasmic goo and in various states of undress. "But can you tell us what's going on here? Because it looks kinda bad."

"It's a long story, guy," Calhoun grumbled. "I'm not sure you're gonna like it."

"All I remember is being recruited to The Future Group," a woman with tousled brown hair and smeared make-up remarked, "and all of a sudden I'm here, and I got an e-mail that I've been fired and have to pay back $1 million dollars in past bonuses? I don't have that kind of money on hand!"

Calhoun glanced across at Kashir.

"Yeah, we bought The Future Group and fired everyone," he confirmed with a shrug. "Seemed like the only way to knock the crazy outta them."

"Well, it worked," McDermott said.

"How did you buy—y'know what? Forget it." Calhoun put his hands up in surrender. "I'm not going to even try."

"But what are we going to do now?" the disheveled man said.

"I dunno," Calhoun dismissed him with a wave, "find another cult."

Seeing an opening, the Octopus Man ran joyously out into the crowd. "Come all ye faithful! Hear the glorious tale of the Cloud Octopus and bring your faith unto his many arms! He has arms for all!"

"Oh, no, you don't!" the Lizard Lady dashed after him, followed by the Freemason, the Leopard Man and the whole host of other weirdos Calhoun didn't care about.

He had another priority: the giant lumbering nightmare that remained glued to the side of The Future Group tower for some reason.

"Dyer took care of the cult, but what're we going to do about the goddamn monster?" Only Calhoun, McDermott, Kashir, and a few straggling citizen soldiers in crushed armor remained behind.

"That's . . . a good question." Kashir rubbed the scraggly hairs on his chin.

"If Korthuu's sticking around, it doesn't matter that we've turned the cult. We need to find a way to send them back to hell or wherever they came from before this shit happens again."

"Stephanie mentioned some sort of statue in The Future Group plaza," McDermott said. "She said it was part of some multi-dimensional hookup."

"Yeah, I remember." Calhoun dug his memories out of his internal filing cabinet. "Something to do with that universal solution. You think we gotta destroy it?"

"Well, Korthuu's already here," Kashir said. "That'd just trap them here with us."

"No, we don't want that . . ." McDermott looked like she was scrolling through options in her mind. Her face brightened when she landed on one she liked. "What if we could use it against them?"

"How do you figure?" Calhoun wasn't sure where she was going with this, but he had a mind to trust her.

"Let's get to the statue and see if we can manipulate it." McDermott started to jog toward the central plaza. "Then we're going to have to rely on faith."

"Oh, great." Calhoun rolled his eyes but followed anyway, along with the rest of the group. "Like that's gotten us anywhere before."

# CHAPTER THIRTY-SIX

## The Call Of Korthuu

Stephanie didn't know where she was. She opened her eyes to the sight of pure light. She looked down at her body. It was all intact and there, even down to her brother's tattered green jacket. But she was in no place. A void of spotless white. And she couldn't remember how she got there. She couldn't remember much of anything, really, except her name.

And all she could feel was a strange calming sensation reverberating throughout her entire body. She had never felt anything like this before. It felt perfect. It felt beautiful. It felt like . . . love.

"Welcome home, Stephanie Dyer," a voice echoed through the void. A voice Stephanie could feel in her bones.

A name danced across her lips. And she remembered.

"Korthuu."

"Yes. It is I, Korthuu. Can you feel the bliss I can create for us? If you accept me into your heart and allow me to consume your essence, this will be your life for the remainder of eternity. Safe within me."

"But what about my friend?" A strange question to ask. She couldn't remember any friend. A different name flew away from her. A name she was desperate to hold on to. But it vanished, replaced by another thought barreling into her brain. "What about my family?"

"You don't remember what happened to your family, do you? Such a tragic tale. A car accident took your parents' lives when you were just a child."

She felt it and knew it was true. "But how do you know?"

"When you gave yourself to me, I scanned your mind. I know what was taken from you so suddenly and unfairly. Here. Let me correct that injustice."

The pure white was broken as two human forms popped up in the distance. A man and a woman, smiling, waving. Stephanie could not make out their features, but in her gut she knew who they were.

"Mommy! Papa!" Stephanie shouted. She felt as if she was five years old again, and she was. Her tiny legs scrabbled across the pure white floor, her chubby little arms reaching toward her parents, who were bending down to pick her up. But the more she moved toward them, the further away they got—until they vanished. Black dots in a sea of white.

"No, Mommy! No, Papa! Don't leave me. Please! Where are you going?"

She was twenty-four again. She wrapped the weathered green fabric of her brother's jacket tighter against herself.

"Where are you taking them?" she shouted into the void.

"Our transaction is not yet complete. Once I have everything I want, you will be free to experience your deepest desires. You will have your family and your world as you truly wish it to be."

"What about . . ." again, the name escaped her. "My friend?"

"Do not worry. He will be here soon. And our pact will be complete."

"What about . . . my brother?"

Stephanie felt a jolt of momentary pain race up her spine.

"Ah, yes, your brother. Missing after the accident. You think him dead, too. But I can provide him to you, sourced from your memories. Everything can be as you wish it to be, when you are with me."

The infinite white space was broken once again, this time with something different. Instead of the smiling, loving face of her brother, one Stephanie only could place fragments of, there stood a void of black. A swirling clouded shadow, radiating nothing but cold emptiness. It was nothing Stephanie could recognize.

"What is that?" she asked.

"No . . ." Korthuu's words rumbled through her mind, although she wasn't sure she was supposed to be hearing them. "That's impossible."

Stephanie sensed something in Korthuu. Something she'd sensed before. Fear. But she could not remember why.

"You!" Korthuu's rage reverberated through the white, causing black cracks to snake down the infinitude. "You mean to destroy me. You and your improvident lackwit of a friend!"

Her friend.

Someone she wanted to remember, but couldn't.

Korthuu's mind shifted, and bits and pieces of Stephanie's memory came popping back. Korthuu was not some benevolent god. It was a demonic hellbeast bent on dominating her reality, and it needed her to do it. Now, it was losing control; it was scared.

Large pieces of the once pristine white world fell away, crashing to the ground and shattering into a million tiny shards of black. Stephanie spun around, disoriented not only by the encroaching black void, but also her newfound memories.

Wait. There. There was the name she was looking for. Her friend.

"Oh, no," Korthuu commanded. "You will not escape my grasp."

The black void space consumed the white sky above Stephanie and was now oozing down the cracks in the wall and across the floor. The shattered pieces of black crystal melted into it as it approached her, a writhing snaking tentacle of absence. Stephanie tried to run, but in an infinite space, she felt like she gained no distance. The black tar of the void grabbed her by the ankle and she fell to the ground. The substance consumed her, pouring itself over her body and into her eyes, ears, and mouth, until all she could see was black.

"You are mine now, child. And there is nothing to stop it. Give in. I have taken your essence and am combining it with my own. You will know nothing. Feel nothing. Remember nothing. Except the will of Korthuu. And your body would obey me."

She tried to speak out; she couldn't. She couldn't even remember her own name. Or what a name even signified. She felt only loss.

"You fool. Nothing can destroy me. I was there at the beginning and will be there at the end. And now, so will you. You are mine now."

She felt nothing, except a few fleeting echoes. Of what? Memories?

"I can feel your last, feeble thoughts. Just like the countless other beings I've consumed across the multi-verse. Thoughts of family. Thoughts of love. It is delicious to see who or what my thralls contemplate in their final moments. It's a lovely tell to their true weakness."

She could no longer comprehend the words Korthuu was saying, but she felt them in what remained of her. Whoever she was.

"So, what little bits remain of your pitiful little self?" Everything vibrated, and Korthuu was everything. "What will you reach out for with your last gasps of sanity? Tell me!"

A pause.

"Who are you going to call?"

A lightbulb turned on in her brain, immolating the darkness. The black exploded away from her, leaving her gasping for breath on an island of white. Things. Items. *Memories* came flooding back. Mostly bits and pieces. From everywhere. Memories of her family. Her brother. Herself. But one familiar voice stood out amongst the rest.

"Don't you goddamn dare."

"I should've expected you to pull something like this."

"You've gotta be kidding me!"

"This is dumb, Steph. Real dumb."

"But I think I need a little dumb in my life. It's really good to have you back."

"You've always been my best friend."

Mike's voice.

"No. No. No. No No. NO!" Fissures exploded their way through Korthuu's dark façade, and the red light of the outside world streamed through. They roared in bewildering agony, as their mental block broke down under the force of her connection to the real world. "What is this? Noooo! What are you?"

As the darkness cleared her mind and soul, she reclaimed her voice. She *had* a voice. Korthuu hadn't taken it from her fully.

"I'm Stephanie Dyer, you son of a bitch."

And she began to smile.

# CHAPTER THIRTY-SEVEN

## A Crippling Fear Of Heights

In a matter of twenty-five seconds, Maureen Whelan had burst through the plate glass windows of the thirty-fifth floor of The Future Group Tower with Michael wrapped in her arms, plummeted several stories, launched her grappling hook up toward the roof, pulled it taut, and rocketed them back up over seventy floors.

Michael was screaming the entire time and only managed to stop himself when Maureen pulled him over the railing at the top of the ninety-eighth floor. He gasped rapidly for air as the wind whipped and stung his face, forcing more tears out of the corner of his eyes.

"Breathe, kid, breathe." Maureen patted him on the back. "And just hope we don't have to do anything like that again."

"Easy for you to say!" Michael yelled. "Where are we?"

"Looks like a few levels from the top. Antenna and Spire maintenance gantries up here mostly." Maureen looked up, grabbed his shoulder, and pointed. "Look."

Michael cleared his eyes with the back of his hand and found what Maureen was pointing at. The massive form of Korthuu's bulging, bubbling skin stood by the other side of the tower, blotting out the glowing red skies with its bulk. The hundreds of eyes and jaws dotting its body were closed, screwed tight, but Michael could see its eyes and teeth roiling beneath as if searching for a way to escape. But two floors up, Michael spotted a bright flash of orange within all that corpse-green skin. Stephanie's old jacket fluttered in the breeze, revealing bits of her prison jumpsuit underneath. She was sitting cross-legged on the ground, unmoving, with Korthuu's wicked arms wrapped around her head.

Michael steeled himself and grabbed Maureen's hand. "We gotta move."

Up they went, their feet clanging against the white metal stairs at a quick clip. The stairways put them at the very top of the building, Floor 100, next to the tower's spire. Stephanie remained sitting, deathly still.

"Steph!" Michael moved toward her, but Maureen clasped his shoulder in a vice-like grip.

"Don't. You don't know what's happening. It might get you too."

Then, the wind, batting them mercilessly since they had arrived, stopped. The flags at the top of tower's flagpole, and Steph's jacket, stopped fluttering. A beam of light pierced through the sky to the left of the tower, coming from the plaza below. It was much like the one that had summoned Korthuu, except this one was a sharp blue.

Michael squinted and put up his hand to shield himself from the glow. "What the hell is that?"

The beam penetrated the sky behind Korthuu and dissipated in a scatter of weak lightning bolts, dispersing through the thick cloud cover.

"Mike!" Stephanie jolted upright, her eyes wide open. Korthuu's arms immediately withdrew from her head, sucking themselves back into the corpulent monster's body. The wind picked back up again, tousling Steph's hair as she clawed at the ground in some sort of disoriented mania. Her eyes, like Michael's, were full of tears. She wiped them away with the sleeve of her jacket. But she was not responding to Michael, who had rushed over and clasped her shoulders.

"Steph! Steph! Are you okay? Talk to me!"

"Uh . . . was . . . what . . . yeah . . ." It took a minute, like Steph was slowly digging words out of her brain. A twinge of pain struck Michael. She was usually so quick to respond with a joke. "I'm . . . I'm okay. Now. I think."

"What the hell happened? Korthuu had you in some sort of death grip. Their fingers were in your ears and nose!"

"Hopefully . . . not any other . . . holes." she struggled to smile.

"No, I think you're good." Michael smiled back. At least she was trying to be normal. That was a good sign. "Korthuu just let you go. Do you know what happened?"

"I think I fought them off somehow and got free."

"Do you remember anything else that happened?"

She paused and looked up before returning his gaze.

"No. No clue. Weird." She turned to Maureen. "How did you guys get up here?"

Maureen waggled her grappling hook gun.

"Aw, yeah," Stephanie said.

"Well, the important thing is that you're safe now," Michael said.

"No," Steph countered, with a burning anger Michael had never seen from her before, "we need to get that . . . that . . . thing out of here. Back into the void. Korthuu can never, ever return."

"Okay, okay." Michael stumbled back a bit, surprised by her outburst. "But how?"

Korthuu's giant form shifted, grabbing onto The Future Group

Tower with their hands. Their multitudinous eyes, once wriggling beneath the surface, shot open, black as pitch but full of fire.

"*Fools!*" Korthuu's energies permeated through the immediate area. Gooseflesh pimpled on Michael's arms and the back of his neck. "There is no escape from the will Korthuu. If you will not join me willingly, then you will be destroyed, and I will take my sanctuary by force."

Korthuu's many mouths snarled, revealing slavering serpentine tongues that lashed out toward the tower gantry and grabbed Michael, Maureen, and Stephanie with prehensile skill. A giant maw, bigger than those that dotted Korthuu's body, opened from within a pocket of their green flesh, and Korthuu began to angle their bodies toward it. Michael attempted to get some words out to Stephanie, but his chest was so constricted, no air could flow through his throat. Nor could Stephanie respond.

As spots began to swim before his eyes and his vision darkened, Michael could hear an incessant clacking from behind Korthuu. Like castanets, but bigger, louder, and angrier. A giant black beak gouged into Korthuu's topside, causing them to let out a pained roar from their collective mouths. The tongues lost their grip and sent Michael, Steph and Maureen falling back onto the tower floor.

Michael pushed himself up on his forearm and struggled to make sense of what was going on. The beak he had seen before had disappeared, and even Korthuu's many eyes were darting around in confusion. The sky churned, turning over from its bright blood red to a deep blue, almost black. Michael could hear the clacking again, and saw the giant beak in the distance. But it did not belong to a bird.

Two bulbous eyes blinked into existence. Then, from within a dark cloud tinged the remnants of lightning, the rest of it emerged. First came the head. Then the legs. Then more of the legs. Then even more of the legs.

A giant, red, flying octopus.

"You have gotta be fucking kidding me," Michael buried his face in his palms as the Cloud Octopus launched itself at Korthuu, covering them with its enormous suction-cupped tentacles.

Korthuu screeched and shot out gangly arms of their own in an attempt to batter the Cloud Octopus into submission. But it didn't seem to want to give in, ripping more holes in Korthuu's flesh with its powerful beak.

"Huh," Steph said. She cleaned out her ear with her thumb. "Looks like the Octopus Man got enough believers to open a bridge to whatever universe the Cloud Octopus lives in."

"How did he get so many so fast?" Maureen asked.

"Well, there's a Sucker born every minute . . ." Stephanie trailed off.

Michael barely had time to roll his eyes before Korthuu let out another shriek. The Cloud Octopus had secured an eight-foothold on the monster's gargantuan frame and was using its jets to lift Korthuu up into the air, which was a bit of a struggle. To its credit, it managed to lift Korthuu up off the ground for a solid minute before tiring and releasing its grip. Korthuu's immense bulk slammed into the midsection of The Future Group Tower, crashing through the glass and steel supporting structure. As he tumbled to the floor that was falling out from beneath them, Michael could feel Korthuu's pained yelp vibrating through his nervous system, and he was sure the others could feel it too, making them altogether more disoriented as they began to plummet to their doom.

"Grab on!" Maureen yelled. "This is going to be a bumpy ride."

Stephanie, in the midst of falling, summoned the wherewithal to wrap her arms tightly around Maureen's chest. Michael had less luck, narrowly missing his chance to grab onto Maureen's thick ankles, and continued to fall, once again screaming the entire way,

"Goddamnit," Maureen grumbled. She streamlined her body to descend quickly and catch up with Michael. Chunks of steel and concrete fell with them, along with the occasional giant swiping tentacle, but

Maureen was quicker than she looked and managed to dodge them with ease, even with Steph in tow. Michael winced as he saw a stray tentacle—he didn't know who it belonged to—swipe into Maureen's airspace, but she was five steps ahead and rolled over it, propelling her and Stephanie even faster downwards. Michael may have been terrified, but he was also a little impressed.

Soon, their velocities matched, and Maureen surprised Michael with her strength by scooping him up with her left hand while simultaneously grabbing her grappling hook gun with the right.

"What're you going to do?" Steph yelled over the carnage. A giant orange tentacle whipped by overhead, slapping some debris out of the air, and smashing into another building.

"I don't know, but whatever it is, you better pray it's going to work!" Maureen yelled back over the onrush of wind.

She looked as if she was aiming her grappling gun, but it could have easily been a random Hail Mary shot. The hook burst forth, propelled by an ejection of carbon dioxide. The arrowhead soared through the air, arcing over an incredible distance despite the falling debris, and found its mark: one of Korthuu's many exposed eyes. The arrowhead squished its way into the liquidy mass and popped it like an oozing black yolk in a dish of a green eggs and ham. Korthuu squealed. Despite the gooey nature of the eye, the hook had auto-grabbed onto something solid. The gun reeled out extra lengths of rope before the hook line went taut, swinging their three-body-system in a long, low arc that brought them all the way down toward the floor of One Future Plaza.

"Tuck and roll, idiots!" Maureen detached the cable and they plummeted the remaining few feet to the ground. Taking Maureen's advice, Steph curled up before slamming to the concrete ground and rolling a few feet. Michael, unfortunately, continued down the stairs, banging him up a bit more.

When he was finally in a position to catch his breath, Michael propped himself up on his arms—one of which he realized was broken—and turned around. The Cloud Octopus had wrapped itself almost completely around Korthuu, suffocating them to the point where they could not breathe. That is, if Korthuu breathed at all. Nevertheless, the once all powerful God of The Eternal Feast stood quiet and still as their gross bulk was lifted off the ground and into the sky, like a jumbo jet made of green fat. A quick blue spark ignited behind the Cloud Octopus, opening a new portal and sending another shockwave out into the city. The Octopus struggled and strained, dragging Korthuu into the portal, which handily sealed itself with a fart-like glorp heard for miles around.

A resounding quiet settled on the city for the first time in so many hours. Michael turned and looked at the gathered masses: Carrie, Calhoun, Kashir, and a host of ordinary citizens in either medieval armor or torn and ravaged clothing. Not to mention the other cult leaders. Where the Leopard Man had gotten a horse from was anybody's guess.

Michael let out a long sigh and made the tentative steps up to join Stephanie at the top of a small set of stairs before the courtyard, Maureen right behind them. They shared a look, and each breathed a sigh of relief. Slowly, Stephanie raised her fist into the air in a gesture of solidarity. The crowd of people before them returned the favor—even Calhoun, of all people.

They'd won. They'd beaten Korthuu. They had all earned some quiet time to decompress.

The Octopus Man pushed his way between Michael and Stephanie. Spreading his arms out, he addressed the gathered masses from the steps of the former One Future Plaza.

"All glory to the Cloud Octopus!"

Authorities later reported that the subsequent cheering did not stop for hours.

# CHAPTER THIRTY-EIGHT

## Lifeline

"Where're we going, daddy?" Marcus Espinoza's eight-year-old daughter sat on the edge of the bed, kicking her feet.

"We're just going on a little trip, Ace," Marcus lied. He didn't know where the hell he was going to go. If Korthuu-in-Craig's-Body was right, there was no place they could hide that Korthuu wouldn't find them eventually. And even in the unlikely event they did defeat Korthuu, the multi-verse was collapsing, which added another existential threat to the ever growing pile of misery that was his life. But he couldn't tell his daughter any of that, so instead he handed her a teddy bear dressed in a tuxedo for some reason. "Go play with Double-O Bear. Daddy needs to finish packing."

"Yay!" Ace leapt off the bed and scampered into the other room. "The name's Bear. James Bear!"

Marcus threw himself back on the bed, narrowly avoiding the corner of his suitcase and let out a long sigh. Just a few days ago, he'd been a head of one of the most successful investment companies of 1997. Now, he was running from an unstoppable inter-dimensional horror possessing his best friend's body. It would have overwhelmed anyone.

The phone rang, shattering Marcus' train of thought. He reached over to the nightstand and put the cordless handset to his ear.

"Hello?"

A gruff, but undeniably female, voice answered. "Is this Marcus Espinoza?"

"Yes, uh, this is he."

"Come outside. I have some words for you."

"But my kid—"

"Come alone. She'll be safe." The line clicked into an empty dial tone.

Marcus put the phone back in its cradle and weighed his options.

"Hey, sweetheart," Marcus called out into the hall. "Could you come here for a second?"

His darling daughter Ace waltzed back in with her bear.

"Daddy's gonna have to go out for a second."

"Where're you going?"

"Just for a little walk before our trip. Can I trust you to be a good girl while I'm gone? Maybe stay in the living room and watch some TV for a while."

She clicked her heels together and offered him a crisp salute. "Yes, sir!"

"Ahaha. That's my little girl. I'll be right back, okay?"

As soon as he was sure Ace was immersed in an episode of Batman, Marcus slipped out the front door of his apartment building. It was gray and rainy, but that didn't matter. He threw up the hood of his sweatshirt and let the water seep into it. Glancing around, he found that there was no one to be seen.

"Ugh."

Must've been a prank caller. Marcus sighed. Whatever, maybe he could at least go down to the corner store and get a soda to drink while he tried to figure out his next move. So Marcus started down the street, staring at his shoes.

Maybe he could move to New Zealand. If everything was going to end, at least he could be somewhere beautiful when it happened.

It was a nice thought for Marcus to have before he was yanked into an alley and slammed headfirst against a dumpster.

"Ow! What the—" Marcus moved to push himself up, but he was stopped by the unmistakable cocking of a gun. He sank back down onto his butt and raised his arms. Looking up, Marcus found himself staring into a pair of blood red eyes inset in gold tubes that jutted out of the face of a skull. It was, for some reason, infinitely more terrifying than the gun pointed at his head. "Gah!"

"Shut up. Keep quiet." A garbled, mechanized voice emanated from somewhere behind the knitted skull mask. "Put your hands behind your head."

Marcus, as usual, did as he was told.

"Good. Close your eyes."

"Who are you? Why . . . why are you doing this?" Marcus stammered, averting his gaze.

"What did you do to my son?" the angry man's voice modulator clipped out at the peaks of his yell. He grabbed Marcus by his collar and yanked him to his feet with a surprisingly superhuman strength.

"What?" Marcus's eyes went wide.

The man ripped off his skull balaclava, and threw it to the ground, the goggle clattering against the wet concrete. As Marcus began to make sense of the whole thing, he realized the person threatening him was not a man, but a woman. The woman who'd made the call. A frightened, angry woman, with tears running down her face and a snarl implying she could rip him in half if she saw fit. And she was really close to seeing fit.

"What happened to Craig?" she yelled.

His name leapt out of Marcus mouth. "You're Craig's mother!"

"You're goddamn right I am! And you're that Marcus character my boy never shut up about!" She yelled and tossed him halfway across the alley with a powerful throw. "What happened to him? It's like he doesn't even know who I am anymore!"

"I can explain. Just let me explain!"

"Stay down," Craig's mother said, keeping Marcus on his knees. "Give me one reason I shouldn't off you right now."

Marcus scrambled to find something—anything—he could say that would stop her from putting a bullet in his brain. All his thoughts raced to his daughter, who wouldn't have anyone to put her to sleep at night. And then he had it.

"The Order of the Steel Knights!"

"What?" Craig's mother lowered her gun.

"Craig told me that story you used to tell him when he was a kid," Marcus said, rainwater pooling in his mouth. "And you're not going to believe how relevant it is."

Craig's mom narrowed her eyes as if suppressing a growl. "Explain."

And so Marcus spent some quality time with Craig's mother—apparently an ex-Marine sniper—in a filthy alleyway, recounting the specifics of Craig's foray into the multi-verse, the idea of a supreme interdimensional hellbeast named Korthuu, the threat of existential collapse, and the unblinking evil The Future Group had become. By the end of his spiel, it was dark and much colder than it was when he had started, and Marcus was beginning to shiver. Sitting in a puddle full of dirty garbage water for the better part of three hours was not pleasant.

"So," Craig's Mom—Maureen—said, "what are we going to do about it?"

"What?" Marcus blinked through the sheets of water that were still pouring down. "There's nothing we can do about it. It's over. Craig's gone. We've lost. Korthuu said so himself."

"Kid, you're going to believe an evil monster from another dimension?" Maureen scoffed. "What'd my boy ever see in you?"

"I . . . I don't know." Marcus looked down. The coldness he felt wasn't all due to the water gathering around his feet. "He loved me, and I failed him. If maybe I had made him feel safe enough, he would've told me everything and I could have saved him. Stopped him from making a bad decision. But I was too wrapped up in my own issues. I wish I could go back and change things. I think"—Marcus cleared his throat—"I think maybe I could've loved him, too."

"Listen, Marcus." Maureen's voice softened; she sounded less like an assassin and more like a mother. "It's not all your fault. I should've been there for him too, but I'd been working so much, I barely had time to speak to him. When it came down to it, Craig had no one to talk to. So whatever this Korthuu thing is, it took advantage of his feelings.

"But the one thing I know for sure is that Craig had a good heart. As naïve as he was, Craig made his decision because he thought he could save the universe from, whatever it was . . . uh, multi-versal collapse. Now, don't you think that we owe it to him, and ourselves, to try to solve the problem? Or at the very least, try to stop Korthuu? Even if there's a sliver of a chance, it's worth taking."

Marcus blinked. Maureen seemed a lot more reasonable when she wasn't pointing a gun to his head.

"I, uh, I guess you're right. But where do we start?"

"I've heard you've got several million dollars in the bank. That can buy a lot of equipment. And I know a few people who can help us go dark. All we need is time."

"That I think we have," Marcus said. "Korthuu said he still needed time to prepare."

"Good. Then we can use that time to plot out our next moves. And see who else out there might be able to help us. Even if Korthuu's brainwashing people, he's gonna make some enemies."

"And the multi-verse problem?"

"One thing at a time, slick," Maureen said. "But I've got a hunch once we solve one problem, we'll be able to solve the other. Take down Korthuu and we might be able to steal back that multi-verse viewer."

"Okay," Marcus nodded. It was a long shot, but Maureen was right. It was better than doing nothing. He just had one last thought. "What about my daug—ACHOO!"

"Whoa, geeze. Bless you." Maureen winced then offered a helping hand. "Here. Let's get you back inside before you die of pneumonia. We've got a lot to figure out, and you being sick isn't going to work."

"F-fine," Marcus sneezed again. "Can we at least get something warm to drink?"

"Sure, okay," Maureen said. "I'll grab us some coffee. How do you like yours?"

# CHAPTER THIRTY-NINE

## Clean Up, Everybody Do Your Share

Michael huddled under the metallic trauma blanket the EMTs had given him, with Stephanie sitting similarly next to him at the back of the ambulance. Once Korthuu's influence waned, those affected by his seduction returned to their normal states, allowing emergency crews to do their jobs once again. The damage to the city was severe, but not unsurmountable. They'd recover, but things would certainly be different.

Stephanie seemed a bit more reticent than Michael was used to. Had something happened when Korthuu had taken her? Michael was afraid to ask, just like he was afraid to ask her about a bunch of other subjects. He thought it would be better if he left well enough alone, so he simply said, "How're you feeling?"

"I'm good, Mike." Stephanie smiled over the cup of soup she had been given. But her smile was different, more rueful than playful. Her unease made him uneasy. "How're you?"

"Glad to be rid of that shitty job." Someone had to make a joke and if Steph wasn't feeling up to it, Michael would handily take up the cause as best he could.

"Hahaha." Steph's laugh was weak. "But what're you going to do for work now?"

"Well . . ." Before Michael could form his thoughts into a concrete proposal, they were interrupted by Rex Calhoun, Carrie by his side. Michael saw a happy twinkle appear in Steph's eye.

"You two doing okay?" Calhoun said.

"Yeah, I think so," Michael replied.

"Good." Rex shut down any further conversation, as if actual feeling would interfere with his programming. "It was . . . a hell of a thing you guys did. I used to think you two were just a pair of screw-ups."

"Aw, thanks, Rexy," Stephanie said.

"Now I *know* you two are a pair of screw-ups!"

"Oh."

"But I've got it on good authority"—he nodded toward Carrie— "that you're smarter than you look."

"Is that a compliment, or . . . ?" Michael trailed off.

"I still don't agree with all of this. The detective agency, the monsters, all that crap. But from where I'm standing, you did a lot of good. A lot of bad, too, but we'll focus on the good. I think it's time I got out of your hair." Calhoun extended a hand toward Michael. "Truce?"

Michael looked at it, unable to comprehend what exactly was happening. Stephanie jumped up, shedding her trauma blanket, and shook Rex's hand, an honest smile appearing on her face.

"Truce!" she said. "I promise you won't regret it!"

"Oh, I promise I will," Rex said. "But you guys are going to have your hands full pretty soon. So, you're going to be out of my hair, too, thank god."

"Wait." Michael found his words. "What do you mean?"

Rex jerked a thumb over his shoulder where Michael could see a throng of people with cameras and microphones amassing amidst vans with satellite equipment sprouting from the roof. The press had finally broken the war zone barrier and were here to report on it.

Rex smiled, which felt uncomfortable. Like seeing a goat smile.

"Good luck with these vultures, kids. You're gonna need it." With a wave of his hand he beckoned Carrie away. "C'mon, McDermott, we've got cops to debrief."

As Carrie walked away, Stephanie snapped twice in the air to grab her attention and then mimed a "call-me" gesture. She smiled before being swallowed up by the crowd of advancing reporters.

"Aw, shit," Stephanie said after they'd disappeared from view, "I didn't give her my number. Do you think Rexy will give it to her?"

"Does Rex even have your number?" Michael asked.

"No." Stephanie frowned. "Shit!"

"Well, you're seeming a bit more like yourself."

"It's . . . been a rough couple of hours," Stephanie confirmed, "but I'm rounding the bend."

Michael looked back at the smoldering remains of The Future Group building. His old job. His old life. Then he looked back at Stephanie. "We saved the world today, y'know?" he said with a knowing nod.

"We sure did," she replied.

"I mean, technically it was the giant octopus, but either way, we did a good job today. And it was a hell of a lot better than my last job. I think I could get used to it."

Stephanie tilted her head, the faintest hint of a smile tugging at her lips. "What're you saying?"

"I'm saying . . . my name's first on our office door for a reason. It's time I earned my keep."

Stephanie threw her arms open for a hug, but she was stopped by the fleet of microphones shoved into their faces amidst the bright strobes of flashbulbs. A barrage of questions came at them so hard and fast, Michael could barely make sense of it all. His head began to spin. Fortunately, Stephanie seemed to have the situation well in hand. She took control of the press gang materializing in front of them.

"People, people!" She raised her hand to steady the stream of questioning. "One at a time. You there, from Channel 7. I love your morning show. Is the weather guy that attractive in real life? Don't answer that. I know he is. You go first."

"Uh, yes," the reporter started, a bit taken aback by Steph's forthrightness, "According to a police spokesman we spoke with earlier, you two are the cause of all this mess. Is that correct?"

"Uh . . . which police spokesman?" Michael asked.

"A Detective Reginald Calhoun. He directed us to you."

"Oh. My. God." Stephanie could barely contain herself. "Reginald? That is amazing! Mike, write that down before I forget." She laughed for a good solid minute before wiping away her tears. She cleared her throat but then continued laughing, waving toward Michael to carry on.

Michael smirked. Steph was definitely back to her old self, and he wouldn't have it any other way. He took over. "Yes, uh, sorry about that. Anyway, Detective Calhoun was not entirely wrong. It wasn't our fault, but we were involved. We're . . . uh"—he hesitated to say it, but knew he had to—"private detectives that had been hired to investigate The Future Group. Apparently, they had secretly been funneling their money into this sort of scary death cult for years in an attempt to raise the giant monster Korthuu. A few concerned citizens helped us defeat it."

"And can you tell us more about the giant Cloud Octopus?" another reporter asked.

"The less said about that, the better," Michael muttered.

A third reporter raised his pen. "And who exactly are you two?

You said you were private investigators?"

"Oh, us?" Michael said, smiling. "We're Duckett and Dyer—"

Stephanie pushed him away to add, directly into the microphone, "Dicks For Hire!"

"What? No! Don't call us that!" Michael pointed to the press group. He hated that name. It was embarrassing! What if his mom found out? "Don't print or broadcast that. Why're you writing that down? Don't write that down! That's not what we're called. That's not our brand!"

But it was too late.

# CHAPTER FORTY

## Business As Unusual

Michael Duckett kicked up his feet on a brand new oak desk. It had been a few weeks since the fall of The Future Group and his loss of professional employment, but he was enjoying every minute of it— despite the fact that his right arm was in a cast.

Ever since the full story broke, the detective agency had been put on the map. They had been fielding all sorts of cases. Well, missing cats, mostly, but work was work. And Michael finally felt like he was making a difference in this world, not to mention having saved it from almost certain destruction. Although Michael didn't agree with Stephanie's branding and had requested new business cards, he had to say, things finally felt like they were falling into place.

That being said, it had crossed his mind that since the incident with Korthuu, he had seen neither hide nor beautiful hair of the mysterious woman and her so-called organization that had set them down this road. And he had not forgotten that she owed him a quote-unquote handsome reward. But what really concerned him was the special request she had also promised him.

"Heyo!" The agency door slammed open and Stephanie waltzed in, her hands overburdened with various goods. "What is up, Mike? I've got some grape slushies from Kashir downstairs. As a thank you, they were on the house!"

"Really? That was nice of him."

"Well, he doesn't know they were on the house, but the spirit is there. I also got us something nice for the office." Steph placed a brown, wrapped rectangular package on the desk before him

Michael tore it open to reveal a framed newspaper front page, with their photo splashed front and center, above the fold. It was a photo that had been taken shortly after they had retrieved the Garbagemobile from the impound lot. Stephanie was making overenthusiastic gun fingers at the camera, while Michael seemed aloof in an attempt to appear cool. A strange sense of déjà vu buzzed down Michael's spine but was quickly put to bed when he read the headline.

### A Couple of Dicks Save The City

"Goddamnit, Steph." He slapped the frame with the back of his good hand. "This is what I was worried about. Everyone is going to call us dicks now!"

Steph shrugged. "I was thinking we could hang it up above the murphy bed."

"Lovely."

"And that's not all! I've also got another surprise for you." She waggled her eyebrows, a sure sign of incoming chaos. "Since we're being swamped with calls and business now, I got us a real secretary."

"Steph." Michael sighed. "Even with what we're earning off all these cat cases, we can't afford to pay a secretary."

"Well, she said she was fresh out of a job, so I took pity on her." Steph waved in Maureen who had been waiting at the door. "Plus, she said she'd work for free."

"I didn't say that," Maureen grunted. "But I have a bunch of ex-fed pensions to keep my head above water, so I could work for whatever drinking money you can spare. The way you guys operate, you might need a bodyguard in the future."

"How about all my shares of The Future Group?" Steph asked. "It's worth around five bucks now, but nobody will take it off my hands."

"Sure. I won't say no to five bucks."

"Well, in that case, I guess you're hired," Michael extended his left hand and Maureen took it in a grip that almost shattered his remaining good fingers. He winced and squeaked out. "Thanks for that."

"Thanks for being willing to work with me even though I almost killed the both of you."

"Water under the bridge!" Steph slapped Maureen on the back. "Now we got a desk for you up front. It's the one with the missing pieces."

Michael's pocket buzzed. He pulled out his phone—the fancy smartphone he'd found in his desk weeks ago. It was an anonymous text. But he'd been expecting a particular anonymous text for a while, rendering it completely non-anonymous.

BACK ALLEY. ALONE. BE INCONSPICUOUS.

Michael nodded to himself, and then announced loudly to the room. "Sorry! Mom's calling! I'm gonna take this outside."

Stephanie, in the midst of explaining to Maureen the intricacies of how she built the desk, scrunched up her face and shooed him away. Michael shrugged and walked nonchalantly out the door.

* * *

Stephanie watched as Michael waltzed out the door to call his mom, leaning out to make sure he was all the way down the stairs before she turned back to Maureen.

"You were right. He's more than capable of taking care of himself."

"I know." Maureen nodded.

"But I'm still worried. I can't let him die. I'd never forgive myself. Maybe I should tell him what I know."

"Kid, you're always going to be worried, because no matter how tightly you try to control him, everything's still out of your control. Nobody needs to be reminded that they're going to die. Best just keep it in your pocket. Don't let it spoil the fact that he values you enough to go in on this crazy detective scheme with you.

"And besides, I don't care what your future self or whatever says is going to happen." Maureen placed a firm, but sweet hand on Steph's shoulder. It warmed her in a way she hadn't felt in years, so she placed hers gently atop it. "Life is chaos. You never really know for sure."

"Thanks, Maureen." Steph sighed. "You have no idea how much I appreciate that."

"Any time, kid. You remind me a lot of me when I was younger."

"Aw, that's sweet."

"Not a compliment. Now how's about you tell me where to get a decent beer around here?"

"I'll do that if you tell me what the hell you were doing with that sexy spy lady and Homeless Joe."

"His name is Marcus," Maureen said before squinting. "And I'll consider it."

* * *

Michael shivered in the cold, dank alley behind the office. He really should've been warmer due to the dumpster on fire across the way, but it only added a rank, smoky smell to the entire area, one of the signature scents of Squalor's Wallow. He puffed on his hands and tried to rub them together before remembering one was in a cast.

"What, you didn't bring a coat?" The Woman emerged from nowhere. Michael would have jumped if his knees hadn't frozen and locked up. "It's almost winter. You'll freeze to death out here."

"I didn't have much time to think, okay? You try getting a sudden anonymous text message sometime."

"I've gotten a few. They were mostly dick pics. Anyway, speaking of dicks . . ."

"Don't call us that." Michael glared at her.

"Sorry. It *is* pretty good branding. I'm just here to thank you for all your help. The world is safe again, thanks to you and Steph."

"Yeah, about that. It's been a while." Michael narrowed his eyes, "We haven't seen you or Homeless Joe—"

"Marcus," she interrupted.

"We haven't seen you since the prison. What've you been up to?"

"I can't answer that question."

"I figured. Well, how about this question: where's our money?"

"Your money?" The Woman cocked an eyebrow.

"Yeah, I'd really not like to live in my office anymore. And you promised a handsome reward, so"—Michael extended his good hand—"make with the cash."

"Right." The Woman looked away, her eyes visible even behind her glasses. "Well, we did have a large amount of money set aside to reward you, but given the amount of damage the whole ordeal did to the city, we kind of had to funnel it to the appropriate support and infrastructure organizations."

"What?" Michael yelled, his breath fogging up his glasses.

"It was either that or let them sue you for billions of dollars in damages."

"I respect your decision." Michael offered a curt nod. "But then why are you here?"

"I'm here to shore up the other part of our bargain." The Woman reached into her jacket and extricated a manila envelope.

Michael eyed it. "You found it? You really found it?"

"Michael, we're a super-secret organization with access to copious amounts of information. Especially now that The Future Group is gone. Of course we found it."

Michael snatched the envelope out of her hands a bit too hungrily. This could change everything. He could finally feel like he was doing something to help. Finally feel like a good person.

"Frankly," the Woman continued, "all we did was a bit of googling. Always look on the second page of the search results. That's where the real gold is."

Michael nodded and reached for the flap on the envelope.

"Now are you sure you want to do that?" the Woman asked.

Michael looked up at her. "What? Why wouldn't I?"

"I know it's none of my business, but if I were Stephanie, I'd view it as a breach of trust."

"It's not a breach of trust. I'm trying to help her."

"Wouldn't it be better if you just talked to her?" The Woman gave him a condescending tilt of her head, as if it were that simple.

"I can't. Steph said she wanted to talk about it, but I don't think she'd actually want to. Stuff like this, the real stuff, it hurts her to think about. I don't know what happened when she merged with Korthuu, but I think they messed with her head. I saw how she acted afterwards. She's my friend. I'd don't want to see her like that ever again."

"What was she like?"

"Sad. Hurt. Far away. It felt wrong." Michael hated even thinking about it. "She was like that the last time we talked about this stuff, so I need to do this on my own. And then, once I'm sure it's the right time, and I've figured everything out and how to say it, then we'll talk. So she'll be able to feel safe and know that I understand."

"Michael, you're smarter than that." The Woman shook her head.

"No, I'm not," Michael said. "I'm really not."

"Well, it sounds like you're trying to spare your own feelings and emotional discomfort. I don't think you're doing her any favors."

"Listen, lady, if you didn't think it was a good idea, why did you give this to me?" He waved the envelope around.

"A deal's a deal." Her voice was full of melancholy. "And I just expected you to know better. Now, if you'll excuse me . . ."

"Wait!" Michael called out to her just as she was about to turn around. "What do I call you?"

She smirked, "Still not going to tell you that."

"What about your organization? Who do you work for?" He wanted something. Any piece of information would feel like a victory.

"Oh, us?" she produced a card with such a slick movement it was as if she conjured it out of nowhere. The Woman flipped it in the air toward Michael, who fumbled with his envelope and caught it. It was a solid sheet of blank, brushed metal. There was only a single word on it in a lighter burnished font. "You can call us STEEL."

"So, does that stand for something, or . . . ?" Michael looked down at the card, cradling the envelope in his cast. When he looked back up, the woman was gone.

"Great," Michael stuffed the metal card in his shirt pocket and turned his attention to the envelope. He flipped it around in his hand, revealing the light pen scrawled on the front.

### Stephanie A. Dyer – Family Relations and Associated Information

Exhaling another cloud of warm air, he rolled up the envelope, shoved it in his back pocket beneath the tails of his shirt, and trudged inside to warm himself up.

# EPILOGUE

## Deeper Underground

The Woman turned her steering wheel with gentle ease, guiding her car onto the freeway. Squalor's Wallow was fine for business, but there was no way she was staying there after dark voluntarily. She felt a little bad for Maureen, having drawn the short straw to babysit those two goofballs. Though, if she was being honest, Michael was kind of cute. Misguided and riddled with anxiety, but cute.

After a few exits, she turned onto an off-ramp that led her away from the lattice of towering cranes repairing the city. Traffic thinned out the further away she drove, eventually dwindling to the odd pick-up or eighteen-wheeler. Eventually, the roads were empty, and the only way forward led to what was, up until recently, the City Penitentiary. In all the commotion of Korthuu, law enforcement had missed the facility quietly dropping off their map into the hands of new, independent management. And the new Chief of the City Police Department, Reginald

P. Calhoun, was up to his eyeballs in paperwork. He couldn't see past his own blind rage.

The Woman maneuvered her car through the rear fences, past the loading dock, and down a ramp that brought her to a newly built underground parking deck. She made sure to grab the box of coffee that was sitting in the passenger's seat—and plenty of packs of sugar—before she got out and strode to the elevator at the far end of the deck. After Duckett and Dyer blasted their way out of the premises, she and her father had mopped up the remaining cultists and took the prison for their own needs. With One Future Plaza destroyed, the ex-City Penitentiary was the only place in the world with the equipment STEEL needed to solve their problem. The last remaining multi-verse viewer. How Craig Breene—or Korthuu—had replicated it was unbeknownst to them, but her father jumped in it almost immediately, remaining there for the last few weeks. That's what worried her.

The Woman keyed in her entry code on the elevator's touchpad—up, up, down, down, left, right, left, right, B, A—and it shuddered as it began to move horizontally backwards. Her stomach shifting in a direction other than expected was a sensation she would never get completely used to.

She stood in silence, her hands clasped over her long wool coat. As the elevator rolled to a halt, her stomach resettled, and she emerged from the dinging doors into a vast open set of offices and sub-departments. When it worked, STEEL worked fast and worked well. The last remnants of their old secret underground tunnel network had been swept away and replaced with actual, workable space. The walls of the entire chamber were of thick brushed metal which acted as an effective faraday cage, keeping out any unwanted electromagnetic radiation and keeping in all internal communications. It was essential for them not to be discovered by The Future Group. But now, with Korthuu gone, she didn't see the need for that level of secrecy. Still, better safe than sorry.

She proceeded across the floor, nodding and giving quick salutes to a few other STEEL agents and scientists in the midst of idle chatter or general paperwork. She had no time to waste. She had to see her father.

Pushing through the main floor, the Woman veered off into a set of dark hallways, remnants of the prison itself. Her father didn't want these touched, as this was where the most sensitive equipment lay. The Woman turned a corner into a holding area that reminded her more of an abattoir or torture chamber than a waiting room. The door was open to the room beyond, and her father sat where he had been for the last few weeks: in the center of the room upon his large, computerized throne. The old red headset sat over his eyes and ears, keeping any trace of the outside world from reaching him while automated wrist-, ankle-, and waist-shackles kept him secured to the throne until he was ready to disengage. Food and evacuation tubes penetrated his body, drawing and pulling solids and fluids out of him so he would not have to leave the chair. His unkempt, homeless appearance was further exacerbated by the fact that he hadn't moved in so long. It didn't help that this very device had been used to brainwash prisoners into Korthuu's service.

The Woman shuddered, and set the box of coffee on the floor, lest she spill it. It was eerie. Like seeing him on his death bed or in a futuristic electric chair. The obsession had absolutely consumed him. Around her father, lining the walls and ceiling of the cube, were enormous towers of computer equipment that blinked, beeped, and whirred, allowing him to run his foray into the multi-verse.

He was determined to find the solution to the problem that the man who was Craig Breene had given his life and sanity for so many years ago. As The Woman understood it, the multi-verse was being destroyed, one universe at a time. Breene had hoped to stop it, but was corrupted by Korthuu in the process. How Duckett and Dyer figured into this was anybody's guess, but recent intel convinced her father of their involvement, and frankly, it had been correct.

The Woman cleared her throat, as if he could hear her over the simulation audio. Surprisingly, his shaky hands steadied, and he manipulated the dial on the keyboard in his lap. The chair beeped and hissed, and with a mechanical clanking, the shackles came undone. The headset and visor lifted off him with a hiss. The Woman could finally see the bleary, clouded eyes of her father again. But the most disconcerting thing—they lacked a clear indication that something was going on behind them. Usually, this effect disappeared after a few seconds as her father's consciousness clicked on again.

"Dad?" she asked. "Are you okay?"

Her father turned to her, and the click she had been waiting for occurred, but not as much as she'd have liked. He blinked and recognized her.

"Oh, God." Another blink. Some of her father had come back, but it still felt like something crucial was missing. "I'm so glad to see you again."

"It's over, dad. Korthuu was defeated. We won." She tried to smile but failed.

"Oh . . . A-Ace," The Woman knew something was wrong when he struggled to say her name. "I . . . I don't think so. I've been investigating all the options I could, but the multi-verse is still collapsing. More and more universes have winked out of existence. In fact, they are disappearing at a faster rate now, leaving no trace behind. It's as if they never existed in the first place. Korthuu was not the source of the instability. They may have actually been one of the things keeping it at bay, culling weak universes. But now we are rushing toward the end more than ever.

"Craig's old calculations only managed a sixty-three percent success rate of saving the stability of the multi-verse. Even with Korthuu gone, even all the new knowledge we've gained over the years, given all the remaining combinations, that number still drops to fifty-four percent. It's not enough. There is no way for us to win. In fact, we've already lost. The fabric of existence is collapsing and the end of everything is unavoidable. There is no one-hundred percent solution."

# DUCKETT & DYER
## Dicks For Hire

Will Return In

# The Mystery of the
# Murdered Guy

# ACKNOWLEDGEMENTS

Duckett & Dyer: Dicks For Hire took four years to come together. Ten if you count from the first time the general idea popped into my head. The fact that I managed to get out a sequel in less than a year from start to finish astounds me, but it's clear that there's no way I could have done it alone.

Emily Spear, my supportive and loving girlfriend. Thank you for making me get up and continue writing when I was being lazy and just surfing Reddit. This book would have never been finished if it weren't for you. I'd still be in my underwear upvoting dank memes.

Andrew Cannizzaro, thanks again for listening to my ridiculous ideas and wading through my early drafts. Most of the emotion and character depth in these books comes from you. The poop jokes are mine and mine alone.

Tareque Powaday. Your amazing covers are what get people to read my schlock. They're bright colorful foliage of my literary venus flytrap. Thank you again for bearing with my nitpicks and demands. I love your art and I wouldn't want anyone else to do the covers to Duckett & Dyer. Here's to an unlucrative seven more books.

To the sketch comedy crew who's kept me writing funny bits to keep me sharp and dumb. Myles Hewette, Sam Bourne, Patrick Reilly, Hattie Hayes, Matt Storrs, Rosa Escandon, Maurice Licorish, Bob Gurnett, Mark Vollinski, Jessie Cannizzaro, Kevin Froleiks – I know only Kevin will probably read this book, but I wanted to thank you all.

Thank you to Roman Levant, my best friend, who's always been supportive with jokes and references no one else will comprehend. It's not often you come across someone like that, so I appreciate you..

Thank you to C.D. Tavenor, who liked the first book so much, he wanted to edit the second. Your work is phenomenal and I hope you don't mind being contracted for more idiocy.

Thanks to the #WritingCommunity on Twitter through which I've gained many actual fans of my work, a possibility I've never even dreamed of. Not to mention all the great reviews and reviewers who've read my work. A special thanks for those who gave me permission to blurb their reviews in the front matter of this book. They all actually liked it!

Of course, thanks to my mother and father. They may not care for what I write, but they're glad that "at least [I'm] doing something."

And a final thank you to my grandfather. He's always been a continual source of inspiration and drive for my writing and I miss him every day.

And thank you for buying the second book in an absolutely absurd series. Without you, I wouldn't be bothering. Thanks for spending a few more hours with Duckett & Dyer. I hope you enjoyed what you read, and if you did, I'd love to hear what you think. Once again, thank you from the bottom of my cold, cold heart.

# ABOUT THE AUTHOR

G.M. Nair is a crazy person who should never be taken seriously. Despite possessing both a Bachelor's and Master's Degree in Aerospace Engineering, he has written comedy for the stage and screen, and is the author of the highly unlucrative Duckett & Dyer series.

*The One-Hundred Percent Solution* is his second novel, and he's on track to make some money off of it in the year 10,000.

G.M. Nair lives in New York City, if you can call it living. Am I right?

You can find him trolling the internet at:

 NairForceOne@gmail.com

 @GaneshNair

 www.ds-df.com